Praise for the novels of *New York Times*
and *USA TODAY* bestselling author

# GENA SHOWALTER

### *The Darkest Passion*
"Showalter gives her fans another treat, sure to satisfy!"
—*RT Book Reviews*

### *Twice as Hot*
"The Showalter name on a book
means guaranteed entertainment."
—*RT Book Reviews*

### *The Darkest Whisper*
"If you like your paranormal dark
and passionately flavored, this is the series for you."
—*RT Book Reviews*

### *The Vampire's Bride*
"Thanks to Showalter's great writing and imagination,
this story, reminiscent of a reality show with all-powerful
gods pulling everyone's strings, will really appeal."
—*RT Book Reviews*

### *The Darkest Pleasure*
"Showalter's darkly dangerous Lords of the Underworld
trilogy, with its tortured characters, comes to a very
satisfactory conclusion...[her] compelling universe
contains the possibility of more stories to be told."
—*RT Book Reviews*

### *The Darkest Kiss*
"In this new chapter the Lords of the Underworld engage
in a deadly dance. Anya is a fascinating blend of spunk,
arrogance and vulnerability—a perfect match
for the tormented Lucien."
—*RT Book Reviews*

**Catch a Mate**

"The versatile Showalter...once again shows that she can blend humor and poignancy while keeping readers entertained from start to finish."
—*Booklist*

**The Nymph King**

"A world of myth, mayhem and love under the sea!"
—#1 *New York Times* bestselling author J. R. Ward

**Playing with Fire**

"Another sizzling page-turner... Gena Showalter delivers an utterly spell-binding story!"
—#1 *New York Times* bestselling author Kresley Cole

**Animal Instincts**

"Bold and witty, sexy and provocative, Gena Showalter's star is rising fast!"
—*New York Times* bestselling author Carly Phillips

**Jewel of Atlantis**

"Shines like the purest gem... Rich in imagery and evocative detail, this book is a sterling example of what makes romance novels so worthwhile."
—*A Romance Review*

**Heart of the Dragon**

"Lots of danger and sexy passion give lucky readers a spicy taste of adventure and romance."
—*RT Book Reviews*

**The Pleasure Slave**

"Definitely going on my keeper shelf."
—*The Romance Studio*

**The Stone Prince**

"Sexy, funny and downright magical!"
—*New York Times* bestselling author Katie MacAlister

# GENA SHOWALTER

## THE DARKEST SECRET

*Lords of the Underworld*

HQN™

Recycling programs
for this product may
not exist in your area.

ISBN-13: 978-0-373-77549-1

THE DARKEST SECRET

www.HQNBooks.com

**Printed in U.S.A.**

I was writing this book
when my cherished friend, Donnell Epperson, died.
She was a woman of unwavering faith and deep love,
who dreamed of being a published author. Tragically,
she died before that dream could be realized.
And that's a shame (or a *Glorious Misfortune,* as she
would have said with a beautiful and slightly wicked
smile). She was truly gifted and utterly dedicated,
and I like to think she was with me as I wrote this.

And so, this one is for you, my friend. And when Jill,
Sheila and I get to heaven, I have a feeling we'll be
arguing about where our mansions are placed. I call
dibs on the middle. Just sayin'. Until then, I continue
to miss you with all my heart. Save me a hug, and
maybe tell the Big Man I'm not so bad. Sometimes.
Meanwhile, it's no secret that I will always love you.

# THE DARKEST SECRET

# CHAPTER ONE

STRIDER, KEEPER OF THE DEMON of Defeat, burst through the towering front doors of the Budapest fortress he shared with a growing cast of friends—brothers and sisters by circumstance rather than blood, but all the closer for it— fighting a rush of undeniable pleasure.

He'd freaking done it, man. *Done. It.* After chasing his enemy cross-continent, bargaining away one of the four godly relics needed to find and destroy Pandora's box— and yeah, he was gonna get spanked hard for that—then, after being eaten alive by insects and at one point (cough) walking into a chick's knife (cough), he'd finally won. And damn if he wasn't ready to celebrate.

"I'm king of the world, bitches. Come in here and bask in my glory." His voice echoed through the foyer, expectant, eager.

No one returned the greeting.

Still. Grinning, he shifted the unconscious female draped over his shoulder into a more comfortable position. More comfortable *for him.* She was the enemy he'd been chasing, as well as the chick who'd oh, so impolitely introduced his pancreas to the freaking hilt of her blade. He could hardly wait to tell everyone that he'd done what they hadn't. He'd bagged and tagged her, baby.

He called, "Daddy's home. Somebody? Anybody?"

Again, there was no response. His grin dulled a bit.

Damn it. When he lost a single challenge, he battled crippling pain for days. When he won, though…gods, it was almost a sexual high, energy buzzing in his veins, heating him, priming him. That kind of enthusiasm called for a playmate. And, hell, twelve warriors and their menagerie of female companions lived here, yet no one had waited around to welcome him home? Even though the grounds were now gated, monitored and someone had had to punch him in, like, five minutes ago?

Didn't that just figure.

But he deserved it, he supposed. Seven days had passed since he'd last texted or phoned. Technically, though, that wasn't his fault. He'd been a wee bit preoccupied, what with subduing his bundle of anything but joy. And on his last update, he'd been told the danger here had passed and everyone could return, so he'd stopped the I-have-to-know-how-everyone's-doing flurry of calls.

So, fine. No biggie. The fact that no one wanted to play actually did him a solid. Now he could take care of a little business. "Thanks, guys. You're the best. Really." *And you can all suck it!*

Strider surged forward. To console himself, he imagined his prisoner's expression when she woke up and found herself trapped in a four-by-four cage. *Now that's the good stuff.* Then his gaze snagged on his unfamiliar surroundings, and the last vestiges of his grin fell away. He stopped abruptly.

He'd been gone only a few weeks, and he'd thought most of the others had been, too, but in that time someone had managed to turn the run-down monstrosity they called home into a showpiece. Once comprised of crumbling stone and mortar, the floor was now brilliant white marble veined with amber. Equally deteriorated walls were now vividly polished rosewood.

Before, the winding staircase had been cracked; now it gleamed, not a flaw in sight, an unblemished gold railing climbing to the top. In the corner, a white velvet-lined chair was pushed against reflective paneling, and beyond that, priceless artifacts—colorful vases, bejeweled trinket boxes and aged spearheads—were perched behind glass cases.

None of which had been there before.

All these changes, in less than a month? Seemed impossible, even with Titan gods popping in and out at will. Maybe because those gods were more concerned with murder and mayhem than interior decorating. But maybe… maybe while Strider had been congratulating himself on a job well done, he'd entered the wrong house? It had happened before.

And talk about awkward. There was no way to explain the cut, bruised and soot-covered baggage he was hauling around. Not without a little jail time. Explaining the blood splatter on his clothing would be a real treat, too.

Nah, he decided a second later. This was the right place. Had to be. Along the staircase wall hung a portrait of Sabin, keeper of Doubt. Naked. Only one person had the balls to taunt badass Sabin with something like that. Anya, goddess of Anarchy and dealer of disorder, who just happened to be engaged to Lucien, keeper of Death. Odd pair, if you asked Strider, but no one had, so he'd kept the opinion to himself. Besides, better silence than the loss of a favorite appendage. Anya didn't take kindly to anyone second-guessing her. About anything.

"Yo, Tor Tor," he shouted now.

Torin, the keeper of the demon of Disease. Dude never left the fortress. He was always here, monitoring camera feed, ensuring the home remained invasion-free, as well as playing on his computers and making their miniature, by-invitation-only army a shitload of cha-ching.

At first, there was no reply, only another echo of his voice, and Strider began to worry. Had something catastrophic happened? A total demon wipeout? If so, why was *he* still here? Or had Kane, keeper of All Kinds of Bad Shit, had a crappy week and—

Footsteps pounded, closer and closer, and relief flooded him. He looked up the staircase, and there was Torin, standing on a zebra-print rug Strider also didn't recall seeing before, his white hair shagging around his devil's face, his green eyes bright as emeralds.

"Welcome home," Torin said, adding, "You shithead."

"Nice greeting."

"You don't call, you don't write, and you want hearts and flowers?"

"Yeah, I do."

"Figures."

Torin wore black from neck to toe, his hands covered by soft leather gloves. Fashion-wise, those gloves were over-kill. To save mankind, though, they were kinda necessary. A single touch of Torin's skin against another's, and hello plague. Guy's demon pumped some kind of disease in his veins, that single touch all that was needed to spread it. Even to Strider. But immortal as he was, Strider wouldn't die from a little cough/fever/vomiting of blood. Not like humans, who would be ravaged, perhaps worldwide, the infection becoming nearly unstoppable. Strider *would* give the illness to everyone he touched in turn, though, and as he moderately enjoyed seducing humans, he relied on skin-to-skin action.

"So, everything good here?" Strider asked. "Everyone fine?"

"Now you want to know?"

"Yeah."

"Figures. Well, for the most part, all's well. A lot of the guys are out hiding artifacts, and looking for the last one. Those who aren't are hunting Galen." Torin took the stairs two at a time and stopped at the bottom, remaining out of striking distance. As always. His gaze flicked to the female, and amusement expanded his pupils, hiding whatever emotion had been banked there before. "So you're the next of us to fall in love, huh? Sucker! I thought you'd have more sense."

"Please. I want nothing to do with this raging bitch." A lie. During their seemingly eternal trek, he'd found himself desiring her more and more. And *hating* himself more and more. She might be sex walking, but she was also death waiting.

Too-pretty-to-be-male lips curved in sheer delight. "That's what Maddox said about Ashlyn. What Lucien said about Anya. What Reyes said about Danika. What Sabin—"

"Okay, okay. I get it." Strider rolled his eyes. "You can shut up now." While he would admit the girl's punked-out style appealed to him, he'd never be dumb enough to try and tap that.

He liked his women compliant. And sane.

*Liar. You like this one. Just as she is.* He wished he could blame his demon for that admission, but... Even now, simply thinking about her, his body was tensing, readying.

Torin crossed his arms over his chest. "So what is she? A human with a supernatural ability? A goddess? A Harpy?"

The guys here *did* have a propensity for choosing females of "myth" and "legend." Females far more powerful than their demons. Ashlyn could hear voices of the past, Anya could start fires with her mind (among other things), Danika could see into heaven and hell, and Sabin's wife, Gwen...well, she had a dark side you saw just before you died. Painfully.

"My friend, what I've got here is a bona fide Hunter." Strider slapped her ass as if a fly was perched there and he couldn't live another second without smashing it. The action was a reminder that she meant nothing to him. Although why he didn't tell his friend *which* Hunter she was, when he'd been so excited before, he didn't know. Actually, he did know. Fatigue. Yeah, he was tired, that was all, and didn't want to have to deal with all the praise. Tomorrow, after a nice long rest, he'd spill everything.

The girl offered no reaction to his slap, but then, he hadn't expected her to. He'd repeatedly drugged her as he'd dragged her from one corner of the world to the other. From Rome to Greece to New York to L.A. and finally to Budapest, leading her brethren on a merry chase as they attempted to save her.

Something they would never do.

*We won!* his demon laughed.

*Damn right we did.* He shivered in delight.

"Hunter?" All amusement fled his friend's face, the light dying in his eyes, turning those emeralds into sharp, deadly blades.

"Afraid so." Hunters. Their greatest enemy. The fanatics who wanted to destroy them. The bastards who considered them evil, beyond redemption, and the scourge of the earth. The assholes who blamed them for all the world's heartache. Best yet, they were the militia Strider was going to send to the hottest depths of hell, one soldier at a time. Or, with grenades, a few hundred at a time. Depended on his mood, he supposed.

"You should have offed her already," Torin remarked. "Now Sabin will want to talk with her."

"Talk" equaled torture in Sabin's mind. "I know he will. That's why she's still alive." She knew things about the gods pulling their strings, and could do things, impossible things, like cause weapons to materialize from thin air. Something only angel warriors could do. Or so he'd thought. Problem was, she wasn't an angel. And not just because she lacked wings. Girl had a temper.

Strider wanted to know how much she knew and how she did what she did.

More than that, he hadn't been able to do his job—aka dispose of Hunter trash—when he'd been alone with her. Every time he'd tried, he'd looked at her beautiful face and hesitated. The hesitation had given way to desire, and he'd started battling urges to kiss her rather than "off" her.

Sabin wouldn't let him get away with that shit. Sabin would ride his ass until he acted. Strider would have no choice but to step up to the plate and knock the ball out of the park. Because… His hands curled into fists. Because this woman, this walking atrocity…

His teeth gritted, and his jaw clenched so tightly the ache shot through his temples and straight into his brain. He experienced the same reaction every time he considered what she'd once done. This woman had helped decapitate his friend Baden, once keeper of the demon of Distrust.

Strider could *never* forget or forgive that fact.

The savage beheading had taken place thousands of years ago, but the pain inside him was as fresh as if it had happened this morning. Along with his friend, a piece of his own soul had died that day, and as the girl had learned during their trek to this fortress, a good portion of his heart had withered, too.

Mercy wasn't something he possessed. Not anymore. Most especially not for her.

He thought he'd killed her in vengeance already, all those centuries ago. Recalled the slash of his blade, the crimson tide of her blood and the metallic stench of death wafting on the air. The sound of her body slamming into rock, her last gurgle of breath. Yet here she was, alive and well and driving him flipping insane.

Maybe he *had* killed her. Maybe she'd been reborn. Or maybe her soul had been stuffed inside another body. Or maybe this chick was more immortal than he was and had somehow healed after the beheading. He didn't know, didn't care.

All that mattered was that she *was* Hadiee of ancient Greece. Well, she called herself Haidee now. From Had-e-ay to Hay-dee. Evidently she'd changed the spelling and pronunciation for "modernization." Not that he gave a shit. He called her Ex, short for Demon Executioner, and that was that.

The proof of her crimes rested in her eyes. Those wintry, callous gray eyes. In the pride that dripped from her voice every time she spoke of that fateful night—*I just loved the way his head rolled. Didn't you?*—and the stark tattoos etched into her back. Tattoos that kept score. Haidee 1. Lords 4.

She deserved everything he and Sabin would do to her.

"I'm taking her to the dungeon," he said, and he'd never heard such a combination of relish and regret in his own voice before. Once again he started forward, throwing over his shoulder, "If you'd be a sweetheart and let Doubty-Poo know..."

"No can do, Stridey-man. There's, uh, something you gotta see." A blast of fear mixed with dread and grim expectation accompanied the words.

Strider halted, one foot raised midair. He straightened, still-sleeping baggage nearly sliding to the ground. Slowly he turned, adjusting Ex, and faced Torin, his own sense of dread sprouting as he spied his friend's now pallid skin. White dusted with tiny rivers of blue. "You said everything was fine. What's wrong?"

Torin shook his head. "No way to explain until you've seen. And I said everything was fine *for the most part.* Now come on."

"The girl—"

"Bring her. She'll be guarded, you'll see." A wave of

Torin's hand, and he was racing up the stairs, taking them two at a time.

Dread increasing, Strider followed, Ex bouncing on his shoulder. If she'd been awake, she would have lost her breath, over and over again, grunting from the pain of having her stomach repeatedly slammed into his bone. She also would have fought him with a skill matched by few.

Too bad the drugs had been so potent. A good fight would have settled his nerves.

What was so important that Torin didn't want him taking a few minutes to lock an abominable Hunter away?

His thoughts splintered the moment he hit the landing.

All he could do was gape. Angels. So many angels. No wonder the house had been redecorated. Divine intervention and all that. Angels did like them some pretties.

They stood along the wall, the only space between them filled by the arch of their wings. White feathers laced with gold, the wings of warriors. Their scents perfumed the air, a collage of orchids, morning dew, chocolate and champagne. They ranged in height, though none were shorter than six foot three, and though they wore girly white robes, their muscle mass rivaled Strider's.

Most were male, but all were demon assassins trained to hunt, to destroy, and when warranted, to protect. Since they didn't rush at him, ripping swords of fire from the air, as he knew they were very capable of doing, he assumed they were here for the latter.

He studied them, searching for answers. Twenty-three in total, but not one of them glanced in his direction. They kept their eyes straight ahead, their stances taut, their hands anchored behind their backs. Not a sound did they make. Not even the rasp of breath.

Physically, they…entranced him. And yeah, it was

embarrassing as hell to admit that, even to himself. But the sheer magnetism of them was stunning. Hypnotic. A drug for his eyes.

They possessed all different shades of hair. From the darkest of midnight to the palest of snow, but his favorite was the gold. So pure, so fluid, a king's ransom that had been melted and mixed with the dazzle of summer sun. Rich, vibrant. Almost...alive. No way he'd be teasing any of them about such prissy locks, though.

They might not be attacking him, might not even be looking at him, but death radiated from them.

Someone cleared his throat.

Strider blinked, Torin coming back into focus. His friend occupied the center of the hallway. Probably had the entire time, only Strider had lost sight of anything but the angels the moment he'd spied them. Yep. Em-bar-rass-ing.

"Why?" was all he asked.

Torin understood. "Aeron and William took Amun into hell on a rescue mission. And yeah, they got Legion out of there. She's alive, healing, but Amun..."

Strider filled in the rest and wanted to punch a hole in the wall. The keeper of Secrets had new voices in his head.

He'd been with Amun for thousands upon thousands of years. Eons, what seemed countless millennia. He knew the warrior's demon absorbed the darkest thoughts and deepest mysteries of anyone nearby. Things long buried, horrific, gruesome. Unwanted, humiliating. Soul-changing. And if Amun had been in hell, where demons roamed in their purest form, his head was now churning with all kinds of evil. Malevolent whispers, wicked images, both drowning the essence of who he was.

Or rather, who he'd *been*.

"The angels?" Strider gritted out. Yeah, he knew it was rude to discuss the beings as if they weren't there, but he simply didn't give a shit. He didn't love many people, but he loved the other demon-possessed residents of this fortress. Even more than he loved himself, and that was a whole hell of a lot.

"They wanted to kill him, but—"

"Fuck no!" he roared. Anyone touched his friend, and they'd lose their hands—followed by their limbs, their organs and, when he tired of torturing them, their lives.

He hefted Ex off his shoulder and into his arms before easing her to the floor and stalking forward, already reaching for a blade.

Defeat sensed his need to destroy and laughed. *Win!*

"Stop." Torin raised his arm to ward him off, even as he backtracked to maintain distance. "Let me finish, damn it! They wanted to kill him, were supposed to kill him, but they haven't. Won't."

*Yet* hung in the air like a noose around his neck. Strider chose to ignore that noose—for the moment—and stopped, already panting and sweating with the force of his instant and white-hot rage.

*Win?* his demon whined.

*No challenge has been issued.* Therefore, he could back off without consequences.

*Oh,* he thought he heard, a whole lot of disappointment in the undertone.

"Why are they here, then?" he snapped, demanding an answer *now.* Or else.

Green eyes grew shadowed as Torin shifted from one foot to the other. His mouth opened and closed, the right explanation eluding him perhaps. "Amun didn't just absorb new memories. He absorbed demon minions. Hundreds of them."

"How? How the fuck is that possible? I've lived with him for centuries, and he's never absorbed *my* demon."

"Nor mine. But ours are High Lords who can bind

themselves to humans. Those were mere underlings, and as you know, they can only bind themselves to, what? High Lords. Which they did, to his. He's...tainted now, a danger far worse than the brush of my skin. The angels are guarding him. Limiting the contact he has with others, ensuring he doesn't leave and...hurt. Himself, humans."

Strider scowled. Amun rarely spoke, containing the secrets he unwittingly stole inside himself so that no one else would have to deal with them, fear them or be sickened by them. A grueling burden few could carry. Yet he did it because there was no one more concerned with the well-being of those around him. So, a danger? No. Strider refused to believe it.

"Explain *better*," he commanded, offering Torin another chance to convince him.

Since they'd reunited a few months ago after centuries apart, he knew Torin was used to his smiles and jokes, but Disease didn't flinch at Strider's new vehemence. "Evil seeps from him. Just going into his room, you'll feel its sticky gloom. You'll crave things." He shuddered. "Bad things. And you won't be able to simply wish the disgusting desires away. They'll cling to you for days."

Strider still didn't care and still wouldn't believe it. "I want to see him."

Only the slightest hesitation, as if the decree had been expected, then Torin nodded. "But the girl..." His words trailed off.

Behind him, there was a rustle of clothing, a feminine moan. Strider whipped around in time to see one of the angels lifting Ex into his arms and carrying her toward the unclaimed bedroom next to Amun's.

He almost rushed forward and ripped her away from the heavenly creature. He'd dealt with an angel before—Lysander, leader of these warriors and the worst of the worst when it came to do-gooders—and knew such beings wouldn't understand the depths of his hatred for the woman. They would see Haidee as an innocent human in need of sweet, tender care. But Amun was far more important than any Hunter's treatment, so Strider remained in place.

"Just so you know, she's worse than a demon," he said, a lethal edge sharpening the truth in his tone. "So if you want to protect your charges, you'll guard her like you're guarding Amun. But don't kill her," he added before he could stop himself. Not that they would have. Still. A guy had to state his wants up front, so there would be no confusion later. "She has…information we need."

The angel paused in his stride, head turning to Strider with unerring precision. Like Torin, his eyes were green. Unlike Torin, there were no shadows in them. Only clear, bright flames, crackling, intense…ready to strike like a bolt of lightning.

"I sense her infection." His voice was deep, with the barest hint of smoke. "I will ensure she does not leave the fortress. And that she continues to live. For now."

Infection? Strider knew nothing about an infection, but again, he didn't care. "Thank you." And hell, had he ever thought to thank a demon assassin for anything? Well, besides Aeron's Olivia.

With a shake of his head, he wiped Ex and everything else from his thoughts and marched forward, trailing behind Torin.

At the end of the hallway, the last door on the right, Torin paused, drew in a sorrowful breath, and twisted the knob. "Be careful in there." Then he moved aside, allowing Strider to breeze past him without a single moment of contact.

First thing Strider noticed was the air. Thick and dark, he could almost smell the brimstone…the bodies charred to ash. And the sounds…oh, gods, the sounds. Screams that scraped at his ears, muted, yet in no way forgettable. Thousands upon thousands of demons danced together, creating a dizzying chorus of agony.

He stopped at the foot of the bed, peering down. Amun writhed atop the mattress, clutching his ears, moaning and groaning. No, Strider realized a moment later. Those moans and groans weren't coming from his friend. They were coming from *him*. Amun was silent, his mouth open in an endless cry he couldn't quite release.

His dark skin was clawed to ribbons, those ribbons tattered and dried with blood both old and new. As an immortal soldier, he healed quickly. But those wounds...they looked as if they'd scabbed over, only to be ripped apart again. And again. And his butterfly tattoo, the mark of his demon, had once wrapped around his right calf. Only now, that tattoo *moved*. Sliding up his leg, undulating on his stomach, breaking apart to form hundreds of tiny butterflies, reconnecting into one, then disappearing behind his back.

How? Why?

Shaking, Strider studied his friend's face. Amun's lashes were fused together as if stitched, and the sockets underneath were so swollen he could have smuggled golf balls in there. Oh, gods. Sickness churned in Strider's stomach, pushing bile into his throat. He knew what that swelling meant, recognized the pattern blunted nails had left behind.

Amun had tried to pluck out his own eyes.

To stop the images forming behind them?

That was the last coherent thought Strider had. The last thought he controlled.

The darkness shrouded him completely, burrowing into him, filling his mind, consuming him. There were knives strapped all over his body, he recalled. He should palm them, use them. Slice, oh, how he would slice. Himself,

Amun. The angels outside the room. Then the world. Blood would flow, an ever-thickening crimson. Flesh would peel like dried, rotted paint, and bone would snap in two, tiny shards falling to the floor, merely dust to be swept away.

He would drink the blood and eat the bones, but they wouldn't be what sustained him. No, he would live off the shrieks and squeals his actions provoked. He would bathe in terror, exult in grief. And he would laugh, oh, how he would laugh.

He laughed now, the chilling sound like music to him.

Defeat wasn't sure how to react. The demon cackled, then whimpered, then sank to the back of Strider's mind. Afraid? *Be afraid.*

Something strong and hard banded around his forearms and jerked him backward, dragging him kicking and shouting out of the darkness and into light. Such bright light. His eyes teared, burned. But with the tears, with the burn, the images in his head washed clean and withered to cinder. Somewhat.

Strider blinked into focus. He was trembling violently, glazed with perspiration, his palms bleeding because he *had* grabbed his knives. Was *still* holding them. Only, he'd squeezed them by their blades, cutting through tendon into bone. The pain was severe but manageable as he opened his fingers and the weapons clattered to the floor.

One of the angels stood behind him, another in front of him. They were glowing from within, like twin suns just freed from a too-long eclipse; he fought to breathe, managed to suck in one mouthful of oxygen, then two. Thank the gods. No brimstone, no ash. Only the scent of beloved—and hated—morning dew. Hated because, with the fresh, clean scent, reality was brought into Technicolor focus.

*That's* what Amun had to endure?

Strider had been given a taste, only a taste, yet his friend suffered with the gloom and soul-shattering urges all day, all night. No one could maintain his sanity when constantly buffeted against that kind of wickedness. Not even Amun.

"Warrior?" the angel in front of him prompted.

"I'm myself now," he rasped. A lie. He might never be the same again.

He looked over the angel's shoulder and saw Torin. They shared a horrified moment of understanding before he returned his attention to the angel and the situation at hand. "Why the hell are you just standing here? Someone chain him. He's tearing himself apart." Strider's throat was raw, grinding the words into broken glass. "And for fuck's sake, get him on an IV. He needs sustenance. Medicine."

The two angels shared a look similar to the one he'd shared with Torin, only theirs was fraught with knowledge only achieved through battle and heartache, before one returned to his post at the wall and the other entered Amun's bedroom.

The one at the wall said, "He has been on an IV before. Several times, actually. They do not last. The needles always find a way free, with or without his help. The chains, however, we can do. And before you demand we clean him and care for him, I will tell you that we have. We brush his teeth for him. We bathe him. We clean his wounds. We force-feed him. He is taken care of in every way possible."

"What you're doing isn't enough," Strider said.

"We are open to any ideas you have."

Of course, he had no response to that. He might be in control of his thoughts again, but as Torin had promised, the need to kill, to truly hurt the innocent, hadn't fled completely. It was there, like a film of slime on his skin.

He had a feeling he wouldn't be able to scrub himself clean, even if he removed every layer of flesh he possessed.

How was Amun going to survive this?

# CHAPTER TWO

IN BRIEF MOMENTS OF LUCIDITY, Amun knew who he was, what he used to be and the monster he'd become. He wanted to die, finally, blessedly, but no one would take mercy on him and deliver the finishing blow. And no matter how hard he tried—and oh, did he try—he couldn't seem to inflict enough damage on his own body to do the deed himself.

So he fought, trying to expunge the black images and disgusting impulses constantly bombarding him, yet at the same time hold them inside. An impossible challenge, and one he would soon lose. He knew it. There were too many, they were too strong, and they'd already burned away his immortal soul, the last tether that had bound them to his will. Not that he'd ever had control.

He'd fight with every fiber of his being, though. Until the very end. Because when those images and impulses, those *demons,* were loosed on an unsuspecting public...

A shudder rippled through him. He knew what would happen, could see the destruction in his mind. Could taste the sweet flavor of devastation in his mouth.

Sweet...yes...

And like that, this newest moment of clarity evaporated like mist. So many images swam through his head, a deluge of memories, and he didn't know which belonged to him and which belonged to the demons—or their victims. Beatings. Rapes. Murders. Rapture in the face of each.

Pain. Trauma. Death. Paralyzing fear that consumed as it destroyed.

Just then, he only knew that fire smoldered around him, melting his skin, blistering his throat. That thousands of tiny, stinging bugs had managed to dig their way into his veins, and they were still feasting on him. That the smell of rot filled his nose, and had infused his every cell. That—

Dead bodies were piled around him, on top of him, smashing and burying him, he suddenly realized. He was trapped, suffocating.

*Help!* he screamed inside his head. *Someone help me!* But no one ever came. Hours passed, perhaps days. His frantic struggling waned until he could only smack his lips. He was thirsty. Oh, gods, was he thirsty. He needed something, anything, to wash away the ash caked inside his mouth.

*Please! Help!*

Still no one came. This was his punishment. He was to die here. Until he came back to life to suffer some more. Desperation renewed his struggle to free himself—but that only made things worse. There were too many bodies, the weight of them drowning him in a ceaseless sea of blood, rot and despair. There was no hope of escape. He truly was going to die here.

But then his surroundings changed again, and he was looking down on that mountainous, decaying pile, grinning and holding another body to toss on top.

This one had died too soon, he thought, gaze shifting to the motionless female soul he held in his scaled, gnarled arms. Souls were as real and corporal down here as humans were up there, and for seventy-two years he'd kept this one chained. She'd been helpless as he'd sliced her piece by agonizing piece. He'd laughed when she'd begged for mercy, revived her when she'd thought to find that same mercy in sleep, and forced her to watch as he did the same to her beloved family, two members he also owned.

So much *fun*…

A female's tears had never tantalized him so exquisitely, and he'd meant to enjoy her suffering at least another seventy years. But he'd gotten carried away this morning, his claws just a little too sharp, the tips sinking just a little too deep.

Oh, well.

He was Torment, and there were a thousand other souls awaiting his attention. Why mourn the loss of this one?

He rid himself of the body with the barest flick of his wrists. She landed, the other damned mortals clanking around her. He waited, expectant, and was soon rewarded. One of his minions, his hungry, hungry minions, crept to the body and began to feast, snapping and hissing at any other creatures who attempted to thieve the delicious meal.

Such a pretty picture they made, the scaled, crimson-eyed fiend and the naughty human who'd dared to die before he'd finished with her. Oh, well, he thought again. Her soul would soon wither, materialize, and solidify somewhere in this endless pit, and if he were the one to find her, he would have another chance to torture her.

Whistling under his breath, he turned and strolled away.

In the next instant, Amun was swept out of hell in a blinding gale of fury and sorrow, Torment no longer, but a female. Human. She huddled in a corner, no more than twelve years old, the harsh material that covered her body like something out of a historic reenactment, tears scalding her cheeks, fear a living entity inside her chest. She was dirty, pale, the straw surrounding her the only source of comfort.

"Have you forgotten how I saved you?" a hard male voice asked. In Greek. *Ancient* Greek.

His booted feet slapped the ground as he paced in front of her. He was on the short side, his face scarred by the pox and his body rotund. His name was Marcus, but she called him the Bad Man. Yes, he'd saved her, but he'd beaten her, too. When her words pleased him, she was given food, shelter. When they did not, she was forgotten, locked away, terrified of being sold as a slave.

She didn't want to be terrified anymore.

He'd plucked her from the hut where she'd lived her entire life. Until he had arrived, she'd been too afraid to leave, even though there'd been no one left to care for her. Somehow, he had known about the terrors that filled her every dream, both awake and asleep—memories no little girl should have, much less replay over and over again, eyes open or closed—and he had promised to help her.

For some reason, she had hated him at first sight, just as she'd begun to hate everything—herself, her hut, the world—but in her desperation, she had believed him. Now she wished she had run.

"Have you. Forgotten how. I saved you? How the evil one wanted you dead, how I whisked you away before he could return? Don't make me ask again."

"N-no, I haven't forgotten," she replied in that same lost language, the words trembling from her throat in a panicked rush.

"Good. Nor will you forget how the evil one infected you. Or what, exactly, the evil one is."

She didn't understand the part about being infected, but the rest had been drilled into her head. "He is a Lord."

"And who killed your family?"

"A Lord." Her voice was stronger now, a flash of mutilated bodies appearing in her mind.

A memory quickly followed, the Bad Man disappearing from view. A memory only three weeks old, and yet, it seemed an eternity had passed already.

"You were promised to someone," her parents' murderer had said, his voice eerie, unnatural, as he'd splashed over the crimson river between their bodies. *He* was the evil one, and something in his voice had caused a blanket of ice to form around her soul. He'd had no face, and his feet hadn't quite touched the floor. He was tall and thin, a black robe swathing him from head to toe, shielding every inch of him, floating around him and dancing in a wind she couldn't feel. "They should have kept their promise."

"Who are you?" she'd asked shakily, terrified and numb all at once. She had only stumbled upon this scene a few minutes ago and hadn't quite processed what she was seeing.

Now, looking back, with the Bad Man's warnings about the creature's evilness ringing in her ears, she quaked. Despite her wonderings, the memory continued on.

"Who I am matters not. Who *you* are is all that matters," the faceless being said. He scooped her up, obviously planning to leave with her, but she fought him with all her might. When he couldn't subdue her, he stabbed her. Once, in the side, barely missing vital organs.

The pain that consumed her was devastating. And yet, with the pain, more of that aberrant cold stormed to life, seeping from her. A cold that didn't just numb. A cold that raged liked a blizzard inside her.

And then, ice actually crystallized over her skin, seeping from her pores. What she was seeing couldn't be real. Couldn't possibly be real.

As the creature strode outside the hut, still holding her, she reached up and pushed at the face she still couldn't see, skin meeting skin. He howled with an agony that matched her own.

For several seconds, neither of them could pull away. Perhaps they were locked together, frozen by the ice. Then he dropped her, and she scrambled backward, bleeding, hurting. Still howling, he disappeared, there one moment, gone the next. Leaving her reeling, uncertain of what had happened and how she'd done what she'd done.

"How are you going to repay these Lords, my darling Hadiee?" the Bad Man asked, drawing her back to the present. She didn't like him any better than she liked the evil one.

Another answer that had been drilled into her head. One she wouldn't forget, one that was as much a part of her as her arms and legs. Perhaps more so, because it was a shield of armor around her, keeping her safe. "Slaughter them all." They were murderers, after all, and they deserved to die.

A pause, silence, and then soft fingers briefly ruffled her hair. "That's a good girl. I'll train you yet."

A split second later, the image inside Amun's mind changed. He realized he was no longer reliving a memory, her memory, but was now staring down at the girl. She was bathed in light, older, a woman now, and sleeping so innocently on a bed of silver silk.

There was something familiar about her name, even though he knew she had changed it. Hadiee then, but Haidee now. There was something familiar about her surroundings, too, but his mind refused to bridge the gap from questions to answers.

She had a shoulder-length crop of pale hair that she'd streaked with pink. Her face was lush in its femininity, despite the silver eyebrow ring she sported. Perhaps because her dark blond brows arched like a cupid's bow.

Lashes thick enough to be a raven's wing fluttered open, one moment fanning over the rise of perfectly sculpted cheekbones, the next framing eyes of pearl-gray, the next, fanning again. She fought to awaken, as if sensing his scrutiny, but failed, allowing him to continue.

Her delicate nose led to lips that reminded him of a

freshly blooming rose. Her skin appeared eternally flushed, as if she were constantly lost to arousal, the undertones kissed by the sun. No, he thought next. Not just kissed by the sun, but *sprinkled* with its rays, as if she was lit from the inside, a thousand tiny diamonds crushed into her flesh. Not like the Harpies, whose luminous, multihued flesh rivaled the brightest rainbow. This woman, this Haidee, didn't actually glow. She was simply beauty personified.

He could have watched her forever, he mused. She was his first glimpse of paradise in what seemed an infinite nightmare. But, of course, even this was to be taken from him.

Though he fought, the image shifted again, orange-gold flames suddenly filling his line of vision. Plumes of smoke curled upward, painting the acrid air with what looked to be a demon's breath.

A city burned in front of him, huts crackling as timber fell and grass disintegrated. Mothers screamed for their children, and fathers lay facedown in the blood-soaked dirt, weapons protruding from their backs. All of them wore the same type of clothing little Hadiee—Haidee now, he reminded himself—had sported. Dark, threadbare linen, rough and stained.

He wasn't the only one watching the destruction. Eleven warriors stood at his sides, their eyes glowing bright red, their skin merely a mask that concealed the hideous monsters lurking underneath. Monsters with sharp-tipped horns knifing from their skulls, poisonous fangs jutting from their mouths, and oozing scales rather than peach-tinted flesh.

Their gore-covered chests lifted and fell with the force of their breaths, their nostrils flaring. Their hands clenched around blades as their thoughts invaded his mind. More. They needed more. More flames, more screams, more death. For only when the entire world was flooded with the blood and bones of these *precious* mortals would they be satisfied. Fulfilled.

Except…

Amun didn't want to kill just then. He wanted to return to the little girl. He wanted to hold her close and tell her everything was going to be all right, and that he would save her from the Bad Man. He wanted to return to the woman. He wanted to curl beside her and hear *her* tell *him* everything was going to be all right, and that she would save him from the demons.

And he would. He would return.

Amun struggled to reach her. He didn't care when skin tore and bone snapped. No, he welcomed the pain. Liked it, even. Perhaps too much. And he didn't care when flames rushed to him, licked over him, hundreds of spiked tongues leaking acid. He welcomed the sting, because with these newest wounds, the bugs in his veins were finally freed. They raced out, crawling all over his body, the bed.

The bed. Yes, he was atop a bed, he thought hazily.

Suddenly he could feel the shredded sheets underneath him, every savage gash carved in his muscles, the pain so much greater than before, and not so welcome now. Worse, steel pressed into his wrists and ankles, preventing him from stanching the flow of blood or shooing away the bugs.

Though every instinct he possessed shouted that he continue to fight, he forced himself to stop thrashing. In and out he breathed, realizing the air was heavy and coated with decay. But underneath the rot, he smelled something else…something crisp, like the earth. Pulsing, vibrant life.

And beneath the flames, he could feel the sweetest kiss of winter ice, soothing his burns, gifting him with tendrils of strength. What—who—was responsible?

He tried to open his eyes, but his lids were sealed

shut. He frowned. Why were his lids sealed shut? And the steel…chains, he thought as the haze began to fade. Binding him, holding him prisoner. Why?

A startling moment of lucidity.

He hissed in horror, even as he clung to every thought now forming in his head, praying he continued to remember. He was Amun, keeper of the demon of Secrets. He had loved, and he had lost. He had killed, but he had also saved. He was not an animal, a brutal killer, not anymore, but a man. An immortal warrior who safeguarded what was his.

He had entered hell, knowing the consequences but willingly overlooking them. Because he couldn't bear to see his friend Aeron hurting, crazed with the knowledge that his surrogate daughter was trapped in hell's torturous blaze. So Amun had gone, and had emerged with hundreds of other demons and souls all trapped inside him, writhing, screaming, desperate for escape.

But he was home now, and he needed to die. *Had* to die. He was a danger to his friends, the world. He *would* die.

There would be no comforting Haidee, nor taking comfort from the woman she'd become, for he could never allow himself to leave this room, his sanctuary. His coffin. And that, he found, was what he would mourn most. Whether he'd encountered her soul in hell and absorbed her memories there, or had stumbled upon her years ago, her voice lost in the dark, thorny mire of his mind until now, he would never know. This was it for him.

This was the end.

*Flames.*

*Screams.*

*Evil.*

Once again they battled for his attention and threatened to overwhelm him.

Amun knew he couldn't hold them off for long. Too

demanding, so demanding… He focused on the earthy perfume and cooling breeze, head automatically turning to the left, following invisible threads wafting in the air. Leading from this bedroom…into the one next to it?

*Power.*

*Peace.*

*Salvation.*

Perhaps he *could* leave this room, he thought then. Perhaps he could be saved. That small sip of salvation, the barest taste…a frosted apricot, juice so sweet his throat would forever rejoice.

He just had to—*flames, screams, evil*—get there. Must…fight. *FLAMES*. Amid the growing black thunder in his brain, Amun jerked at his bonds. *SCREAMS*. Already torn flesh surrendered, and already broken bone dusted to powder. *EVIL*. But he couldn't pull himself free. He'd already used up his strength, he realized. He had nothing left.

*FLAMES, SCREAMS, EVIL..*

As he slumped onto the mattress, he laughed silently, bitterly. He'd lost, and so easily, too. He'd truly, finally lost. He couldn't even call for his friends. A single word spoken, a single sound made, and everything inside him would spew out, his clash against the evil all for nothing.

*FLAMESSCREAMSEVIL.*

Closer…closer now…

A shocking burst of hope as that sense of defeat shattered.

If he couldn't reach whoever was in that bedroom, perhaps he…she…they…could reach him.

As the evil swamped him once more, Amun shouted as soundlessly as he'd laughed. *Come to me!*

# CHAPTER THREE

*COME TO ME!*

The desperate male voice invaded Haidee Alexander's mind, a thriving fire amid a raging ice storm, dragging her from a cloying sleep and into total awareness. She jerked upright, panting, wild gaze scanning, mind cataloging her options in seconds, just as she'd trained it to do since being captured by the demon. Unfamiliar bedroom with one window, one door, offering two possible escape routes.

The door, varnished to a luxuriant shine. Scratches around the handle, meaning it was well-used. Probably locked. The window, thick glass, unstreaked by hand or bird. The pane wasn't nailed shut, then. Couldn't be, not to maintain that level of cleanliness.

Window, best bet.

Alone. Had to act now.

Riding a cloud of urgency, Haidee threw her legs over the side of the bed and stood. Her knees instantly buckled, too feeble to hold her weight. Not normal. Usually she could awaken and five seconds later be ready to run a marathon. A this-is-the-only-way-to-survive marathon.

This weakness… How long had she been out this time?

She lumbered to a shaky stand, trying to find her balance as she replayed the happenings of the last weeks through her head. She'd been overpowered by Defeat, the demon she'd been hunting. He'd carted her to what seemed a thousand different locations, trying to lose her boyfriend, Micah, and his crew of four. Hunters, all of them.

*Don't think about that right now. You'll lose focus.*

Escape. That's what mattered.

She tripped her way to the window, but just before she tugged on the pane, she stilled. In all their days together, Defeat had never left her side. He hadn't even trusted her to go to the bathroom or shower by herself, but here she was, on her own.

So, where was he now?

Two options. Either the demon had reached his final destination and was confident enough in the surrounding security to venture off on his own, or someone had stolen her from him.

Next thought: if someone had stolen her, they wouldn't have abandoned her. They would have wanted her to know their intentions. Good or bad.

So. Defeat had her where he wanted her. The door and the window were probably wired, so there was a very good chance an alarm would sound the moment she touched either one.

Would an army of demons come gunning for her?

Probably. But she didn't care. She had to try. Giving up wasn't in her nature.

Haidee gripped the warm edge of the panel and shoved. Cursed. Nothing, no movement. Not just because her fingers were as weak as her knees, but because the pane was sealed. She'd been wrong about the cleanliness factor, but at least she'd also been wrong about the wire.

Still. She'd have to find another way out. And she would. She'd been in far worse situations than this and survived. Hell, *thrived.*

Steeling herself, she peered outside to note what she'd have to overcome once she left this place. The sun shone brightly, amber rays causing her eyes to tear. She wiped each drop away with the back of her wrist. No girly weaknesses allowed. Her prison rested high on a mountaintop, a barbed gate—electric?—stretching skyward and wrapping around the perimeter. She'd encountered similar gates in the past and knew this one would be impossible to climb without inflicting so much damage she'd die on the other side. If she even made it over.

Still. There were hundreds of trees, each more lush and green than the last, their limbs stretching in welcome. Those limbs would hide her, their leaves draping her and allowing her to search for a way to bypass that gate. And if there *wasn't* a way to bypass it, she'd forgo cover and climb. Bottom line, death was preferable to staying here and being tortured by a demon.

Okay. So. New plan. Shatter the glass and shimmy to land. Easy.

Yeah. Right. *I've never been that lucky.* Haidee twisted and surged through the room, her steps not getting any smoother. Clearly, whatever drug Defeat had repeatedly injected into her vein still poured through her.

*Concentrate, woman.* The spacious chamber boasted a king-size canopied bed with a white swath overlaying the top and falling to the floor like clouds sprinkled with fairy dust. A floral print love seat and a small glass table perched in a tiny alcove, illuminated by a chandelier weeping with glittering crystal. None of which she could throw.

To the left was a freshly polished desk and matching chair. No paperweights or knickknacks rested on the surface, and the drawers were empty. To the right was a full-length mirror surrounded by an ebony frame. Both were bolted to the wall. Next she tried the door. As she'd suspected, it was locked.

Panting, fury blooming, she kicked the bench at the foot of the bed. The heavy wood didn't move an inch. And shit, that *hurt!* She yelped, hopping and rubbing her stinging toe. Someone had removed her shoes, leaving her barefoot. Something she wished she'd noticed before.

Damn, damn, damn. The luxury and wealth here made a mockery of the hovel she'd scrimped and saved and finally managed to buy for herself, yet there wasn't a damn thing she could use to aid her escape. What the hell was she going to do?

*Come to me!*

The tortured, pain-filled voice overwhelmed her senses, the words like licks of fire, somehow heating her up. A voice? Heating her? Could be a hallucination, yeah, but she'd seen and experienced all kinds of weirdness throughout her too-long life to simply write this off.

"Who said that?" She spun, fighting a wave of dizziness and automatically reaching for the blades she kept anchored at her thighs.

Only silence greeted her—and she sported no weapons. Defeat had taken her knives, guns and poisons, foolishly thinking he'd triumphed. But that's what he—it—did. Broke down the opponent through any means necessary, destroying all thoughts of achieving victory, no matter the cost of surrender.

Not that he'd broken her.

He'd learn. Haidee was unbreakable.

*Come to…me…* Weaker now, riding a tide of despair, but no less urgent.

Not a hallucination, she thought. Couldn't be. That heat… So, who was he? A prisoner like her? There was something oddly familiar about his voice, as if she'd heard it before and it had made an impression. Yet she couldn't specifically place it. Was he a Hunter? Had they met during training? At one of the thousand debriefings she'd attended?

*Come…*

Her ears twitched, and she turned, following the sound

of his voice this time, determined to help him, just in case he was a Hunter as she suspected.

*Come...please...*

There. She frowned. A wall. Was he on the other side? The fact that she'd heard him certainly suggested he was nearby.

Slowly she approached the wall. She padded her hands along the smooth, delicate paper, finding no hint of a doorway, and yet... Haidee dropped to her knees, gaze zeroing in on a tiny gap between crown molding and floor. A small crack of light seeped through.

No, not light. Not fully. Woven with that stream of light and dancing dust motes was a wisp of black, a writhing phantom, curling up, inching toward her.

With another yelp, she scrambled backward. The black tendril followed her, avoiding her pants and her T-shirt to reach the skin bared at her wrist. But when it touched her, a screech rent the air and the...thing was sucked back through the crack, returning to the other room.

What. The. Hell?

Had she just met one of the demons, stripped of its human cloak? Was *that* what tormented the man who'd called her? Probably.

Her fight-or-flight instinct screamed *flight.*

Haidee replied, *Screw you, flight! I won't leave a man behind.*

Teeth grinding, she scraped her nails over the wallpaper until she created a groove. Then she began ripping, tossing the pieces she extracted over her shoulder. She worked feverishly and finally revealed enough of the wall to find the outline of the door.

No knob. Of course.

Through faint scrape patterns on the floor, she knew the door had once opened from the right. Which meant there would have been a knob at one point. She had only to find where the demons had spackled over the hole its removal would have left behind....

She scraped the center of the right side, cringing at the grating sound she created, until flecks of white chalk began to embed in her nails. Bingo! Clawing harder, deeper, she removed the spackle as fast as she could. Took half an hour to reach the other side, and by then, ice coated her entire body in a chilly sheen.

Her arms trembled violently, her sense of urgency increasing. She was swiftly using up her reservoir of strength and knew she wouldn't be able to stay on her feet much longer.

When she collapsed, she wanted to be outside, the man with her.

Haidee latched her fingers around the edges of the hole and jerked. The door eked open a mere fraction of an inch. Fighting disappointment, she gave another jerk—only to be rewarded with another fraction. *Get in the game, Alexander. You can do this.* Deep breath in, hold, hold... As she exhaled, she tugged so hard she feared her spine would snap. Finally. Real movement. Not much, yet just enough. When the door stopped, it stopped hard. She lost her grip and fell to her ass.

Pinpricks of starlight dotted her gaze, but when the crackling orange and yellow washed away, she focused on the gap she'd created. A sweet sense of victory flooded her as she popped to her feet. Her knees rebelled with every step forward, but she didn't pause.

She squeezed her way through the opening, shirt snagging on a sharp protrusion, then ripping as she just kind of fell into the other room. When she balanced, she quickly took stock, readying herself for anything. Another bedroom, this one a mix of light and dark. There was a thrashing man on the only bed, smoke rising from him, undulating.

Her gaze locked on the smoke, and she gasped. It was as beautiful as it was horrifying. An ocean of crumbled black diamonds, punctuated by the occasional sparkle of paired rubies—like eyes, watching, lethally intent—and damning flashes of white. Sharp, like fangs.

*Come on, come on. Time's wasting.* For some reason, looking away actually hurt, shooting a pain from her temples to her belly, but she did it, refocusing on the man and closing the distance between them. The moment she reached him, bile scalded her throat, and she nearly lost her last meal. Fruit and bread that Defeat had grudgingly given her. All those injuries…

What had the demon done to him? *Peeled* him? Lit him on fire? He was—

Oh, God. Oh, dear God. Eyes widening, she covered her mouth with shaky hands. No. *No!*

Despite the savaged body, the swollen, nearly unrecognizable face, she knew who writhed before her. Micah. Her boyfriend. Same dark skin—what remained of it—and same muscled frame. Same inky hair he constantly smoothed from his brow. No wonder she'd recognized that battered voice.

*Oh, God.* The demon must have caught him while he'd chased after her, trying to save her.

Tears rained down her cheeks, crystallizing into ice as they fell. She almost crumpled into a sobbing heap. She'd dreamed of this man long before she'd ever met him. Had *loved* him long before she'd ever met him. She'd thought him a memory that hadn't quite been wiped clean after—

*Nope. Don't go down that road, either.* Those kinds of thoughts would paralyze her as nothing else could. Micah. She'd think only about Micah now. He needed her.

About seven months ago, she discovered he wasn't simply a memory or even a figment of her imagination. He was real. She'd thought, *Surely this is a sign we're meant to be together.* A point further proven when they were both assigned to the same demon-hunting mission in Rome, and then again when he'd asked her out, as attracted to her as she was to him. She'd said yes without any hesitation.

Except the real man hadn't lived up to her imaginings.

There'd been no bone-deep connection. No earth-shattering awareness. She'd blamed herself, and rightly so, and had tried to force the bond. Because of her visions, she'd known—*knew*—on a level she didn't quite understand that he would make her happy. That he was her future. That he could at last melt the unnatural ice that still swirled inside her.

So she'd stayed with him, all the while thinking the connection would soon spark. It never had. And though they were still seeing each other and were totally exclusive, she'd always held a little piece of herself back. She hadn't even slept with him yet. But now...*connection.* Sizzle. And it was everything she'd expected to feel for him.

Here, now, she thought she might never again be whole without him. As if she'd finally found the last piece of a puzzle.

Guilt suddenly swarmed her. She hadn't been the best girlfriend, holding herself back as she had, yet still he'd searched for her, still he'd challenged a Lord of the Underworld for her. And now, he might die for her.

"Oh, baby," she managed to croak past a constricted throat. "What did he—" they? "—do to you?"

She reached out, the shadows hissing as they inched backward, away from her, away from him, as if afraid to be near her. She paid them no heed. As gently as she was able, she slid one of Micah's pulverized hands through the steel cuff that bound him. The amount of blood and the crushed bone allowed for an easy glide and also had her swallowing bile at an astonishing rate.

Could he recover from this? Could anyone?

Thankfully, her touch seemed to calm him rather than hurt him further. The thrashing became less violent, and he eventually relaxed against the mattress. Haidee moved to the other side and freed his other wrist. By the time his ankles were unchained, the slightest hint of a smile curled his lips.

Her chest contracted at the sight of it, both an agony and a blessing. He was damaged, but he was alive. Would he be grateful for that, though? He might never be able to fight again.

Didn't matter. She had to save him.

Biggest problem: she couldn't carry him. He was too heavy. And he certainly couldn't walk. She didn't have a medical degree, but she'd bet a fortune that half the bones in his body were broken. Still. She couldn't leave him behind, either.

She studied him more intently, praying for a solution. Instead, what she found had her gasping in outrage. Those *bastards!* Of all the cruel things they'd done, this was the worst. They'd branded him. Etched a jagged-winged butterfly—the mark of their demons—into his calf. Just to taunt him.

"I'll make them pay, baby." Her hands coiled into tight fists, ready to strike. "I swear it."

At the sound of her voice, he shifted, angling toward her. He even tried to reach out, the muscles in his forearm bunching with the strain. The action proved to be too much for him, and the arm hung uselessly. A second later, the thrashing started up again.

Cooing, Haidee eased beside him and smoothed away the hair sticking to his brow, just as she knew he liked. The first moment of contact, she experienced a jolt of undiluted heat. The ice that was her constant companion, a part of who and what she was, cracked. Droplets melted, dripping. Instantly Micah calmed, his sweat drying as if he'd absorbed her deepest chill.

Nothing like that had ever happened before, and the sensation disconcerted her. A side effect of what had been done to him, perhaps?

*Bastards,* she thought again, her molars gnashing together. In this life or the next—and she was always given a "next"—she *would* punish them.

Spiderwebs suddenly wove in front of her eyes, gossamer threads laced with a shot of fatigue. Determined, she swept them away. She couldn't deteriorate. Not now. Micah needed her.

*Haidee?*

His voice startled her, but she quickly recovered. "I'm here, baby. I'm here."

A soft sigh echoed, a whisper of contentment. The breathy sound stroked her—even though his mouth had never moved and his lips had never parted. Impossible. Right?

"Micah? How are you talking to me?"

*Sweet, sweet, Haidee.*

Again, his mouth hadn't moved, but again, she'd heard him. And she knew she wasn't imagining his voice. She couldn't be. She'd heard him before ever entering the room.

That could only mean… Her eyes widened in astonishment. He was speaking inside her mind. Had been speaking inside her mind the entire time. That was new for them, too, and far more disconcerting than the heat.

How was he doing it? How could the Lords have caused this?

*Reason it out later.* "I'm going to look for weapons, okay? Something, anything." Could she even stand? Her muscles were vibrating, her veins filling with sludge. "And then I'm going to find a way—"

*No! Don't leave.* There was a panicked pause. *Need you. Please.*

"I won't leave the room, I swear, not without you, but I have to—"

*No! No, no, no!* Babbling now, his body tensing. *You have to stay.*

"Okay, baby, okay. I'm here. I'll stay." Soft, gentle, the promise left her before she could consider the consequences. Not that they would matter. She would rather hand herself over to Defeat, gift wrapped on a silver platter, than cause this man any more grief. "I won't budge from this spot. Promise."

*Need you,* he said again, barely audible this time.

"You've got me. You've always got me." She stretched out, mindful of his injuries, and curled herself around his fragile frame, offering what comfort she could. She knew what it was like to suffer alone. She didn't want that for him. Ever.

Perhaps this was even a blessing in disguise. Micah probably wouldn't survive his wounds if he left the bed anytime soon. And this way, when the demons returned— and they *would* return, they wouldn't leave her for long— she would be here to fight them, to keep them from hurting him even more.

Yeah, they'd strike back and probably kill her. And yeah, she gagged, thinking of what would happen to her after that death, a fate so much worse than being stabbed, shot, or even burned alive. All of which she'd endured before.

She'd told herself she wouldn't consider what happened after she died, but she didn't stop herself this time. Not even when fear swept through her, consuming her, chilling her.

If she managed to kill any of the Lords, they would be eternally lost, but she would be reformed, returned to the age she was now, minus any good memories she'd built of this lifetime, consumed only with the bad, with the hate. It was an agonizing process that made her scream and beg and pray for an eternal death of her own.

A process that had taught her to avoid death at all costs. But this time...she would die willingly, eagerly, taking as many Lords as she could with her. And then, *then* she could return for the rest of them.

Then she could avenge Micah.

# CHAPTER FOUR

AMUN BLINKED OPEN HIS EYES. Or tried to. The action proved difficult, since his lashes felt as if they'd been glued together. And maybe they had been. If one of his friends had punked him, he was going to retaliate. With scissors. He kept tugging and finally managed to separate top from bottom. Immediately his eyeballs burned and watered, everything around him seemingly smeared with Vaseline.

Worse, the light seeping in from the only window still managed to lance his retinas like blade-tipped lasers. He turned his head away from the reflective glass and studied his surroundings as best he could.

He frowned—and damn, that hurt, tugging and splitting multiple cuts on his lips. He was in his own bedroom, but...there was a hole in the wall. A hole that led into the chamber next door. A hole he hadn't made, and to his knowledge, his friends hadn't, either. He liked to think they would have asked his permission before *redesigning* his room like that.

How was he here, anyway?

Last thing he remembered, he'd been deep inside hell, fire crackling all around him as he fought evil spirits and basically got the shit kicked out of both his body and his mind. Demon thoughts and human memories had bombarded him, like bombs going off inside his head, and they—

Were still there, he realized, frown deepening. The dark

thoughts and memories were still there, but though they were churning, agitated, they remained at a distance, as if afraid to gain his attention. Why?

A feminine moan stroked his ears, shocking him into concentrating.

Amun stiffened, his attention shifting again, this time landing on his mattress. Or what should have been mattress. Beside him was a woman. A very beautiful woman who was curled on her side, facing him, her warm breath caressing him. One of her arms was bent over his stomach, as if she couldn't bear to let him go, with her hand resting over his heart. Monitoring the beat?

That arm was tattooed from wrist to shoulder, completely sleeving her. He saw faces—human—each one glowing with life and love. Numbers, too. And dates, maybe? Though, if so, some of those dates were from *way* back. There were also names: Micah, Viola, Skye. And phrases: *Darkness always loses to light* and *You have loved and been loved.*

He knew her. Somehow he knew her. How—

The answer slid into place. Haidee, the one from his visions, or whatever they'd been. The little girl he'd yearned to comfort, and the woman he'd longed to touch. She was here.

How was she here?

He lifted his hand to smooth the pale hair plastered on her cheeks, and his muscle went death match on his bone, both aching in protest. Damn. What the hell was wrong with him?

As carefully as he was able, he moved his arm closer to his face, every inch an unsteady milestone, but not stopping until he had a clear look. Seeing the ruined flesh, the knotted muscle, he wanted to curse.

He'd been chained, maybe tortured. By Hunters?

Had they tortured the girl, and his friends had rescued her, too?

As rage sparked inside him at the thought of her mistreatment, his gaze returned to her. She hadn't moved, was still sleeping so peacefully. Dark circles marred the delicate tissue under her eyes. There were a few smudges of dirt lining her cheeks and a bruise on the underside of her jaw. Signs of wear and tear, but not torture. The rage muted to a low simmer.

*She's fine. And you'll defend her.* Or rather, he would defend her until she healed and he had to send her on her way. He wasn't safe to be around anymore. Not for long.

*For now, though, she's yours.*

Suddenly she jolted upright, her gaze swinging left and right. "Who said that?" Without waiting for a reply, she threw her legs over the side of the bed and stood. She raced to the window.

What was she doing? *Haidee,* he mentally tsked, *you shouldn't be running around like that. You need time to mend.*

As if she'd heard the thought, she spun around and faced him. Eyes of the sweetest pearl-gray widened as they studied him from top to bottom. "Oh, baby. You're getting better. Thank God!"

Baby. She'd called him baby. The first endearment ever to be directed at him, and his ears soaked it up like nectar from the heavens.

"I didn't mean to fall asleep. I'm so sorry." She tripped back to his side. "We have to get out of here. Can you walk?"

*I don't think so.* Both of his femurs were cracked, if not broken entirely. He recognized the heavy ache underneath the muscle. Besides that, he was home. He didn't want to leave.

"Okay, okay. We'll think of another way, then." Even as

she spoke, she scanned the room a second time. "I thought I'd have to fight them from the bed, but they must not have come back." She offered him a fleeting smile. Fleeting, but like a ray of sunshine all the same. "Their mistake."

He blinked. That was the second time she'd—correctly—responded to something he hadn't spoken aloud. *You…hear me?*

"Yes. I know, I know. It's weird." That gaze never stopped scanning. For weapons? An escape route? "I was surprised, too. I don't know how it's happening, but I'm grateful. If I hadn't heard you from next door, I would have left without you."

No one had ever heard him like that. No one. He'd always been the one to know what others were thinking, and he found he was…uncomfortable with this new development.

How was she doing it? Could she hear *everything?* All the secrets floating through his head? Could she even hear his whimpering demon? What about the others, the new ones who liked to scream? Or could she only hear what he projected at her?

"Can you still not speak?" she asked gently.

Test time. He allowed the answer to form in his mind, but he kept a firm mental hold on it.

"Can you?" she insisted. She reached out and traced a fingertip along the seam of his lips, careful, so careful not to hurt him. The you've-just-reached-the-freezer-section coolness of her skin delighted him.

She hadn't heard, he realized, even as he shivered at her silken touch. Such a surreal moment. She acted as if she knew him…liked him. Baby, he thought, dazed all over again.

*No. I still can't talk.* He pushed the words at her, watching for the minutest reaction.

An angry sigh escaped her, and the corner of her lip

curled in disgust. "Those bastards. Did they do something to your voice box?"

Bastards? *No.* She'd heard that time. Which meant there *were* limits. Thank the gods. No one, especially such an innocent human, should have to listen to the evil inside his head. No one, especially such a fragile female, could survive its gloom. Even now, Amun wasn't sure *he* could.

"Do you remember what happened?" she asked. "How you got here?"

He shook his head, slow, measured, trying not to open up any more wounds. Problem was, he was utterly covered in abrasions. The smallest action tugged too-tight skin and split scabs.

"Okay, then." Her next sigh was sorrowful. Her hand remained on him, as if she couldn't bear to sever contact. "I'll tell you what I know."

He nodded to encourage her, winced.

"Be still, baby," she said, all concerned mother hen and determined commando. "Just listen, okay, and try not to panic." She drew in a deep breath, then slowly released it. "The Lords of the Underworld have us. We're in a structure on top of a hill. Their fortress in Buda, maybe? I didn't see any landmarks to verify my suspicions. Though why they'd risk bringing us here, I don't know. Last I heard, this was where they were keeping two of the artifacts. You think they'd want us as far away from those as possible."

The artifacts. There were four, and each was needed to locate, and thereby destroy, Pandora's box, saving him and his friends from certain death. Besides decapitation and other violent demises, that box was the only thing that could separate man from demon, wiping man from existence and unleashing the then-crazed demons on an unsuspecting world. This woman knew two of the artifacts were here—the All-Seeing Eye and the Cage of

Compulsion—yet she expected the Lords to be *upset* that Amun, a Lord himself, was near them.

She didn't know he was a Lord, he realized. She thought he was a…Hunter?

Like…her? All that disgust, all that anger directed at the Lords…the notion seemed likely. But, if she knew him, why didn't she know who—what—he was? And if she *was* a Hunter, why would his friends have placed her inside his room?

His gaze skidded to the hole in the wall. Maybe his friends didn't know she was here. But…

She thought she knew him, and he definitely recognized her. At least somewhat. He knew her name. Haidee. Could picture her face softened by sleep, so lovely. He knew they'd met somewhere, interacted in some way, but not where or when.

For once, his demon wasn't spewing out answers.

This was so damn confusing, and his weakened condition wasn't helping. Maybe she had tricked him into thinking they'd met, so he'd be more inclined to help *her*. But again, how? Why? The artifacts? Would anyone except a Hunter be after them?

His stomach twisted into little knots. There was only one way to find out the truth about this beautiful woman whose presence alone both muddled and cleared his brain. That way was dangerous, the possible consequences severe.

He didn't want to go that route, but he didn't feel he had any other choice. Normally he could read the thoughts of those around him; so far, he'd heard none of hers, despite the fact that she could hear his. Therefore, he needed to deepen the connection between them, push past any mental shields she might possess and peek into her mind, glimpse her memories.

Amun would be careful. He wouldn't let his demon wipe her brain clean—the biggest complication of all. Secrets liked to play, to steal memories and leave the victims with nothing but static. Amun would pull away the moment the fiend tried to do so. Unless she proved to be a Hunter, of course; then all bets were off.

Gritting his teeth against the pain he knew he'd feel, Amun lifted his arms. Gods, the sharp lance, the burn, worse than he'd expected. When he'd reached high enough, he allowed his hands to fall onto Haidee's shoulders.

"Stop whatever you're doing," she admonished. "You're hurting yourself."

Just that small action caused him to moan and groan inside his head. *Need...a moment. Must...*

"Must? What do you need, baby? Tell me, and I'll take care of it."

Baby, again. She'd "take care" of it, of him, as if she cared. Truly cared. He couldn't soften, no matter how much he liked the way she treated him. *Touch your...temples,* he said, guilt suddenly flooding him. He'd just requested her aid for her possible downfall.

Did she have any idea what he could do?

"You getting kinky on me?" she asked with a chuckle. She probably meant to distract him from his pain. She did, just not the way she'd intended. Her jest had his gaze fastening on her lips, imagining the thrust of her tongue inside his mouth.

His body reacted, blood heating, pooling between his legs. Damn it! *Just...need...temples.*

"Okay, okay. I'll help you."

No, she didn't know. Her fingers wrapped around his wrists, so cool, so welcome—so steady—and lifted without any hesitation. No questions about his motives, his intentions. She trusted him absolutely. When his hands reached her temples, she flattened her palms, pushing his closer, providing skin-to-skin contact.

"Like this?"

*Yes.* Such faith. *Too* much. He told himself he was disgusted by that, not delighted. It was a trick to distract him, surely.

Her lashes fluttered closed, and she nibbled on her lush bottom lip. Such straight, white teeth. Once again his body reacted. He wanted those teeth on him…lower…moving up and down on his shaft. He wanted her hands reaching out, tugging at his balls. He wanted her tongue flicking over the slit of his erection, tasting.

*I need to get laid,* he told himself darkly.

The corner of Haidee's lips quirked. "Do you now? I'm invited, I hope," she said with husky entreaty.

Shit. She'd heard. And she wanted to join him. Wanted him deep inside her, rocking them both to satisfaction. *Don't think about that now.* He'd forget he needed to learn about her and simply drag her on top of him. Besides, she could be lying, purposely distracting him as he'd suspected.

"I won't if you won't," she said with a warm chuckle.

*What?*

"Think about having sex."

Damn it. He had to stop talking to himself. She heard every unshielded thought.

How did his friends stand him? He constantly read their minds, knew their every private—and mostly pornographic—contemplation. They rarely chastised him, however, and never made him feel like a nuisance. He'd always figured they didn't care. They must have found a way to hide their true feelings from his demon, though. No way they *liked* his ability.

He owed everyone in this house an apology.

Amun forced his mind to quiet and his own lashes to close. He'd done this a thousand times before, the process as ingrained as breathing. He'd done it for Sabin, his leader. For their cause. He blanked his mind and darkness enveloped him, then he concentrated on his senses. Her skin, cool and soft. Her scent, so earthy. He could hear the rasp of her next exhalation…focused on the chilly breath wafting over him…allowed his demon to reach out…

Colors exploded, chasing away the black. Suddenly images began to take shape. He saw a sky of the brightest azure, a lush green meadow, untouched by time. A scattering of silver stones. Trees missing their leaves, but with sleek, twisted branches. Two little girls running and laughing, playing chase, both wearing lovely pink linen robes, flaxen curls streaming behind them. Sisters. Both possessed hearts practically bursting with love.

Secrets purred in delight.

The reaction struck Amun as odd. Such an innocent memory, and not what the demon usually favored. Why did the fiend even care about this?

The image suddenly shifted, day replaced by night in an instant, leaving only one of the girls. Older now, her gray eyes sparking with tentative joy, as if she was afraid to hope but couldn't help herself.

Her skin was sun-kissed and glowing with health, her cheeks rosy with vitality. She wore a linen robe of lavender this time, flowers of the same color pinned through her hair. Those curls…like ribbons of the very moonlight surrounding her.

This was a past version of Haidee, Amun realized as a gentle, spice-laden breeze caressed her. She stood at the edge of a veranda, looking down into a dappled, crystalline pond. She bore no tattoos, no streaks of pink in her hair, no piercings; she was innocence and optimism wrapped in an utterly stunning package.

"Are you nervous, my sweet?" a female voice asked from behind her.

Haidee turned, startled from her reverie. "I love when

you call me that," she replied sincerely. "Especially since you did not like me at first."

"No. But that soon changed, did it not?"

"It did. And yes, yes. I'm nervous, but excited, too."

They spoke in Greek.

Ancient Greek.

He'd heard the language before, Amun thought, and recently. When? Where?

The scene continued to play on, and Secrets continued to rifle through Haidee's memories, dabbling here and there, the girl completely unaware. Then there was a purr, and Amun knew. Answers. His demon had found the answers.

No new images sprang up, not yet, but what the demon learned, Amun learned, too. Always. So, between one heartbeat and the next, he knew that Little Haidee and Sleeping Beauty Haidee were one and the same. They were *this* woman. And this woman was—

*Responsible for Baden's murder,* he realized.

In a flash that lasted no more than a second, Amun saw Baden, hair soaked with blood and plastered to his scalp. Bodiless. He saw Haidee—*Hadiee*—as she'd once been, golden hair streaming down her back, naked, tanned skin luminous in the moonlight despite the hate radiating from her and the crimson-splatter all over her. He saw her friends, Hunters, swarming, battling *his* friends.

Horror blanketed him. The woman he'd lusted after had helped kill his best friend. The woman he'd thought to defend had helped snuff out the kindest soul he'd ever known. The woman he'd cradled at his side had destroyed the one man who'd stood between easily broken mortals and feral, foaming-at-the-mouth immortals still consumed by the evil of their new demons. The man who'd said, "Save the humans, do not hurt them."

Baden had been the first to find himself in the darkness.

Baden had been the one to help the others do the same. Baden… Baden… Amun's chest constricted so painfully, the barest hint of a gasp left him. He hadn't made a single noise as the new demons had ravaged him, over and over again, but now he was helpless to hold the sound inside. Baden. Gone forever, because of this woman.

Each warrior had loved Baden like a brother, and each had felt as if they were his greatest confidant. That's where the true beauty of the man had lain. His ability to captivate everyone around him. Which had been a miracle, considering the nature of his demon, Distrust.

Now, Amun held one of Baden's killers in his hands. Cupped her temples as he'd once cupped Baden's.

"Are you okay?" Haidee asked him, all concern and sweetness. Her grip on him tightened.

His horror was followed by a quick burst of confusion. How was this possible? She'd died. Hadn't she? Yes. Yes. *She. Had. Died.* Hunters had used her as Bait—dressed her up like a pretty, helpless doll, sent her knocking on Baden's door, begging for help. She had lured him straight into slaughter. The rest of the Lords had arrived just before he'd lost his head; they'd attacked. But even if they had arrived a few minutes sooner, they would have been too late. All the pieces of the game had been set.

Amun remembered the blood, the screams. Remembered Strider victoriously lifting Haidee's head when the battle had finally ended, and like Baden, she'd been without a body. Not even an immortal could recover from that. Otherwise Baden, more alive than anyone he'd ever known, would have risen from the grave long ago. Instead, the man's soul was trapped somewhere in the heavens.

The horror intensified to a shattering level. Amun couldn't bear to remember. Not this. Because the longer he wallowed in the past, the more likely he was to lose his tether on the other deep, dark emotion buried inside him.

Rage. He would destroy the fortress in a way Maddox, keeper of Violence, never had, ruining their home stone by precious stone.

His hands fell away from Haidee and flopped to his sides. Her past faded, as did his own, and he could only stare at her, this present version, hate blending with his horror—then completely overshadowing it. Yet even with that earth-shattering hatred flooding him, the lust remained undiminished.

His body simply didn't care what she'd done.

The pink tip of her tongue swiped over her mouth, leaving a sheen of moisture. Dust motes sparkled around her, and with the pink streaks in her hair and the haze of his vision, she looked like an X-rated fairy-tale fantasy come to dazzling life. Her shirt hugged her breasts, and her nipples were pearled into decadent peaks.

"What *was* that?" she breathed, unaware of the change in him.

*What do you mean?* The question snapped like a whip, lashing out before he could reason what to do, how to proceed.

"The…memories. Of me as a child, then as me as an adult, on the veranda."

She'd seen what he'd seen, then. That had never happened before, either. And yet, she made no mention of Baden—but then, Amun hadn't truly pictured his friend, had he? No, not true. He had. There'd been a split-second glimpse. She just hadn't noticed, then, the other memories holding her attention captive.

Therefore, she would have no warning, no way to prepare herself for his retaliation. And he would. Retaliate. He needed to punish her, needed to hurt her. So very badly.

Still she didn't seem to notice the darkness of his emotions. Gray eyes wide, she shook her head. "I've never remembered the good parts of my lives. Those memories are always taken from me."

Lives. As in, more than one. Had she been reborn more than once? Was she here to finish the job she'd started all those centuries ago? To cause the destruction of everyone he loved?

How had she gotten here? Why hadn't she tried to kill him already? Why did she treat him with such affection? He'd never had to wonder about someone's motivation before. He knew the truth, always. Knew what those around him most wanted to hide. This uncertainty was maddening, increasing the depths of his rage.

Answers first, he decided. Except, he had no idea how to urge her in that direction.

"Whatever you did...however you did it..." Wonder consumed her expression, lighting her up. "Thank you." With a shaky hand, she brushed a budding tear from the corner of her eye. *"Thank you.* I knew I'd once had a sister, but I hadn't known what she looked like."

*And the other vision?* Could he trust a single word out of her deceitful mouth?

"I have an idea, but I'm not sure." Slowly she smiled, a vibrant smile of white teeth and untamed joy. "Maybe... maybe when we're safe we can do this again? I can find out if I'm right."

The smile he'd seen before, that barest hint of delight, should have warned him of the devastating impact a full-on smile would cause. It hadn't. He sucked in a breath, lost in her—and never wanting to be found. The gray of her eyes lightened so much he could see tiny flecks of blue. The rose in her cheeks deepened, his fingers itching to discover if the color warmed her flesh, or if those cheeks were as deliciously chilled as the rest of her.

He couldn't soften, he reminded himself darkly. Couldn't crave her in any way.

"What?" she asked, suddenly unsure. She'd finally noticed the change in him. "You've never looked at me like that before."

*How am I looking at you?* Like he wanted to stab her? He would. Soon. For Baden. For the others who still mourned the loss of their friend.

"Like I'm…edible." She leaned down, her breasts rubbing his chest, her breath fanning over his ear. "I like it," she whispered.

He could only sit there, wanting desperately to grab her, hold her there—to choke her, he assured himself—but unable to make his useless body cooperate. Then, as if she hadn't just sent a thousand bolts of white-hot need—to choke her—through him, she straightened, returning them to the business at hand.

"Okay. So. We can't leave yet, which means we have to prepare. Maybe…maybe we can blockade ourselves in here. That might buy us some time."

Leave? She meant to leave with him? Without the artifacts she'd mentioned? Without trying to pry information out of him? That made no sense. Unless…

*Prepare for what?* His execution?

"The Lords." She popped to her feet and slowly spun. "I'll have to shut the door between the rooms." As she spoke, she rushed to the wall. She hooked her fingers around the edge of the "door," and pulled.

*Scraaape.*

Gradually, the hole closed. Haidee then shoved the dresser against the exit he hadn't known about, preventing anyone from opening it from the other side. Well, anyone of normal strength. She did the same to the front door, using his vanity.

Amun watched her, no closer to answers now than he'd been before traipsing through her head. Perhaps even further away. She was serious about protecting him. Despite who and what he was.

"If you continue to heal so rapidly, and they continue to stay away, we might be able to fight them when they finally bust inside. We can escape. And I know, I know. Our motto is 'die if you must, but take as many Lords as you can with you.' And I was totally prepared to do that when I thought you couldn't be moved. But sometimes it's better to get out and come back later, you know?"

*You hate the Lords?* he asked, just to discover what she'd say.

"Hate is a mild word, don't you think?" She never ceased her efforts to blockade them.

She had told the truth. Shocking. *Why?*

"I have my reasons, and you have yours." She attempted to wrench the mirror from the vanity. Hoping to shatter the glass and use the shards as blades? "We don't talk about them, remember?"

*No. I don't remember.* Now, what would she say to that?

Finally she paused, her sharp gaze whipping to him. "You don't remember our past?"

She thought they had a past. *No. Should I?* Carefully, he had to tread carefully.

Her eyelids slitted, evidence of the predator that lurked inside. "I swear to God, baby. I'll make them pay for every injury they inflicted on you."

Baby again. And she meant to seek revenge on his behalf? He still couldn't, wouldn't, soften, but something was wrong here. The knowledge changed the direction of his rage. She wasn't pretending to like him; she actually liked him. And when Amun looked past his own emotions, he realized Secrets sensed no malice in her. Not directed at him, at least. And even as unreliable as the demon had been since Amun had woken up, he found he couldn't refute that.

Haidee's fingers curled over the mirror's frame so tightly her knuckles leached of color. After a few seconds of deep breathing, she released the wood and straightened.

*What are you doing?* he asked.

"We need weapons." Her gaze circled the room—she did that a lot, he realized, and thought it was a defensive instinct—before landing on his closet.

She strode forward, disappeared inside. He had multiple weapons stashed inside, but he knew she wouldn't find them. No one could hide things quite like Amun. What he wanted to remain unseen, remained unseen. Soon she exited with one of his shirts wrapped around her fist, and that was all. Still, satisfaction radiated from her. Barely a second passed before she reached the mirror and punched, punched again, a hard *jab, jab.*

"They have a whole wardrobe in there," she said. "This room must belong to one of them." The glass shattered against that second thrust, and she released the material from her grip, letting it float to the floor.

*One of them,* she'd said. As he'd suspected, she hefted several shards, tested their weight, turned them in the light. With a nod, she sheathed several in her pockets.

*Haidee.*

She jolted as if startled. "I'm sorry. Yes?"

*Who...am I?*

"You don't know your name, either?" A frown darkened her expression. "Your name is Micah. We've been dating for about seven months."

Micah, like the tattoo on her arm. Micah, her "baby." That's who she thought he was? *And I'm a Hunter?*

"Yes."

*Like you?*

"Yes." So easily admitted, without a care. Unless she

was a grade A actress capable of fooling a demon, she truly believed what she said, that *he* was Micah, a Hunter.

Knots formed in Amun's stomach, then sharpened into daggers, cutting at him. So there it was. Proof, by her own admission, that she was his enemy. He needed to kill her before she discovered the truth about him. *Before* she thought to fight him, to hurt him when he couldn't really defend himself.

And as she'd just locked them inside this room, effectively trapping herself in his presence, all he had to do was summon her over, wrap his hands around her pretty neck, choke as he'd already wanted, and twist. He might be weak, the action might pain him, but he wouldn't back down. He couldn't.

*Haidee,* he projected to her, the word a croak, even in his mind.

"Yes?"

Don't do it, part of him cried. She was sweet and lovely and utterly luscious.

Secrets might even have whimpered, eager to return to her mind and play rather than destroy.

The other part of Amun recalled her past deeds, her current motto. "Die if you must, but take as many Lords as you can with you." The moment she realized he wasn't this Micah—Amun's hands fisted, how he despised the bastard...for no other reason than he was a Hunter—she would attack. There would be no stopping her if he failed to act. And fast.

Determined, he lifted his chin. *Come here.*

# CHAPTER FIVE

PANTING FROM EXERTION, those drugs *still* playing havoc with her body, Haidee strode to the bed. She placed a sharp glass shard on the nightstand, within Micah's reach, then stuffed one under his pillow. Never hurt to have two weapons at your disposal, rather than one.

Then she searched the nightstand, surprised she hadn't thought to do so before. She found all kinds of goodies inside. Toothpaste, a toothbrush, mouthwash, antibiotic ointment, bandages and wet wipes. None of which made sense. Or had the Lords wished to torment Micah with what he couldn't have or use?

Well, she would show them! She made use of the wash and wet wipes and helped Micah do the same, cleaning them from top to bottom, even intimately, which left her blushing—hello, big boy—then applied the ointment to his wrists as gently as she was able.

He watched her, silent, his dark eyes intent but unreadable. She hated that he didn't remember her or their relationship. Not that there was a lot to remember, but months ago they'd reached an understanding. They'd get to know each other before they had sex, but they'd get to know each other without discussing their pasts; they'd also vowed that no matter what, they wouldn't see other people.

Why had he agreed to that? she wondered now. At the time, she'd thought he respected her, hoped to ease her skittish nature. But had she not had those visions, *she* wouldn't have agreed to such an arrangement. Because with the restrictions laid bare like that, she realized they hadn't had a relationship. They'd had a tolerance.

That would change, she vowed. He'd come after her, fought to get to her and endured horrendous torture on her behalf. He deserved everything she had to give. So, she would give.

When she finished, she put everything back inside the drawer. "Now. The shards will cut your hand if you use them," she said, easing beside him, "and with as much blood as you've already lost…" Her voice trailed off. She didn't want to remind him of his frailty. He was a warrior to his soul and might think to prove his strength if she pressed too forcefully. "What I'm saying is, only use them if absolutely necessary. Okay?"

He might be healing physically, and at an astonishing rate she couldn't explain, but her worry for him hadn't faded. He'd been savaged and mind-fucked in the most terrible way. He would be a different man now. Was already showing signs of change.

He'd always been an intense man, and that intensity had deepened and darkened over the past few months, frightening everyone around him. Moods had blackened around him before he'd ever spoken a word. Even hers. Now, he was just as intense, but the darkness had faded. He actually *lightened* her mood.

Before, the thought of sleeping with him had disturbed her. She'd felt as if she would be cheating herself of… something. The sizzle, she supposed.

And maybe if she'd felt that sizzle she would have felt comfortable discussing her past with him. She'd never told him that she'd lived before, that she'd died before. She'd never told him what happened to her after she died. That she'd lived far longer than her seemingly twenty-odd years. That she'd had hundreds of lives but couldn't recall any detail that didn't involve blood, pain and death. That she'd tattooed herself so that she would have *some* link to the good things that had happened to her.

To her knowledge, she'd never told anyone.

One, she didn't trust people. Ever. Not even Micah, not fully. Two, when your business involved killing anyone with a supernatural ability—because that ability could mean possible demon contamination—you didn't admit to having a supernatural ability of your own. And three, the less people knew about her, the easier it was to return from the dead as someone else.

Yet, she thought she might like confessing all her secrets to this man. Even though he was more distant than ever—such clipped responses to her every word. Even though he was harder than she'd ever seen him—he'd endured so much, yet he barely seemed to notice his pain. They were connected in a way they'd never been before, and he'd been so gentle with her. More than that, she felt safe with him. And desired.

Yes, he'd desired her before. But that desire had been tempered with a bit of hesitation. Now, nothing would stop this man from getting what he wanted. If she rebuffed him, she thought he might help her see the silliness of that. In a good way, of course. His protective instincts were too honed for anything else. Look how tenderly he had caressed her cheeks.

And there were physical differences, too, she realized. His lips seemed fuller, but of course, that could be from the swelling. His lashes were definitely longer, his eyes now so black you couldn't distinguish pupil from iris. His shoulders were wider, the ropes of muscle in his stomach more numerous.

She knew the Lords had branded him with their butterfly, but what if they'd done more than that? What if they'd somehow possessed him with a demon and *that's* why he carried the mark? The moisture in her mouth dried as she recognized the possibility for what it was: likely.

Galen, leader of the Hunters, had found a way to pair a human with a demon. Maybe the Lords had, too.

*Haidee.*

She blinked as that husky voice penetrated her thoughts, then forced her suspicions to the back of her mind. Scaring a man in this condition wouldn't be wise. Or maybe he already knew, but didn't know how to tell her. Did he fear she would turn away from him if she learned of his possession?

*Haidee,* he repeated.

"Sorry. My mind wandered. Twice." She slid closer to him, not stopping until her hip met his.

He grimaced as he pulled himself into a sitting position. This close, she could feel the heat of his skin. So much heat she'd never encountered its like. Another difference. He'd never been this warm before. Otherwise, she would have finally given in and slept with him, even without the sizzle; she wouldn't have been able to help herself. Nothing was more delicious than the sweet burn of him.

*Haidee,* he snapped again.

Again she blinked into focus. She had to stop traveling these unwanted mental paths. "Sorry. What do you need, baby?"

*To touch you.* He managed to raise his hands on his own this time and cup her temples.

More of his heat enveloped her, his skin like a live wire against hers. She shivered and leaned into his grip, practically purring. Surprise flashed through his eyes—eyes now flickering with sparks of red. Oh, yes, she thought, hopes plummeting completely. He had been possessed. He knew. And he hadn't expected her to desire him.

Poor darling. As if she would ever betray him. He couldn't help what had happened, and she wouldn't reject him for it. Besides, her war with the Lords had never been about their demons, but about their actions.

Micah hadn't infected her. He hadn't killed her family.

*Blood, a river between her mother and her father. Both helpless...dead.*

She shook off the memory before it could tug her into a pit of despair.

"If they did something to you, something...evil, I'll help you through it," she told him gently, flattening her hands over his. Touching him was definitely a need. "I won't turn you in to Galen or Stefano. I won't betray you. No matter what. And if you start to...do things, bad things—" like lashing out, killing indiscriminately "—well, I'll take care of you myself." Mercifully. And only after she'd done everything in her power to purge him of the demon.

She'd loathe herself, would probably replay the act again and again with every new lifetime she experienced, but she would do whatever was necessary to save innocent families from the blood-fate hers had received. Even destroy herself and the only source of her happiness.

"Do you understand what I'm telling you?" she asked gently.

Again surprise flashed in his eyes, adding tiny pinpricks of amber light to the dark irises. Thankfully, the red was gone. *Something evil. Like...?*

Another shiver danced through her. She was coming to love the times his voice drifted through her mind, as warm as his body. "A...demon possession."

He tensed. *Tell me everything. How you got here. What your purpose is.*

At least he hadn't flung her away for guessing the truth. Nor did he seem afraid of her. Good. "Okay." She lowered his hands to her lap, clutching them tightly. He didn't protest. "The demon of Defeat, the one hosted by the Lord named Strider—I don't know if you remember him from the pictures we've seen?"

Micah merely blinked at her.

She continued. "He was in Rome. He had the Cloak of Invisibility. We spotted him, chased him. He managed to capture me." Bitterness seeped into her tone. She'd been such an easy mark. "I think he meant to kill me, but for whatever reason, changed his mind. A few times, I even caught him looking at me like…you know, like he wanted me, but that can't be right. He detests me. Anyway, he brought me here. Put me in the room next door to you. I heard you calling and basically clawed my way through the wall to reach you."

He offered no reply, but his expression was tense.

How long had he been here? she wondered as guilt torched her insides. She should have fought Strider harder. Should have escaped and found Micah before he'd been beaten. He suffered now because of *her*.

She'd never be able to make it up to him, but God, did she want to try. "Micah?" Gaze never leaving his beautiful, savaged face, she scooted even closer to him. She placed their twined hands on his waist as she leaned in…closer still…and softly, gently, pressed their lips together. "I'm so sorry you're here. I'm so sorry for everything that was done to you."

At first, he gave no reaction. Not to her words and not to her kiss. He still didn't reply. Didn't flinch from pain or encourage her to deepen the contact, either. Then he stiffened, his fingers squeezing at hers. Then he inhaled deeply, as if he couldn't get enough of her scent. *Then* he canted his head and opened his mouth. Not just welcoming her, but encouraging her.

Moaning, she slipped her tongue past his lips, past his teeth, and jerked at the sudden bolt of arousal that speared her. His taste was minty from the wash, but spiced with a dark drug, luring, tempting…demanding a response. A response she couldn't deny. Her breath grew shallow, her nipples pearled and every cell in her body smoldered with the sweetest kind of fire.

*More,* she thought.

His tongue met hers, rolled and coiled, danced and sparred, the heat spreading, intensifying. And then he was moaning, pressing more fully, thrusting his tongue as if their mouths were having sex.

She'd kissed him a few times before and had been disappointed in each of the experiences. This time, there was no disappointment. There was shattering excitement, sultry danger and heady bliss. Her fingers moved of their own accord, up, up, tangling in his hair. Soft, silky hair, the strands baby fine.

*More,* he said this time, the single word a growl inside her head.

"Oh, yes." More. She never wanted this to end. She had a mind filled with bad memories, yet as she swallowed his exotic flavor, she was swept away by him, the past forgotten, the present a thrill and the future something to anticipate. So *good.* "I don't want to hurt you. Don't let me hurt you."

*Stopping's the only thing that will hurt me.* The kiss must have caused an adrenaline reaction in him, something, because the next thing she knew, he had enough strength to heft her up, forcing her to straddle his lap.

His erection pressed against her needy core, hard and thick, and she gasped. Good? No longer an adequate word. The earth freaking *moved.* Unable to help herself, she rubbed against him, arching forward and back. Each time she hit him, each time they connected, she released a groan of need. Nerve endings did the sizzling thing, pleasure rushing through her in heated waves.

*More.*

"Please." Her voice was little more than a needy whimper.

One of his hands dove past the waist of her pants and cupped her ass. Skin-to-skin, a white-hot brand of possession. His other hand rode up her spine and latched onto the back of her neck. In the next instant, he spun her, basically tossing her on top of the mattress and looming over her, his weight smashing into her.

The kiss never even paused. Over and over his tongue worked hers, feeding her the ecstasy she needed but also making her ache. Didn't help when his hips began a slow grind against her clitoris, that hand on her ass forcing her to rise up and meet him, to slide up and down his shaft. The friction burned, burned so damned sweetly. She'd never experienced anything like this.

*We shouldn't be doing this.*

For her, it was too late to care about their surroundings, the danger. "I need you."

*Yes.*

She would have laughed at how easily he'd been convinced to continue, but at the moment she cared about only one thing. Climax. Her nails scoured his back, probably drawing blood. She tried to temper her reaction, to calm before she erupted, went wild and injured him further, but couldn't. The ache…was consuming her, driving her, fogging her brain.

"I need…" Haidee wound her legs around his waist and locked her ankles. He palmed her breast, rolling her nipple between his fingers. Even through her shirt and bra, she could feel the heat of him. The fiery brand. "I need…"

*Me. You need me.*

AMUN WAS LOST.

He'd placed his hands around Haidee's neck ready to snap the bone in two. She'd looked over at him with those eyes of pearl-gray, lashes long and sweeping, lips soft and pouty, pink locks of hair falling over her forehead. She'd talked of saving him...then a dark emotion had claimed her expression. One he hadn't been able to read, but one he'd hated.

She had leaned into him, somehow innocent in a way he'd never been, apologized to him as if his pain were somehow her fault, and he'd forgotten his body's wounds. His forgotten everything. He'd been helpless to do anything but accept her lips against his. Then he'd breathed her in and accepting hadn't been an option, either. He'd needed to possess her. Own her. Taking everything. *Giving* everything.

He hadn't understood the desires, still didn't understand them, but he couldn't bring himself to care. The moment their tongues intertwined, his body had become a storm, and this woman had become his only anchor.

Now, all the demons inside him—so many voices, so many thoughts and urges—lurched frantically, unable to remain at the back of his mind. They did not like her, had tried to hide from her, but now they were desperate to stay away from her. He sensed their agitation, their fear, but they were being pulled toward her unbidden, as he had been. They resisted.

He hadn't resisted. He'd simply given in.

Now he struggled to tether the demons, to keep them in place as Haidee writhed in his arms, the decadent chill of her skin teasing his palms. Soon he had trouble even remembering to do that. She was undiluted pleasure in his arms. A demon in her own right, consuming him, driving him.

Just then, he realized he didn't care that she was a Hunter. Didn't care that she meant to harm his friends. That she *had* harmed his best friend. This was...necessary. She tasted like the Water of Life found only in the heavens.

Pure, fresh, crisp. And when she bit at his lips, no longer concerned with being gentle with him, too passion-crazed to care, like him, his thoughts derailed, realigning to his first goal: possessing her. Totally, completely.

He pried his fingers from her ass and slid his hand to the front of her. Panties. Cotton. Damp. *Nice.*

*Mine,* he thought next and still didn't care about the consequences. He would care later. Tomorrow, maybe. Here, now, she was his. Desperate to feel her most feminine core, he shoved those panties aside. More than damp. Slick, ready. Gods, the way she wanted him…

A groan rose from low in his throat and rumbled out. He stiffened for a moment, fearing what might follow even so slight a sound, but his mouth remained focused on Haidee and her thrusting tongue, no words forming.

Relaxing, he tunneled through her folds, found her clitoris and pressed with the heel of his hand. She cried out, hips shooting off the bed, nails scoring his back.

*This is good. You like this.* They should have been questions; they emerged as statements of fact.

"Yes, please. More."

Hearing her beg was a climax all its own. *What do you want? What do you need?* What else did she like?

"You. Just you." Her eyes were closed, her tongue swiping at her lips to find his taste. Oh, yes. She was as lost as he was.

*Has it ever been this way before? Between us?* The moment he asked, he stiffened. He didn't want to know. He didn't—

"God, no. We were terrible before."

He fed her another kiss to show his approval, and that surprised him. Amun wasn't like Strider, possessive to the extreme. He'd never minded sharing *anything.* Had never gone caveman on a woman before. Had never claimed one as his very own. Actually, he hadn't had a lover in hundreds of years. To always know what they were thinking, what they truly thought of him, truly wanted from him... It had gotten old fast. So he'd concentrated on the war with the Hunters and what he was good at: killing. But Haidee...

He wanted to be her best. Her only. Didn't want her thinking the old "Micah" was better. Didn't want her thinking about any man but Amun.

"You are...this is...amazing."

*Gonna make you so happy you said that.*

Amun worked his way down her throat, nipping, licking, sucking. Until he reached her nipple. Tenderness was abandoned. He bit through the fabric of her shirt, tugging the little bud into the fiery heat of his mouth, even as he shoved a finger deep, *deep* into her sex.

Another cry left her, renting the air. Every muscle in his body clenched, savoring the sensation. Holy hell, but she clasped him tight. Seed leaked from the slit in his cock; he was hungry for her, for this, for more, so hungry. He added a second finger, moving in and out, in and out. She writhed, she begged some more.

The demons grunted hysterically as they gripped the tether he'd created, trying desperately to stay inside him as she pulled at his hair—as though she was pulling on them again. And yet, agitated as they were, they still could not overtake his mind.

Haidee's head thrashed left and right. "So close...just a little more...and I'll... I have to... I need... Please!"

He couldn't let the beasts near her. Not that they wanted near her; they were still fighting. He should stop this, stop the madness, but he had to taste her. He *needed* to taste her. Life wouldn't be worth living if he didn't.

She was panting, little beads of ice crystallizing over her skin as he worked his way down. An oddity he barely registered. Sweating ice? Her T-shirt was rucked up to the middle of her bra—cotton, white, pretty—the flat plane of her stomach and the dip of her navel revealed. Gorgeous. Had a woman ever been so gorgeous?

As he ripped the crotch of her panties, paving the way for his mouth, he licked into her navel. Her belly quivered. Her knees pressed into his sides, squeezing. Had he been human, she would have cracked bone.

He kissed his way to her zipper. Barrier. He couldn't allow a barrier. Another rip, and the pants were gaping open just like the panties. Then he was peering down at her, at a tiny triangle of pale curls, the rest of her pink and glistening. His. Ready.

*Liiick*. Holy hell, he thought again. *Nothing* had ever tasted this good.

Another cry left her, this one hoarse and broken. She released him to reach behind her and grip the headboard, her back bowing. Surprisingly the demons calmed, but only slightly, the pull on them somewhat eased, allowing them to go back into hiding.

The door handle rattled.

Amun was dimly aware of the possible intrusion but unconcerned. *Liiick*. Heaven and hell wrapped in temptation, leading him straight to his downfall. Addicting him. Consuming him. Owning *him*.

The door handle rattled again.

This time, there was a flicker of rational thought in his head. Someone meant to enter his bedroom. Friend? Foe? Didn't matter. He had to wait to finish tasting her.

The intruder would pay for that. Painfully.

Haidee must have sensed his growing disquiet, because she opened her eyes and said, "What are you—" Her mouth floundered open and closed as she gasped in horror. "Your eyes. They're completely red. Glowing."

What she didn't say: *demon*. She'd known he was possessed, no matter what she thought his name was, and had claimed she would shield him from Hunters. But this must be her first true confirmation.

There was no time to placate her. *Someone comes.* He swiped the glass shard from the nightstand and whipped around. Haidee jolted upright, the spike of glass under the pillow already palmed. She tried to right her ruined clothing as another rattle sounded.

An instant later, the person on the other side decided to take things to the next level. Wood split from the hinges as the door was savagely kicked, the vanity in front of it skidding to the middle of the room.

A scowling Strider strode inside, knives in both hands. All the demons inside of Amun danced into a sudden frenzy, Haidee forgotten, rushing back to the surface. Torment...punish...pain...blood...suffering...must have. Needed.

Something else struck him. Something that had nothing to do with the demons, but everything to do with a long-buried instinct. Safeguard. He would safeguard the girl. Her taste was still in his mouth, and he needed more. Still had to have more. If she were hurt, he couldn't have more.

Wrong, that thought was wrong, but he couldn't banish it. Instinct demanded; he heeded. *Go!* he mentally screamed at the warrior, but Strider didn't hear him. Or didn't care.

When Strider spotted Amun and Haidee on the bed, lower bodies still twined around each other, he blinked. His jaw even dropped. And if Amun wasn't mistaken, there was a flicker of fury over his expression.

*Will safeguard,* Amun thought, scowling at his friend. No matter what.

"You bitch," the warrior growled to Haidee. "What the hell did you do to him?"

# CHAPTER SIX

HAIDEE JUMPED TO SHAKY LEGS, breath sawing in and out of her mouth. As she'd predicted, the glass shard she held had already sliced through skin, blood dripping to the floor. She barely noticed the sting or the loss.

Without her there to cushion him, Micah hit the mattress face-first and grunted, but she paid him no heed. She couldn't. Not if she wanted to get him out of this fortress alive.

And shit! This showdown couldn't have happened at a worse time. Desire still pumped through her veins, thick and heavy, dulling her reactions and making her limbs feel weighted with rocks. Her chest felt hollowed out, and her muscles ached. Perhaps she could have dealt with those things, but her mind was as clouded as if she'd popped a dozen different pills, a mix of sedatives, stimulants and aphrodisiacs.

She could only blame Micah. His kisses had been CPR to her soul. He'd made her come alive. Split apart. Forget everything and every one. Common sense had abandoned her. So had survival instinct. She'd *never* ignored her survival instinct before. All she'd been able to think about was him. His touch, his taste. His tongue lapping between her legs. God, she could fly apart simply thinking about that heady caress. In seconds, he'd reduced her to an animal state, where nothing had mattered but sensation.

*Now isn't the time, remember?* The doorway was open, offering a straight shot into the hallway. Either she or

Micah could run, but not both. One of them had to deal with the demon.

Hopefully Micah would understand what she wanted him to do.

"Not smart, coming in here on your own," she said to taunt the Lord into an emotional response. What she'd learned about him during their time together? He was always quick to anger, and that anger made him easily distractible. "You ready to die?"

For once, he didn't react. His gaze darted from her to Micah, Micah to her. He radiated a mix of rage, concern and disbelief.

Micah didn't move.

Why wasn't Micah moving? Damn it. If he would move, she could attack. Defeat would have to fight her. Micah was simply too weak to see to the battle himself.

She opened her mouth to challenge Defeat but closed it with a snap. She'd challenged him a few times during their trek. *Bet you can't catch me if you let me go.* He'd let her go. And he'd caught her, pissed beyond imagination. *Bet you can't just stand there while I stab you.* He'd let her stab him. And rather than pass out from blood loss, as she'd hoped, he had then returned the favor. He'd stabbed her thigh to keep her from bolting while he healed.

He'd then stitched her up, shocking her. Still. His determination to win every challenge gave him strength, more so than usual, and she couldn't have him stronger than usual right now. Not while she battled the fog. So, as they stood there facing each other, both deliberating how to handle the coming fight—and there *would* be a fight—she was very careful not to issue another challenge. Not even a challenge to *lose* the fight.

She'd made that mistake only once.

*Bet you can't lose a fistfight to a girl.*

He had allowed her to punch him, and he hadn't fought

back. Therefore in his mind, he had just lost a fistfight with a girl. She'd run off while he'd struggled to breathe—'cause yeah, she'd gone for his trachea—and he'd had to track her down. When he finally caught her, he'd trussed her up like a Thanksgiving turkey, gagged her and started drugging her.

And if she had tried to speak past her gag, he would have removed her voice box. No question.

"What the hell did you do to him?" Defeat repeated, dark, deadly.

"What did *I* do to him?" She assumed attack position: legs apart, knees slightly bent and ready for her leap. The cold, already so much a part of her, seeped out, sheened her skin. With every exhalation, mist created a cloud in front of her face. All the while, she mourned the loss of Micah's heat.

She still didn't know why she froze like this. Still didn't know how. All she knew was that the ability manifested with her emotions, sometimes strengthening her, sometimes weakening her. Today, she felt empowered.

"Me?" she went on. "What the fuck did *you* do to him?"

"If *she* hurt him…" A muscle ticked below his dark blue eyes, and he finally kicked into motion.

If *she* hurt him? What a joke! "This is gonna be fun. I've been *craving* a go at you." One step, two, she moved toward him, determined to meet him in the middle.

*No!*

In a sudden blur of motion, Micah sprang from the bed and flew past her, tackling the demon-possessed warrior and sending both men toppling to the floor. Grunts and groans soon echoed. Slashing arms and vicious kicks ensued. They rolled, they struggled, they assaulted each other ferociously.

She'd never seen Micah fight so dirty. He went for the

eyes, the throat and the groin, biting and ripping flesh, fists hammering. Defeat, though, merely deflected each of her man's blows. He never tried to cause harm. Why? Something else she'd never seen—a Lord of the Underworld backing down. And this one, Defeat... Something was wrong. Had to be.

Haidee stood there, numb, watching the bloodbath, sick to her stomach and unsure what to do. *Apparently, he's not too weak after all.* Like him, she didn't run from the room. God help her, she wasn't leaving without him.

What should she do? If she threw herself into the fray, she might cut Micah instead of the Lord. They were moving so quickly...twisting and turning, flying apart, springing back together. And if she accidentally delivered Micah's death-blow...

Damn it. What the hell should she do? she wondered again, no closer to an answer.

"What the fuck is going on?" Defeat demanded between punches. "Stop. Amun, you have to stop."

Amun?

She'd heard the name before, knew it belonged to one of the Lords, but she couldn't connect the name with a face. And because she had memorized all the names and faces of her enemy, she knew that could only mean one thing.

There was one immortal warrior the Hunters had never been able to photograph or even sketch throughout the years. Not that they hadn't tried. They'd snapped pictures, but those pictures had never turned out, had always been blurry. And when they'd drawn what they'd thought was his face, they'd later realized they'd done nothing but scribble on the page.

Amun was also the Lord most people forgot the moment they walked away from him. He was the immortal the Hunters knew the least about. Maybe because Amun was possessed by the demon of Secrets.

All the Hunters really knew about him? He had dark hair and dark eyes, and he was tall and muscled. That little bit of information had been acquired through *centuries* of observation.

Had this Amun died, his demon given to Micah? Did Micah now carry Secrets inside him? Was that why the Lords had chosen Micah? And he was demon-possessed. She no longer had any doubts about that. Those red eyes... peering down at her...hungry...craving...raging... She shuddered, then scowled.

This was another sin to heap on an already mountainous pile. Another crime to hate the Lords for.

Had they wanted someone with the same physical characteristics as their friend Amun? Probably. How amused they must have been, using a Hunter to house one of their disgusting demons.

*Don't think about that, either. Get yourself in the game, woman.*

Haidee shook her head, clearing her mind, thankfully thinning the fog. The two men were on their feet now, throwing punches, falling backward into the walls, causing dust and plaster to waft through the air, then reconnecting and tossing each other into furniture. They were a blur of motion, brutal, like wild animals fighting over the only snack in the jungle. Wood chips were scattered across the floor, some even swimming in little pools of blood.

*Blood, a river between her mother and her father. Both helpless...dead.*

Again she had to shake her head, dislodging the memory.

"Amun," Defeat snarled. "For gods' sake! I'm your goddamn friend. What the hell are you doing?"

In the next instant, Micah's thoughts hit her. *Must kill. Must safeguard.*

The words were sluggish, lower in volume than the

ones that had come before them, and she realized he was weakening. His wounds were opening, seeping, dripping all over the room.

"She's a Hunter," the demon continued in that outraged tone, "and she's my prisoner."

*Mine!* blasted through her head. *Not yours. Never yours. Mine to safeguard.*

Could Defeat hear him? Probably not. Otherwise, he would have been backing out of the bedroom and running for his life. There had been barbwire in Micah's tone, the tips laced with poison.

But then, Micah's thoughts switched direction. *I have to stop this. Why am I doing this? I love this man.* Confusing, wrong, but again, those thoughts switched direction. *Must kill. Must safeguard.*

Micah snarled low in his throat, the sound rumbling through her mind as he punted Defeat into the already crushed vanity. More wood chips scattered. Red sparked in Defeat's eyes, a gnarled mask of bone and scales falling over his features.

He was turning, she thought with dread. From immortal to demon.

"Win," he growled now, and there was another voice fused to his. One that was guttural, raw. Determined.

Shit. She knew that determination. No longer would he pull his punches or deflect Micah's. Now he would fight to win.

He closed the distance and threw his meaty clubs around, a jackhammer of lethal purpose. Not once did he miss. Micah weakened further, wobbling on his feet, his eyes beginning to swell shut as his head whipped left then right, alternating as Defeat switched fists.

The fact that Micah had lasted this long was astonishing, proof of his own determination, but he wouldn't last much longer. He couldn't. Not at the rate Defeat was delivering blows, and not with the already ravaged condition of his body.

She had to risk hurting Micah, she decided. There was no other way. Which meant she had to put herself in front of him, probably take a few blows before she was able to strike. No problem there.

Better she die than him, even though he was now tainted. He was tainted, yes, but he wasn't evil. That kiss…no, he wasn't evil. And if she was killed this day, she would come back; she would remember him. Not the kiss, that had been too good, and all her favorite things were always wiped, but this fight. She would recall the blood, her fear…her despair. But if Micah died, he would be gone forever.

Haidee stiffened, preparing to jump, waiting for the perfect moment. A thought suddenly hit her and she hesitated. If Micah turned his sights on her or even struck her accidentally… Oh, God. If she died, she wouldn't remember why he'd done so when she awakened, only that he had—and she would come back to kill him just as she planned to come back and kill the others. If he survived this, they would be enemies.

Defeat landed a particularly vicious blow to Micah's side, causing him to wheeze.

Worth the risk, she decided in the next instant. He was teetering…falling…

At last Haidee jumped forward, hooked her arm around Micah's waist and threw him with all her might. *I'm sorry, baby.* As he stumbled to his knees—away from the action—she used her momentum to spin and duck, swinging her right fist at Defeat's groin. Contact. He doubled over, oxygen bursting from his bleeding lips. She used her other hand, the one clutching the fragment of glass, to slice across his stomach. *No mercy.*

As she straightened, she landed a hard right to his chin. His head jerked backward, and he grunted, blood and teeth spewing. She aimed the glass at his throat, but only managed to slash his shoulder as he pivoted.

His narrowed gaze landed on her. He could have hit her just then. He didn't.

Firm hands suddenly gripped her waist from behind and tossed her. Through the air she soared, flailing for an anchor, wondering what the hell had just happened. The makeshift weapon flew from her clasp, then she was bouncing on the bed, realization setting in. Micah was aware enough to know who she was, aware enough to want her out of harm's way. Sweet of him, but that wasn't going to stop her. He'd done his part. Now she would do hers.

Before the bouncing stopped, she was throwing her legs over the side of the bed and straightening, once again intending to knock Micah out of way. Only, she saw that he had somehow tackled Defeat and now straddled the warrior's prone body, punching...punching...

Between whaling fists, Defeat groaned and babbled. "Lost...lost...no, gods, no...lost..."

For several moments, she could only blink, watch. Micah had done it. Despite his injuries, he'd won. Against an immortal. *That's my man.*

*Seriously? You're going to victory lap* now? Haidee forced herself into motion and rushed to Micah. She latched onto his surging elbow. He could have shrugged her away, batted her off, could have swung at her with his other arm, but he didn't. He faced her. What she could see of his glowing red eyes locked on her, tormented, agonized.

*Didn't want to hurt him...couldn't stop...couldn't let him hurt you.... Why couldn't I let him hurt you?*

The words echoed in her mind. *Didn't want to hurt him. Why couldn't I let him hurt you?* Courtesy of the demon? Was the demon trying to convince him that he liked the Lords? Didn't matter, she supposed. They'd deal with it. Later. Along with everything else.

"Come on. We don't want to free his demon right now." She tugged him to his feet, and God, he was heavy. "We have to leave before the others come." They'd be pissed when they saw what had been done to their friend. She didn't want Micah punished for that. And they would punish him. She had no doubt. Even though he was currently part of their group.

She ushered him to the doorway but had to pause there to wind her arm around his waist. He was stumbling, barely able to remain standing on his own.

"You can do this, baby. Come on."

*Where are...we...going?*

"If we're lucky, no one will be around and we'll find a way outside." Dragging him through the doorway left her shaking and ice-sweating. He was bleeding all over her, giving her more and more of his massive weight. How she maintained her grip, she didn't know. What she did know after taking two steps to the right?

They weren't lucky.

Her eyes widened as she stumbled to a halt, Micah moaning, nearly falling. She held tight. They were surrounded—but not by the demons she'd expected. Robed warriors filled the entire enclosure, wings of white and gold outstretched. Scowls lined every single one of their faces, but even still those faces were glorious, radiant. So beautiful...so majestic...dazzling her. She couldn't look away. No matter how hard she tried, she couldn't look away. Exquisite...

Angels. These men were angels.

Maybe she and Micah *were* lucky. Maybe Galen had sent reinforcements to rescue them.

"Help us," she beseeched. "The demons captured us, and we're trying to escape."

A lovely dark-haired male stepped forward, hard gaze pinning her in place more forcefully than any of the others.

"We were told to wait out here." His voice was just as thrilling as his face. A sensual breeze, an exotic caress. "We did so. We were told not to interfere with what happened inside the room. We did not. But now you have come to us. Now we interfere."

Realization cut like a knife. The angels hadn't been sent by Galen. They were helping the demons. Horror barely registered before Micah was ripped from her grip. She'd never seen the angels move, had been too riveted by the one in front of her, but losing her man snapped her from that lost, dreamy haze.

With a scream of outrage, she kicked the angel in the chest. He stumbled backward only a few steps. She spun, reaching for Micah. Her voice must have snapped him out of his pained, weakened stupor, because, as two angels dragged him down the hall, farther and farther away from her, he blinked open his swollen eyes.

When he spied the distance between them, he roared. Loud and long and ragged, but only she seemed to hear him. No one else paid him any attention, no one else cringed. As she elbowed her way to him, the angels attempted to grab her. She twisted and squirmed for freedom.

All the while, Micah fought his captors. Soon, the two holding him weren't enough. Soon, she wasn't pegged as the biggest threat. The angels turned their attention to the warrior, all but one needed to subdue him.

*Haidee! Haidee!*

Before she could reach him, the one that had remained behind caught her, strong arms banding around her and squeezing tight. Breathing became a thing of the past. Still. Her struggles never ceased.

Micah's didn't either, she noted as she was at last carted out of the hall. "I'll come back for you," she screamed. "I swear I'll come back."

## *CHAPTER SEVEN*

STRIDER FUCKING *hurt*.

He hurt everywhere but especially his gut. Maybe because Ex had sliced him open from hip to hip, spine to navel. The angels had had to stuff his insides back, well, inside. They'd even stitched him up and tended his feverish, sweat-drenched body for three solid days.

He would have healed sooner if he'd won the fight with Amun and Ex like a big boy. But he hadn't. He'd lost. And so his pain had been magnified a thousandfold, and he'd been too weak to do a damn thing about it. Talk about humiliating!

Now he was still bed-bound and propped against pillows, but at least he was awake and aware. His demon was silent, too afraid to poke his head from the shadows of Strider's mind and lose another challenge until they'd recuperated sufficiently.

Torin sat in a chair in the far corner, and Zacharel, the black-haired angel Lysander had left in charge, leaned against one of the metal posters of Strider's bed. Both were watching him, waiting. Clearly impatient.

Could a guy not suffer in peace?

This room was supposed to be his sanctuary, his private escape, but he'd opened his eyes a little while ago to find Torin pacing beside him—and not out of concern, the curious bastard. Zacharel had been exactly as he was now. Unmoving, gaze penetrating.

"What happened?" Zacharel asked. His voice mesmerized

even as it repelled. The undertones were lilting, almost melting—and yeah, it was still embarrassing as shit the way Strider reacted to these angelic beings—but everything else about that voice was cold, uncaring, detached.

Like his eyes. A vivid jade-green, they should have been welcoming, should have reminded Strider of summer. Or hell, even of Torin's wicked sense of humor. Instead, those eyes were green ice. There was nothing inside them. No emotion of any kind. Not good, not bad, just a spiraling abyss of emptiness.

Strider had met some freaky immortals over the centuries, had thought he'd seen everything, but this one…no. There were none like him. Nothing fazed him. Strider had a feeling he could stab the angel in the heart and Zacharel would merely glance down before continuing on with whatever he'd been doing.

"Demon. Concentrate. What happened?" Zacharel again, and he didn't raise his voice in the slightest. See? Emotionless.

"For gods' sake, Strider," Torin snapped. "Open your damn mouth and form some words. While you're at it, stop staring at the angel like he's a tasty treat." Not so emotionless.

Strider's cheeks warmed with a flush. He'd leave the tasty treat comment alone since he was too foggy to come up with a decent response. And no, Zacharel didn't react to it.

"I went to the girl's room. She wasn't there, but I saw where she'd peeled back the wallpaper and found an old doorway that led into Amun's bedroom. She barred it. So I went to his door, but she'd barred it, too. That one I kicked in." And he'd expected to find Amun headless. Or, at the very least, Haidee under the dark influence of Amun's new demons.

The rage he'd felt at the prospect…the despair. And

yet, neither had compared to the jealousy he'd experienced when he'd discovered the truth. A jealousy that had shamed him. One, he couldn't be attracted to Ex. Two, Amun was his friend. He should have sheltered him from the temptress's wiles.

"And?" Torin prompted, exasperated.

"And he was awake, lucid." At least for a little while. Until Strider had approached the girl. Then Amun the Demonically Insane had returned. "Surprisingly, the black phantoms were gone and stayed gone." He didn't mention that Amun had been on top of Ex, with his hand down her pants, his face aflame with pleasure.

Hers had been, too. So much pleasure.

She hadn't fought the warrior. She had encouraged him, begged for more. A trick, Strider had thought. Surely she had planned to lure Amun into a false sense of security and then strike.

But when Strider had approached her, determined to stop her from hurting his friend, Amun had attacked him. And when Strider had tried to defend himself, *Ex* had attacked him. To *aid* Amun.

What the fuck, man? He hadn't understood at the time; he'd been too busy trying not to die. Now he thought he got it. Ex had wanted to leave with Amun. Which meant she'd planned to take him to her Hunters so *they* could kill him.

Still. That didn't explain why Amun had defended her. Why the warrior had touched her so intimately.

Strider had known the dude a long, long time. They'd fought together, hung out and partied together. And by "partied together" Strider meant that Amun had watched him party and guarded his back. Amun didn't sleep around, was usually the most reserved of the warriors, and was sometimes as boring as shit. The good kind of boring, though. You knew you could rely on him for anything. He was solid, a rock, and you always knew where you stood with him.

He wasn't prone to angry fits, was the most levelheaded guy Strider knew. He would rather take a bullet himself than watch his friends take one. Yet, to protect a murderous bitch, he'd attempted to splatter Strider's brains all over his bedroom floor.

Amun must not have recognized her. Hell, would anyone? Centuries had passed, she no longer looked like an innocent maiden in need of a strong warrior's aid, and as many freaky places as they'd been, they'd met other women named Haidee. The fact that she'd somehow regrown her head maybe mighta kinda sorta have also prevented his friends from realizing who she was.

Part of Strider was glad she hadn't been recognized. The stupid part of him that didn't like the thought of anyone hurting the woman.

*You planned to sic Sabin on her. Remember?*

Yes. And maybe he would have done it. Maybe not.

Strider hadn't even told Torin her true identity yet. He didn't know why. He'd only said she was a Hunter and had left it at that.

And, okay, yeah. Maybe that had been a halfway decent decision. Maybe Ex's efforts on Amun's behalf were real rather than faked. The day Strider had captured her, he'd gotten a glimpse of her boyfriend and had been floored to note the similarities between the Hunter and Amun. Was still floored. As swollen and disfigured as Amun's face currently was, she probably thought the men were one and the same. If that was the case, she wouldn't have been taking Amun to Hunters to torture him but to save him.

Had she realized the truth yet, since he'd called Amun by name? Or had she been too preoccupied?

"For gods' sake!" Torin tossed up his arms, dragging

him from the thorny pit of his thoughts. "What's wrong with you, Strider?"

He leveled a brutal scowl on his friend. "I'm healing. Can't you see the gaping hole in my stomach?"

"You are fine. Now, as you were saying. Amun looked into your eyes during your conflict, yet you felt no evil urges?" Zacharel asked, returning them to the only subject that mattered.

Conflict. Such a mild word for the handing-of-the-ass Strider had received. "Right. No urges." Then or now.

Torin scrubbed both of his gloved hands down his tired face. "Well, the shadows are back. Came back that very day, in fact, the moment the angels got him back in bed. And now he's worse. He worsens every hour. Silently moaning, always thrashing."

"But he was fine when you walked into his bedroom?" Zacharel insisted.

Did he seriously need to repeat himself? "Yes."

"With the girl?"

Shit! "Yes, damn it. With the girl."

Zacharel gave no reaction to Strider's outburst, of course. "While you were absent from the fortress, we tried exorcism, burning him as close to death as possible, hoping the spirits would unbind themselves and leave. They didn't. We even tried a cloud cleansing, a—"

"A what?"

"Don't ask," Torin said dryly.

"But," Zacharel continued, "none of those things made a difference. Yet if you looked at him and felt no evil, the girl did the impossible. She forced the demons into submission. That means she is the key."

Confusion caused Strider's brows to knit together. "The key? The key to what?"

"Amun's sanity. He needs her. He must be with her."

Both Strider and Torin gaped at the angel.

Torin was the first to recover. "She's a Hunter." Disbelief and fury coated his tone.

"Yet that mattered not to Amun or the demons," Zacharel pointed out. "Where is your joy? Your friend now has a chance of surviving."

A chance. Grim words when they should have been hopeful.

The day Strider had busted into Amun's room, the angels had been talking of finally killing the insane warrior. They'd given the Lords enough time to fix him, they'd said, and the Lords hadn't fixed him. The phantoms had begun to seep into the hallway, trying to escape the angels, the fortress, and enter the world.

Strider wouldn't allow that. He wouldn't allow Amun to be harmed, either. But he *really* wouldn't allow Ex near him. "The day I arrived, you said the female was infected. What did you mean by that?" He would have asked before, but after visiting Amun that first time, he'd been kind of busy sandpapering his skin off in an effort to expunge the evil.

"I have not been given permission to share those details," the angel said, his frostiness not thawing a single degree.

Zacharel cared about permission? Shocker. "Who do you need permission from?"

"Lysander."

Of course. The head honcho. "Well, where is he?"

"With his Bianka. They were arguing, and he gave her possession of their cloud. No one is to disturb them for any reason. There are neon signs all around the palace saying so."

Okay. Strider didn't really understand a word of that. A cloud palace? Why would Bianka's possession of it matter? There was no one bigger or stronger than Lysander—except Strider. And unless Bianka went total Harpy on Lysander, which she wouldn't do because Harpies were supposedly physically incapable of harming their consorts, there was no way the petite stunner could overpower the angel.

Unless, of course, Lysander *wanted* her to overpower him. Aha. Now Strider understood what Zacharel had meant. The two were engaged in a sexual marathon, and Lysander had given control to Bianka. They may not see him for several years. One thing Strider had learned about the Harpy when she'd visited the fortress was that she enjoyed power and didn't relinquish it easily.

Lucky Lysander.

Strider could have tasted a Harpy of his own, he supposed, since Bianka had two single sisters. Taliyah and Kaia. Taliyah was the ice princess, as seemingly emotionless as Zacharel, but Strider had never been interested in her. Now, Kaia on the other hand, well, she was the wildfire. He'd been interested. *Really* interested—until she'd slept with Paris, keeper of Promiscuity. Strider had decided then not to bother with her. Who could compete with a freaking god of sex?

To be honest, Strider was sick of competing in the bedroom all the damn time. Sick of having to be the best lover his partner had ever had. It had gotten old. There was nothing wrong with a guy wanting to lie back and let the woman do all the work for once.

If Defeat had been awake, the demon would have said, "Win." Strider almost wished the little shit *would* speak up. Woulda been nice to trample on his feelings by shouting, "Shut the hell up!" The bastard had gotten Strider into this mess, after all.

"And…he's off again," Torin muttered wryly.

"Am not." Strider flipped him off. "Tell me this at least," he said to the angel. "Can the girl, being infected as she is with something you stupidly won't tell me about, contaminate Amun? Make him worse?"

A moment passed in silence as the angel considered the question. And wouldn't you know it? He gave no reaction to the word *stupidly*. "No."

All right, then. Strider would forget about Ex's "infection." For now.

"So what are we going to do about Amun and the girl?" Torin asked, getting them back on track. Again. He leaned back in his chair, resting his ankle against his knee, hands twined over his middle. A casual pose, if not for the lines of tension branching from his mouth.

Zacharel eyed the keeper of Disease as if he'd lost his brain when he'd gained his demon. "We will test our theory, of course. We will put her back inside Amun's room."

"Hell, no!" Strider snarled. And not because those sparks of jealousy had instantly lit back up and now poured through his veins like streams of acid. "He's defenseless, and she'll hurt him."

"She didn't before."

"That doesn't mean she'll be a tame house cat next time!"

"If things continue as they are, I will kill him." The words were so simply stated, Strider had no doubt Zacharel meant what he said. "Your choice. I will be satisfied one way or the other."

Not really a choice at all, the bastard. He had to know that. "I'll have to clear out Amun's room and remove..." Shit. "Everything except the bed." Anything could be used as a weapon. As he'd already learned. "The window will need iron bars." Hunters were notoriously adept and wily. Look what Ex had done with a simple piece of glass.

His stomach ached in remembrance, the scab pulling tight.

"Maybe we should break her hands, too," Torin suggested, shocking the sweet loving hell out of Strider.

He was usually the voice of semi-reason. "I don't want her able to snap his neck or pluck his eyes while he's defenseless."

Zacharel shrugged, drawing attention to the breadth of his shoulders—and making Strider grit his teeth in annoyance that he'd noticed. What was wrong with him? Men were not his personal preference. "She didn't before," the angel remarked.

"That doesn't mean she'll be a tame house cat next time," Torin repeated, mimicking Strider's earlier you're-a-moron tone.

"That's when she thought she could escape with him," Strider forced himself to say. Because deep down, he *still* didn't like the thought of hurting her. He lost more IQ points every day, he decided. "This time, she'll know there's no way she can free herself. She'll know she's helpless and needs to curry our favor."

Torin's eyes widened. "You're actually voting to leave her be? A Hunter? What'd she stab you with? A magic wand laced with Prozac?"

"No, I'm not voting to leave her be." Damn it! He had. "Fine. We'll break her hands." He wasn't going to argue about her treatment. She deserved what she got, and he would just have to pacify himself with that knowledge.

"One other thing to consider," Zacharel said. "Amun fought to reach her, and all of my warriors were needed to subdue him. If you hurt her, I think he will object. And if he objects, I think many in this household will be injured. But again, I give the choice to you."

How magnanimous of him, Strider thought dryly. Zacharel had a gift for ripping your rationale apart with only a few words. But…Torin couldn't force the issue now.

Still. Prick that he was, Strider wasn't exactly ready to back down yet, no matter that he was getting what he'd originally wanted. Zacharel irritated him, and part of him hoped to irritate the guy right back. At least garner *some* kind of reaction.

"If we decided we wanted it done, would you be the one to do the breaking?"

"Of course," Zacharel said easily.

Strider blinked at him. Not the answer he'd expected. Feet shuffling, maybe. A little waffling, for sure. "But you're an angel. Aren't you supposed to be defenders of humanity or something?"

"She is not exactly human."

"Then what is she?" The question whipped from him, his eagerness to know unparalleled.

"I do not have permission to tell you."

The eagerness deflated like a balloon, and Strider gnawed the inside of his cheek to keep himself from snarling. When Lysander finally crawled his way out of wild Bianka's bed, Strider was going to have a long chat with him. He suspected daggers would be used between every word.

"We won't damage her," Strider finally said. "And I have a few conditions. I have to be the one to escort her to Amun." Just as soon as he could walk. He didn't like the thought of anyone else putting their hands on her. She was—not his. "Also, I want a camera in the room." The words emerged harder, harsher. "We'll monitor what goes on twenty-five, eight."

Torin nodded, his expression half satisfied, half steeped in guilt. "I'll have them placed and recording within the hour."

There were cameras strategically hidden throughout the entire fortress just in case Hunters snuck past their gate and traps, but not in any of the bedrooms. They'd all agreed. If the enemy could bypass everything else and enter one of the rooms, the Lords deserved to die. Privacy was *that* important.

If Amun ever regained his senses completely, he'd be pissed as hell about the new cameras. But better his fury than his murder.

Zacharel straightened from the post. "I'll inform my men of what is to transpire." With that, he turned with the fluid grace of a dancer and strode from the room.

A dancer? Seriously?

Strider's cheeks heated a whole hell of a lot more than before.

When Torin made no comment about his blush, he relaxed against his pillows. As a sigh left him, he realized how tense he'd been in the angel's presence. Now he scanned the bedroom, allowing the familiarity of his surroundings to comfort him further. His weapon collection decorated the walls, everything from ancient swords to modern-day firearms.

Only thing hanging on the wall that wasn't a weapon was the portrait just over the bed. No. Not true, he thought then. The portrait *was* a weapon, too. Of seduction. In it, Strider was utterly naked and whisking through the clouds like an avenging angel. He was holding a teddy bear in one hand and a stream of pink ribbons in the other.

Anya had given him the nearly life-size monstrosity as a joke. But the joke was on her. He loved the damn thing.

"Where are the others?" he finally asked. "The other day you told me they were out and about, but not where exactly. Or why. I've had a little time to think this through, and I realized they don't need to keep the artifacts out of the fortress anymore. The Hunters aren't swarming us like before. Word on the street is they vanished, which is bizarre, but Cronus says not to worry—and yeah, I talked to him, he just popped in the other day for no apparent reason—so I'm not worried. Which means you aren't, either. Which means the boyz are away for a different reason. Right?"

Torin's sigh was an echo of his. "It's just too dangerous around here, what with the angels being demon assassins and Amun visiting the dark side. Aeron, Olivia, Legion, William and Gilly are the only ones still here. Not because I need help, but because they're too weak to leave. And well, Aeron has taken the blame for Amun's condition and refuses to leave him. Not that you've paid any of them a visit, you slacker."

Gods, he was, wasn't he? "Thank you for shoving me down the shame spiral. How are they?"

"The guys are still recovering from Hell Week, and the girls are taking care of them. Well, except for Legion. She refuses to get out of bed."

Aeron must be worried about her, too. Strider really should have checked on him. On all of them. *I'm a self-absorbed prick.*

"The rest of the crew is spread out," Torin said, "and I no longer have their locations. I told them not to tell me anymore, to just check in at least once a day so I'd know they were alive."

"Why don't you want to know where they are?"

"With the little Hunter here, the less I know about them, the better."

True. "So, any news? Gossip?"

"You want gossip, you've come to the right place, my man." Some of the tension drained from Torin's features as well, and he rubbed his hands together. "Ashlyn's pregnant."

He rolled his eyes. "I know, moron."

"Yeah, but did she know she's carrying twins?"

"No shit?"

"No shit. A boy and a girl. Fire and ice, Olivia said." Olivia, the angel. She wasn't like the assassins currently living here, but a joy-bringer. Aeron's joy-bringer, in fact, and the girl did her job well. The somber bastard had never been so...smiley, for lack of a better word. It was straight up weird. "Can you imagine twin demon hellions running around this place?"

"No." Strider had never spent any time with kids and wouldn't even know how to hold one. Or what to say to one. Or what to do when one vomited on his favorite sword. But damn if he didn't get a kick out of imagining his friends struggling to cope.

"Oh, and get this. Gideon married Scarlet, the keeper of Nightmares."

"You're kidding." Fickle Gideon? Married? Scarlet was gorgeous, yeah, and feisty as hell. Powerful, too. And Gideon had been a tad bit obsessed with her when she'd been locked in their dungeon. But marriage?

*Everyone* in the fortress had lost IQ points, it seemed.

"He couldn't have waited until I got back to sign on for double occupancy?" Strider mumbled. "What a great friend."

"*No one* was invited to the ceremony, if you catch my meaning."

"Well, the decision to get hitched is gonna give him nightmares." Strider snickered. "Get it? Nightmares?"

"Har, har. You're a borderline fucktard, you know that?"

"Hey, I'm not going to apologize for being on my A game. Why don't you step up to the plate and join me, Junior League?"

Torin ignored him. "It's weird, don't you think? Two demons hooking up?"

Strider peered at him, blinked. "I can't believe *you* just said that."

"Why?"

"One word—Cameo. And you. Okay, so three words."

Torin snapped his teeth at him. "Whatever. We were talking about Scarlet. Which brings me to more gossip. Turns out she's the only daughter of...wait for it... Rhea."

What? *Rhea?* And he hadn't known? Strider had been *way* more self-involved than he'd realized. Rhea was queen of the gods, the estranged wife of Cronus, and the bitch helping Galen, keeper of the demon of Hope—and an all around asshole—leader of the Hunters. "How'd Gideon take the news?"

"Well, he tried to kill his mother-in-law."

"Sweet. But such romantic gestures aside, our boys have gotta start picking their significant others with more care. Gwen is Galen's only kid, Scarlet is Rhea's. What's next?" A Hunter? A participant in Baden's killer?

Yes, he was a fucktard.

"I'll tell you what's next," Torin said. "Lucifer's brother."

"Come again."

"Did no one tell you? William is related to Lucifer. And Lucifer is the devil, in case you didn't know."

"Come *again*."

The corners of Torin's lips quirked with amusement. "I know. Whacked out as hell, but kind of fitting."

He wouldn't ask again. He wouldn't. "How?" Damn! The question escaped before he could stop it.

"Don't know. William refused to spill. Needless to say, things have been pretty festive around here. So, anyway. You're back, and you're kind of healthy, so I can ask the question I've been holding in for three days. Where the hell is the Cloak of Invisibility? I looked through your stuff, your room, but couldn't find it."

Oh, shit. Now it was his turn to drop a news bomb. "About that..."

# CHAPTER EIGHT

HAIDEE PROWLED THE CONFINES of her cell.

She had no idea how much time had passed since she'd been pushed inside. She was alone. Food and water had been brought to her only once. The fruits and nuts and crisp, clean water had somehow curbed her hunger completely, strengthening her in a way she couldn't explain.

Oh, and the food had been delivered by an angel—a freaking *angel* living in a demon's den. That still had her reeling. But she now knew beyond a doubt she was in the Budapest fortress. As they'd dragged her down here, she'd spotted wear and tear from a recent bombing. A bombing she hadn't been involved in, but one she'd heard all about.

Enough time had passed for Micah—"Amun," Defeat had called him—to have suffered countless fates. Torture, relocation, even death. The thought of each had sent her into a near hysteric state. She'd clawed the walls until she had no nails left. She'd beaten the bars until her knuckles had cracked and swelled. She'd screamed for answers until her voice had fractured.

Now, in the silence, all she could do was think, one sentence echoing over and over again. Defeat had called him Amun. *Was* he Amun, a Lord? Or was he Micah, a Hunter?

He'd known her, shouted for her help. That had to mean he was Micah. But, on the flip side, he hadn't known anything else about her. Not their history, not their purpose. That had to mean he was Amun.

Argh! The back-and-forth, was he or wasn't he, was driving her as crazy as her confinement. Could he be a mix of both? Amun's demon stuffed into Micah's body? Because really, two men couldn't look that much alike. Could they?

No matter the answers, she wasn't leaving without him. Even though, deep down, a part of her suspected the worst. That two men could easily look alike—especially if powers beyond a human's comprehension were involved. That he was Amun, that he'd always been Amun. That Micah was someone else completely, out there somewhere, still searching for her, and she was simply trying to convince herself otherwise so she wouldn't feel guilty.

That kiss…something else she couldn't get out of her mind. Micah had never kissed her like that. Fiery, consuming. Necessary.

Despite the danger they had been in—*were* in—she would have allowed him to strip and penetrate her. She would have met him thrust for wild thrust, taking, giving, *claiming*. She would have clung to him, desperate for more, for everything.

Hell, she would have crawled inside him if she could have. She'd wanted them fused, never able to part. How crazy was that? A kiss had never affected her like that. Never. A *man* had never affected her like that.

Always before, she had remained detached. From everyone. Maybe because she'd known the people around her would die, while she would continue on, eternally brought back from the grave. Maybe because there was darkness inside her. So much darkness. A living entity, as real as the ice that flowed through her veins, a presence in the back of her mind, muted but always there, urging her to despise people, places, life, death. Anything, everything.

For the first time, she hadn't had to fight to feel or garner affection. She had looked at Amun—

*That's how you think of him now? Amun?*

Yes, she realized. Somehow he was Amun to her now. Micah didn't fit those fuller lips and wider shoulders. So, she had looked at Amun, and sensual awareness had sizzled inside her. Connecting them. She had heard his voice inside her head, and that sensual awareness had deepened.

And if he really was Amun, not Micah, she *should* feel guilty about what had happened between them. She should be horrified that she'd succumbed to her enemy. Should be devastated that she'd let him give her more than an explosive kiss; she'd let him lick between her legs, and she had loved it. Had been begging for more.

Guilt and horror were not what she felt, however. Well, not completely. She felt them, but she was still consumed by desire.

Forgetting the fact that Amun was the enemy, she wasn't a cheater. And yet, had he walked through her cell, she felt pretty certain she would have thrown herself into his arms.

She scrubbed a shaky hand down her face. What was happening to her common sense? Her well-honed self-preservation instincts?

Micah was the first boyfriend she'd allowed herself in centuries, and only because she had dreamed of him first. But she hadn't needed him, hadn't been lost without him. She paused and peered down at her tattooed arm. At his name, branded so deeply into her flesh. *M-i-c-a-h*. She traced the letters with a scabbed fingertip. There was no leap in her pulse, no hum of desire.

She thought the name Amun.

Goose bumps broke out over every inch of her skin. She licked her lips, her mouth suddenly flooded with moisture.

See? Reaction. Always. And that wasn't good. Not good at all.

What if…what if she hadn't dreamed of Micah? What if she'd dreamed of Amun? Did that mean Amun was a bad memory trying to surface? Or, like the visions he had showed her of her past, was he something good?

Neither made sense, really. One, in the visions, she knew the man she saw was her key to happiness, to freedom. Two, how could a demon-possessed immortal, responsible for the travesty that was her life—and her parents' and sister's deaths—be something good?

She kicked back into motion, her sure strides eating up the distance from one cell wall to the other. A better question: How could a demon-possessed warrior be the one thing she craved? The one thing she didn't think she could live without?

*Live. Without.* The words echoed through her mind, and she stumbled to another halt. Her stomach twisted, sharp little knots forming, cutting. No. No, no, no. She purposely kept her home and belongings sparse, her friendships casual. That way, she could pick up and leave without a moment's notice or regret.

She could live without him. She *could*. He was a mystery right now. A mystery she needed to solve. That was all.

Another complication sprouted. If the warrior she craved was Amun, he wouldn't want her when he discovered the truth about her. The fact that he'd kissed her meant he hadn't realized who she was and what she'd done to his friend, Baden. When he did, he would want to kill her, not pleasure her.

*But he knew you were a Hunter. You told him.* Still. Easier to forgive a run-of-the-mill Hunter, she thought, than the Hunter who had helped behead his friend—and planned to do the same to all the others.

Footsteps suddenly resounded. Haidee swung around, facing the cell door. She tensed, waiting, dreading. A few seconds later, the blond, blue-eyed keeper of Defeat rounded the corner and approached her prison. Bile burned a path up her throat. His pretty features were devoid of emotion, but his skin was pale, the tracery of his veins evident.

Though her heartbeat sped up, thumping erratically, she didn't back away, wouldn't act the coward.

"How are you feeling?" she asked, just to taunt him. "Have a tummy ache?"

Both of his sandy brows arched into his hairline, his eyes glittering dangerously. His gaze perused her from top to bottom, purposely lingering at her breasts, between her legs. "I'm feeling like I can do anything I want with you." Calmly yet brutally uttered, his threat clear. *"Anything."*

That wasn't the answer she'd expected, and she scowled at him. But then, she should have known he wouldn't simply endure her snide remarks. He always had to one-up her. So. Enough pleasantries.

"Where's the warrior?" she demanded. "The one I was with?"

"You mean Amun, keeper of the demon of Secrets?" So calm, so certain. "Or your boyfriend?"

Secrets, he'd said. Just as she'd suspected. The confirmation explained so much. The knots in her stomach twisted into themselves, sharpening further. Still, she wouldn't confirm or deny what she knew. "Maybe that's what you want me to believe. That he's masquerading as a Hunter, while in reality, he's really your friend." The words croaked from her. "Or maybe you just want me to hate my own boyfriend. Maybe you want me to hurt him and afterward, you'll taunt me, laugh at me."

"Now why would I want that, huh? If he's my friend, demon-possessed like me, yet I told you he wasn't, that he was your man, you would do your best to watch over him. And I would want my friend watched over, wouldn't I?" Strider propped his shoulder against the bar, and though his head was turned, his hard gaze remained fixed on her. "But if he isn't, if he *is* your boyfriend, why would I give the pleasure of killing him to you, even for a joke?"

Her chin lifted a notch, her stubborn core refusing to be cowed. Despite his sound reasoning. "Why would you admit he was your friend, then? Thereby placing him in danger?"

"So I've admitted he's Amun, have I?"

No, he hadn't. He'd only questioned *her* thoughts on the matter, probably trying to confuse her. "I don't care who he is." Either way, he belonged to *her*. That was a fact she couldn't argue, even with herself. "I just want to see him, make sure he's okay."

"Want, want, want." He tapped a finger against his chin. "Who said anything about giving you what you want?"

She popped her jaw, still refusing to show him emotion. "Why are you here, Defeat?"

"We'll get to that in a minute. First, I have some questions for you."

"And I have every intention of answering them," she said, sugar sweet.

"You will if you want to see your...man again." The last was gritted, as if the prospect bothered him.

"You just told me I wouldn't get what I wanted."

"No, I didn't. Think back. I asked you *who said you would*."

True. Bastard. But would he honor his word? The Lords of the Underworld were not known as givers in her world. "After you just taunted me with never seeing him again, you expect me to believe you'll escort me back to his room if I give you answers you won't believe anyway?" Or bring Amun here, she thought, but didn't say the words aloud.

No reason to put ideas into his head if they weren't already there.

He shrugged. "You're right. I was merely taunting you. Can you blame me, though? You bring out the worst in me, and I struck back."

She wanted to yell at him to continue but remained silent, waiting.

"So," he prodded. "We gonna do this? Answers in exchange for a little sightseeing?"

"Yes," she gritted out. She had no other recourse. He might be lying, but she was willing to risk Hunter secrets on the hope that he'd follow through. And that's what he would demand, she thought. Secrets. "Let's hammer out a few details before I start spewing info. *When* will you take me to him? A few years from now?" She wouldn't put such a trick past him.

A muscle ticked below his eye. "I'll take you immediately following our conversation."

"As if you'll keep your word," she said, raising her chin another notch. She might be willing to risk everything, but that didn't mean she would be stupid about it. The terms needed to be laid out flat, ironed and starched. Just in case. To do that, she would have to provoke him. Some things had to be offered without her prompting.

His eyes narrowed to tiny slits, the top and bottom lashes catching and twining. "Challenge me, then. Challenge me to keep it."

Like that. Had she challenged him on her own, he would have punished her. "Is he even alive?" Even asking, she wanted to cry. *You* can *live without him,* she reminded herself. She just didn't want to.

Oh, God. He already meant *that* much to her? Despite who and what he might be? Despite how he would hate her?

"Yes," Defeat said. "He is. Though his condition has worsened."

Her heart thumped against her ribs. "How many questions? There has to be a limit."

He gave another negligent shrug. "Five. And your answers had better be truthful."

*How will you know if they are or aren't?* she almost asked, just to taunt him as he'd taunted her, but she didn't. The outcome of this was too important. "All right. I—I challenge you to take me to see Micah—Amun—after I answer five questions honestly." If he punished her for the challenge, anyway, it would be no more than she deserved for allowing him to trick her.

Defeat's pupils gobbled up his irises as he jerked his head once in a stiff nod. "I accept." His hands fisted. "Satisfied?"

She'd seen that reaction before, recognized it as what he'd claimed. Acceptance. "I'm as satisfied as I can be in a place like this."

Those pupils continued to grow, as if she'd said something provocative. And maybe she had—a virile man would see her words as an invitation to satisfy her physically, and this man was more virile and invitation-happy than most—but it had been unintentional. She wasn't attracted to Defeat. He was beautiful, yes, but he lacked Amun's intensity. She also wanted to throw up in her mouth a little every time she looked at him.

"What's your first question?" she demanded.

He didn't hesitate. "What the hell are you?"

She didn't pretend to misunderstand. "I'm human."

Fast as lightning, he struck out, his fist pounding into the bar and rattling the very foundation of the cell. "Already you're lying. You can materialize weapons out of thin air. That's not something humans can do."

She gave no reaction to his fury. "If I can, why haven't

I produced one since being here? And I promise you, I would have sliced your throat from end to end if I'd had even the slightest opportunity during our trek."

Now a muscle ticked in his jaw, but at least he didn't strike out again. "An easy boast, almost believable. Maybe you just wanted a ticket into this fortress."

"To do what? Expedite my torture?"

"You were Bait once. Maybe you're meant to be Bait again."

"Then you were an idiot to bring me here," she lashed out.

His nostrils flared with the force of his renewed fury, but he said nothing else.

"This is getting us nowhere," she said, as calmly as she was able. "The weapons didn't simply materialize when we were in the jungle. I hid them from you until I found the opportunity to use them." And that was the God's honest truth. "That, and you're kind of a dumbass."

He exhaled, the breath seeming to drain his fury. "Well, that's an improvement over stupid and idiot."

Gentle, amused teasing. From him. Shocking. Or was he trying to throw her off balance? "I answered. *Honestly.* So, second question."

The gentleness faded, only a single thread of the amusement remaining. "If you're human, how are you alive? I watched you die. Which is a nice way of saying I fucking murdered you!"

"I've been reanimated." She didn't mention how or how many times. He hadn't asked. "That's two. Next."

He shook his head. "Not done with that one yet. If you've been reanimated, and I'm guessing that's just a fancy way of saying you were brought back to life, a god aided you. Only a god has the power to reanimate a body after a beheading. And even then, I'm not sure it's possible."

Silence enveloped them. He stared at her pointedly. She stared back.

"Well?" he demanded, spreading his arms as if he were the last sane man in the universe.

"Well, what? You didn't ask a question."

The muscle in his jaw started ticking again. "Who aided you?"

Aided was not the word she would have chosen. Cursed, maybe. "A creature very much like you. I think. I didn't see it, only know I had a reaction to it the first and only time it touched me." And that's all she would say on the matter. Even if he asked for more. "That's three. Next." Why hadn't he asked her about the Hunters?

"Rhea, then," he said, as if that explained everything.

Haidee schooled her features, unwilling to show him the depth of her confusion. Rhea, the supposed queen of the Titans? Haidee had heard of her, of course. A small group of Hunters even worshipped her. But why did Defeat assume the woman was responsible for Haidee's curse? Or "infection," as the Bad Man had called it? "Two more questions to go. Better make them good."

"When I saw you with…him, kissing—" he'd almost said a name, she realized, but had managed to stop himself in time "—were you interested in him as a man or as a possible escape route?"

Of everything Defeat could have asked, why that? "Why the hell do you care?"

His traced the tip of his tongue across the seam of his lips. "I don't believe our bargain involved explanations on my part."

Fine. "The man."

There was a beat of silence before he gave her a reaction. A flash of that fury, quickly gone.

"He's always been the gentle one, you know," Defeat said almost absently. "He's rarely ever displayed a temper.

Has *never* hurt one of his friends. And he would be horrified to know what he did to me." As soon as he realized what he'd said, what he'd admitted, he scowled at her, as if the confession was her fault.

She pretended not to notice. "You have one more question. And did I forget to tell you that if *you* lied to *me*, I would personally reacquaint your spine with a shard of glass?"

He stared at her for a long while, studying, searching for something. Whether he found it or not, she didn't know. Then he spoke, soft, gentle. "Why did you help kill Baden, Haidee?"

She sucked in a breath. Of everything he could have demanded to know...how dare he ask *that?* As if he didn't already know the answer. As if he hadn't rallied to destroy her, all those centuries ago. As if he would enjoy hearing her pain and her heartbreak.

Just like that, all the hate inside her exploded to the surface, and she stomped to the bars, placing herself within striking distance. She didn't attack him but dared him to attack her.

He didn't move, just continued to stare at her.

"Why did I help kill him?" She threw the words at him as if they were weapons, and maybe they were. "Because he took what I loved most. And don't try to lie and say he didn't, that I'm confused, or misremembering. I *saw* him. I was there."

"He—"

"I'm not done! Why else did I help kill him? Because he represented what I despised most. Because he deserved what I did, and he knew it. He *wanted* me to do it. And not once, not once in all these years, have I ever regretted it."

Again, silence. Those blue eyes glittered far more dangerously than before as he reached inside his pocket.

Haidee expected a dagger to the stomach but still didn't back down. Physical pain might dull her emotional anguish.

He merely keyed the lock. The cell door swung open, the hinges squeaking. "For some reason, you calmed...our boy before. He's worse now, and we need to know if you can calm him again."

Him. Amun. So, she thought, furious all over again, Defeat had meant to take her to the warrior all along. She hadn't had to answer a single question. She'd been tricked, just not the way she'd thought. What a fool she was. "And what is it, exactly, that I calm him from? How is he worse? What the hell did you do to him?"

"I'm going to take you to him," the demon went on, ignoring her. Either he was unaware of her volatile emotions or he just didn't care. "But if you harm him, Haidee, I *will* kill you. And I'll make it hurt in a way you can't even imagine."

THE MOMENT DEFEAT led her down the hallway to Amun's bedroom—a hallway still filled with towering angels and their outspread wings—she heard the warrior's voice inside her head and forgot everything else.

*Haidee!* That single word was a tormented wail. *Need... you...please...*

How long had he been calling for her? Why hadn't she heard him before now?

*Haidee!*

She'd uncover those details later. Right now, he was in pain, so much pain, and nothing but helping him mattered.

Wrenching away with all her strength, she broke free of Defeat's hold and rushed forward. No one tried to stop her. Not the angels and not the Lord. She expected Amun's doorway to still be splintered from Defeat's vicious kick, but someone had fixed the metal and wood, both now blocking her entrance.

She twisted the knob—unlocked, thank God—and raced into the bedroom, quickly slamming the door shut behind her. She tried to flip the lock in place and noticed it had been removed. Shit! Something else to worry about later. Tiny beads of ice dotted her skin, and her knees knocked shakily as she pivoted. Then she saw him. He was thrashing atop the bed, just like last time.

Finally, she was with him again. He was alive. But for how long? He was worse, Defeat had said, and Amun had barely survived the last set of wounds.

*Haidee...please...*

So weak, suffused with all that pain. "I'm here, baby. I'm here." Acid flowed through her as she stumbled toward him. Some distant part of her brain noticed that every piece of furniture but the bed had been carted out. Then she was standing at the edge of the mattress, peering down at him, and all thoughts fled.

He moaned inside her head.

"I know. I know you hurt."

*Haidee?* Not quite so pained now.

"Yes, baby. Haidee's here."

He sighed with the barest hint of relief.

The shadows had returned, were even then dancing around his once again savaged body. His eyes were swollen shut, his hands bloody and torn. The wings of his butterfly tattoo were...moving, breaking apart, forming hundreds of other butterflies. Those, too, danced over him, up his thighs, on his stomach, his pectorals, his arms, then disappearing behind his back.

In that moment, she was absolutely certain the man she watched was Amun rather than Micah. Which meant the Lords wouldn't hurt him. *Thank God*. The intensity of her relief was stunning.

*What's wrong with you?* she wondered again. Now that her worries over Amun's possible torture and execution were proven unnecessary, she couldn't forget or refute two simple facts. This man had never been a Hunter. This man was her enemy.

*She* should kill him. She should add to her tally and be all the closer to evening the score. Like Baden, Amun deserved whatever punishment she dished. The vile things these men had done in ancient Greece… Still. She couldn't force herself to hurt him. He was too battered, too pitiful. Had sought only to protect her.

*His attitude will change. You know it will. The moment he's well, his friends will tell him who you are. He'll go for your throat faster than you can say, "But I spared you."*

She'd worry about his hatred then. For now, for better or worse, she and Amun were connected. Later, she would search for answers, find out how and why. Maybe she could even convince herself she'd never had visions of him. And then…maybe then she could find a way to cut the ties that bound them. If he didn't do it first.

Until then…

She would do everything in her power to save this man, just as before.

Even the thought was a betrayal to the Hunters. A betrayal Micah would take personally. But that didn't alter her plans, and that, she realized, drove home the knowledge that her relationship with him was over.

She was shocked by her lack of unhappiness at the prospect. Shocked further that she didn't wish things were different. She just wished there was a way to let him know. Gently. She desired another man, a demon-possessed man at that, and Micah deserved better than she could ever give him.

She sighed, the relieved sound an echo of Amun's. It was nice, having *something* figured out. If only healing Amun proved to be that simple. She reached out and brushed the sweat-soaked hair from his brow. Those dancing shadows screeched, darting away from her and burrowing under Amun's skin, even as the warrior leaned toward her, seeking closer contact.

What did that darkness represent? What did it mean? Definitely something evil, as she'd first suspected. Amun obviously hated it, cringing as the last thread of gloom faded inside him.

*Haidee, my Haidee.* Another sigh wafted through her head, this one laced with contentment. *Don't leave me.*

"I won't leave you." Her trembling intensified as she climbed in beside him and wrapped him in her arms. "I'll be here as long as you need me."

IN HIS OWN BEDROOM, Torin watched Haidee on one of his computer screens. Haidee. Come back to life. Who would have thought? And why hadn't Strider told him? The questions lost their importance between one heartbeat and the next. His eyes widened as the shadows scrambled to escape her touch. He'd never seen anything like it and had no idea what it meant.

He did know one thing. She wasn't human, as she'd told Strider. No mere human could frighten demons as she'd just done. And they *were* frightened of her. They'd hidden inside Amun, rather than try and escape him as they'd done from the first.

"So what the fuck is she?" he muttered.

SCOWLING, STRIDER BARRELED his way inside Amun's chamber. How eager Haidee had been to reach the warrior, her sworn enemy. And now Strider saw her sprawled on the bed, curled into Amun's side, tenderly smoothing his brow. As if she wanted to be there. As if she was glad to be there. Helping a Lord.

*She thinks Amun's her boyfriend, remember?* Of course she was glad. Of course she was helping.

"Ex?" he growled with more force than he'd intended.

Her gunmetal gaze shifted and locked on him warily. "What?" There was nothing wary about her voice. That single word snapped at him with more force than even he had used.

Clearly, she wanted him to get out and leave her the hell alone.

His molars gnashed together, and he beat down the tide of jealousy that suddenly raged through him. Jealousy. Jealousy over a Hunter. A Hunter he'd always planned to kill. Why couldn't he simply be happy that Amun now had a chance to pull through?

Because Haidee was going to make Amun miserable. And if the big guy fell in love with her, he just might abandon his friends to be with her. Which would get his ass killed for good. Ultimately, she would betray him.

*I won't let that happen. Ever.*

*Win,* Defeat said, sensing the challenge.

*I will.* Strider raised both of his hands. In the left, he held a syringe. In the right, chains. They'd been waiting in the hallway, but she'd been too damn concerned for Amun to notice. "You didn't honestly think you'd have free rein with him, did you?"

# CHAPTER NINE

AMUN DRAGGED HIMSELF FROM the tangled web of his mind and forced his eyelids to open. First things he noticed: the taste of frosted apricots filled his mouth, there was a wonderful chill inside him, cooling the fires that had raged, and an earthy perfume wafted into his nose every time he inhaled.

Second thing: sunlight streamed through the window, the heavy curtains parted and the blinds slatted to welcome every single bright ray. His eyes teared and burned, but at least those tears washed away the hazy shield seeming to cloak the entire room, allowing him a clearer view.

Third thing: Strider reclined in a cushy chair he'd placed just in front of Amun's bed, watching him with an intent, almost forbidding expression.

Strider's mind was blank, and purposely so. The warrior knew Amun could read every single one of his thoughts. Everyone here knew it. Which was why, when they wanted privacy—because Amun simply couldn't stop the flow of their innermost secrets, no matter how much he wanted to—they had to wrap themselves in darkness and silence.

"How do you feel?" Strider asked, his timbre scratchy and rough.

Even though the new demons were rattling against his skull, Amun had no trouble understanding. He tried to raise his hands to sign his reply. *Like shit, for the most part.* The apricots, the chill, both overshadowed the worst of his pain. Only, his arms refused to obey the mental command. Why? His head turned to the left, gaze sliding to his wrist. Scabbed skin, dried blood. Fingers swollen, nails ruined.

Suddenly memories flooded him, Secrets stretching to wakefulness inside his mind, enjoying the unveiling of what his inner defenses would have liked to keep hidden.

Hell. Those other demons. The dark flashes, the vile urges. Haidee. The knowledge that he should kill her, the inability to do so. A taste of heaven, her body writhing against his, her hands all over him, her sweet cries in his ears. Strider. Battle, blood. Hating himself for hurting his friend and shielding a Hunter. Failing to reach the girl when she needed him. The return of the demons, the dark flashes and vile urges. No Haidee. No heaven.

Grim expectation mixed with white-hot rage and bone-numbing fear, all filling him as he jerked himself upright. The bedroom spun, a sharp lance of pain tearing through his temples. He didn't care, remained upright. Where was she? Dead? The thought left him sick to his stomach.

No. No, he assured himself desperately, and he felt Secrets's agreement. She couldn't be. That earthy perfume belonged to her, as raw and basic as his need for her. He had to find her. Had to make sure she was okay, that no one had hurt her.

*Even though you meant to kill her yourself?*

He ignored the simple, rational question and experimented with his range of motion, lifting one leg and rotating his ankle. He grimaced, then repeated the process with the other leg. He grimaced again. Both legs fell back onto the mattress with a hard thump. The bones had woven back together, but they were still fractured.

"Whoa." Strider pushed to his feet, the chair skidding

behind him. "What the hell do you think you're doing? Lie down. You're still recovering."

Amun hardly ever despised his inability to speak. Silence was his choice, his way of righting the wrongs he'd committed all those centuries ago, of helping the innocents so much like the ones he'd once slaughtered. Not to mention his friends. They had enough to worry about. But just then, he wanted to shout—*the girl, where the hell is the girl*—uncaring that the moment he did, all the secrets inside him would spill out, hurting everyone who heard them. Not physically but mentally, and that was a far worse pain to bear. He knew that very well.

Not even the warriors he lived with would be able to tolerate knowing when other men desired their women. Nor would they be able to tolerate the disgusting things their enemies had planned for their loved ones. Friendships would be destroyed, jealousy a constant companion, and paranoia would follow their every step.

Amun could deal because he'd spent thousands of years learning to distance himself from the visions and voices in his head, blocking emotions before they could even form. Not this newest onslaught, of course. He'd never experienced anything like this and had no idea how to cope. Had no idea how he was lucid now, the new demons cowering in the back of his mind. Unless…

Haidee.

Her name whispered through his mind, a plea, a prayer, his demon sensing the truth, even as Amun struggled to accept it. Was she responsible? The first time, as well as now?

The first time he'd tasted frosted apricots, he'd come to his senses. Now he tasted apricots again, and his senses once again returned. Couldn't be a coincidence. His desperation to find her intensified.

He threw his legs over the side of the mattress, hinges

squeaking. Every muscle he possessed knotted and ached, clamping tightly on those fractured bones.

"Amun, damn it. You've been bed-bound for days, recovering from your wounds and our little experiments. Stop before you—"

Agitation somehow making his motions fluid, he twisted to face his friend, lips pulled over his teeth. Most of what Strider had said confused him, but he left it alone. Finally forcing his hands to work, he jerkily signed, *I'm sorry I hurt you. Sorry I challenged you before. But I have to find her. Where is she?* If they'd hurt her, he didn't know what the hell he'd do. Didn't know how she affected him like this. Didn't know why he cared what was done to her, whether she was responsible for his recovery or not.

Secrets whispered, *She is fine,* and despite the low volume, the High Lord still managed to be the loudest voice in his head. At the same time, Strider sat back down and said, "She's there." His tone was hard and unbending as he motioned to the left with a tilt of his chin.

Amun noticed his friend didn't have to ask who "she" was. He followed that tilt with his gaze, and hissed in an agonized breath. She was on her knees, her arms chained above her head. That chain was anchored to his ceiling, offering just enough slack to keep her spine erect. Her head lolled forward, her chin pressed into her collarbone.

The length of her blond-and-pink hair shielded most of her dirt-smudged face, but he could see that her eyes were closed, her long, curling lashes fanning down.

His lips parted in a silent roar as he at last pushed to a stand. *She is not fine!* His knees almost gave out, his stomach almost rebelled, but fury and reckless determination gave him strength.

"I drugged her," Strider said as if to soothe him from a violent temper. "She'll recover."

That didn't fucking matter! What mattered was that

something had been done to her. How long had she been tethered like that? Unconscious? Helpless? Amun stalked to his friend, stumbling twice, and held out his hand, palm up. Secrets began prowling restlessly. Because they were closer to the girl?

Strider knew what he wanted and shook his head. "She's a Hunter, Amun. She's dangerous."

He waved his fingers, insisting. He would challenge Strider if necessary. Would do anything for what he wanted.

"Damn it! Do you care nothing for your own safety?"

Again he waved his fingers.

"Fine. You can deal with the consequences on your own." Scowling, but perhaps sensing the depths of Amun's resolve, Strider reached inside his pocket and withdrew a key. He slapped the metal into Amun's still open palm.

Immediately Amun spun and stomped to Haidee. He tripped twice more along the way, but not even that slowed him. Secrets, he noted, had ceased prowling, was utterly still and completely silent now.

Only those years of blunting the fiercest edges of his emotions kept his ire inside as he twisted the key into the lock. The metal unsnapped, freeing her. She sagged forward without a sound, arms falling heavily to her sides. She would have kissed the floor if Amun hadn't caught her. His arms despised him, sharp pains still shooting through him, but he didn't care. At the moment of contact, the screams inside his head—muted though they'd been—quieted altogether, the demons determined to hide from her, as if they feared the pulling would start up again.

Gently, so gently, he fit her against his chest and lifted her into his arms. The chill of her skin delighted him anew, and he couldn't help but remember the glide of that skin against his, caressing, stroking, the friction unbearably sweet.

Raw desire, brutal in its intensity, suddenly consumed every inch of him. He fought past that clawing need and carried her to the bed. He eased her down, then fit the covers around her slight frame and peered down at her. How fragile she looked, her cheeks a bit hollowed, her lips chapped, her skin pallid. How vulnerable she was, unable to defend herself from any type of attack.

She would hate that vulnerability, he thought, not needing his demon's help to recall the way she'd constantly scanned her surroundings, how she'd vigilantly searched for a weapon. How she had defended him with her very life.

*Because she thought you were her human boyfriend,* he recalled next. He despised the reminder. Did she know the truth now? Would she fight him when she woke up? He thought he would prefer that. Better her loathing than her acceptance of him as another man.

He would be liked for himself or not at all.

Amun stilled as he realized where his thoughts were headed. Permanency. Keeping her. The moisture in his mouth dried, and he felt like he was swallowing cotton mixed with Haidee's glass shards. He couldn't, wouldn't, keep her.

When his friends learned what she'd done, that she was the one who had helped kill Baden, they would demand her head. He could try to talk them out of it, but they wouldn't be denied. He knew that beyond any doubt. And if he chose her, placed her needs over theirs, they would never forgive him. Hell, he would never forgive himself. Baden deserved better. *They* deserved better.

*Don't think about that now.* Head spinning with the tide of conflicting emotions and urges flooding him, he climbed into bed beside her, fit her against him, and faced Strider with narrowed eyes. The warrior was watching him, blue eyes ablaze.

*She's more than a Hunter,* Strider thought, clearly knowing Amun would hear. *She's responsible for Baden's killer.*

Amun knew the warrior wanted to keep that particular revelation just between them—strange that he hadn't spoken aloud, considering no one else was in the room—but he was glad. The fewer people who knew about her, the safer she would be, and this way, no one would overhear. Then Secrets informed him that Torin knew, also. That Strider simply hadn't realized. Amun was shocked to his soul that neither man had killed her already. Shock that nearly burned him alive, chasing away the sweetest kiss of her chilled skin. Because she lived, Amun had assumed he was the only one who had figured out her past misdeed.

"Well?" Strider demanded

In reply to his previous statement, Amun merely nodded.

The warrior's nostrils flared with outrage. "You knew?"

He gave a second nod.

"I shouldn't be surprised. You always know everything. But fuck, man! You're still treating her like a goddamn treasure." The words were gritted as he tunneled a hand through his hair and paced. "You picked her over me, damn it."

There was no response that could exonerate him, even another apology, so he offered none. And in the silence, Amun began to hear more of Strider's thoughts. Thoughts the warrior couldn't snuff out quickly enough.

*She's mine. To kiss, to kill. Whatever I decide. Damn her, how has she tied me in knots like this? I despise her.*

Amun's hands curled into fists. *Mine,* he wanted to shout. He didn't. Such a confession would only dig his hole of guilt and shame deeper, so he kept his lips pressed into a tight line.

*Why haven't you harmed her?* he signed stiffly. Because Strider desired her, too? Such desire was completely unlike the war-hungry man, though. Only Sabin, their leader and keeper of the demon of Doubt, was better able to place the campaign against the Hunters over his personal needs and wants. So Strider's hesitation to strike had to stem from something else. Or rather, it had better stem from something else.

Amun had never felt more capable of murder than he did at that moment, thinking of another man putting his hands on Haidee.

Guilt…shame…he fell into the hole anyway.

His friend plopped back into the chair, gaze never leaving him. "We don't know how, but she calms you, clears your mind, even makes the demons cower."

So. As he'd suspected, Haidee was responsible for his recovery. The knowledge was as upsetting as it was welcome.

"She has to be near you, in the same room, for…whatever she does to work," Strider went on. "We still don't know how she's doing it, but we've carried her in and out of this room several times to test the limits of her ability. Once she reaches the hallway, your torment begins all over again."

"Experiments" suddenly made sense. Was her ability the reason he felt bound to her? Because she somehow did what he couldn't, frightening the demons into submission? Was that how she affected him so strongly, his body a slave to desires he didn't want to feel?

That question led to another, one far more distressing than any that had come before. Was this how Baden had felt when he'd opened his door one moonlit night and found Haidee outside, begging for help?

The memory opened up in Amun's mind, courtesy of Haidee, he was sure.

*I'm frightened,* she'd said, tears glistening in her eyes, her lower lip trembling. *I think someone's out there, following me. Please escort me home. Please.*

He beat it back until he saw only black. He didn't want to go there. Other questions began to pop up, each more damning than the last. Had Baden looked at her lovely face and felt at peace for the first time since his possession? Was that why he'd simply bowed his head when the Hunters had surged from their hiding places and attacked him, welcoming his own death?

Jerkily, he signed, *Can she hear your thoughts?*

"No." Strider blinked, shook his head in confusion. "Can she hear yours?"

Amun nodded stiffly.

"Can she hear everything? Even your demon...s? Even your *demons*."

No. Thank the gods. *Just what I allow her to hear.*

Strider propped his elbow on the arm of the chair, a triumphant gleam suddenly glittering in his blue eyes, intensifying the blaze already banked there. "We can use that to our advantage."

Of course the warrior immediately went to tricking and defeating the girl.

"Sabin will—"

Amun hissed before he could stop himself. *No.*

Again Strider blinked in confusion.

*No,* he signed a second time. *You will not mention this to Sabin.* He barely stopped himself from adding, *Ever.*

"Amun, you know I can't—"

*Not yet. You won't mention it* yet. Amun had chosen to follow Sabin while they'd lived in the heavens, soldiers for the god king, even though Lucien had been the one in charge. No one could strategize like Sabin. No one was fiercer. No one was better suited to getting an unpleasant job done.

After they'd opened Pandora's box and found themselves cursed, as well as stuck in the land of the mortals, half of his friends had continued to follow Lucien. The other half had decided to follow Sabin. Amun hadn't changed his mind. He'd gone with Sabin because no one hated Hunters more.

For the first time in all the centuries since, he regretted that decision.

Amun had often helped his friend torture their prisoners for information, but he hadn't enjoyed the screams or the blood as Sabin had. Still. He'd known that what they were doing was necessary to their survival.

Now he knew, deep in his bones, that no matter what he said, the moment Sabin learned Haidee's true identity, he would stride into this room and calmly but surely strip her of her pride, her peace of mind and even her will to live.

"I'm not going to keep this from him, Amun," Strider said. There was no emotion in his tone. His voice was dead now, his tenacity clear.

*Give me a day with her, then.* A day wasn't going to be enough, he realized in the next instant. Not because he desired her. Which he did. Oh, did he desire. More than he should, more than he'd ever desired another. There was still no denying that fact. Never before had he placed someone else's welfare above that of his friends, and an enemy at that. No, a day wasn't going to be enough because she'd called him "baby" and he wanted so badly for it to be true.

He scrubbed a hand down his sore, swollen face. The endearment had been meant for another man. That should have lessened its appeal. It didn't.

Still. He was going to protect her, he thought. From

Sabin. From all of them. She was the reason Amun's sanity had returned. Therefore, he had to keep her safe. And if he was going to keep her safe, at least for a little while, he needed to set a few rules. Like, no more thinking about how soft she felt in his arms. Like, no more tapping into her sweetest memories. Like, no more kissing her.

The first time had been the last time. No matter how succulent she'd tasted. No matter how passionately she'd come apart for him. No matter how much he yearned to sink inside her, slipping in and out, slowly at first, then increasing his speed, pushing them both to feverish heights. *Shit.* He wasn't supposed to be thinking about her, and he damn well wasn't supposed to be lusting for her.

"Why do you want a day?" Strider demanded. "A day's not going to change anything. Besides, Sabin's not going to kill her, knowing she's responsible for your improved condition."

Sabin *would* torture her, though. *Because I would rather pamper an enemy*—even the one responsible for Baden's murder, he added for his own benefit—*than endure the darkness and the visions.* Selfish of him, yes, and another reason to hate himself, but that wasn't going to stop him.

*Another* reason to hate himself? he mused then. An odd choice of words. Amun didn't hate himself and never had. He didn't like some of the things he'd done over his endless lifetime, but hate? No. Unlike some of the other warriors, he wasn't filled with guilt over his past, either. He'd killed innocents, yes. He'd razed cities to the ground, that, too. But he'd been a puppet, his strings pulled by his demon. So how, then, was he to blame?

Because he should have been stronger? That was what some of his friends thought about themselves. Not him. No one would have been strong enough to stop those demons.

Because he'd helped open Pandora's box, and deserved

the punishment that led to his need for destruction? Nearly all of the Lords thought that, but again, Amun didn't. Everyone made mistakes, and that had been one of his. You paid the price and then you moved on.

And what of Haidee? he wondered. Was her mistake forgivable? Had she paid the price? Should he move on?

His jaw clenched. He ignored that line of questioning, focusing instead on what he'd do once his day with her was over—or if he wasn't even given a day. No matter what, he wasn't going to allow Sabin to have her. When the time came, Amun would simply cart her out of the fortress. And once they left, no one would be able to find them. His demon could do more than steal secrets from those around them. His demon could *keep* secrets. Distorting memories, even before they were created.

If Amun wanted to disappear forever, he could disappear forever.

He could hide Haidee until he learned how to control the new demons himself. Then...then he didn't know what he would do with her. Bring her back, he hoped. Do what needed doing, he prayed. Because if he failed to learn the answers he needed, he would be stuck with Haidee forever, destroying his friends.

*Plus,* Amun added, *I plan to talk to her. Learn more about her effect on me.*

"Who are you trying to fool? Yourself or me? We both know that's a lie. You're not thinking with you brain right now, my man." The last was snapped, as if the warrior had reached the end of his patience. "You want to fuck her, end of story."

Well, Amun had reached the end of his patience, too. *What we both know is that you aren't thinking with your brain, either.*

There was a momentary splash of astonishment over Strider's face before the warrior smoothed his features into a blank expression that matched his earlier tone. "Stay out of my head."

*Control your thoughts,* Amun signed. *I know you desire her. Now I'll hear you admit it.*

The tip of Strider's tongue traced over the straight line of his teeth. "Fine. I want her. But I'm not going to do anything about it. I'm not going to let it stop me from winning our war." At least he didn't try to deny his feelings. "Can you say the same?"

Amun merely raised his chin. *I can't say anything.*

"Funny. That's not what I meant and you know it."

*Well, that's all you're going to get from me.*

"Fine," Strider snarled, pushing to his feet. "I'm leaving before you provoke my demon any more. You've got your day, but I'd be careful if I were you. When you least expect it, she's gonna go for your head. Guaranteed. And maybe that doesn't concern you. Maybe you even want to die. Yeah, I saw what you did to yourself. But guess what? Not for a single moment are any of the rest of us ready to deal with your loss. So why don't you think about that before you put your life on the line for our enemy?"

# CHAPTER TEN

TWO SECONDS AFTER STRIDER barricaded himself inside his own bedroom, he had his phone in hand and was texting Lucien. He couldn't deal with this. He'd reached his bullshit limit.

At fortress. Come get me. Now.

It was nice, having a friend who could flash from one location to another with only a thought.

Within five minutes, his friend materialized a few feet away from him. Lucien was winded, barreled chest rising and falling shallowly. A sheen of sweat covered his entire torso. His mane of black hair shagged around his severely scarred face, and his multicolored eyes were bright. He was shirtless, his butterfly tattoo practically crackling with electricity on his left shoulder. His unfastened pants were barely staying on his hips. To top it all off, tension radiated from the man.

"What the hell were you doing?" Strider asked from his closet. He'd already strapped himself with weapons, but a few moments before had decided a couple more blades wouldn't hurt. Well, wouldn't hurt *him*.

One of Lucien's black brows practically knitted into his hairline. "Who the hell do you think I was doing?"

O-kay, then. Lucien had been in bed with Anya. For a moment, Strider almost forgot how pissed he was with Amun and Haidee as he savored the fact that he'd just cock-blocked the keeper of Death. Almost. "Anyone ever tell you that you shouldn't check your messages while you're rolling around in bed?"

"Yes. Anya. And believe me, I'm going to pay for this." His deep baritone was amused and excited rather than fearful at the thought of incurring his volatile female's wrath. "Here's a news flash for you. No matter what I'm doing, I check my messages when I'm worried about leaving my friends at home with a contingent of angels, when one of my men is sick, or when a Hunter is in residence. And when all three are happening at once? I check even when I don't have messages. So. What's wrong? Why did you summon me? Amun okay?"

Strider shoved an extra clip for his .22 into his pocket as he abandoned the confines of the walk-in. "Amun's great. Better. The problem's me. I gotta take off for a little while." For his sanity, yes, but mostly for Amun's safety.

Amun had lifted the fragile Haidee into his battered arms and carried her to his bed. He had tucked her under the covers, so careful not to jostle her, and climbed in beside her. Strider didn't think Amun realized this, but the warrior had caressed the woman during their entire conversation, as if the need to touch her was already ingrained in his soul.

A sense of challenge had begun to rise inside of Strider. For Haidee, a godsdamn Hunter. Worse, a godsdamn killer. He'd wanted to win her from Amun and claim her for his own, and the want had been far more intense than his usual "that's mine and I'm not sharing" mind-set.

If Strider stayed here, he would eventually give in. He wouldn't be able to help himself. His demon would badger him constantly, and in the end, he would fight his friend, hurt his friend—because no way in hell would he pull his punches like he'd done the first time—and hate himself.

Hate. Huh. He'd *never* hated himself. If anything, he'd always liked himself a little too much. Once, a human female had even accused him of picturing his own face while he climaxed. He hadn't denied it, either, and next time he'd slept with her, he'd made sure to scream, "Strider" at the pivotal moment.

She hadn't appreciated his sense of humor, and that had been the final nail in their relationship coffin. He was too intense, too jaded, too warped and too...everything for most women to take for long. But so what. He was made of awesome. Anyone who couldn't see that wasn't smart enough to be with him, anyway.

Haidee, though... She would be able to take him. With her strength of will, her courage, her unbending and reckless spirit, she would match him. Maybe even surpass him.

*That is the key player in Baden's murder you're thinking about.*

Hadn't mattered to Amun, he thought darkly. Why should it matter to him?

Fuck! He hated those thoughts.

*Hated.* There was that word again.

"—listening to me?" he heard Lucien ask with exasperation.

"Sorry," he muttered. "Say again."

Sighing, Lucien strode to the bed and sat at the edge of the mattress. Strider's gaze followed his friend, picking up little details about the room along the way. He hadn't cleaned in a few days, had been too busy guarding Amun, so his clothes were scattered throughout. His iPod hung from his nightstand, the earbuds wrapped around a lamp.

How the hell had it gotten there? Oh, yeah. He'd tossed it over his shoulder last night, uncaring where it landed.

"Torin texted me and told me Amun was doing better, but damn," Lucien said, once again dragging him from his thoughts. "You scared ten years off my life."

"You're welcome. Eternity's too long, anyway."

"Not when you're with the right woman."

He experienced a flash of jealousy that so many of his peeps had found the "right woman" already. And damn it, he was as sick of being jealous as he was of everything else.

"Talk to me," Lucien said. "Let me help you, whatever's going on."

"Nothing to talk about." He needed to forget Haidee, lose himself in another woman, in the heat and wetness of her body. An *appropriate* woman. Someone inexperienced, though not a virgin. Someone he wouldn't have to work his ass off trying to win, then work his ass off again to please. "I need a break, that's all."

"You summoned me with a 'now' because you need a break?"

"Yeah. You've been on break for weeks, it seems. Let someone else have a turn."

Silence, thick and heavy, enveloped them. Lucien studied him, and whatever he saw in Strider's expression caused him to lose his air of irritation. "All right. I'll take you wherever you want to go. For Torin's sake, someone needs to take your place before we leave. He'd never admit it, would even deny it, but he needs some help running this heap."

Gods, he loved his friends. Lucien wasn't going to question him further. Was just going to give him what he'd asked for.

"I'd do it," Lucien continued, "but I'm busy. I haven't been vacationing as you seem to think. I've been—and currently *am*—guarding the Cage of Compulsion in a place Rhea can't reach. And I can't tell you where that is. Torin asked me not to say anything since there's a Hunter in residence."

The cage was one of the four godly relics needed to find

and destroy Pandora's box, and in desperate need of that guarding. Strider knew that wasn't the only reason Lucien refused to move back into the fortress. The god queen was out for blood, and the man didn't want his Anya in any more danger than necessary. Strider could dig. "William's here," Strider said. "He can—"

Lucien was already shaking his head. "He's useless. He grows bored too easily to be relied upon. He'll forget whatever duty he's promised to perform and head into town for a little some-some."

Some-some. Someone was picking up his woman's vernacular. "Apparently he's related to Lucifer. That has to count for something."

"Believe me. I know who he's related to," Lucien replied dryly. "That doesn't change anything."

"Yeah, but he's strong. No one will want to mess with—"

Again Lucien shook his head. "Nope. Like I said, he's unreliable. He'll think of himself first and everyone else not at all."

"I know." William wasn't demon-possessed. He was a god, according to himself, and had spent centuries locked in Tartarus—a prison for immortals—for sleeping with the wrong woman. Hundreds of them, in fact. He'd even slept with Hera, the former god king's wife, and had been stripped of some of his supernatural abilities as further punishment. Exactly what those abilities were, he wouldn't say.

Strider liked the man, even though, as Lucien had said, he looked out only for himself. Even though he could turn on you in a heartbeat, stabbing you in the back—or rather, the stomach—as Lucien had experienced firsthand.

*My kinda guy,* Strider mused. And since William wasn't wanted here, maybe he'd want to leave with Strider. Strider made a mental note to text him before taking off. Never hurt to vacation with a friend.

So. Who did that leave to guard the fortress and those inside? "Kane and Cameo," he said with a nod. Disaster and Misery. "Since Amun's better, they can return from wherever they are."

Lucien pondered for a moment, then nodded in turn. "All right, then. It's settled."

"One more thing. Tomorrow I need you to contact Sabin." Strider planned to be too wasted to be coherent. "He needs to return, too, and meet the female Hunter up close and personal. But don't call him until tomorrow, okay?"

While Torin had apparently been texting, Strider had been calling both Lucien and Sabin every day, giving them updates on Amun's health. Only thing he hadn't told them—yet—was Haidee's identity. He didn't know why. He'd certainly meant to share, but every time he'd tried, the words had congealed in his throat.

All he knew was that he still wasn't going to tell them. Like him, they'd find out the truth as soon as they talked to her. And when they did, Strider wouldn't have betrayed Amun's trust, but would still have done all he could to safeguard his friend from the murdering bitch's influence.

Shit. He was getting worked up again, fighting a need to stomp back to Amun's room and do some damage.

*Win?* Defeat asked.

*Oh, no. We're not going there.*

"Consider it done," Lucien said.

"Good," he replied, tangling a hand in his hair. "'Cause I really need this break."

Once again Lucien asked no questions. He merely straightened and gave another nod. "Pack while I hunt down the lucky twosome and bring them home."

"No need to pack." He had his weapons. That's all he needed.

For the first time during their conversation, Lucien's lips twitched into the semblance of a smile. "Twice you've said you need a break. We both know nothing will change in a day or two. You'll still be stressed, on edge. So I want you gone for at least two weeks, and that's a nonnegotiable requirement if you expect transport. Pack."

Death didn't wait for Strider's reply. He simply disappeared.

Strider packed.

WILLIAM THE EVER RANDY, as the shitheads here had started calling him, lay propped on his bed, a mountain of pillows behind him. His covers were tucked around his waist and legs, cocooning him in a way he despised but refused to complain about because his Gillian Shaw—nicknamed Gilly, also nicknamed Little Gilly Gumdrop, though only *he* was allowed to call the seventeen-year-old human that last one—was responsible. She had a huge crush on him, and she had thought "tucking him in" would soothe him.

Unlike the tucking in, he'd done everything he could to discourage the crush. She'd told him she wanted to date a nonsmoker, so he'd immediately taken up the habit. Was even now sucking a disgusting cloud of ash into his mouth and blowing smoke in her too-appealing, perfectly sunkissed face.

She gave a delicate cough.

Tragically, the smoke failed to diminish the loveliness of her features. Big, wide eyes of the purest chocolate. Sharp cheekbones that hinted at the passion she would one day be capable of giving. A pixie nose, slightly uptilted at the end. Lush pink lips. And framing all that beauty was a cascade of midnight hair.

With a sigh, he smashed the cigarette butt into the ashtray beside him. Maybe it was time he took up drinking.

"Liam," she said softly. Her nickname for him. A name he would kill anyone else for using. Maybe because it was hers and hers alone. She sat beside him, her hip pressed against his, warm and soft and completely feminine. "I have a question for you."

"Ask." He could deny her nothing—except a romantic relationship. Not only because she was too young, but because he...well, he liked her. Yeah, shocking. William the Perfect—a much more suitable name for him—friends with a female other than Anya. The world should have ended.

But, in many ways, Gilly truly was his best friend. When he'd returned from hell, unable to care for himself, she had done so. She had fetched his food, endured his dark moods as the pain became too much, and washed his sweat-soaked brow when necessary.

If, when she reached maturity, he was foolish enough to touch her, their easy camaraderie would be ruined. She would be forever disillusioned about the kind of man he was. He didn't want to disillusion her.

She deserved a man who would give her the world. All William would give her was pain.

So, become involved? Hell, no. Not now, not later. He wouldn't allow himself to hurt her. Ever. He was many things—a womanizer, a killer. Callous, sometimes cruel, always selfish and dark in a way no one inside this fortress knew. But this tiny little beauty had been through enough in her short life. Physical abuse, and so much worse. She'd run away from home, had lived on the streets, taking care of herself when loved ones should have ensured her safety.

After Danika and Reyes, the keeper of Pain, had hooked up, Danika had brought her here. William had taken an instant liking to her. She'd needed someone to look out for her, and William had decided to be that someone. For now. That meant destroying those who had destroyed her innocence and later helping her find a man worthy of her love. That meant resisting her.

Lids heavy over those exotic eyes and lashes so thick and curling they seemed to be reaching for her brows, she traced some sort of design on the covers beside him. At last she found the courage to ask her question. "You're cursed by the gods, but I don't know *how* you're cursed. I mean, I tried to read your book. Anya let me borrow it, I hope you don't mind, but the pages were weird."

The subject he hated more than any other. His curse. The only person he'd ever discussed the particulars with was Anya, and then only because they'd been cell neighbors inside Tartarus, and he'd needed something to do while the centuries ticked by. When they'd later escaped, he'd made the mistake of showing her the book that detailed everything he'd told her, as well as his only chance for salvation.

He shouldn't have been surprised when the naughty goddess had stolen that book—and now threatened to rip the pages out every time he pissed her off. Nor should he have been surprised that she'd given Gilly a peek. Anya had taken over the girl's care, too, and knew how the sweet little human felt about him. But damn it, his secrets were his own.

"Liam?"

Resisting was pointless. And gods, he was pathetic. To not even put up a fight? Sickening. "The book is written in code," he explained. A roundabout fuck-you from Zeus, he mused. A "here's your salvation—not." He had yet to find the key to unlocking that code. He knew it was out there, though. It had to be out there. He couldn't believe otherwise. Even though he was afraid to find the key, afraid to know more about his curse.

"Yes, but *how* are you cursed?" she repeated.

He shouldn't tell her. He knew what she was doing. Trying to find a way to save him. Still. She needed to know the truth. Maybe then her crush would at last crash and burn. "All I know is that the woman I fall in love with will unleash—" He pressed his lips together. The woman he fell in love with would unleash every evil being he had ever created. And he had created some monsters. *That*, he wouldn't tell her. "She will kill me," he finished. That, too, was the truth.

Her eyes widened as she lifted her gaze to his face. "I don't understand."

"The curse isn't completely mine. I share it with her." Whoever she was. "Once I fall in love with her, she'll lose her mind. She'll think only of my demise, and she'll make sure it comes to pass."

Another gift courtesy of that too-cocky shit, Zeus. Good news was, the joke was on the now deposed king. William had never fallen in love and never would. There was only room in his heart for one, and *he* was that one.

"I would never hurt you," Gilly said softly. And before he could reply, not that he had any clue as to what to say, she added, "Let's backtrack a little. The book contains a way to save you? And her?"

"Maybe." He gently chucked her under the chin. "Don't even think about it, Gumdrop. The curse is one of blood, which means *someone* has to die. If I'm saved, the one who saves me will be the one to die in my place. That isn't going to be you. Understand?"

She didn't speak, but she didn't nod, either. Nor did her gentle expression change. That scared him. The thought of dying should have freaked her out. The thought of her dying did freak *him* out.

With more force than he'd intended, he said, "Be a good girl, and go get some rest. You've got circles under your eyes, and I don't like them."

Finally. A reaction. Her mouth pressed into a mulish line, and as well as he was coming to know her, he prepared himself for pure, unbending stubbornness. Whoever she ultimately ended up with was going to have his hands full. Poor bastard.

Dead bastard. William might kill him just for fun.

*Don't go there.*

"I'm not a little girl," she gritted out. "So stop treating me like one."

"You *are* a little girl," he replied easily, rolling his eyes for good measure. She was, and that was a fact.

She stuck her tongue out at him, proving his claim. "The boys at my school don't think so."

He would not react to the sight of that tongue. Or to the provocative words. "The boys at your school are dumb."

"Hardly. *They* want to kiss me."

A flicker of rage took residence in his chest. "You better not encourage them, *little girl,* because I will hurt them if they ever try anything with you. You're not ready for that kind of relationship."

"And I suppose you get to decide when I'm ready?"

"Exactly." Smart, his little gumdrop. "In fact, as soon as I think you're old enough, I'll let you know. Until then, keep your lips to yourself or you'll regret it."

"Oh, really? Give me a hint, then." There was steel in her voice rather than amusement. "What age do you consider old enough and just how will I regret disobeying you?"

A wiser man would have kept his fat mouth closed. "Three hundred. Or so," he added, giving himself room to work. "And believe me, you do not want to find out."

"First, I'm human," she snapped. "I'll never be that old."

"I know." And he didn't like that fact, he realized. She had eighty years, give or take a few, but no more. And that was only if she wasn't run over by a car. Or beheaded by a Hunter.

Damn it. If he had to sign on with the Lords for a permanent place in their army just to look after her, he was going to be annoyed. He had shit to do, places to be.

"Second, I'm not afraid of you."

She should be. The things he'd done over the years....The things he would do in the years to come.... "Let's forget the fear for now. By your own admission, you're a puny human. Which is another reason you need to rest." He gave her a "gentle" push off the bed. "Go. Get out of here."

She hit the floor with a *hmph,* then popped to her feet. She peered down at him for a long while. He let her look, silent, knowing what she saw. A black-haired, blue-eyed stunner who had broken more hearts than he could count. He prayed that she, like all the others before her, wouldn't overlook the fact that *his* heart had never been breached. That she wouldn't see him as a challenge, as tamable...as worth any risk.

His phone beeped, disrupting the quiet and signaling a text had come in. She glanced at the phone on the nightstand, then at him.

"Go," he said more firmly.

"Fine." She spun and strode from the room, leaving William with an odd, hollow feeling in his chest. Damn it, he thought again.

Another beep sounded. He pushed Gilly to the back of his mind and lifted the little black device to read the screen.

Screen name "Stridey-Man" asked, Want 2 vacay w/ me?

William snorted as he typed. Romantic getaway for 2? UR not my type, dickwad.

Only a few seconds passed before the second message arrived. Fuck U. I'm everyone's type. So U in or out? 'Cause I'm thinking about hooking up w/ P, wherever he is. U'd just B extra baggage.

Leave the fortress. Leave Gilly and her dark, too knowledgeable eyes. Leave her staggering hope for something he couldn't, wouldn't, give her. Leave her probing questions, her gentle touch. Some1 taking UR place here at fort? he typed. Much as he wanted to escape, he wouldn't leave her helpless.

K & C are gonna come back. Last chance. In or out?

This time he didn't hesitate. In.

Stridey-Man: Knew U couldn't resist me. B ready in 5.

Right on. Make it 10. I want 2 style my hair for U. U know, just how U like it.

Stridey-Man: ASSHOLE.

He snickered, having more fun teasing Strider than he'd had in a long, long time. ?? U up for a lil stop before we play??

Stridey-Man: Where?

Locale deets later. Alls U need 2 know is I plan 2 murder Gilly's fam.

He'd wanted the deed taken care of long before now, but his little jaunt into hell had altered his plans. The demons down there had nearly eaten through his arm, and the stupid limb had only recently healed. Plus, Amun had promised to go with him and tell William about the mom and stepfather's deepest secrets and fears so that William could make the road to dead frightening and painful.

Only, Amun was still whacked out of his mind and William was tired of waiting.

Stridey-Man: Rock on. But now U only have 8 minutes 2 do UR hair.

Trust the cocky Strider to agree to a brutal massacre without asking dumb questions like "why" and "how."

William untucked the covers and stood, making a mental list of everything he'd need for the coming trip. A few blades, serrated and nonserrated. A vial of acid. A bone saw. A spiked paddle. A cat-o'-nine-tails. And a bag of Gummy Bears.

Gods, but this was going to be fun.

# CHAPTER ELEVEN

HAIDEE LUXURIATED IN THE now-familiar warmth enveloping her, branding her all over again, as the hazy dream took shape in her mind. Moonlight surrounded her, illuminating the veranda she stood upon, as well as the pond she studied in the courtyard. Fireflies hovered over the clear, dappled water like fallen stars that had finally found a new perch. A cool breeze ruffled the wild tumble of her hair, and her lavender robe—her *wedding* gown—danced at her ankles.

She could hardly believe this day had arrived.

Solon had actually married her. After a rocky start and courtship, he'd vowed to love and cherish her in front of his friends and family. Even though he was a powerful noble, she was not, and he could have kept her as a slave. But that arrangement was unacceptable, he'd said. As his wife, no one would ever hurt her again. Even after he died.

For that alone, she would have fallen in love with him. Except, she'd already loved him. He was older than she by sixteen years but strongly built nonetheless. He had only ever regarded her with kindness, had never raised a hand to her in anger, even though his first reaction to her had been one of tension, and had never allowed his visitors to abuse her.

He'd begun to cosset her soon after buying her at the slave market, some eleven years before. She'd been a child then, still devastated by the loss of her family, terrified by the new fate that awaited her and confused by the numbing cold that had never left her. A cold that had saved her from being raped, time and time again. Most men couldn't stand to touch her.

And perhaps that was why Solon had never demanded sexual favors in return for his kindness. At least, that's what she had assumed. Until six weeks ago, when he had asked for her hand in marriage.

"Are you nervous, my sweet?" a familiar voice asked from behind her.

She turned, heart accelerating with dizzying speed. Leora, friend and equal until this very day, was now supposed to be her servant. Gray hair frizzed around her aged features, and she wore the same coarse sack Haidee was used to wearing.

If Leora was here, that meant the time had come. That meant her husband had summoned her, was ready for her. Her *husband*. "I love when you call me that," she replied sincerely. "Especially since you did not like me at first." No one had. For that matter, no one ever did.

"No. But that soon changed, did it not?"

Yes. Just like with Solon. "It did. And yes, yes. I'm nervous, but excited, too."

Finally, she would be allowed to show Solon the depths of her gratitude for him.

Leora arched a too-thin brow. "And you know what a man does to his new wife on their wedding night?"

"Yes." At least she thought so.

She had squeezed her eyes tightly closed when the guards at the market had raped the other slaves. The screams, though… Haidee shuddered, momentarily lost in the pain and humiliation she had been helpless to stop, no matter how much she had struggled against her chains, no matter how much she had prayed and cried and hated.

Deep down, she knew bedding Solon wouldn't be

like that. He would be tender, patient. He was kind and sensitive, and he would ease any fears she harbored.

"Then I will not keep you a moment longer," Leora said with a soft smile. "Your man awaits."

The old woman turned, her bones creaking, and ushered dream Haidee inside a torch-lit hallway, toward the gynaeceum. The master's bedchamber. Alabaster columns stretched on each side of them, the arching doorway—their final destination—looming closer...closer still...

Real-life Haidee cried out, reaching for the innocent girl she'd been, trying to grab her, halt her. "No. Don't go in there." She had never remembered what had led to this point of her memories, but she suddenly knew what waited beyond that entrance. "Stop! Please, stop!"

Neither female paid her any heed. Closer...

*Haidee.* A male's hard, determined baritone filled her head. Equally hard bands wrapped around her forearms, white-hot and inexorable, shaking her. *Wake up.*

Haidee fought the voice, just as she fought the dream. "No!" Her arms flailed, her legs kicked. If she could prevent herself from going inside that bedroom, she could save herself thousands of years of guilt and pain. "Don't go in there! *Please!*"

Closer...

As Leora slowed her steps, she glanced over her shoulder and offered Haidee another sweet smile. They had finally reached the door. Leora stepped aside. A trembling, unsuspecting Haidee reached out—

—was somehow floating, suspended—

—was tightening her fingers around the edges of the curtain—

—was being straightened out, placed on her feet—

Before she could enter the room, cold water hit her full-force, soaking her from head to toe and shocking her into reality. Haidee sputtered, blowing droplets out of her mouth. Her eyelids fluttered open.

Out of habit, she immediately took stock of her surroundings. She stood inside a shower stall. Unfamiliar. Spacious, tiled, the faucet speckled with gold filigree. She glanced down at herself. She still wore the new T-shirt, jeans and underclothes Strider had given her before chaining her. Her feet were still bare. Dark arms ripped with muscle were wrapped around her waist, holding her upright.

She stiffened, began to struggle. Panic gave her weakened body strength, her heart pumping blood through her veins at an astonishing rate. Yet, no matter what she did, she couldn't budge those meaty arms.

*Easy. Easy now. Are you okay?*

Amun's voice, steady though concerned, uncompromising though tender. He was the one holding her, she realized. Instantly the fight abandoned her, and she sagged against him, resting her head in the hollow of his neck.

If he was standing, that meant he had recovered. She was so relieved she could have sobbed. She'd spent several days trapped beside his bed, drifting in and out of consciousness. His stupid friend had carted her in and out, in and out. Just when Amun would stop thrashing, about to awaken, Defeat would move her. When the bastard would finally take her back, Amun would be worse than before. Each and every time.

Now he was aware, lucid. For good. Now she was free.

Now they were touching.

*Nightmare?* he asked.

"Yes," she managed to croak past the sudden lump in her throat. "How did we get here?"

*Later.*

She thought she remembered vowing that she wouldn't

allow herself to touch him again. Wouldn't allow him to touch her. Both were dangerous. And maybe she had, maybe she hadn't. Nothing seemed real just then. But when one of his arms moved away from her, she had to cut off a whimper.

To her surprise, he didn't abandon her. He merely reached forward and twisted the faucet before straightening and holding her again. A few seconds later, the temperature of the water warmed considerably.

*Tell me about the nightmare,* he said, gripping the hem of her T-shirt and lifting.

She could have protested. Instead, she raised her arms and allowed him to whisk the material over her head. This moment was so steeped in fantasy, so...necessary, she wanted only to follow it to its end. "I saw the vision you showed me the other day. The one on the veranda."

*I thought that was a good thing.* He unfastened her jeans and pushed them to her ankles, then picked her up and kicked the denim out of the tub, leaving her in her bra and panties.

"I saw what came after." Another croak.

With one hand snaked around her waist, propping her up, he used his other hand to palm a bar of soap and began lathering her skin. *But you were so happy at the beginning.*

So intimate a task, so shattering a topic. Yet, despite who and what he was, she had never felt more comfortable with another being. He didn't try to arouse her as he cleaned her, careful of her cuts and bruises; he merely performed a basic task.

"Yes," she said.

*Tell me,* he repeated. Once her skin was washed free of dirt and grime, he massaged shampoo into her hair. The scent of sandalwood bonded with the rising steam.

She opened her mouth to obey, but the words tangled

on her tongue. If she spoke them, she realized, she would fling herself back to the past, back to that dark, dark day that had forever changed the course of her life—and his. She would lose the tranquility of this moment.

Tranquility she desperately needed.

"No," she finally said. "Not now. Later. Please."

*Our later is filling up.*

"I know."

She expected him to push for answers, but he merely ducked her head under the spray of water and rinsed the suds from her hair. Clearly he understood a woman's needs because he coated the thick strands with conditioner, gave the cream time to do its job, then gently rinsed her hair again.

*There. All clean.*

"Thank you."

He didn't switch off the water or even move from where he stood behind her. He simply continued to hold her, strong fingers tracing circles just below her navel, his chin resting atop her head.

Still he didn't try to arouse her. Not once did he pluck at her pebbled nipples or brush his fingertips over her sex. Yet, with every second that passed, her skin became more sensitized, a primitive need unfurling inside her and overshadowing that thick cloak of fantasy.

Reality was better.

Still. She had to resist. For every reason she'd already noted and the thousand others she hadn't yet considered.

Took every ounce of strength she possessed, but she stopped herself from lifting her arms, curling them back and digging her fingers into his scalp. Stopped herself from angling her face up to his for a kiss. Bottom line, despite everything else, he didn't desire her. He couldn't. Not when she was practically bare, covered only by thin strips of white cotton, and he'd had his hand all over her, yet had never tried to arouse her.

Suddenly that wasn't the comfort it had previously been.

Had he figured out exactly who she was? Was that why he no longer wanted her?

No, he couldn't know. Otherwise, he wouldn't be taking such good care of her. Most likely he'd just decided kissing a Hunter, any Hunter, was wrong.

"Amun, I have to—" she began, stopping when he stiffened. What had she said?

*You know my name?*

Her nerve endings flared with trepidation. "Yes," she whispered.

*So you know who and what I really am.* A statement of fact, not a question. *You know I'm not your Micah.*

No reason to deny the truth. "Yes." Another whisper.

*And yet you of all people let me hold you like this?*

Something about the absolute confusion in his tone alerted her. She replayed his words. "You of all people," he'd said. Oh, God. She'd been wrong, she thought dizzily. He knew. He'd already known she was a Hunter, yes. She'd told him. Now, however, he knew the rest, the worst of the details. He knew about her part in Baden's death.

Why hadn't he killed her already?

The moisture in her mouth dried, and her knees began to tremble. "Defeat—Strider told you who I am. What I've done." She was proud to note that no emotion filled her voice, only arctic steel.

*No. I discovered the truth on my own. You were Hadiee then, but are now Haidee. Whoever you were, whatever you are, you were there when Baden was slain.*

Confirmation. "And yet you of all people hold me like this?" As she snapped the question, understanding dawned. This was the calm before the storm. He'd merely shown her the pleasure she could have had but now would be forever denied.

A bitter laugh escaped her. In a lifetime of regret and pain, he had no idea that denying her would simply be more of the same. That he wouldn't break her. Wouldn't ruin her. No matter what he did, she'd already experienced worse.

Amun spun her around before severing all contact. Their gazes locked, black fire glittering down at her. She gasped as another realization struck. He hadn't been unaffected by touching her. Far from it. Lines of tension branched from his eyes and mouth. His lips were pulled taut over the straight white pearls of his teeth. His breath emerged shallow and fast, his nostrils flaring.

Wait. Did he want her? Or was he simply pissed?

The swelling had gone down in his face, revealing a rough beauty that shocked her further. His skin was like the richest coffee mixed with the slightest dollop of cream. Those gorgeous black eyes were framed by a thick fan of silky lashes, lashes longer even than hers. He had an aquiline nose, regal and proud. His cheekbones were so sharp they could have cut glass. Lips that would have been considered cruel if not for their soft pink color glistening with moisture.

His chest was bare, scabbed in striking patterns of four. Claw marks, she thought with a shiver. His own? Hers? His nipples were small and brown, beaded. Rope after rope of muscle descended the torso of a man who had honed his strength on the battlefield rather than inside a gym.

He wore sweatpants that hung low on his waist, revealing the barest hint of dark, springy curls on his groin. And when she saw that the rounded head of his penis stretched past the material, semen pearling from the slit, she swallowed, her gaze jerking back up to his face.

He was the gentle one, Strider had said. Yet she'd never seen a man look quite so fierce.

*How did you get me mixed up with him?*

"You guys look a lot alike. Weirdly alike."

*Was he immortal?* Pause. *You know I'm immortal, right?*

"Yes, I know, and no, he's not. Believe me, I would have known. He was injured time and time again, but he healed as slowly as any human."

*So our likeness is a mere quirk of fate? Doubtful. I was created by Zeus, fully formed, and I've often wondered if the former king had simply looked down from his perch in the heavens, picked out a face he liked and boom. But that creation happened thousands of years ago, so my face had to come first.*

"And so you think someone else created Micah? Someone who saw you?"

*Yes.*

"Then how is he human?"

*There are gods, humans, demigods, and then creatures in between. He could be any number of things.*

"Well, maybe Zeus saw past, present and *future* faces, and picked from those. Or hey, maybe Micah's your son, and you just don't know it. I'm sure you've picked up a few humans in your time."

*Not possible.*

"Why? Accidents happen, even with immortals."

*I haven't been with anyone in a long time. Like, a century. And if he looks to be my age...*

She couldn't hide her relief. He hadn't been with anyone in over a hundred years. Same with her. "Oh. Well, maybe he's a descendant of yours. Maybe it's just one of those strange, unexplainable things. Or hell, maybe—"

*Okay. Maybe you're right,* he allowed. *Doesn't matter, anyway. We're on opposing teams.*

"Very true."

*So why did you change your name?* he asked, switching gears.

"The simple change of spelling helped me blend in as society changed around me," she said. "Plus, there are more Haidees than Hadiees, and I didn't want to be spotlighted for any demons that happened to be looking for me."

*If you wanted to blend in, you shouldn't have done so much to stand out.* His gaze raked her hair, her tattoos.

She stiffened at his obvious censure. What did she care if he found her appearance lacking? Except for the ache in her chest, she didn't care at all, she told herself.

*How are we connected?* he demanded, switching the subject again. Bye-bye distraction. He'd asked an excellent question. How *were* they connected in mind and body?

"I—I don't know." Her cheeks flamed when she heard the stutter. She had fought and won too many battles to count. This man would not intimidate her.

*Why can't I harm you?*

Had he tried? The thought unsettled her. "Maybe for the same reason I can't harm you."

*And that is?*

*You're the sweetest form of temptation. I know the spicy decadence of your kiss. I've ridden your fingers and want to ride them again.* Not that she'd make such an admission aloud. "I don't know. I've had the opportunity, though," she reminded him. "Several times."

A sigh slipped from him, easing some of his tension. *But you soothed me instead. Protected me.*

She nodded. "As you did for me."

For a long while, only the pattering of the water against the porcelain could be heard. Part of her was glad they knew about each other. That she didn't have to wonder what would happen when he discovered her secrets. The other part of her had never been more frightened.

They knew, but if they pursued each other anyway… there could be no excuses for their actions. For their stupidity. Their friends would blame them, perhaps begin to hate them. And for what? No matter what they did, there could never be a happily ever after for them.

She must have retreated into her mind—a shocking discovery, that, since she never allowed herself to drop her guard—because she never saw him move, but suddenly his hands were clamped onto the flare of her hips. Another gasp escaped her as their gazes tangled anew.

Amun backed her up, pushing her under the waterfall, then walked through the spray himself, not stopping until she was smashed against the tiled wall. And even though they weren't touching anywhere but her waist, the heat of him wrapped around her, sinking past skin into bone. Her nipples hardened, aching for contact.

He looked capable of anything just then. Most especially of driving her to the brink of passion, of madness.

*Stop this before it's too late,* she commanded herself. A single brush of his lower body against hers, and "too late" would happen. She knew it. After their last kiss…

She flattened her palms on his chest, felt the erratic rhythm of his heartbeat. A harried rhythm that matched her own. "I can't be with you this way. Until I've spoken to Micah." Oh, God. Had she really said that? Had she really just pushed the qualification out of her mouth, trying to pave the way for them to be together? Even for a little while?

Seriously. What the hell was wrong with her?

Amun's eyelids narrowed, hiding his irises. That should have lessened the dangerous magnetism of him. It didn't. She doubted anything could.

*Why?* The single word was snapped, demanding an immediate response.

"I have to tell him it's over between us." That was the only honorable thing to do. For all her faults, she truly wasn't a cheater. But God, even talking about this, she was undermining everything she'd already decided, not to mention her resolve to leave Amun alone.

*You would end your relationship with him in favor of me? A demon-possessed warrior you've sworn to murder?* He laughed without humor. *I'm not as foolish as you apparently think I am.*

She was the foolish one. They would never be able to trust each other, and with good reason. That still didn't stop her from saying, "Yes." See? Foolish. She wanted to be with him. Despite everything, even her reasons for pushing him away, part of her needed him and that part clearly would not be denied.

His false laughter died quickly. *Your relationship didn't stop you from kissing me before.* Now his voice was a growl of frustration.

"I didn't know who you were then."

He pondered that for a moment, then nodded. *Fine. I'll give you that. But how do I know this isn't a trick?*

Nope, no trust. Not that she blamed him. "You don't."

*And how do you plan to speak with this Micah?*

"I'll call him." How else?

Water droplets rained down Amun's hard expression. *And during the conversation, I'm positive you won't speak in code and inform him of your location. I'm equally positive he won't try to swoop in and save you. Of course, that means I'm positive he won't then try to capture everyone inside this fortress.*

"No." She shook her head to emphasize her denial. "I would break it off with him. No more, no less."

Intense need flickered over his expression. Need blended

with possessiveness and primal instinct, with hope and helpless indecision.

No one had ever looked at her like that. As if she were a treasure, wanted in the most primitive of ways—as if she were a bundle of dynamite that could detonate at any moment.

So badly she wanted to glide her hands to his back, lock her fingers together and jerk him into the soft line of her body. Then she'd feel his hands settle on her bottom and heft her up, forcing her to wrap her legs around him. She'd grind against the long, thick length of his erection until they were both screaming from the pleasure. Already she was close to begging for it.

Amun's hands fell away from her, dropping heavily to his sides, and he straightened. The water cascaded over him without mercy, shielding his features from her view.

*Never going to happen, Haidee,* he said flatly. *A simple fuck isn't worth the consequences.* With that, he left her alone in the shower.

His crudeness and cruelty shouldn't have surprised her, but they did. They hurt her, too. She'd been willing to try to make something work between them; he hadn't. He never had. His eyes had been cold, distant as he'd reduced her to "a simple fuck." She'd never been more to him, would never be more. There were too many obstacles between them.

She wanted to hate him. God, did she want to hate him.

Instead, Haidee did something she hadn't done in hundreds of years. She sobbed like a baby over the cruel fate she'd once again been dealt.

# CHAPTER TWELVE

AMUN STRIPPED OUT OF HIS WET sweatpants, toweled off, dressed in a T-shirt and jeans, then waited for Haidee to emerge from the bathroom. He didn't have to wait long, yet the time apart seemed infinite. When she entered the bedroom, he saw that her features were annoyingly blank, though her eyes were pink and a bit puffy. Had she… cried? His chest constricted painfully at the thought, and he nearly stalked to her, nearly took her into his arms. To soothe her.

His hands curled into fists. She couldn't have cried. To do so, she would have had to care about him. She didn't care about him. Therefore, he couldn't allow himself to believe a single tear had fallen from her beautiful eyes.

So why did his chest still ache?

He forced his thoughts to clear and his gaze to move away from her face. A fluffy white towel was wrapped under her arms and hit just above her knees. Obviously she had removed her bra. He saw no telltale straps. She'd probably removed her panties, too. They'd been so wet. So wonderfully wet.

The constriction in his chest migrated south. He knew what she looked like under all that cotton. Breasts that would fit in his hands. A soft though concave stomach. Hips that flared perfectly. He'd desperately wanted to grip her there and force her to rub against his erection, over and over again. Even now, she tempted him. Even? Hell, especially now.

*Clothes are on the bed,* he told her, turning away before he forgot the reasons he'd left her alone in the shower. Even in his mind, his voice was rough. And yeah, it still shocked him every time he "spoke" to her without having to sign the words.

The connection between them was the very reason he'd opted to tell her the truth about himself, about what he knew concerning her past. He'd decided to show most of his cards before she glimpsed them on her own, hoping she'd then reveal her own cards.

He hated that his demon had gone silent the moment he'd touched her and hadn't spoken up again. Secrets was always either quiet or agitated around her, and he never knew which he'd get. What bothered him most was that the demon probably could have discovered everything about her. Except, though Amun could cast his voice into her head, he couldn't read her the same way he read everyone else. He would've liked to chastise Secrets for that, but didn't. He chastised himself. What was the use of having a demon if a man couldn't use the damn thing's abilities?

Wasn't like he could use the other demons, either. They'd experienced the opposite reaction when he touched her, shrieking and scrambling for a new hiding place.

Behind him echoed a light patter of footsteps, then the rustle of clothing. He wanted to watch Haidee dress. He was desperate to see those curves again. All of her curves this time. Through the white cotton of her bra, every bit of fabric drenched, he'd seen those firm breasts crested with rosy nipples perfect for sucking. And those matching panties...

His spine went rigid as another hot blistering wave of need savaged him. Between her gorgeous legs, at the apex of her thighs, she'd had a little tuft of hair slightly darker than the flaxen mass above. He'd almost dropped to his knees, almost dove in and feasted, shoving those unwanted panties out of the way and tasting the essence of her femininity. Gods, he remembered the sweetness of her. Knew the heaven that awaited him.

He needed to think about something else before he cut the tether of his control and fell on her and took her. He couldn't take her. As he'd promised her, he would not allow himself to touch her again.

He blanked his mind. There was one thing guaranteed to piss him off and keep his hands to himself. Her tattoos. Just the thought had him biting his tongue until he tasted blood.

In the shower, he'd gotten a peek at the travesty that was her back, and each marking had turned portions of his desire into boiling rage. If any part of him had ever doubted who she was, the tattoos there convinced him otherwise.

She kept score, Baden's death proudly etched into her flesh. And the four Hunters the Lords had supposedly killed? He didn't know, but he would. How he would acquire the information when her secrets were her own, he didn't know, either. But again, he would.

Perhaps he'd seduce the information out of her.

*Seduce.* Instantly, his mind and body returned to lusting after her. Seducing would involved touching.

Perhaps his "no touching" vow had been premature.

Really, why handicap himself? He should have her. Often. As many times as the urge struck him. Until he obtained the answers he craved. Until he worked her from his system. Until he realized that she hadn't called him *baby* while he'd held and cleaned her because the endearment was clearly reserved for her precious Micah.

Red suddenly dotted Amun's vision, just as it had done in the shower when she'd spoken the bastard's name, and he drew in a deep breath. Hold…hold. Slowly he pushed the oxygen through his nostrils.

Micah could very well be a descendant of his, as Haidee had said. The idea intrigued him. He'd never thought to have a blood-related family. However, the idea of that blood-related family being his enemy, well, *that* he didn't like. Wasn't like he and Micah could sit down and have a heart-to-heart, either. Besides the good versus evil thing, there was Haidee.

They both wanted her.

Amun should have taken her in the shower, despite her fragile protests, and pounded the worst of his emotions straight into her. And those protests of hers *had* been fragile. So fragile he could have bent his head and blown on the hammering pulse at the base of her neck and her reasons for denying him would have snapped beyond repair.

There were no doubts in his mind that she'd hungered for him, too. Her pupils had been blown, her lips parted as she'd struggled for air. She probably hadn't realized that her nails had sunk into his pecs the moment she'd flattened her trembling palms on him, fingers curling, some part of her desperate to be connected to him, eradicating all hint of distance.

The action, small though it was, had been a claiming, and he'd reacted violently. Not that he'd shown her. That boiling rage had been his only link to sanity.

Over the years he had pampered the few women he'd been with, and given them what time he could, as well as attention and fidelity. Even when they hadn't given him the same—and had then tried to hide their actions from him. As if they could. But he liked seeing a female light up because of his special treatment. He liked knowing he was the cause of their happiness.

He knew his friends considered him calm, without a temper. Normally he was. But when he looked at this woman, this supposed enemy, this unexpected savior, something hard and primal seethed inside him, knocking at the door of his restraint. He felt like a godsdamn cave-man, wanting to carry off his woman and hide her from the rest of the world. Wanting to put his body between hers and anyone who dared threaten her. Wanting to tie her to his bed, keep her there forever, keep her ready for him.

Wanting to soothe her even as he ravaged her.

The desires were dark and sultry, insidious as they snuck past his defenses and wrapped around his every cell, changing the very fabric of his being. He was Amun no longer, but Haidee's man.

That title was not something he could tolerate. Not for long, at least.

Still. He was on the right path, he decided. If he had her, he would tire of her. How could he not, when she was who she was? And when he tired of her, when the new-ness of her touch and taste and scent wore off and he no longer needed her to beat the demons back to maintain his good sense, he could do his duty and slay her. But until then...

He would just have to continue protecting her.

The rustle of clothes died, and he pivoted on his heel, facing her. A smart man would never have given an enemy his back in the first place. But then, a smart Lord would never have allowed a Hunter to live long enough to dress.

Haidee stood by the side of the bed, arms hanging at her sides, her hands empty. His gaze raked her, and he told himself the perusal was necessary, that he needed to check for hidden weapons. The pink T-shirt and jeans she had donned belonged to Gwen, another petite female, but still they bagged on little Haidee. Despite her feminine curves, she was too thin.

Irritation joined his other emotions. Over the past how-ever long Strider had been in charge of her care, the war-rior had most likely given her enough food to survive. No more, no less. She'd probably lost pounds she hadn't been able to spare. That would change now that Amun was in charge. Causing needless suffering wasn't his style.

She had toweled off her hair as best she could, but still the blond-and-pink locks dripped onto her shirt, wetting the material covering the delicate frame of her shoulders.

"What now?" she asked in her raspy voice.

She hadn't shifted under his scrutiny, he realized. She had stood still, allowing him to look his fill. Perhaps she'd studied him, too, because tiny flickers of the mating heat had returned to those distracting eyes.

He liked that she liked the look of him. Usually, with Paris and Strider and, hell, Sabin around him, women found the roughness of his features too…well, rough.

*Sit down*, he told her. *Now we talk.*

"More talking?" She didn't sound enthused.

*Yes, more talking.* He would not allow her to irritate him into forgetting what needed to be said, he vowed. *Sit.*

With only the barest hint of hesitation, she obeyed. She perched at the edge of the bed, folding her hands in her lap.

*Thank you.* Now, it was time to show her the rest of his cards. Her reaction would dictate their next course of action. Amun spread his legs, braced his knees and prepared to defend himself from attack.

"What are we going to talk about?"

*Me. You guessed my identity, but I doubt you know exactly what that means. So here it is, flat out. I'm possessed by the demon of Secrets.* He waited for a reaction; he didn't get one. In the shower, he'd merely played with the details, never actually admitting he was possessed.

"And?" she demanded.

No, he would not allow her to irritate him. *And you know about immortals, but do you know anything about the heavens and hell?*

"I know they exist."

That was a start. *Recently I ventured into hell to rescue a friend.*

She gulped. "You rescued another demon?"

*In a way.* Legion had been demon, but had bargained with Lucifer for a human body. A human body she still possessed. *She wasn't—isn't—evil. Well, not totally—and she was being tortured.*

"She?"

Did he detect a note of jealousy or was that wishful thinking on his part? *Yes. During the few days I spent down there, I was...overcome by demon thoughts and urges.*

When he offered no more, she nodded.

*Those thoughts and urges are a part of me now, driving me...*

"Insane?"

Now he was the one to nod, though his was stiff. *Only when I'm with you do those things become manageable.*

Wariness fell over her lovely features like a curtain, but she didn't attack. "Why me?"

*I have no idea.*

"Guess."

He released a sigh. *Perhaps for the same reason I can project my voice into your head.*

"That tells me nothing," she said, pursing her lips.

How adorable she was, just then. A pouty princess. The thought made him frown. *Whether we like it or not, there is something between us. Maybe, because of that, the demons know what I know, and they're afraid of you. Afraid of Hunters.*

"Maybe. So...you hate these thoughts and urges?" Her question was soft, almost hopeful.

Why hopeful? Because she wanted to believe the best of him? *Yes. Beyond anything.*

She peered down at her lap, where her fingers were linked and now twisting together. He hadn't expected such calm. Not from her, a demon-hater, when he'd just admitted to being poisoned by all kinds of evil.

Was she playing him? Lulling him into a false sense of relaxation? If so, what was her ultimate goal?

He should know; his demon should know. More than ever he hated that he couldn't read her. Hated that the two times he'd peeked inside her mind, he'd seen her smiling. Heard her laughing.

Hated, because the images were branded inside him, a part of him, haunting him. Hated that even so, he craved another glimpse.

"Why did you tell me this?" she asked.

*Because of my affliction and your affiliation, we can't stay here. I'm a danger to my friends,* he told her, expecting her to argue. If she remained in one location, her associates had a better chance of finding her. *And you, well, you're a danger to them, too. As much a danger as they are to you.*

He didn't want either group to find her. Plus, his twenty-four hours were almost up, and every noise outside the door had him stiffening. Sabin was liable to burst into the room with a flamethrower at any moment.

"Yes, we need to leave," she replied, thick lashes finally lifting. "So where do you propose we go?"

Such pragmatism was admirable. Combine that with the *we* and the heat of her gaze, and she presented a powerful aphrodisiac. *You wish to stay with me?*

"Of course."

There was no "of course" about it. *Why* did she want to stay with him? His suspicious soul floundered for an answer, and found only one: she *was* playing him. Perhaps she even meant to lead him to her fellow Hunters, just as she'd done to Baden.

Amun's hands curled into fists. Fists so tight and hard his already damaged knuckles cracked from the strain.

"Amun?" she prompted.

His name on her lips…another aphrodisiac. *We will go to the only place I can purge the thoughts and urges.*

Her eyes widened. "You can purge them?" Once again she sounded hopeful, as if she truly cared.

Though the prospect rocked him to the core, he revealed only mild surprise. *While you slept, I spoke with someone in the know.* And the conversation had pissed him off royally.

"You must return to hell," the angel Zacharel had said, unconcerned, when Amun sought him out.

*What?* Amun had mentally shouted. When he remembered to sign, his motions had been jerky. *My little jaunt into hell is the reason I'm like this. So returning isn't really a solution, is it?*

"You took the demons out, now you will take them back in."

*No.*

A shrug. "Then you will forever be chained to the woman's side. Not that forever will be long. Not for you. Without her, the spirits overcome you, and the next time you are overcome, you will die by my hand."

*If getting rid of the demons is as easy as going to hell, why didn't you take me back already?*

"I did not say it would be easy. Nor did I say returning *with me* would be helpful. You must take the girl."

*No,* he repeated.

"Your choice, of course. I have no qualms about removing your head."

It was impossible to argue with so logical and uncaring a being. *How do I get them out of my body once I "take them back in?"*

Zacharel had walked away without answering, without

offering even the slightest hint. Why? What was Amun supposed to do when he got there? How long was he supposed to stay? Exactly where in the endless pit did he need to go?

*He told me the only way to free myself was to return to hell,* Amun said to Haidee now.

"Return to…hell? As in the fiery pit of the damned?" The last was uttered in a horrified whisper.

*Yes. And you're going with me.* He waited for her to protest, to fight him. She didn't, not yet, and he relaxed. Somewhat. He couldn't subdue her, defend her *and* search for a way to liberate himself. *You won't burn,* he assured her. *I won't allow the flames to reach you.*

"If we go," she said with a tremor, "will there be anyone with us?"

*If,* she'd said, and he relaxed a bit more. *No. We'll go alone.* He desperately needed the muscle and support— because gods knew, he'd barely survived last time, and he'd had two trained warriors with him—but he wouldn't place his friends in danger. Not from the demons, and not from Haidee. Besides, that would defeat the purpose of whisking Haidee out of their midst. *Why? Do you wish to take someone with us?*

Her lips pressed together in that mutinous line, and he suspected he'd somehow hurt her feelings. No, surely not. She would have to care about him, he reminded himself, and she didn't.

"Will you—will you allow me to have a weapon?" The word *allow* choked from her, and he doubted she'd ever spoken it before.

*Yes, but if you attempt to use it on me, I will strike back in kind.* Perhaps a lie, perhaps not. He valiantly hoped she didn't try to test the claim.

Silence stretched between them, an oppressive cloud he couldn't shoo away. He gave her the time she needed, though. He was asking a lot from her and offering very little in exchange. Of course, he would have to force her if she refused him—they truly had no other options—but until she did, he would let her think the decision was hers.

"All right," she finally said on a sigh. "I'll do it. I'll go with you."

No fight at all.

Once again he was thrown, but this time he couldn't hide the intensity of his shock or the earth-shattering cascade of relief. Then his suspicions flared. What did she hope to gain, placing herself in danger to help him regain his senses? Or did she plan to go simply to gather intel? Yes, he thought with a nod. That was far more likely. She was a Hunter, after all, and finding ways to destroy demons was her business.

Hunter. The blasphemy echoed through his mind, and he cringed. *Stop reminding me.*

"Stop reminding you of what?" she sputtered, obviously confused by his sudden bout of disgust.

*Nothing,* he muttered. He nearly apologized but bit the words back. He would not apologize to this woman. Ever. He had *some* pride, at least. *We'll waste no more time.*

Amun strode to the door and knocked. Behind him, he heard Haidee gasp, her clothes rustling again as if she had pushed to her feet. A few seconds later, the lock clicked from the other side, and the wood squeaked open, revealing the angel Zacharel. Black hair in perfect order, emerald eyes devoid of all emotion. White-and-gold wings arched over his shoulders and swooped down his robed sides.

"Yes," the warrior said. The greeting should have been inflected with a question, but surfaced as a mere statement.

*We are taking you up on your offer of transport,* Amun signed.

Zacharel offered no hint of his thoughts. "I'll gather the necessary supplies. Be ready to leave in five minutes." With that, the door shut, locked.

Amun rested his forehead on the cool wood, reminded for a moment of Haidee's skin. Hell. He was returning to hell when he'd sworn never to go back. In a deep, dark corner of his mind, he thought he heard Secrets whimper.

Thousands of years ago, Secrets had fought to escape hell—and won. And yet, Amun kept taking him back. At least the other demons remained calm, neither crying nor cheering in regard to his plans. But then, they were more afraid of Haidee than anything else.

"Why can't you speak?" she asked, slicing through the tension he hadn't realized had sprouted anew.

*My demon,* he replied, offering no more. He straightened and turned to her. Mistake. She *had* stood, and as always, he was struck by the delicacy of her features, the passion that lurked under her glowing skin. More than that, his mouth watered for a go at those breasts, that stomach, those legs.

He shouldn't have dressed her in the T-shirt and jeans. He should have dressed her in a shapeless sack.

"Because you carry the demon of Secrets, you can't speak?"

*Yes.* Had he ever thought to find himself in this position? Sharing his own inner mysteries with a Hunter?

"I don't understand. Why does your demon prevent you from speaking?"

She wasn't curious about him, he knew, but was merely fishing for information to perhaps share with her people. Still. He answered. *I open my mouth, and everything the demon has discovered, every dark deed of those around us, every bit of information that could ruin families and friendships, slips out.*

"So you *can* speak?"

What did that matter? *Yes.*

"But you choose not to?"

*Yes, damn it. Why do you want to know?*

Amun's uncustomary outburst didn't faze her. "It's just…it's a good thing you're doing. Very sweet."

So unexpected was the praise, he could only blink at her.

"No one else can hear your voice? Inside their head, I mean."

*No. Just you.* Bitterness had crept into his tone, and he could do nothing to mask it. Not that he wanted to. Let her hear. Let her know.

Twin pink circles stained her cheeks, and she cleared her throat. She eased back onto the mattress, prim once again. "So how did you guys hook up with angels?"

A change of subject. Wise of her, yes, but foolish of him to offer more truth. *A friend of ours married their leader.* More like Bianka had claimed Lysander as her property, but Amun wasn't sure Haidee would understand that kind of sentiment.

"An angel and a demon? Married?"

*Pretty much.* As stone-cold as Lysander was, the term "angel" seemed just about as appropriate as "fairy godmother." The term "demon" fit Bianka perfectly, though. Her soul was darker than Amun's, but in the best possible way. The Harpies were so open, so honest about their mischievous nature, they were a delight to be around. At least for Amun. For a while, he'd even considered pursuing Bianka's twin sister, Kaia. War had gotten in the way. *Speaking of angels, you should know that your precious Galen isn't one. He—*

"Okay, let's agree right now not to talk about your friends or mine," Haidee interjected angrily. "It'll only make us angry with each other. We should focus on the mission."

So she considered Galen a *friend* of hers? Of course she did, he thought next, and wanted to punch something. The leader of the Hunters wanted every Lord of the Underworld—excluding himself—dead and buried. Because of Baden, Haidee had to be a prize among prizes for the keeper of Hope. Or was it possible Galen didn't know who she was?

Amun's teeth gnashed together—he was doing that a lot lately—grating the top layer into a fine powder, but he nodded. *Very well. There will be no talk of our* friends.

"I just, I don't want us to fight," she said. "And just so you know, Galen isn't a personal friend."

"Time is up," Zacharel's hard voice proclaimed before Amun could reply.

At the vocal intrusion, he whipped around, at the same time moving in front of Haidee to act as her shield. The door was still closed. He frowned until the angel simply stepped through the wood, a backpack dangling from his hand.

He'd possessed the ability all along, yet had only now opted to reveal it. Why?

"I will take you to the place your journey must begin," Zacharel said. As with all angels, there was an undeniable layer of truth in his tone, and Amun couldn't doubt a single thing he uttered. "But know that Lucifer is angry that he was thwarted in his quest to destroy you and yours through Legion, and will be out for eternal blood. Be wary, trust nothing and no one."

*I never do.*

"Except, perhaps, each other," the angel added.

Amun glanced over his shoulder, and he and Haidee shared a look.

Zacharel nodded in approval. "I can promise you that

your last journey through the underworld was nothing compared to what you will soon face. In reparation for his role in Legion's freedom, Cronus has returned it to its former glory."

*Why would he—?*

The angel held up his hand, halting Amun's tirade. "It was either that, or return Legion."

*He made the right choice, then.*

"Let's see if you still agree when you get there. Monsters you've only heard whispered about, you will soon encounter."

Haidee stood, her cool hands flattening on Amun's lower back. He had to bite his tongue to stop his moan of pleasure. Finally, contact. He felt as if he'd been waiting forever to feel her, any part of her, again. That she now offered comfort…comforted him.

Gods, he really was pathetic.

*You won't allow any of my friends to follow us?* he signed.

"Correct. I will ensure you and the girl remain undisturbed by them."

Amun took no offense. If anyone could keep the brutes here from getting their way, it was this hard-as-steel creature. *Thank you.*

"Now. Something else you should know." A breeze ruffled the golden down streaked through the angel's wings like a flowing, molten river. "With the changes, there are now six realms you must pass through before you even reach the gate—and the gate is another obstacle altogether."

Haidee stepped to Amun's side, but didn't break contact. "How will we return here when we're done?"

Zacharel's green gaze briefly shifted to her. "Should you save Amun, you will have nothing to worry about. Should you not, you will never leave."

The ominous warning rang through his mind. Then Amun shrugged. They would save him; it was that simple. *We'll find a way,* he told Haidee.

Her hands trembled against him, but she said no more.

*What about weapons?* he signed. *Food?*

"Everything you need is in here." The angel tossed the pack, and Amun caught the too-thin, too-light duffel with ease. "Good luck to you, warrior."

The moment his fingers wrapped around the straps, his surroundings completely fell away. From light to murky dark, the smooth white walls were replaced by jagged stone stained with crimson splatter. Bones littered the equally rocky ground, and the temperature instantly flared hundreds of degrees—or so it seemed.

A cavern, he realized, deep in the earth. And there was no sign of Zacharel—no dainty hands on his back. Fighting a rush of panic, Amun swung around. He relaxed, but only for a second. Haidee was a few feet away, hunched over and vomiting. Beside her rested a toothbrush, toothpaste and bottle of mouthwash.

Amun closed the distance between them before he realized what he was doing. With one hand, he smoothed her hair out of the way. With the other, he stroked her back, trying to comfort her as she'd comforted him. Flashing from one location to another in a mere blink of time affected some but not others. She, apparently, fell into the "some" category. The angel must have known she would.

As strong as she usually was, the weakness probably appalled her.

*The sickness will soon pass,* he told her. Even as he soothed her, he thought perhaps she had infected him with a toxic mix of hunger, stupidity and unwanted tenderness—and *he* would never find a cure.

She spit, wiped her mouth with the back of her trembling hand. "Thank you. For not kicking me while I'm down."

*I'm not a monster, Haidee.* Yet.

"I know," she said weakly. "Otherwise, I wouldn't be here."

She, apparently, suffered from the same toxic mix.

That did not bode well for their mission.

# CHAPTER THIRTEEN

"BEFORE WE GET STARTED, let's see what we've got to work with," Haidee told Amun after she disinfected her mouth. Twice. She ducked her head as she walked away from him so that she wouldn't have to see his expression.

He'd had his hands on her the entire time. Did he regret it? She'd vomited in front of him. Did he find that amusing? She had responded to him, goose bumps breaking out over her skin. Did he feel smug?

He offered no reply, and she experienced a wave of hurt. A wave she ignored because it was stupid. He wasn't her boyfriend, wasn't a tame pet dog, and was merely using her, the enemy, to stay calm.

Still. Would a "that's smart" or "are you okay?" have been amiss? After all, she had agreed to venture into hell with him. Was actively trying to reach the fiery pit *for* him.

And because of that, she was alone with him, she thought, suddenly dazed by the way things had worked out. She was completely, utterly alone with the demon-possessed immortal who set her body on fire. The demon-possessed immortal who would probably try to kill her after they found a way to free him from the evil that plagued him. The demon-possessed immortal she should despise, *did* despise, but couldn't convince herself to hurt, even in the smallest way.

The demon-possessed immortal she still craved.

Frowning, she crouched in front of the backpack the

angel had given them. Her hand shook with the force of her nervousness as she unzipped and parted the folds. What she saw, or rather, what she didn't see, had her sputtering.

"It's empty!"

Pounding footsteps resounded, then Amun was crouched beside her, grabbing the pack and searching inside. She heard his growl whisper through her mind, low and rumbling.

He scrubbed a hand down his face, the rough action leaving his forehead red and scraped. *The angel wanted us to fail, then. He...lied. I can't believe he lied.*

"Well," she replied, chin lifting, jutting stubbornly. "We won't fail." They'd survived too much already.

*No. We won't.*

Their gazes locked together in a suspended moment of agreement and awareness. At least, she thought awareness was the other surprise battering between them. It was for her. She saw the strength in every line and curve of his face, the determination glittering in his eyes, the need parting those soft lips. Only he never reached out, never touched her. In the shower, he'd promised her he wouldn't, and he was obviously—tragically—a man of his word.

Silent now, Amun pushed to his feet and turned away from her, shattering the tranquility of the moment.

Haidee straightened, and her trembling increased. He'd known who she was before their shower, yet still he'd treated her with care. He'd held her, caressed her, he'd even gotten hard simply being near her. He'd peered at her lips with utter longing, as if he couldn't exist another moment without lapping at her tongue.

What had changed since then?

The fact that she'd mentioned breaking up with Micah? Well, a man who truly desired her would have been over-joyed by her suggestion. Yet Amun had stomped away from her and hadn't lowered his guard since.

Men! She would never understand them.

*Come,* he said, starting forward without looking back.
*I want to leave this area. We've been here too long for my
peace of mind.*

They were in hell, or near enough. She doubted she'd
know peace ever again.

"I'm right behind you." As she followed him through
the yawning opening of the cavern, she anchored the
backpack's straps on her shoulders. No reason to toss it,
and a thousand reasons to keep it. They could store rocks
inside, even bones, and use each as weapons. If they lucked
out and found berries or nuts, they could store the food
for later. Still. That damn angel! He must be a demon in
disguise, tricking them the way he had. And if she ever
encountered the bastard again, she would probably knife
him.

In fact, for what seemed an eternity, she distracted herself by considering all the ways she would torture him. A
knee to the groin, an elbow to the cheek. A hard kick to
the skull. When that began to bore her, she switched her
mental target to Amun. But soon that, too, lost appeal as
she and Amun trekked through the underground tunnel,
the scenery unchanging. Only the growing soreness in
her muscles and the constant ache in her booted feet indi-
cated the passage of time. The leather of those boots was
well-worn but not fitted to her arches, and blisters quickly
formed on her tendons.

She endured without complaint for a little while longer,
but really, she hated the suffocating silence between them,
every second laced with tension. If they were going to work
together, which they needed to do if they hoped to succeed
in freeing Amun, she had to break through whatever was
angering him.

So she asked the first question that popped into her
head. "Do you have a girlfriend?" The moment the words

were spoken, fury raced through her. The thought of this man belonging to someone else…kissing someone else… his intense arousal focused on someone else…

*No,* he said, and she relaxed.

Haidee nearly reached out and petted him as a reward. She kept her arms at her sides, though, as they rounded a narrow corner, the walls thinning yet again, practically scraping at her. He might rebuke her, and she'd rather endure the silence than that.

*Did you ever kiss Strider?* The question lashed from him, surprising her, and if his tone had been tangible, she suspected she would have been cut to the bone. *Or…do more?*

"No! Never." She might have abandoned her vengeance quest with Amun, but the same courtesy did not extend to his friends. Them, she still wanted to kill. Amun, she just wanted to kiss again. Soon. Maybe. Definitely. Except—

Damn it! She'd left the toothbrush and toothpaste back in the cave. Next time she and Amun did a little hooking up, she wanted to taste—argh. If he had his way, they were never going to hook up again. She glared at his back, considered raking him with her nails. To him, she wasn't worth the risk. Any risk.

Part of her admired that. His friends were important to him. Momentary pleasure was not.

Some of the tension left him. Was that what had been bothering him? she wondered. The thought of her with Strider? She stopped glaring at his back, and again considered petting him. If he didn't like the idea of her lip-locking his friend, she had to mean a little something to him. Right?

The other part of her *really* admired *that.* He could overlook his (justified) prejudice in favor of desire for her and only her.

*All right, then,* he said, pacified.

"So what gave you that stupid idea that I'd made out with the keeper of Defeat?" She'd meant to ask gently and certainly hadn't meant to use the word *stupid,* but then she'd remembered Amun's snotty attitude the past few hours and her irritation had taken over, speaking for her.

*You spent some time with him. Alone. You were desperate to be free of him.*

Irritation morphed into anger. "I'm a lot of things, Amun, but I would never use my body to get what I wanted. Even freedom."

There was a beat more of silence, then, *You did with Baden.*

Oh. Yeah. He was right, and there was nothing she could say to defend herself.

Back then, she'd been so filled with hate and fury that she would have done anything, *anything*, to destroy one of the Lords. And she had. She had stripped in front of Baden, as if she'd wanted to bed him in thanks for his escort home. And as he'd looked her over, distracted, she had signaled for the waiting Hunters.

"I learn from my mistakes," she said softly. Helping to kill the warrior hadn't been the mistake, but she did regret the way she'd gone about it. She'd lied to Strider about feeling nothing. She even regretted the pain her actions had caused the man in front of her, which was one of the reasons she had willingly placed herself in danger.

A confusing realization. That meant she more than wanted him; that meant she cared for him. Why did she care for him? She didn't know him, not really. She was attracted to him, yes. She'd already admitted that, over and over again. She was somehow linked to him, yes. She couldn't stop thinking about his mouth on hers, then between her legs, yes, that too. Oops. That was part of her attraction to him. Anyway. None of that required caring.

Yet she had done everything in her power to stay with him. Be with him. Spend time with him. Aid him.

She sighed.

*What?*

He hadn't turned around to ask, and her gaze ate up the strong expanse of his back. Without her emotions in the way, she was able to truly *see* him. Such dark skin, so many layers of muscle. He had no scars now, and his only tattoo was the butterfly. Which she couldn't see at the moment; it must have returned to his leg. She marveled at the thought of a living tattoo, slipping and sliding from one corner of his body to the other, then shook her head and told herself to concentrate.

He was talking to her now. She didn't want to lose this opportunity.

"I dreamed about you before I met you," she confessed. "But I didn't know who—" or what, she mentally added "—you were. That's why I began dating Micah. I thought…"

Amun's shoulder blades pressed together in a jerky motion as he straightened. *You thought* he *was* me?

"Yes. And before you start insulting my intelligence, remember that you guys look a lot alike."

*So how do you now know you dreamed of me rather than him?*

Because of the way Amun made her feel. Connected, aware. Alive. Burning from the inside out when she'd only ever known cold. To confess the truth was to make herself vulnerable—more than she already was. To confess was to give him power over her—more than he already had.

"I just do," was all she said. "If I hadn't calmed you, would you have killed me when you found out who I was?" She tried to maintain an impassive tone, but the tremble in the words gave her away.

There was a terrible pause that crystallized the oxygen in her lungs. Then, *Yes*.

At least he was honest, but wow, that hurt. *You would have killed him if you hadn't dreamed of him,* she reminded herself. True. That failed to ease her hurt, though. He'd kissed her, damn it. Intimately. A little loyalty would have been nice.

*Illogical.*

Distracted as she was, she tripped over a stone and stumbled forward. She had to anchor her hands on Amun's waist to steady herself. Instant, amazing heat. As always. He didn't pause, but he did stiffen.

*Stay alert, Haidee.* He spat her name like it was a curse.

Maybe it was. "I'm trying. *Amun*. We've been walking for a long time and don't seem to be getting anywhere. I'm tired, hungry, and oh, yeah, I'm also saving your ass. Propping me up when I fall *without complaining* is the least you can do to repay me." Even as she scolded him, she vowed to do a better job. She straightened, severing contact—mourning the loss, again as always—and studied her newest surroundings.

They had maneuvered into a type of hallway, the bloodsplattered walls tall but not broad. The floor tilted, sending them deeper underground with every step. Dust layered the warm air, and in the distance she thought she heard a steady *drip, drip*.

*You're right,* he said. *I'm...sorry.*

The apology was gritted, like the words tasted foul. Didn't matter. She'd take it. Anything was better than nothing. Just ask her stomach.

"Do you know where you're going?" she asked, her voice echoing around them.

*No.* A clipped tone, and, if she wasn't mistaken, a roundabout command for silence. Then he surprised her by adding, *All I know is that hell is down, so that's the direction we're heading.*

A chimp could have told her that, but she kept her mouth closed as they stepped through another opening. Another cavern. The walls stretched, allowing easier, freer motions. Finally, they were getting somewhere. And shockingly, there was thick, dewy foliage sprouting from the rocks. Nice, she thought, until something hissed at her. She yelped, twisting to discover the source.

A pair of narrowed red eyes glowed from the round head of a snake, forked tongue dancing over sharp, dripping fangs. She opened her mouth to scream, but a tide of dizziness slammed through her and only a moan escaped.

Somehow she remained on her feet. "N-nice snakey snake," she whispered, palms rising to proclaim her innocence.

The creature launched at her neck. *Not* nice. Her reflexes were too slow to save her.

Amun's thick, corded arm whipped out, fingers wrapping just below that open, waiting mouth, wrist twisting, snapping head from scaled body. When he opened his fist, the reptile floated lifelessly to the ground.

"Th-thank you," she rasped. The dizziness hadn't left her, and now her heart felt distorted in her chest, a smashed organ hammering against her spine rather than her ribs.

*Welcome. Now* I've *saved* your *ass.* His gaze never shifted to her, nor did he massage her neck in comfort, as she suddenly craved.

"We're not even close to even, big boy."

*I didn't say we were. Let's keep moving. I don't like this area.*

They started forward again, and this time, Haidee kept one hand wrapped around the waist of his pants, afraid to let go. He didn't chastise her, and she was grateful. She hated snakes. Hated, hated, *hated.* Maybe because a

Hydrophis Belcheri had killed her once, its poison spurting acid straight into her veins, making her writhe and beg for mercy she had never found. Not even in death.

"Hurry," she said. "I don't like this area, either."

*Then you're really not going to like what my demon just told me.*

"Oh, God. What?"

*We've just entered the Realm of Snakes,* Amun said grimly.

Sweet heaven above. "Please tell me the Realm of Snakes refers to the sweet little garden variety, and that we'll only encounter one or two of them."

*The Realm of Snakes refers to the sweet little garden variety, and we'll only encounter one or two of them.*

Though she knew he was lying, his dry baritone caused her lips to twitch and some of her fear to fade. "Good, that's good. So what else did Secrets tell you?" Fingers crossed she didn't have a panic attack after his next words.

*That we shouldn't look directly into their eyes because they can hypnotize us into believing we actually want them to bite us.*

The fear returned full-force, but at least the dizziness now made sense. Hypnosis. Shit. Control was one of her most prized possessions. Too well did she know the horror of being without a choice. For days, weeks, whatever, she'd been Strider's prisoner, allowed to do only what he wanted her to do. Before that, every time she'd died, losing pieces of her memories when she finally returned to life, she had known only consuming hate and a driving need to destroy. And long before *that,* she'd been a puppet of the evil one, then the Bad Man, then the Greeks who had enslaved her.

"I'm not sure I can do this," she whispered.

*Just pretend the snakes are demon-possessed warriors. I'm sure you'll do fine.*

Ouch. He'd struck more sharply than the snake. Tears momentarily burned her eyes, but she blinked them back. No weakness. Especially when she deserved such a stinging remark. Once, she might have even been proud to hear it. Once, but not today.

"And why don't you pretend they're innocent humans?" she said softly. He, too, deserved to be cut down, and she couldn't let herself forget.

Another bout of silence thickened the air between them. Until he sighed and admitted, *I shouldn't have said that. I'm sorry. Again.*

The second apology, offered far more poignantly than the first, was so unexpected she was shocked—and softened. "I'm sorry, too. And I understand why you did," she admitted. "I took something from you. Something you loved."

*Yes. And we took something from you?*

"Yes."

He waited for her to elaborate, but she never did. She'd already told him she wouldn't discuss the past with him, and she'd meant it. There was nothing he could say to ease the hurt, and a million things he could say to increase it.

*I won't let anything happen to you while we're here, Haidee. You have my word.*

Again he shocked her. Silly thing was, she believed him, and not just because he needed her. He may not like her, but he'd taken responsibility for her welfare. No matter the circumstances, his responsibilities were clearly important to him.

Something else to like about him.

The deeper they walked, the more lush the vines became, until there was no gap between leaf and limb, tree and cave wall. There was only mile after mile of what seemed to be a tranquil forest.

How many snakes lurked nearby? Waiting? Hungry?

Oh, God. *Bile, rising again…*

Soon steam was wafting from the leafy greens, limiting their range of vision. She inhaled deeply, scented sulfur and something else, something sweet. The conflicting aromas left her gagging and swaying with another bout of dizziness. Was she being hypnotized again and just didn't know it?

"Help," she managed to whisper, hating that she was already losing control of herself. Her knees were knocking, about to give out. "Amun."

In the next instant, he had turned, his arm winding around her waist and holding her up. *What's wrong?*

Her lashes fluttered shut, suddenly too heavy for her to keep open. "Don't know. Head…spinning…" He was so still against her, she couldn't even feel his heartbeat or the rise and fall of his chest. Couldn't feel his heat, that amazing heat.

*There's ambrosia in the air, a substance very harmful to humans, but you aren't…*

"Human. Yes. I am."

*I don't understand. You died. Now you're alive. You can't be human.*

The dizziness intensified, pulling her under a dark, dark wave. No matter how hard she fought, she couldn't swim to the top. "Amun…"

*Haidee. Listen to my voice. Stay with me.*

"Can't," she wanted to tell him. No sound emerged.

*If you pass out, I'll strip you and touch you again. Do you hear me? I'll view it as an invitation to take you.*

Before she could tell him the invitation wouldn't have an expiration date, that his "consequences" were not a threat but a delightful prospect, the darkness swallowed her completely.

DAMN THIS. Amun hefted Haidee over his shoulder, barely registering her slight weight. He did, however, register the fact that her breasts were smashed into his back. Because of her unusually cool body temperature, her nipples were already pebbled.

She'd been behind him for what seemed an eternity, touching him fleetingly yet awakening every nerve ending he possessed. Despite the danger, he'd almost stopped a dozen times, desperate to taste her again, to hear her moan his name. His, and no other.

When she'd confessed that she had only dated that bastard Micah because she'd mistaken him for Amun, she'd almost found herself pressed against the cave wall, her jeans and panties ripped away, his shaft pounding its way home. Control had been maintained through a wish and a prayer only.

Confounding baggage. How was he supposed to callously use her and work her from his system when she treated him with such…sweetness? When she responded to his barbs with hurt rather than venom?

Secrets still couldn't read her mind, but the demon had begun to sense the absolute conviction in her every word. She believed everything she said. Of course, the demon also retreated every time Haidee touched him. The coolness that so delighted Amun terrified his companion. *All* of his companions. Since leaving the fortress, the other demons had yet to try to influence him in any way. Why?

Damn this, he thought again, striding forward. Didn't matter why. He needed this woman.

A little dizzy himself, he shouldered his way through the foliage. He'd whisk Haidee to safety if it killed him. And it just might. If he was affected by the ambrosia in the air, how much damage would the substance do to her?

Through Maddox, Amun had learned that humans simply couldn't tolerate ambrosia, a drug meant only for immortals. They were better off being injected with tainted heroin. Haidee hadn't ingested the substance, had only breathed in the fumes, so Amun told himself she would be okay.

Was she human, though? She truly believed she was and could very well be, despite the fact that she'd risen from the dead. But surely she was more than she realized. That unnatural coolness, her mental connection to Amun, the way she corralled his demons, each bespoke something beyond mortality.

Still. To be safe, he wanted to get her out of this forest as quickly as possible. All he had to do was find the entrance to the next realm. Which, if he wasn't mistaken, would be the Realm of Shadows. So far, all he could see were trees. Trees, trees, trees. They surrounded him so completely they were like a second layer of clothing.

Soon he was panting from exertion. His dizziness increased, and he tightened his hold on Haidee. They didn't touch skin to skin, merely cloth to cloth. Perhaps if he slid his hands up the hem of her pants and gripped her thigh properly, her temperature would stave off the dizziness the same way it staved off the demons.

*Follow your own advice and stay alert. No touching the girl.* A single touch, and he'd become lost to the lust again.

Branches slapped at him, slicing his cheeks. He shook his head, clearing his thoughts. The action must have roused Secrets. Instantly agitated, the demon prowled through his skull, hatred for this place welling up.

Voices suddenly wafted to Amun's ears.

*Come closer, warrior...*

*Welcome to our home...*

*We won't hurt you...much...*

Thoughts soon followed, filling his mind.

*They'll taste so good.*

*Maybe she'll scream just the way I like...*

The snakes were closing in, ready to strike. To kill. He couldn't fight them with Haidee dangling so precariously over his shoulder. She would take the brunt of the action, her body acting as his shield, and that he wouldn't allow.

Not knowing what else to do, he stopped and eased her to the ground—no sudden movements—then fit the backpack she still carried around her neck, shielding the sensitive area as best he could. As he slowly, so slowly straightened, he withdrew two of his blades, metal whistling against leather.

That must have been the starting bell for the snakes.

Dozens of crimson eyes leveled on him... Fangs flashed bright white.

He tensed.

The snakes launched forward.

# CHAPTER FOURTEEN

*NOW THIS IS THE SHIT,* Strider thought with a slow grin.

A few hours ago, Lucien had flashed him and William to Paris. The guy, not the city. Though the evening had only just begun, Paris had been well on his way to ambrosia intoxication, already laughing like a loon. So rather than cart him off and start hunting Gilly's parents to play a little game of slice and dice, as planned, and rather than leaving him behind in such a vulnerable condition, Strider and William had decided to take care of Paris—aka down a little ambrosia themselves—and head out as a unit in the morning.

Brotherly love and all that. *The things I do for my friends.* Not that Strider was intoxicated. He was the sober one.

He reclined on a delightfully cushioned lounge in the sprawling ranch Paris had rented. In Dallas, Texas, of all places. Promiscuity had decked himself out, too, wearing a Stetson (weird), no shirt (understandable), unfastened jeans (smart) and cowboy boots (weird again). Dude looked ready to rustle cattle or something.

At least the girls Paris had invited to party with him were more sensible. They wore bikinis.

Best of all, as the girls swam in the moon-and-lamplit pool, laughing, playing, Strider was reminded that he'd always preferred females with big boobs and lots of makeup. He was able to forget all about only-a-handful

Haidee and how lovely and delicate she'd looked in Amun's arms. Arms that should have been *his*. But whatever.

"I call dibs on the topless one," William said from Strider's left, throwing back his ambrosia-laced beer. "And the one wearing dental floss." He'd changed his mind five times in the past ten minutes. As of now, he had dibs on every single female in sight.

"That's a thong, moron," Paris slurred from Strider's right.

They reclined in lounges, too, the only cocks within miles of this little henhouse.

The girls were in front of them, some using the concrete rim around the hourglass pool as a dance floor. Gods love this modern era, because the females weren't afraid to grind on each other.

"If the thing riding up her ass is a thong, whatdya call that string across her nipples?" William countered.

"A string," Paris said, then nodded as if confirming his own genius. "And by the way, I get first pick since I rounded 'em up and brought 'em here, and I call dibs on the topless one."

"Where'd you get 'em, anyway?" Strider asked. Funny. His own words were slurred.

"Strip club downtown," Paris replied, finishing off his latest bottle of jack. "Throw enough money around and you can have anything you want. Except, maybe, fried Twinkies. I can't find those anywhere."

William tapped two fingers against his chin. "You had any of 'em before?"

"Fried Twinkies?" Paris nodded. "Only once, but I've never forgotten the experience. It's like heaven in your mouth, man."

"Fried— Paris, you dumb bastard." Exasperated, William shook his head. "I meant the women."

Exasperated himself, Paris splayed his arms. "How

would I know whether or not the women have had a fried Twinkie? I only just met them."

"Dear gods." William pinched the bridge of his nose. "Have you. Slept with. One of. The women. Before?"

"Oh. Sure, I have. And shit. Why didn't you say that to begin with?"

"Finally," William said. "We get somewhere. Who?"

Because of his straight-up awesome demon, Paris couldn't screw the same woman twice. Sure, he weakened unbearably if he failed to roll around in the sheets at least once a day, but that was a small price to pay for unlimited nookie.

"Like I remember," Paris replied.

"Your cock always remembers."

"Well, we're currently not speaking, so…"

"And we come to yet another dead end." William's sigh was somehow as wry as his tone. "You're just gonna have to take who I give you and deal."

"Like anyone would pick you over me."

William blustered over the insult. "You just wait and see. I'll have every single one of them eating out of my hand."

"Only if you find one of those delicious fried Twinkies," Paris snapped.

Strider rolled his eyes. Egotistical morons. Anyone with a set of eyes could see that Strider was the pretty one in their little threesome.

His demon immediately recognized the challenge and stretched, gearing up to do whatever was necessary to ensure that statement was true. *Win?*

*Down, boy.* He didn't need the hassle tonight.

"Hey, William," a beautiful blonde frolicking in the water called. "You said you wanted to taste me when I got wet. Well, I'm very, *very* wet," she ended with husky entreaty. "Come taste me."

"You're not quite wet enough, honey bun. Keep playing, and I'll let you know when you're ready."

For all his own dib-calling the past few hours, William hadn't touched a single female yet. Strider had, though. He'd already taken the one with blue streaks in her sandy-colored hair upstairs. For forty-five minutes he'd unleashed his sexual needs on her willing body, making her moan and scream and writhe. He'd even made her beg.

Clearly, he'd been the best she'd ever had. Not that he'd ever doubted that would be the case. Not that he'd waited several minutes after the loving was done, tense, expecting to double over in pain since he hadn't laid his patented moves on her, had just acted on need.

When he and Defeat had realized they could add another name to their ever-growing list of completely satisfied females—not that they remembered any of the names—Strider should have shot right into another climax. But the rush of victory hadn't done anything for him. He hadn't felt any better about his situation. He might even have felt worse. Like, hollowed out or something.

The girl had fallen asleep immediately afterward, thank the gods, because if she'd tried to talk to him, he would seriously have cut off his ears. Sex, good. Conversation, bad. He should have let her rest, but he hadn't trusted her enough to leave her unattended, so he'd carted her back outside and placed her on a lounge—on the opposite side of the pool, where she was still sleeping. A guy couldn't be too careful.

Still. She hadn't been a challenge, not in any way, really, and he'd liked that. Liked being able to relax. With Ex, the challenge would *always* be there, influencing everything he did, so he would always be on edge. Of course, that would also mean the pleasure of finally winning her would be unparalleled, because the harder the battle, the sweeter the victory.

Not that he gave a shit about that now. He just wanted to take the easy road, damn it. He deserved the easy road for once. Even though he was learning the easy road sucked.

"Why don't you join us, Paris?" a brunette called silkily, dragging Strider's mind back to the party. She sat at the edge of the pool, her feet dangling in the crystalline water. She nibbled on her bottom lip as she swirled a finger over one of her bared nipples. "I've wanted to get my hands on you ever since you first said hi to me."

A few others sighed dreamily, as if remembering that very thing. As if Paris's "hi" was the most stimulating conversation they'd ever had the privilege of enjoying.

"I've been watching you all this time," Paris responded in a rumbling purr, "and as you can guess, I'm practically on fire to have you. But I gotta get myself under control before I can trust myself to even kiss you."

The girls giggled.

Such a smooth talker Paris was, flattering without hurting a single feeling, yet doing exactly as he desired. Staying just where he was without inviting anyone over. But his desires were stupid, Strider thought. Did Paris want to spend the night alone and untouched?

And what the fuck, man. Was Strider dog food? Where was his shout-out? Where was his "come over here and play with me?" Or maybe they thought he only wanted the sandy-haired wench. Well, he wanted the topless one.

*Win.* Defeat stretched a little more, practically humming about the possibility of trying to steal the girl's affection away from Paris.

*Damn it. Can't I have a single night to myself?*

The demon replied with more humming. Meaning, hell no.

*I gave you a victory tonight already.*

*WIN.*

*Fine. One more.* But it wouldn't be the fight his demon wanted. Frowning, Strider pointed to the shortest female in the group. "You."

Her eyes widened with pleasure. "Me?"

She was slightly older than the others, putting her in her early thirties, with black hair and green eyes. He kinda wished she were a blonde, but she had a few tattoos scattered across her back—birds rather than words and faces, not that he cared—so he figured she would do. Not that he was particular or anything, or going for a specific type. He just knew what he wanted, and there was nothing wrong with that.

"Yeah. You. C'mere, honey," he said, crooking that finger and motioning her over.

She giggled and jumped to a stand. Several of the other girls threw her jealous scowls as she closed the distance and plopped onto his lap, and he nodded in satisfaction. Now that was more like it.

*There's your one more, you little shit.*

Defeat quieted, happy with the win but bored by the ease of it.

Strider sighed. Earlier, this female had taken a dip in the water, and her gold-foil bathing suit was still damp. She fit her ass right over his semi-erect penis and leaned back, stretching out against him. Her large—really large— breasts jutted up, her nipples beaded underneath the fabric of the suit, and she squirmed against him, trying to rub him into full arousal.

Suddenly he wished he'd kept his mouth shut. He didn't want to be rubbed—or talked to. Damn his irresistible sexual magnetism.

"Easy now," he told her, gripping her hips to ensure she slowed down. "I need a few minutes to recover from the excitement of having you here."

Thankfully, she stilled. She twisted just a little, peering

up at him through heavy-lidded eyes. "Want me to turn around?"

She smelled of peaches and cigarette smoke. "Actually, be a good girl and get me another beer from the kitchen." He hefted her to her feet and gave her tight ass a pat. "I need to rebuild my strength or I'll never be able to keep up with a woman as talented and beautiful as you."

The action startled her, and she yelped, then threw a narrowed glance over her shoulder. "Beer?"

"Yeah, and sometime tonight," he prompted, not wanting to give her time to question him further. "That's a sweet girl."

"Grab me one, too, sweetness," Paris called. "Don't pop the lid, though, all right?"

With a huff, she flounced inside. The kitchen sat right next to the patio, the glass doors allowing him to watch her as she dug into the fridge, turned and stalked back out. By the time she reached him, she had calmed down.

When she tried to sit back on his lap, he confiscated the beers and gave her a little push toward the pool. "Watching you swim is about the sexiest thing I've ever seen. Show me that swan dive again, and transport me right back to heaven."

"But I thought you wanted… If you're sure you don't…"

"I'm sure. I'm practically drooling just thinking about how graceful you are."

Her shoulders squared proudly, and she raced off to do just that. Strider tossed Paris his beer.

"I just had the best idea ever," William said the moment they were alone. Well, as alone as three guys could be with a backyard filled with strippers. He grinned evilly. "Let's give Maddox a ring."

Paris had dumped a baggie of ambrosia in the new bottle and had just taken a swig. The liquid caught in his throat, choking him. After banging a fist into his sternum, he regained his breath and said, "You mean *propose* to him? To grumpy ole Maddox? Shit, Willie, why didn't you tell us you're a masochist who swung that way? You're so delicate, he'll rip you to shreds the moment you climb into his bed. Plus, he's hitched himself to Ashlyn. You try to lay a move on him, and that sweet thang will rearrange your face."

Rolling his eyes, William withdrew Paris's cell phone from the pocket of the swim trunks he'd borrowed. "I mean call him, you idiot. What's with you tonight? Permanent brain damage? We'll breathe heavily and ask him what he's wearing. I bet no one's phone sexed him before."

"Hey!" Paris frowned as he eyed the small black device. "I had that stashed in my bedroom."

"I know. That's where I found it when I was snooping through your things." As always, William was unrepentant about his sins. "So who has the titanium balls to actually do it, huh?"

Defeat raised his arm like a schoolboy, the only kid in class who knew the answer to the seemingly impossible mathematical equation on the board.

*Enough from you already! You had your "more."*

"Why Maddox?" Strider asked. If anyone could kick his ass over the phone, it was the keeper of Violence. The warrior would probably find a way to reach through the line and strangle him the moment he started describing all the naughty things he supposedly planned to do to him.

William flashed his perfect white teeth. "Because he'll curse the most, and that'll make me laugh the hardest. Now, are you in or not?"

"Give me that effing phone," Strider grumbled, opening his palm and waving his fingers.

"Effing?" William laughed with genuine amusement. "You ever realize how polite you get when you're hammered? And you know what they say. A man's true character is revealed when he's toasted. So you gotta face facts, man. You're a closet gentleman." He shuddered. "Loser!"

"The heck I am!"

Even Paris laughed at that.

Strider snatched the phone out of William's hand and started dialing. Yeah, Maddox—like every other warrior— was on speed dial, but Strider didn't know the order Paris had them listed and he didn't want to ask. If Strider wasn't first, he didn't want to challenge the bastard to fix the mistake.

A few seconds later, Strider realized he'd dialed the wrong number because some dumb kid answered with a "What's up, yo?"

Strider quickly hung up and tried again, carefully pecking at the keys. After the first ring, he switched to speaker.

Maddox answered a few seconds later, his voice raspy with the force of his panting. "Something wrong, Paris?"

William and Paris were on the edges of their seats, peering over at Strider with utter glee. He hadn't seen either warrior that happy or relaxed in a long time, and he realized they had needed this vacation as much as he had.

Strider blew into the mouthpiece, then moaned as if he were buried deep inside a woman's body. He tried not to grin.

"Paris?" Maddox asked, confused. "You there? You okay?"

Both warriors tried to cut off their laughs, smashing their knuckles into their mouths, but snorts managed to escape.

"You naked, big boy?" Strider asked in his best imitation of an aroused female. "Because I am."

More snorting followed his words.

"Strider? And don't try to deny it. I recognize your voice. What the hell are you doing with Paris's phone? I thought you were in Rome. And furthermore, what the hell does it matter if I'm naked or not? You have exactly two seconds to explain or I'm going to reach through the line, rip your tongue out of your mouth and—"

There was a pause, static, a muttered, "Give me that," by an indignant female. Then the normally quiet and reserved Ashlyn was demanding, "Did you just drunk dial my husband?"

"Yes, ma'am," Strider said, and the other two finally burst into laughter, falling back in their chairs, their bodies shaking with the force of their mirth. "A guy's gotta have some fun. Even if it's the fun he puts in his own funeral. So is he? Naked, I mean."

"No, for your information, he is not. He's working out. I, uh, kind of incited him to rage so he's beating the crap out of a brick wall."

The laughter continued for several minutes, until even Ashlyn was chortling. "You boys are incorrigible. This isn't funny! He'll probably destroy the other wall when we hang up."

"Good. He needed to get out of bed and finally do something besides—" Strider stopped himself before he said something else Maddox would rage over.

"Besides pleasuring me?" Ashlyn finished for him, anyway. "You'll change your mind when you next see him. Lately, he's a nervous wreck about the babies. He's picking fights with everyone he meets and has even been arrested. Twice. We're going to make our way back to the fortress in the next week or so. He needs you guys. Because, and please don't laugh when I tell you this, if we're alone much longer I'm going to murder him in his sleep."

Strider chuckled. "Bet you're wishing you hadn't saved him from his death curse." Once upon a time, Reyes had been forced to murder Maddox every night and Lucien had been forced to escort his soul to hell. Ashlyn managed to reverse the curse, sparing them all.

"A little peace and quiet isn't too much to ask for, you know?" she said loudly. Then, in a softer tone, she added, "So everyone's good?"

"Don't be nice to them," Maddox barked in the background. "You need your rest, and they interrupted."

"Oh, hush," she replied. "If you had your way, I'd be resting every minute of every day. And like I can really rest while we're outside, in the middle of town, while you destroy another building. Besides, I miss them and want to talk to them."

That shut Maddox up. He could deny his precious Ashlyn nothing.

"We're great. Me, Willie and Paris are on vacation. Together," Strider added. He relaxed against his lounge, his free hand anchored under his head, wondering if he'd ever have such an easy relationship with a woman. "*You* guys good? No trouble lately?"

"Besides Maddox's temper? Not even a hint of it."

He didn't ask where they were or what, exactly, they were doing. Besides destroying public property. He didn't want to know. Ignorance was bliss. Besides that, if Hunters ever managed to pull their heads out of their asses and capture him, he wouldn't have any secrets to spill.

Secrets. Amun. Ex.

His jaw clenched. *You weren't going to think about them, remember?* "How are Stride and Stridette?" Friend that he was, he'd taken the massive burden of picking names for the twins upon himself.

"He's means Liam and Liama," William called, but a shadow then passed over his features, his grin fading.

"Madd and Madder are kicking like professional soccer players," she replied, her voice softening with love and affection. "I swear, we're gonna have our hands full when they finally get here."

"By the way, you've ruined a perfectly good prank call with all this baby talk, Ash," William scolded her.

"Seriously," Paris said with a nod.

She laughed with unvarnished delight. "No more than you deserve, boys."

"Hang up the phone, woman," Maddox suddenly said, grim. "Someone's coming."

"Uh-oh. I have to go now," she said and hung up before anyone could reply.

Strider tossed the phone to Paris, who missed. "Think they're in trouble?"

"Nah," Paris said, plucking the device before William could. "The someone who's coming is probably Maddox himself."

"Yeah, he's probably dragging her back to wherever they're staying so he can make a prank call of his own," William said, adding, "on her body."

Before Defeat could throw in his own supposition, Strider changed the subject. "So now what are we going to do?" Out of habit, he scanned his surroundings.

The girls were watching them, he realized, confused by their amusement but clearly charmed by it. They were wearing dreamy expressions, as if they were already planning a triple wedding.

"I guess we could grab a female or two and head to our bedrooms." Paris didn't sound enthused by the prospect. At least he wasn't going to deny himself his daily dose, though.

"Yeah," William replied, and he actually sounded depressed.

Strider knew Paris's problem. The woman he had desired above all others, the first woman he'd ever been able to have sex with more than once, had died in his arms, gunned down by her own people. Hunters. Like Ex.

This time, Strider didn't even attempt to cut off his thoughts of her. Yet. Had she been among the shooters? Probably. There was no bitch more coldhearted. Literally. He'd never met anyone whose body was as cold as that girl's—except those he'd sent to the morgue, of course. Like he'd once sent Ex.

Was she cold because she was still dead? Was she akin to the walking dead?

The possibility was worth considering. Later. Right now, he wanted to figure out William's unusual somberness. A much safer topic. Was there someone the warrior wanted but couldn't have? Someone he'd lost? Was that why he was so hands-off when he used to be a worse degenerate than Strider? Seriously, he hadn't touched a single stripper. Not even to slap a rump.

"So am I the only one who sees the dead girl at Paris's feet or what?" William asked conversationally.

Strider and Paris stiffened in unison. Dead girl?

Strider was the first to find his voice. "What do you mean?" He looked, hard, but saw no hint of a dead... anything.

"Is this a joke?" Paris demanded, and there was no denying the menace in his voice.

"No joke, I swear." William held up his hands, all innocence. "She showed up a few minutes ago and just kinda threw herself on the ground beside your chair. Dude, she's got her hands wrapped around your ankle." His gaze remained in the same spot, as if he were studying her.

"She's got dark hair and dirt-smudged skin. Or maybe those are freckles. She's wearing a ripped white robe and black wings are growing out of her back. Ohhh, she's got nice hands. Look at those things. I bet she does all kinds of naughty things with them."

Paris was on his feet a second later, wild gaze darting over the concrete surrounding his chair. "Where is she? Where, damn it?"

A frowning William pointed at the exact spot Paris was standing. "You're on top of her. Hey, girl. Girl. I don't think he can see you. Or feel you. I don't think grabbing on to him like that is gonna help you."

Paris jumped back and, with an urgent moan, fell to his knees, patting the area in question as if he were putting out a fire. "I don't feel her. Are you sure she's here?" Desperate, uttered in a rush.

"Uh, yeah." William's brow furrowed several seconds before smoothing out as comprehension dawned. "I guess I never told you guys, but I see dead people. Oh, and look. There's Cronus."

Cronus, the god king. Strider's eyes widened, but he saw no bright light to announce the sovereign's sudden appearance. All remained as it was. No, not true. Paris had stiffened, fury bathing his face, his teeth bared in a fearsome scowl.

Cronus had given them medallions to hide them from the gods, but had since taken them back, saying the Lords had abused them. Meaning, Cronus wanted to know where they were at all times. Here was proof.

"Hey, buddy. How you doing?" William waved. "You taking the girl?" Pause. "Wow, you're brave. Doesn't look like she wants to leave with you." Another pause. He didn't seem to care that he was having a conversation with himself. "Okay, then, but go easy on her. I think Paris likes her. Well, bye." He waved again.

Paris listened, growing more and more agitated. At the "bye," he launched himself at William, his roar shattering the ease of the night.

# CHAPTER FIFTEEN

HAIDEE FOUGHT THROUGH THE thick, black cloud in her mind, hearing grunts, groans and hisses in the distance. Heavy eyelids blinked open, and through a misty haze she saw a tall, muscled warrior standing over her, a solid leg on each side of her hips. Amun. Her sweet Amun.

He slashed his serrated daggers with swift proficiency, his wrists arcing as his hands overlapped, quickly sailing apart and nailing a target. Or several targets at the same time. Thin, scaled bodies—snakes, she thought groggily—fell all around her, crimson rivers flowing under her. In death, their red eyes were fixed on her, their fangs forever bared but useless.

Those bodies continued to rain as Amun continued to slash, and a more fantastical display of male aggression and skill she'd never seen. But no matter how many reptiles he killed, more flew from the tangle of limbs, desperate to bite him. Many had already succeeded. His arms were covered with tiny punctures, his own blood dripping and blending with theirs.

None of the snakes had reached her, however. Every time one of them angled in her direction, either from in front or behind, he noticed and attacked. He protected her, even though he left his sides wide open to do so, allowing several other sets of fangs to sink deep.

She should help, do something, anything, but her limbs refused to obey her command to move. She drew in a deep breath—the air, so sweet, so pungent—trying to find her center, trying to tap into a reservoir of strength. Only lethargy greeted her.

Amun was panting, sweating, probably tiring and definitely needing her to do—her eyes were closing again…*open, damn it*…closing…thoughts fragmenting… darkness.

THE NEXT TIME HAIDEE managed to pry open her eyelids, she saw wide, rocky walls painted red with blood and de-picting horrific images that blurred at her sides as she… floated? Even from the swift glimpses she was afforded, she managed to spot three stabbings, two rapes and count-less burnings.

Worse than the images, however, she saw an actual human body hanging from the domed ceiling, crows eating at its rotting flesh. What. The. Hell?

Hell. The word echoed in her mind, rousing her memory. She had entered hell with Amun. Her dream man. Her enemy. Her obsession.

Her head felt too heavy to turn even the barest inch, so she moved her gaze instead—and found herself peering up at his beautiful dark skin. He cradled her in his arms, his chest littered with tiny, seeping holes. He stared straight ahead, his chin jutting stubbornly, his lips pressed into a thin, mutinous line.

He must be in pain, she thought, yet he carried her with careful, easy steps, doing his best not to jostle her. Such tenderness…such a darling man.

Would she ever figure him out?

She tried to open her mouth to thank him, to apologize for not aiding him in the Realm of Snakes, for actually hindering him, but no words emerged. Her lips refused to even part, lethargy still pumping through her at an alarm-ing rate. Damn it. She owed him *something*.

He must have sensed her internal struggle, though he

never looked down, never slowed his gait. *Easy now,* he said, that husky voice wisping through her mind. *Don't try to talk. Sleep, heal.*

That. She could give him that. Obedience, just this once. Or again. With him, the lines had always been blurred. She closed her eyes and let the darkness once again consume her.

HAIDEE STRETCHED HER ARMS over her head, back arching, legs kicking out. In the back of her mind, she knew she'd grown used to hard, twig-laden ground, cramped cells and general discomfort. But, oh, not this time. The mattress beneath her was soft and smelled deliciously of peat smoke and flowers. And sweet Lord above, she heard a crackling fire, felt wave after wave of delicious heat caressing her skin.

Only two things marred the luxury of the moment. A dull headache throbbing in her temples, and a gnawing sense of emptiness in her stomach. Both demanded attention. Now. She blinked open her eyes, taking stock. She was sprawled on her side, lying on a bed of soft, colorful petals. Inside a murky, barren cave. Had Amun picked the flowers from the forest and brought them here, just to ensure her comfort?

Amun.

She jolted upright, heartbeat accelerating with gratitude, delight and awareness. So much awareness. He sat only a few inches away, within striking distance. Perhaps he was coming to trust her. A fire blazed in front of him, creating a symphony of music and heat. His bare back was to her. As she'd noticed before, he bore no tattoos, no scars. She saw only the ridges of his spine and a wide span of muscle and scabs. From the snakes, she realized. The snakes he'd saved her from.

"Where are we?" she asked, surprised by the raw quality of her voice.

He didn't move, didn't even twitch with alarm at the sudden interruption. *We're between realms, I think. We're safe, though. I scouted ahead, and there's nothing and no one for miles.*

"Thank you," she said softly. "For everything."

He nodded. *You have to talk to me, Haidee.* Slowly he twisted so that his hip pressed against hers, and they were facing each other. *I wasn't sure how the ambrosia in the air would affect you. I wasn't sure if I needed to try and purge it from your body or leave you be.*

She knew she needed to reply but couldn't. Not just yet. She wanted to savor this moment with him, no animosity between them.

He was just so beautiful, his dark, fathomless eyes probing all the way to her soul. His lips, though taut with tension, could lure a woman to her own downfall. As long as she could have those lips on her body, that tongue licking, sucking and tasting, destruction hardly mattered.

More than embodying physical perfection, he was courageous, caring, protective. How could anyone consider him evil? Least of all herself?

Honestly. How could she ever hurt him? Even if he decided he no longer needed her and opted to punish her for her past sins? She wouldn't be able to blame him. He just wanted to survive, as she always had.

And what if Baden had been just like him? she suddenly wondered, causing sickness to churn in her stomach. What if she'd helped kill an innocent man? Not that Baden had been innocent back then, but what if he would have matured into a dedicated warrior like the one in front of her?

What if they were *all* innocent? The sickness intensified. Strider had spent those seemingly endless days with her, yet he hadn't raped her, hadn't tortured her, hadn't hurt her as he could have. He'd threatened her, yes, but then, she had threatened him. She had even hit him, stabbed him. He'd retaliated, once, but not as fiercely as he should have.

*The Lords of the Underworld are the epitome of evil,* Dean Stefano, the modern-day version of the Bad Man, the first Hunter she'd ever encountered, had always said. As right-hand man to Galen, who rarely made an appearance, he was currently in charge of the troops. *They must be eradicated before their poison spreads. To you, to your loved ones. How many of your mothers have died of cancer? How many of your teenage daughters have been violated? How many of your spouses have betrayed you?*

When someone had balked about killing another living being, Stefano had added stiffly, *Killing a demon isn't murder. Demons are animals, and those animals would slaughter your entire family without a single pang of remorse. Like a starving lion or bear. They attack and ravage thoughtlessly. Never forget that fact.*

Wasted breath, she'd thought every time she'd heard that speech. Haidee hadn't needed convincing. A demon *had* slaughtered her entire family. Not just once, but twice.

She'd always blamed the entire lot of them because, to her, a demon was a demon and evil was evil. Now, with the proud, compassionate Amun so close to her, she at last saw the flaw in her logic. Evil destroyed. These men hadn't destroyed her when given the chance, yet destruction had always been *her* ultimate goal.

How many times had she tried to eradicate the Lords? Had she even cared about the methods used? No.

A wail of regret suddenly caught in her throat. What if *she* was the evil one?

A firm arm slid under her knees and another wrapped

around her waist. A moment later she was being lifted and lowered. After that, she was leaning against Amun's massive chest, her cheek pressed into the hollow of his neck. Gently he caressed her hair as if she was beloved rather than despised, as if her emotional state mattered.

*What are you, Haidee?* he asked again, voice as gentle as his touch.

She'd never discussed her…infection with another living being. Ever. Not even Micah. But this was Amun. Her Amun. As tears burned her eyes, she relaxed against him, flattening her palm against the heart beating so swiftly in his chest. He'd saved her; he deserved to know the truth.

"I'm not exactly sure," she whispered. "Human, I know that much, but something else, too. I *can* be killed just like anyone else. Bleeding out, disease, starvation. But each time I'm killed, I come back, exactly as I am now."

*You've died before? I mean, I know you died that once, but you've actually died several times?* His tender stroking never ceased.

"Yes. More than several, though. I lost count a long time ago. Still, no matter how long I manage to stay alive in one incarnation, I never age past this point. I guess my age just kind of froze after the very first death."

*So what happens after you die?*

She shuddered. "It's horrible. You'd think the pain of dying would be the worst, but no. The pain of rebirth, or whatever it is, is devastating. I'll feel my life slipping away, float in darkness for what seems an eternity, but then, when the light comes…" She shuddered again. "The light swallows me, burns me to my soul, but not with fire, with ice, and my body will begin to rejuvenate. I'm like a mother giving birth—to myself. My bones feel like they're being injected with acid, every muscle spasms and my skin feels like it's being poured back on."

Those warm fingers curled around her nape, the caress

becoming a massage. Again, his touch was tender, and yet, as aware of him as she was, her sensitive flesh prickled, her nipples beaded, and an ache bloomed between her legs. How she wanted this man.

She had always assumed discussing the past would be difficult. And never had she imagined doing so with one of the demon-possessed warriors she'd fought so diligently to obliterate. The words flowed smoothly, however. "When the pain finally leaves, I always find myself in the same location. Greece, in a cave next to the water. I won't remember any of the good things that happened to me, yet I'm aware that the memories were taken. Not that that makes any sense. I'll know who I am, every terrible thing that's ever been done to me, every terrible thing *I've* done, and the hate… God, Amun, I'm always filled with so much hate. For the first few years of a new life, that hate is the only thing that drives me."

He rested his chin on top of her head, his warm breath ruffling strands of her hair, tickling. *How long have you been alive this time?*

"About eleven years."

*Why have you never come after us before?*

She should lie. The truth would destroy the tranquility of this moment. He deserved the truth, though. After everything, he deserved the truth.

"I have come after you," she admitted. "A few years ago, some of you were in New York. I helped burn down your home. And then, a few months ago, in Budapest, there was a shootout. I was there."

*No, I mean, in one of your other lives. I've been around a long time, yet this is the first time since ancient Greece that I've encountered you.*

He wasn't going to take issue with her confession. He wasn't even going to acknowledge it as the travesty it was. The realization was staggering. "I always remain in seclusion until I've got the hate under control. And even then, I have to wait until I can pass myself off as someone else before I can rejoin society and the Hunters, which means waiting until the people who might have known me are dead."

*How do you know who they are, if most of your memories are taken? And how you are Haidee now, if you've changed your identity?*

"I've come back so many times, and with so many years apart, I'm often able to reuse the same name. As for the rest, I keep records inside my cave, files detailing everything I've been through in one lifetime. I also send newspaper clippings, photos, that sort of thing, to a mailbox nearby."

*That's smart.* His sincerity warmed her as surely as his touch.

"Thank you." She lifted her arm, drawing his attention to her tattoos. She'd never done this before, either. Never explained what the etchings meant. If she and Amun were ever going to make a relationship work, though—*you want a full-blown* relationship *now?*—one of them had to take that first, trusting step.

"See this?" she asked, ignoring her question to herself. With her free hand, she traced a circle around the only address amid the faces, phrases and dates.

His fingers curled around her wrist, slowly turning her arm, allowing him to study each of the surrounding tattoos. He rubbed the pad of his thumb over Micah's name, as if he could wipe it away. Just then, she wished he could.

*Yes,* he said. *I see.*

"That's where my mailbox is."

At first, he didn't respond. Then his breath emerged raggedly and he stiffened. *Don't tell me anything else about how you survive. Okay?*

"O-okay," she said, confused. "Why?" Because he'd

feel obligated to tell his friends, but didn't actually want them to know? Yes, she realized a moment later. That was exactly why.

The thought of possible betrayal should have sent her leaping out of his lap. Instead, she cuddled closer. He was still trying to take care of her.

*Who's the Bad Man?* he asked, changing the subject.

Hearing a nickname she'd only ever thought jolted her. "How did you know about him?"

His thumb brushed the side of her jaw, and she shivered. *I had a vision of you. Like the one we saw together, of you on the veranda. Except in this one, you were a little girl. Everyone else, I can read their minds, but you...I have only ever seen snatches of your life.*

First, he could read all minds but hers? That was kind of...disappointing. She wished he could see all of her, *know* all of her. If anyone could help her sift through her confused emotions and conflicting desires, it was this man. "The Bad Man was the first Hunter I ever met. He found me after my parents were killed."

*Blood, a river between her mother and her father. Both helpless...dead.*

Oh, no. No way in hell would she allow that hated memory to resurface now. "He saved my life after... someone like you tried to kill me. He thought I'd come in handy." She laughed bitterly. "He was right, he just didn't know it. I was nearly a teenager when he sold me in the slave market after failing to train me. But after I died the first time, I remembered his lessons and that's how I later hooked up with the Hunters."

*And that's when you helped kill Baden?* Simply asked, with no hint of his emotions.

Goodbye, sweet, stolen moment. If any topic could ruin their ease with each other, it was that one. Still. She nodded, tears once again burning her eyes.

*Who did we take from you that drove you to hate us so deeply?*

Again, there was no emotion in his voice. Not anger, not condemnation. Far more stunning, his question offered her absolution. A justifiable reason for her actions. He would never know what that meant to her, how profoundly that affected her.

She couldn't help herself. She pressed a kiss on the pulse thumping at the base of his neck. "My parents. My sister. My…husband."

*Husband?*

"Yes."

His arms tightened around her. *Before, you mentioned only one of us had done the deed. Do you know…do you know which of us it was?*

That hesitancy…he feared he was the culprit, she realized. "I did not see the face of the one who killed my parents and sister, but I do know it wasn't you or any of your friends. He was a demon-possessed warrior, though. As for my husband…" She sighed. "I'm not sure exactly who was responsible, but I do remember seeing your friends the night of his death."

He tipped up her chin and met her gaze, his black eyes deep pools of regret. He didn't speak, and neither did she. Earlier he had offered her absolution, and with her silence, she now did the same for him.

He nodded in understanding, in thanks, and released her chin. His hand slid into her hair, his fingers combing through the strands. *Do you know the story of how I came to be demon-possessed?*

"I think so. You and the others stole and opened Pandora's box, unleashing the demons that were trapped inside. The gods decided to punish you, and rightly so," she couldn't help but add, "by bonding each of you with a demon of your own."

THE DARKEST SECRET

*That's right.*

"Why'd you steal the box, anyway?"

*Zeus asked Pandora to guard it rather than asking us, and we were...upset.*

"Insulted, you mean." Men and their pride, sometimes the reason nations fell.

*Yes. We wanted to teach the god king a lesson, show him our worth.*

"And did you?"

*Hardly. We showed him exactly how stupid we were.*

She fought a grin. At least he saw and accepted the truth.

He lifted a lock of her hair to his nose and breathed deeply, a moan of satisfaction drifting through her mind. *The reason I brought up the box was to tell you that there were more demons locked inside than there were warriors to punish for unleashing the evil. Those that remained were placed in the prisoners of Tartarus. An immortal prison,* he explained.

Ah. She knew where he was going with this. "So the man who killed my parents and sister might have been released from that prison."

*Or escaped. Yes.*

"And whoever killed my husband could have escaped, as well?"

*That, I don't know. I wish otherwise, but... If you saw us that night, I'd say there's a ninety-nine percent chance we were responsible.*

No excuses, just brutal honestly. With countless lifetimes steeped in mystery, she appreciated such unvarnished probabilities. She kissed his pulse a second time, letting him know the admission hadn't propelled her into a rage. His sandalwood scent consumed her senses, reminding her of their shower. Which reminded her of their almost-kiss.

Which reminded her she was in his arms and had only to stretch up to press their lips together.

*Have you seen the man who—have you seen him since?*

She blinked. *Concentrate.* While she'd been opening the doors to her body's desires, Amun had been focused on the being responsible for her family's demise, still determined to look out for her. "A few times," she hedged. More like a hundred.

*When? Where?*

"Each time, just before I die," she admitted. Always a prelude to the end of her current existence, as if he poisoned whatever life she'd managed to build for herself. But as many times as she'd seen him, she'd never fought him. And she'd wanted to fight him, so badly. He would simply reveal himself, that dark robe dancing around his ankles, his feet not quite touching the floor. He would watch her, hate dripping from him. He would curse at her. But he would never touch her or allow her to touch him. Then, he would disappear.

*I need to think on this,* Amun said.

Her stomach chose that moment to rumble, and her cheeks flushed with embarrassment.

Once again Amun lifted her up, but this time he placed her on that bed of petals. Instantly she mourned the loss of his arms, his heat. *I need to find you something to eat. I was afraid the snakes would harm you, even in their deaths, so I brought none of their meat with us.*

Always taking care of her, her Amun. "I wish that stupid angel had packed a few protein bars and bottles of water," she said, snappier than she'd intended.

Beside her, the pack in question plumped up with a whoosh. She and Amun shared a confused glance. Frowning, he leaned over, unzipped the panels and reached inside. He withdrew a handful of protein bars.

His frown deepened as he upended the bag and dumped out the contents: more protein bars, followed by bottles of water. Just like that, his frown softened with hints of relief and wonder.

*Ask for something else,* he commanded.

Haidee lumbered to her knees, not daring to hope. "I wish the pack had sandwiches and fruit."

The sides of the pack expanded a second time before sandwich after sandwich fell on top of the bars, each encased in a clear plastic wrapper. And when those stopped raining down, apples and oranges began to drop and roll. Haidee's mouth watered.

"I want wet wipes and a change of clothes. I want weapons and toothpaste and a toothbrush—" they'd left those behind "—and a first aid kit for Amun's wounds." As she spoke, each of the requested items joined the pile.

Giddy, she sorted through the food, picking out what she wanted to eat. Once she had a ham sandwich and apple in hand, she practically inhaled them. Then another sandwich, then an orange. She drained two bottles of water. Every bite, every drop was heaven. And when she finally finished, too full to shovel in another crumb, she cleaned herself as best she could with the wipes, brushed her teeth—God, that felt good—and finally allowed herself to glance over at Amun. Breath caught in her throat.

The firelight caressed him lovingly, bestowing a golden tint on his dark skin. A tint she hadn't noticed before. He was watching her, a strange, bemused expression on his beautiful face, and a half-eaten apple in his hand. Obviously he'd cleaned up, too, since his face was no longer streaked with dirt.

"Let me bandage your wounds," she said quietly.

The bemused expression vanished, his pupils expanding, his nostrils flaring as if he suddenly scented prey. Her eyes widened. What had she said?

*Your concern for me is nice, but to bandage me, you'll have to put your hands on me. I want your hands on me for a different reason.*

"I—I...okay."

*Come here.* There was such force, such command in his tone, she didn't even think about refusing.

She crawled to him, quickly closing the distance between them. He set the apple aside, but he didn't touch her. He simply peered at her. Waiting. Expectant. She rose to her haunches, breathing him in. The sandalwood was now layered with the peat smoke.

She was supposed to bandage him first, right? Then touch him *for a different reason.* "I—I forgot the supplies." They were around here somewhere, and—

*Forget the supplies again. You're going to kiss me now, Haidee.*

His heat was like a thick vine around her. She found herself almost in a trance as she straightened and said, "Yes." Finally. Another kiss. Exactly what she'd craved. Forever, it seemed.

*A kiss between you and me and no other.*

"Yes." A plea from deep inside.

*Do it, then.* His voice snapped like a whip, daring her even as it warned her.

It was then she realized that, on some level, he was still fighting his desire, exactly as he had in the shower, just before he'd walked away from her, and that even when their tongues were rolling together, he still meant to resist her, to maintain distance.

She wasn't going to let him.

If she gave her all to their kiss, he had to give his all, too. That was only fair.

"I—I won't kiss you," she said, shivering as his eyes narrowed to dangerous slits. "I mean, I won't do it because I'm grateful to you, and I won't do it to distract or soften you. I'll do it just because I want you. So get ready. Because I expect the same from you. If you can't do the same, walk away now."

# CHAPTER SIXTEEN

*I'LL DO IT JUST BECAUSE I want you.* As Haidee's soft, shattering words echoed in Amun's mind, he stopped waiting for her to take the lead, stopped waiting for her to physically prove her desire for him, thereby atoning for her rejection of him in favor of Micah in the shower.

*I can give you what you want,* he told her, voice raw.

Her lips parted on a relieved gasp.

He didn't want her relieved; he wanted her mindless. With a moan, he crushed his mouth to hers, one hand at her nape, one on her ass, and jerked her into the uncompromising line of his body. Immediately she opened for him, welcoming the hard thrust of his tongue into those wet, satiny depths. He tasted mint and apple, both frosted like ice cream. Both fueling his need.

During their talk, he'd meant to ask her about the unnatural chill of her skin, but as she'd spoken of death and pain, he had focused only on that. On finding a way to save her. There had to be a way. And there had to be a reason she kept coming back.

How many times had she died? he'd wondered. In how many ways? Not knowing tortured him, but he had a feeling that knowing would utterly *destroy* him. No matter what she'd done in the past, she hadn't deserved to suffer as she clearly had. Especially more than once. The fear in her eyes as she'd spoken of being reborn into the same body...he never wanted to see it again.

And could he really blame her for her hatred of him and

his friends? A demon-possessed immortal had slain her family, her husband. Amun would have reacted the same way, lashing out at everyone responsible, even the slightest bit. At the time of Baden's death, Haidee had known only that the Lords were violent, crazed, capable of any dark deed. *Of course* she'd sought to destroy them.

He'd done the same to her. To her colleagues.

Now, as Amun looked back without any taint of guilt, fury or despair, he knew three things to be true. Haidee had lost her family. He had lost a friend. He wasn't going to hate her for that loss anymore. Since she'd fought her way into his bedroom, so sweetly caring for his wounds, the sentiment hadn't sat right with him, anyway. He'd had to force the issue.

Now, he wanted all of her. He wouldn't, couldn't, settle for less, his need to touch no longer about tiring of her or freeing himself of this obsession, but about gratifying her.

"Amun," she rasped, and the sound of his name on those pleasure-giving lips nearly undid him. "You...you stopped. Why did you stop?"

Amun. She'd called him Amun. He lifted his head and peered down at her. Her mouth was red, swollen and glistening with moisture. Her tongue flicked out to capture the lingering flavor of him. His shaft throbbed in response, desperate to feel the clench of her inner walls.

Her hands rested on his shoulders, her nails already cutting. He was panting, sweating despite the cool breeze wafting from her.

"What's wrong?"

*You always called me "baby" when you thought I was... Micah.* Just then, he had trouble even thinking the loathsome name. The scope of his understanding extended to Haidee and only Haidee. Besides being a Hunter, the bastard had held her, tasted her, and while Amun knew he was being irrational, he despised every man who'd ever had this pleasure. *His* pleasure. *Yet you call* me *by my name,* he finished darkly.

Her expression softened, illuminating the delicacy of her features. "The only person I've ever called baby is you."

Well, okay, then. That was acceptable. He reclaimed her mouth in a rush. Their tongues rolled together, taking, giving, their teeth scraping. Hands began roaming, every new touch increasing their fervency. He cupped her breasts, her nipples beading under his palm, and he moaned.

"I wish they were bigger," she said between licks.

Her breasts? *Why?*

"Men like bigger."

Someone had made her self-conscious, he realized, and he wanted to kill that someone. *This man likes these.* He squeezed. They were small, as she'd implied, but firm and wonderfully tipped. And they truly were the sweetest little morsels, as *he* had implied. *They're perfect.*

In fact…he whipped her shirt over her head and ripped the front clasp of her bra. The backpack would provide her with another one. As the material sagged apart, he caught a glimpse of nipples the prettiest shade of pink he'd ever seen.

*You're so beautiful.* He sounded drugged, didn't care.

"Th-thank you."

He bent his head and sucked one of the little pearls harder than he'd intended. A gasp escaped her, but she didn't push him away. No, she tangled her fingers in his hair and held him against her.

He switched his attention from one to the other, laving them equally until goose bumps broke out over her skin. Until her belly quivered in anticipation every time he moved. Until breathy groans were falling from

her lips, interwoven with his name, with pleas for mercy—
for more.

Amun hadn't had a lover in a very long time, but he
hadn't forgotten the basics, and he'd never been so driven
by instinct. *Touch, taste, possess, own.* He could have
been a virgin, and he would have found a way to please
this woman, because making her come wasn't simply a
desire. Making her come was a necessity.

Her pleasure was his pleasure, and that's just the way
it was.

*Touch...taste...*yes, taste. He straightened, meshing their
lips. He had to taste her again.

He wanted to go slowly, to savor every inch of her. To
learn what she liked, what she didn't. But just as before,
with a single kiss and a few caresses, the passion between
them went nuclear. Those roaming hands clutched, nails
scraped. He rubbed his erection between her legs, and she
arched into every slide.

After everything she'd told him, he felt as if he could
lose her at any moment. As if someone would take her
from him, and she would wake up in that cave in Greece,
unable to remember him or this kiss.

They were both shirtless, and when her breasts brushed
his chest, he hissed out a breath. The kiss never slowed,
their tongues continually rolling, seeking, demanding. *Possess...own...* He cupped her ass and slammed her against
him, the rubbing becoming a frantic seeking. A fever.

No, not a fever. His blood was on fire, true, racing
through his veins with a swiftness that would have killed
a lesser man, but the woman he held was becoming colder
with every second that passed. Her skin was like ice, her
mouth the storm, and as he sucked on her tongue, that icy
storm filled *him*.

The demons had been hiding in the back of his mind,
afraid to make themselves known. Now they shrieked,

her touch affecting them as if they'd just been hooked to an electric generator. Each one—and gods, there were hundreds—scrambled through his head, doing their best to avoid the renewing of Haidee's pull...the unavoidable cold.

Finally the kiss slowed...slowed...and then Haidee leaned back. "Are you okay?" Soft knuckles stroked his cheek.

*Just need...a moment...* Amun closed his eyes and settled on his haunches, inhaling unhurriedly, exhaling with care. Every muscle in his body was locked in a desperate tug-of-war with his bones, lancing thousands of aches through every part of him. All at the same time. From the demons, yes, but also from unfulfilled desire. He hadn't been ready to stop.

"My internal thermometer gets the better of me sometimes. I'm sorry. I didn't mean for it to—I could feel it... I'm sorry," she said again, a trace of misery in her tone. "I'll control it, I promise."

*No apologies,* he told her. *You did nothing wrong. Besides, I like it.*

He wasn't sure why the demons were calmed by her one moment, then roused by her the next. He wasn't sure how she pulled on them or why they reacted that way, but he would puzzle over the answer later. With the distance between him and Haidee—minute though it was—the heat returned to him and the demons ceased fighting so stringently. For the moment, that was enough.

Secrets, though, had remained unaffected throughout the entire ordeal. Amun didn't think his soul-companion had liked the change in temperature, but the beast hadn't been—and still wasn't, because yes, Amun planned to have another go at his woman—screeching in fear.

His woman.

The phrase delighted him in a way he never would have

expected. But she was. His. In every way that mattered—and soon in every way imaginable. His friends wouldn't understand. Might even hate him, might consider him a traitor. He couldn't make himself care. Just then, her well-being came before his own.

The change in his mind-set was radical, even to him, and he wasn't quite used to it yet. That didn't lessen the impact, though. He'd held her in his lap, listened to her story of loss, had heard the heartbreak in her voice, and something inside him had broken. He'd begun to comprehend the truth. They were alike in so many ways. Determined, constantly bombarded by the worst the world had to offer—people, places, circumstances—yet finding joy where they could.

He wanted this woman. Would have her. And yeah, maybe he was driven purely by desire right now, convincing himself of feelings he wouldn't normally entertain to ease the shame of being with the enemy, but he didn't think so.

"Maybe it's best that we stopped," she whispered on a trembling breath. "I—I still can't sleep with you."

Amun's eyelids sprang open, and he knew flickers of firelight showcased the dark menace in his eyes. *Because of him?* he demanded.

"Yes. I won't cheat."

He popped his jaw. *When did you last sleep with him?* With every new word, there had been an increase of rage in his voice.

"I didn't. Not once."

The rage vanished in a blink. Had she said *yesterday,* he would have wanted her still—he doubted anything could change that—but knowing Micah hadn't touched her in that way stoked his new sense of possession. *When you dated him, you thought he was me,* he reminded her.

"Yes."

Amun gripped her hips, urged her forward and rubbed against her. *Then you are cheating on me by staying true to him.*

She moaned, her eyelids drifting to half-mast. When he forced her to steady, she nibbled on her bottom lip, white teeth sinking deep. "Maybe I am, but there's still a note of dishonesty there. So, no sex. Not until I tell him we're over. But…"

But Amun could kiss her, she was saying. The rage returned full-force. *Kissing is a form of cheating, Haidee.* He knew how he would react if he caught her kissing another man. Blood would flow.

Her shoulders sagged, her expression suddenly tortured. "You're right. I'm sorry. I know you're right. You just make me so…hot. We'll stop, then. For good. Until—just until."

*Break up with him in your mind. Now.*

"In my heart and in my mind, he and I are done already. But I have to tell him, Amun. He deserves to know. I know you won't believe me, but he's a good man."

Amun had just realized he would do anything to protect this woman, even give up life as he knew it, simply to be with her. Yet she couldn't let go of an old boyfriend for him. Not completely. While part of him admired such loyalty, the other part wanted that loyalty directed only at himself.

No sex, she'd said, and now, because of what he'd said, no kissing, either. Well, then, by the gods, he would do everything else. Scowling, he caught her by the back of her knees and jerked, tossing her to her back. She landed on the flower petals, their softness cushioning the blow. Before she could suck in a breath, he was atop her, shoving her legs apart and fitting himself against her.

*Don't cheat me, Haidee. Don't cheat me. Please.*

She groaned, as if in pain, and then she settled.

"I—I—maybe I'm a terrible person, but I need you to kiss me. Please."

*Not terrible. Perfect.* In that moment, he found he could deny her nothing. So, kiss her? Yes, even though he'd thought to balance the scale. Their mouths met in a frenzied tangle, licking, sucking, biting. As promised, she kept her temperature under control. Still cold, but never freezing. How she did so, he didn't know. And he didn't like that she couldn't let go completely, that she had to remain guarded.

When this was over, he vowed, when he'd gotten rid of the demons inside him, he would have her. All of her. The cold and every inch of her luscious body. Even her heart. He would shield his own, of course—wanting her, needing her, that was fine, but he would be owned by no one—but by gods, he absolutely would have hers.

He unsnapped her jeans and kicked them down her legs…off. She didn't protest, didn't try to stop him. She trusted him not to cross the line she had drawn. Again he found himself torn, liking that she trusted him, hating that she didn't crave more from him despite everything against them, as he did. Hating that she had him addicted to her, but didn't seem to be addicted to him.

Well, he would just have to change that.

Amun kissed and nibbled his way to her breasts and once again laved her nipples. When she was writhing, hips lifting, greedy for a touch, any touch, he worked his way to her navel. There, he tormented her with fleeting, gentle bites while his fingers toyed with the band of her panties, at her waist, around her thighs, but never stroking where she needed him most.

"Amun…baby…please."

Begging now. Good, that was good. What he'd wanted. Yet, his body ached with such unfulfilled desire, he wasn't sure he would live through this encounter. Sweat beaded on his brow, his skin pulled taut and consuming need blistered him inside and out.

*I'm going to taste you again. Take you to the end this time.* Finally he kissed her between her legs, flicking his tongue against the damp fabric of her panties.

Her hips shot up, and she cried out uninhibitedly. "Yes!"

*You're going to give me everything.*

"Ye—no." She undulated, seeking more of his mouth. "I can't."

*I know. But soon.*

"Soon. Yes, soon."

With that promise ringing in his ears, he ripped the material away and feasted on her. At the first true glide of his tongue, she screamed with absolute abandon. He tasted her femininity and those frosted apricots he'd scented the night they met. He'd thought himself on fire before, but this…this burned him alive.

His cock filled to the point of bursting, and he ground himself into the hard floor, pumping as if he were already inside his woman. She tugged at his hair, not to pull him away but to urge him on.

He licked inside her, feeling those tight walls close around his tongue. He sucked and swallowed, laved and flicked at her clitoris. Soon she wasn't just writhing, she was making love to his mouth, moving against him, legs finding their way to his shoulders, heels digging into his back.

*Hands over your head,* he commanded, and he was immensely glad he could speak into her mind, that he didn't have to stop what he was doing.

"Wh-why?"

*Do it.*

Hesitantly she released him and drew her arms high.

*Clasp the rock behind you.*

This time she obeyed without question.

*Don't let go.* He grabbed her thighs, lifted, and twisted her so that she faced the ground. Twisted himself, too, ramming himself beneath her, but still between her legs. Her body fell back on him, her core directly over his face. Her grip on the rock kept her from smashing face-first into the petals, but didn't save her from the increase of pressure his mouth caused as his tongue sank deeper than before.

"Oh, God. Amun!" Tremors rocked her, vibrating into him.

*So wet. So perfect.*

"Amun. Please, more, need, *want.*"

With one hand, he clasped her hip. With the other, he stroked his cock. And as he worked her, he worked himself, pretending they were making love. She pumped against him, up and down, her essence all over his face, and he matched her with the movement of his hand.

*So damned good.* Had he ever experienced something this good? Impossible.

"Hurry! Have to…almost…need…"

Him. She only needed him. He released her hip and reached under her, never ceasing his carnal attentions. On either of them. Feverish, he impaled her with two fingers.

Tight. She was so tight. And as he slammed those fingers deep, so deep, she convulsed around him, pulling him even deeper.

"There!" she shouted, the climax razing her voice as every muscle she possessed clamped down, trying to hold him inside.

Feeling her spasm around him sent him over the edge. He erupted, hot seed jetting onto his stomach. And when the last of the shudders left her, when the last drop of come was squeezed from him, she rose on her knees, panting, severing that intimate contact. They moaned in unison at the loss.

She scooted down his chest and collapsed atop him. Though his first thought was to clean them both, he couldn't bring himself to move her. His arms wound around her, and he held on, knowing he would never be able to let her go.

His head was (somewhat) clear, so he couldn't blame desire for the possessiveness. She was his. Now... always.

# CHAPTER SEVENTEEN

FOR HOURS, HAIDEE AND AMUN alternated between sleeping, eating, kissing and talking, careful not to mention their pasts, their circumstances or their future. They were just a man and a woman, their hands never far from each other. Through it all, Haidee remained in a state of bliss, joyful in a way she knew she couldn't afford.

For her, joy never lasted.

This joyful stretch ended when Amun released her to build a campfire—and didn't return to her side. He fiddled with the backpack, then pulled out two robes, his motions rigid.

*Angel robes,* he said (just as rigidly). Without looking back at her, he placed the white one at her side. *The material will clean you. It'll even untangle your hair when you lift the hood.*

A simple robe could do all that? Wow. "Thank you."

*Welcome,* he said as he tugged the material over his head. And damn if the dirt smudges on the back of his neck didn't disappear. *Now, we do what needs doing.*

"You mean, now we play the quiet game?"

*Among other things.*

This formality…how she hated it.

He had given her the sweetest, most agonizing orgasm of her life, playing her body in a way that conquered all doubt, all inhibition. Passion had filled her so inexorably, she hadn't been able to hold it all inside. She had erupted, barely managing to temper the ice. Her body was now so hyperaware of this man that the ache, the need for him, never left her. Constantly her stomach quivered and her skin tingled.

His name might not be tattooed on her arm, but she was nonetheless branded by him.

While they'd touched, there'd been no hesitation on his part. That had astonished her. He hadn't withheld pleasure, hadn't whisked her to the brink and walked away, leaving her empty, hollowed. Even though he'd been angry with her. No, he'd been almost…reverent as he'd caressed her, as if they were lovers in every sense of the word rather than enemies.

She didn't want to be his enemy. Not now, not ever again. But she could think of no way to repair the damage she'd done to him. He hadn't killed her family, another demon had. He wasn't the one who had killed her husband, she was almost positive of that. Another demon must have. Probably one of his friends. Still, it was Amun she had punished, taking someone he loved from him.

She hated herself for that. Wished she could go back. Wished she had never walked into her husband's bedroom that fateful night. The night everything had changed for her. But she couldn't and she had, and she hoped that maybe, just maybe, she could make Amun understand the pain she had experienced. That wouldn't be enough to earn his forgiveness, but perhaps it would offer an absolution she wouldn't find otherwise.

Sighing, Haidee donned the robe. Only a few seconds later, she realized Amun hadn't done the thing justice. A bar of soap hadn't touched her, but as the material settled over her, she'd never felt cleaner. Amazing!

Her gaze returned to him. He was peering into the flames. He should have looked like a monk, but even draped by the shapeless cloth as he was, he looked wicked and sensual and so damn powerful.

He'd mentally distanced himself, but she didn't let that stop her. She settled in front of him, trying not to tremble. He didn't spare her a glance, but reached inside the backpack and withdrew an apricot.

"I'd like you to do something for me," she said. "Think of it as an extension of the quiet game."

He had been in the process of biting into the fruit. His hand stilled and at last he faced her, his dark eyes wary. *Can it wait? We've been here too long. We need to leave.*

Suddenly he was in a hurry? Hardly. "No. We have to do this now." If they waited, she might lose her nerve.

He nodded stiffly. *Very well.*

Haidee squared her shoulders and lifted her chin. "You've seen a small piece of my wedding night. Will you…will you now watch the rest?"

His wariness intensified, and it was almost painful to see. *I can't control what secrets the demon shows me, Haidee.*

"But you can try." He had to try.

*I don't think you're understanding me. To show you* anything, *I would have to use my demon.*

"Yes, I do understand that. I'd still like you to try."

He studied her. *May I ask why?*

So polite, when he still clearly wanted no part of this. Did he fear she planned to show him a time she'd spent in another man's bed? Did he think she planned to punish him for being what he was? "You can ask, but I won't tell you." She didn't want him refusing, and he would if he knew the truth going in.

Probably not a smart move on her part, though. He would have to trust her. Blind trust, at that. Something a Lord could never give a Hunter.

A sigh wafted through her mind. *All right. I will try.*

The acquiescence surprised her, and for some reason, that surprise seemed to irritate him.

*Are you ready?* he snapped.

"Yes." No. Butterflies danced through her stomach. "Yes," she repeated for her own benefit.

Motions stiff, Amun set the juicy apricot aside and fit his strong, callused hands against her temples. As always, he was as warm and welcome as a summer day. But now that she'd had those big hands on her breasts, between her legs, inside her, having them placed so innocently was the most decadent of tortures.

She wiggled to get closer to him, settling only when their knees were touching, his wild scent surrounding her. If he did indeed tap into her memory, he would see one of the most painful experiences of her too-long life. A recollection that never failed to tear her up and leave her broken heart bleeding. She would need his strength.

*Concentrate on your breathing,* he said, and she jumped at the gentle intrusion in her mind. *And close your eyes.*

Every friend she had would have called her stupid for trusting a demon like she was about to do, but she didn't care. Amun had given her the necessary blind trust, she could do no less. Her eyelids fluttered closed, hiding the features she'd come to crave, and she drew in a large quantity of oxygen. Slowly she released every molecule.

*Good girl.*

On her next inhalation, she felt tendrils of something... warm and dark drifting through her, rattling her mind as the wind often rattled the leaves on trees. She had experienced this before, but she'd been drugged, lethargic, and unaware of what that warmth and darkness represented. Now she knew—and tried not to panic.

She had asked for this. She wanted this.

But she didn't stay calm for long.

*Demon,* she thought wildly. Her heart crashed into her ribs, threatening to burst from her chest.

Blindly she reached up and wrapped her fingers around the solid warmth of Amun's wrists. In and out she continued to breathe. She held on as tightly as she could, not to push him away, but to remind herself that he was with her. That he wouldn't let his beastly half hurt her.

And, to be honest, the demon had never really tried. Actually, the demon had *helped* her, revealing her sister's beautiful face, showing her the joyous minutes before her husband's death. Why had the creature done that? Why had it shown her *good* things? Weren't evil beings supposed to focus on the bad?

Though she couldn't fathom the answers, she relaxed. And as the rigidity melted from her spine, colorful images began to flash through her mind.

Once again she saw her little sister's cherubic face, smiling back at her as they raced through a lush meadow. Innocent, carefree giggles echoed between them, and for a moment, only a moment, the cold completely washed from Haidee's body, leaving her drenched in radiant heat.

The image shifted—*come back!* she mentally shouted, not yet ready to be separated from her sister again. But then she saw the adult version of herself standing on that long-ago veranda, lavender wedding gown draping her slender frame, her golden curls practically glowing in the moonlight.

This was it. What she wanted to show Amun—what she dreaded showing Amun.

"Are you nervous, my sweet?" her former servant said, pulling her back into the vision.

Haidee watched herself turn, heard herself reply to Leora. A conversation followed, dragging into eternity. When would they quiet? When would they—?

The old woman pivoted on her sandaled heel and led

Haidee inside a torch-lit hallway. Toward the master's bedchamber.

This was it, she thought again. Haidee's grip tightened on Amun, tremors rocking her. Just as before, the arching doorway loomed closer...closer still...only this time, she didn't try to stop herself.

Closer...

As Leora slowed, she smiled over her shoulder. Finally they reached the door, and the servant stepped aside.

Haidee wanted to vomit as she saw herself reach out. Saw her fingers curl around the edge of the curtain and move the material aside. Her shoulders squared as she stepped inside the chamber, the curtain falling back into place behind her.

At first, the Haidee in the vision couldn't make sense of what she was seeing. But the smell, oh, God, the smell... metallic, coppery...mixed with the stench of emptied bowels. She knew that smell very well: death.

Once white walls were splattered with crimson. On the floor, her husband lay in pieces. Hysteria bubbled inside her as she spun. The carnage—there was no escaping it. Solon...a piece here, a piece there, a piece everywhere. The words filled her mind, her encroaching madness making them a song. Her knees knocked together, and dizziness nearly drowned her. Frigid breath sawed in and out of her nose, uncontrollable now.

Then she saw something far worse than the carnage.

In the center of the room, the creature from her nightmares floated above a coagulated puddle of blood. Just as before, the black hood was drawn over his face, shielding his features. But in the midst of the shadows, she could see the glowing red of his eyes.

Slowly he lifted one arm, a single gnarled finger extended in her direction. Rage pulsed from him, so much rage, enveloping her in malevolence. Hate followed. So much hate.

The eeriness of his presence jolted her out of her quiet horror, and she screamed. Screamed and screamed and screamed. She couldn't stop herself, even though each new wail scraped her throat raw. She pressed her palms over her ears. That didn't help. Still the screaming ravaged her.

The creature floated toward her, and she at last quieted. So close…almost upon her…she scrambled backward until she hit the wall. Just before he reached her, several black-clad men stormed from the terrace and into the room, their weapons raised.

"There!" one of the men cried.

"He was right! The demon's here!"

Demon? He? How had "he" known?

They pounded toward her nightmare, blades raised, ready to hack him into bits, just as he'd done to her husband. Oh, God. Her husband. Maybe the creature hadn't killed him after all, because there were others just like him in the room, and now they exited the shadows, their eyes glowing bright red.

The creature disappeared before either the humans or the others could reach him.

Beside her, the curtain swished open. Haidee's knees gave out as Leora and the guards that Solon had ordered to remain nearby stormed inside. There were so many of them, and in their haste to discover what had happened, they failed to see her. She was kicked forward, Solon's blood soaking her beautiful gown.

The guards attacked the men from the terrace *and* the shadows, clearly blaming them all for their master's murder. Metal whistled through air, swords clanged together, skin *popped* as it ripped and men grunted in pain. Then *another* set of warriors flew into the room. They, too, came from the terrace. They must have scaled the side of the house. They were far bigger and more muscled than any of the others—and their eyes glowed that same shade of evil-red as every one of Solon's possible killers.

"More demons!" someone shouted.

"These must have followed us!"

"Hunters," one of the new warriors growled, the word somehow echoing with a thousand other voices. Each of them tormented. "Die. Will die."

A new battle began, this one a macabre dance of glinting silver and sharpened claws, and body after body fell around her. Even the aged, defenseless Leora was struck down, a dagger protruding from her chest. There were more grunts, many agonized moans and brutalized screams, each blending with the renewal of her own. She couldn't breathe, had to breathe. Had to escape.

More servants and guards rushed into the room, but they, too, quickly became victims of the bloody battle. Breathe, breathe. Haidee tried to scramble away, to hide, but the floor was so slippery, blocked by all the fallen, and she gained no ground. And then someone fisted the back of her robe and dragged her to her feet. Oh, God. This was it, the end.

In reality, Haidee braced herself, knowing what came next. She tried to distance herself from the scene, to pretend she was only watching a movie. That the people dying around her were actors, that their pain was faked.

That's when the scene slowed, and, through Amun and his demon, she was able to see things she'd never noticed before. Suddenly, the players had names, faces she recognized. There was Strider—Defeat—lost to his demon and slashing at a Hunter. There was Lucien—Death—his mismatched eyes colder than the ice storm inside her.

She'd seen pictures of him over the years, and knew he was now scarred. But he wasn't scarred as he fought with lethal menace, and his beauty was breathtaking. Or would have been, if someone else's blood hadn't dripped from his mouth. He'd just ripped a man's throat out with his teeth.

Sabin, Kane, Cameo. Gideon, Paris, Maddox. Reyes. Baden, his red hair actually crackling with living flames. Aeron, his black wings outstretched, the ends as sharp as daggers. All but Torin and Amun were there. No, not true, she realized as her gaze caught on the man who had grabbed her robe.

Amun. Amun held her.

So dark, wild in a way she had never seen him before. His eyes, like twin rubies plucked from the fires of hell. His lips, etched into a permanent scowl. His teeth, sharp and white and almost…monstrous. His cheekbones were sliced open, bone revealed.

He had one arm anchored around her waist, preventing her from bolting. Not that she could have. Her muscles were paralyzed with fear. Even as a Hunter leapt toward them, sword raised.

Amun swung her behind him—and a sword that had been arcing toward him cut her from one side of her throat to the other. A scream of agony gurgled from her as her legs gave out. But she didn't drop to the floor; Amun still held her. He turned then, and the real Haidee registered the glint of shock that suddenly consumed his features as he saw what had happened to her.

She'd always thought the man holding her had used her as a human shield, but just then, she realized he'd tried to save her. Even then. Even lost to his demon.

In the vision, she sagged from his now-loosened grip, her world going dark.

That was the first time she died.

But even then, the vision didn't fade. Amun's memory must have picked up where hers had left off, because the fight continued around her lifeless body. She watched as an enraged Amun stepped over her and ripped into the man who had killed her, tearing him from limb to limb, just as Solon had been torn.

Amun made sure the rending *hurt*. The Hunter screamed with every new slice, horrified pleas for mercy. But mercy wasn't something anyone in that room would experience. And because Amun was distracted by his task, another Hunter managed to sneak up on him and make a play for his head.

Fast as he dodged, the blade merely cut into his neck, nicking him. With a roar, he spun around, arm rising to bat the offender away. The Hunter had already repositioned himself, however, and slashed once again. This time, the blade struck true, hitting spine, and Amun's throat opened up all the way.

Blood poured, and he collapsed, his body beside hers. They were facing each other, and his blood mingled with hers, pooling between them, soaking into their wounds.

Binding them, from that moment on?

Seeing their friend down, the other Lords became all the more enraged—and all the more vicious. The remaining Hunters and guards were soon felled in the most savage massacre she'd ever witnessed. And when it was over, the warriors panting, sweating, but far from calm, they gathered Amun and dragged him from the chamber, the home.

Finally the vision faded and Haidee's mind catapulted back to the present. She was still seated in front of Amun, but ice had crystallized over her skin. Either he hadn't noticed, or hadn't cared, because his hands were still flattened against her temples, the only bit of heat she felt.

With a moan, he severed contact, tiny ice crystals flying in every direction. His expression was tormented, and his eyes sparkled with red. Strangely, seeing the red didn't scare her. Even with the memory of what had happened so long ago still playing through her head.

*I'm so sorry, Haidee. So sorry.* His voice was as tormented as his expression.

"Why?" The single word scraped her raw throat, her voice hoarse and broken. Had she screamed during the vision and just hadn't realized it? "You did nothing wrong." She knew that now. Was amazed by it. He'd done everything *right*.

*The Hunters must have been chasing the other demon. And I don't know if the robed creature killed your husband or if it was one of the Lords who reached the bedroom first. All I know is that I was part of the group that arrived last. I wasn't trying to hurt you,* he rushed out. *I swear to the gods I wasn't.*

"I know. Now." Just as she knew he had almost died for her, avenging a veritable stranger. God, she'd wanted to absolve herself with the memory. She'd only managed to weaken her case.

She had destroyed this man for nothing. For nothing!

*I never saw your face that night. I saw a frightened female and tried to move her—you—from the battle. But I put you in the middle of it instead. You wouldn't have died if I'd left you on the floor.*

He would not feel guilty about that. She wouldn't let him. "You don't know what would have happened to me, Amun. You can't—"

*Don't try to make me feel better. Don't try to comfort me. Gods, I don't deserve it. Don't even deserve to be here with you. You, helping me. Me. The man who placed you in the path of a blade.* A bitter laugh left him as he flexed and unflexed his hands. *All these centuries, I've never understood why the others allowed themselves to be filled with remorse over actions they hadn't been able to control. Meanwhile, I'm the worst offender of the lot.*

*Because of me, you died. Because of me, you came after Baden.*

That was not the reaction she'd expected or wanted. "Amun, I—"

He tore his gaze from her and pushed to a stand. *If you want me to summon the angel, I'll find a way to do so. He can return you to your...friends. You don't have to do this. Don't have to help me.*

"I'm not leaving you," she told him, angry now. "And you saw for yourself that you weren't the one who killed me. You tried to save me. More than that, I blamed you when I—"

*You blamed me, and rightly so!* He swiped up the backpack, commanded it to provide clean clothes for both of them and then tossed her a shirt and jeans. *The robes are good for the caves, but not for movement. You need to change. We're leaving.*

"Listen to me. I wrongly blamed you and—"

*We're done discussing this. Change. Now.*

He'd never, ever treated her like this, even when they'd first discovered who the other was, and she had no idea how to reach him, how to make him understand. Shaking, Haidee removed the robe and tugged on the new clothing. "We—we can't leave yet. Not until we know what we'll be facing." She claimed the backpack and said, "Give us instructions for successfully navigating the next realm."

When she reached inside, she found a small, yellowed scroll.

Without a word, Amun took the backpack and settled the straps over his shoulders. With every second that passed, he seemed even more removed from her, and still she didn't understand. She didn't blame him for what had happened, so why did he blame himself?

Because he'd failed? Because he feared failing again?

"Amun," she said, trying again to reach him. She *had* to reach him.

*Come,* he replied, striding from the cave, forcing her to follow or be left behind.

The scroll crinkled as she unwittingly tightened her grip. "I'm not going to let you shut me out," she said, knowing he couldn't hear her but feeling better just saying the words.

She forced herself to relax and trail after her man—and he was her man, there was no question of that now—as he headed into the unknown.

## CHAPTER EIGHTEEN

VACATION SUCKED. Strider sat in the passenger seat of the caddy William had stolen, peering out at the barren landscape and waning sunlight. This was the road trip from hell.

After the debacle with the invisible girl, who just had to be Paris's obsession, Sienna, Paris had flipped his ever-loving lid and attacked William for not preventing the god king from leaving with her. It had taken all of Strider's strength—and a dagger through his friend's broken heart—to defeat the hysterical warrior.

Afterward, bleeding and far from calm, Paris kicked Strider and William off his ranch, along with the strippers. But Paris had soon realized Sienna could escape Cronus again and return to him, and without William, he wouldn't be able to see her. So, the injured Paris had tracked them down and insisted on coming with them. Not a difficult task since they'd merely hiked to the mailbox at the end of his driveway and decided to rest. For a few hours.

Ambrosia hangovers sucked as much as vacations.

They'd been on the open road for countless hours, and for most of those hours Paris had shouted for Cronus, issuing threats and generally annoying the hell out of everyone. Finally, though, he'd quieted and now slept fitfully in the back seat, blood loss having drained him. Just before falling asleep, he'd vowed to call Lucien and demand the keeper of Death flash him to the heavens when his injuries healed.

Paris was going hunting for his female.

That kind of obsessive desire for one specific woman wasn't smart, and Strider acknowledged that he himself had been speeding in that direction with Ex. Unlike Paris, he had willingly given the woman up, and suddenly, he was grateful. Had he continued down that path, he eventually would have fought Amun for her.

Fighting a friend for a woman was the epitome of stupid. Wrong on every level.

One, he valued his friendships. Two, no woman was worth the trouble she caused when he knew he would one day lose interest in her. Three, a Hunter *really* wasn't worth the trouble she caused. Four, sex was sex. A man could get it anywhere, as proven by his time at Paris's ranch.

He sighed and concentrated on the shitty scenery. Trees. Rolling hills. And—oh, hells yeah. A convenience store, dead ahead.

"Pull over," he commanded.

"What?" William flicked him a now's-not-the-time-to-joke glance. "We just got a little peace and quiet and you want to ruin it all just to piss? You're *such* a baby."

"Red Hots, dude." He'd ruin *anything* for a mouthful of those. "Now pull the fuck over."

"Oh, Gummy Bears. You should have said so."

The car merged right, hit the service road and finally halted abruptly in front of the twenty-four-hour shop. Burly truckers hustled in and out, as well as families traveling the countryside.

William jerked a thumb toward the backseat. "What about sleeping beauty?"

"He's not gonna kill himself while we're gone."

"Do you have *any* self-preservation instincts?" Ice-blue eyes glittered with sardonic humor. "I meant, what if he wakes up, steals our car and abandons us?"

"Easy. We steal a truck and play chase. I've always wanted to drive a big rig."

"I like where your head's at, Stridey-Man. Maybe we'll do that anyway."

Out of habit, Strider performed a perimeter check before exiting. During the drive, when he hadn't been lost in thought, he'd been watching for a tail. So far, so good. Not once had he spied anything suspicious. To be honest, that was kind of disappointing. He'd expected Haidee's boyfriend to come after him. Shit, the guy had sworn to spill Strider's guts and remove each of his limbs. Oh, well.

He and William entered the store side by side, then split up. They still wore their swim trunks, but they also wore T-shirts and flipflops, so they weren't totally inappropriate as they strutted down the isles, grabbing what they wanted. Still. People stared. Maybe because they were giants compared to everyone else, both in height and muscle mass. Maybe because of the telltale bulge of weapons at their waists. Or maybe because William opened a bag of Doritos and ate while he shopped. Hard to tell.

"You see any Gummy Bears?" William called.

Strider balanced five boxes of Red Hots and five boxes of Hot Tamales in the cradle of one arm as he scanned the racks. "Nope. Sorry." He grabbed a few Twinkies for Paris and threw them on top of his pile. They weren't fried, but hell. Women ate sweets when they were nursing broken hearts, and Paris was definitely acting like a woman. Guy would be grateful for anything.

Strider was snickering to himself as he mixed a suicide at the soda fountain. Paris, acting like a woman. What was new about that? When the fizzing liquid reached the rim, he popped the lid and straw in place. Hard to do one-handed, but he managed it. He sipped. *Nice.*

Behind him, gasps resonated. He whipped around, expecting trouble with William—only to spy a scowling

Lucien with his hand resting on the shoulder of a stunning redhead. She was a tiny little thing, only reaching his
shoulder, but damn was she curved. Her breasts strained
the lacy tank. Her waist flared around low-rise jeans.
*Really* low-rise. So low it was obvious she wasn't wearing any panties. She couldn't be. Her legs were lean and
long enough to lock around his back.

He wanted to curse.

"Kaia?" Strider blinked, certain this was only a nightmare. A Harpy, the deadliest race on the planet. Here.
Stinking up his vacation even more. And he'd thought the
night couldn't get any worse.

"Oh, yummy. A Big Gulp." She closed what little distance there was between them and jerked the cup from his
kung fu grip. Then, without waiting for his permission,
she slurped the contents. "Thanks."

*Not a challenge, not a damn challenge,* he told his
demon.

Still. Defeat perked up inside his head. Thank the gods
the beast didn't urge him to act. Yet.

Kaia's features wrinkled with distaste. "Yuck! What is
this stuff? Battery acid?"

"It's a little of every kind of soda they've got," he gritted, reaching out his free hand and waving his fingers.
"Now give it back and tell me what you're doing here."

Her sensuous lips pulled back from her teeth as she
hissed, her gray-gold eyes flickering with incandescent
striations of silver and deep, dark lines of black. "Mine."

*That wasn't a challenge,* he mentally shouted.

Defeat practically twitched against his skull, a wee bit
agitated but still not insisting Strider do anything.

He allowed his arm to fall to his side. Harpies could
only eat what they stole or earned, everything else made
them sick, so he knew she had to take what she could,
when she could. He also knew Harpies were as possessive

about their stuff as he was, and Kaia now considered the drink hers. But if she pushed any more, his demon *would* want him to do something. Strider knew it, felt it. Yet there was no damn way he could challenge a Harpy in front of humans. That was something better done in private— where he could have his ass handed to him without being humiliated in front of others.

"I asked once, but I'll do it again. What are you doing here?" He switched his focus to Lucien before she could reply. "What's she doing here?"

Lucien met his stare and gave a pitying sigh. "She was bored, so she called me and asked me to take her to you, and because I like my testicles where they are, I decided to indulge her."

"Take her to *me?*" Strider thumped his chest to make sure Lucien and Kaia understood who "me" was. "Why me?"

Neither responded to his question.

"My friend, I wish you a good night. She's your pain in the ass now," Lucien said, and after saluting Strider with the same irreverent pinky wave Anya was fond of giving, he strode out of the store to find a nice, deserted corner outside where he could disappear without witnesses.

Strider returned his attention to Kaia. She fluttered her lashes at him, all innocence and feminine wiles. If he hadn't sparred with her a few times in the past, if he hadn't known exactly how dirty she fought, going for the groin at every opportunity, he might have believed the act. Even knowing, he had a hard time convincing himself of her extraordinary ability to deceive.

She was here for a reason, and he wasn't going to like it.

His only consolation was that he liked looking at her. Truly, if the gods had asked him to design a female, Kaia would have been it. She had a deceptively delicate bone structure and long red hair that curled to her waist. She had the face of a wicked pixie, the fangs of a pissed off snake and the body of a porn star, minus the implants. And her skin, oh, gods, her skin.

All Harpies possessed skin like hers. Like polished opals and crushed diamonds, glinting with all the colors of the rainbow. They had to cover every visible inch with cosmetics and clothing because men became slobbering fools whenever they saw that skin. Strider had caught a glimpse only once—during one of their practice sessions, her shirt had ridden up to her navel—and he'd instantly lost control of his body. He'd become consumed by the need to penetrate her.

She'd covered herself before he had attacked, and the urge had passed. Eventually. Even then, remembering, he wanted to strip her, take her.

No way. No way in hell. She might be the loveliest female he'd ever beheld, but she would be more trouble than a Hunter. She was a consummate liar and an unrepentant thief. She killed indiscriminately, and well, she was stronger than him. Talk about embarrassing!

Plus, the first time she had visited her sister Gwen at the fortress, Strider had noticed several of the warriors eyeing her as if she were a lollipop. She hadn't seemed to notice or care, and he hadn't wanted to compete for her affections. He'd made the right decision, too.

He still couldn't believe she'd slept with Paris.

Paris. Ah, okay. Her need to find "Strider" was beginning to make a little sense. He was with Paris, so what better way to spend time with the warrior without admitting what she really wanted?

That didn't bother Strider, but damn it all to hell, he didn't like being used. "If you're here to win Paris's everlasting love, you've already failed. He now knows beyond any doubt that Sienna is still out there, and he's desperate to reach her. You're not going to make him jealous by cuddling up to me and you're not—"

"Will you just shut up?" Kaia snatched a box of Red Hots and popped open the lid.

He snatched it back before she could eat a single one, and Defeat purred with satisfaction.

"Hey!"

"Mine," he snapped. Enough was enough.

Rather than attack him, she merely anchored her free hand on her perfectly shaped hips. "Lookit. I didn't want to kick things off this way, but you're being an asshat. So here it is. Paris was a one-time thing and not just because he can't ever come back for seconds. Yeah, he gave me about a bazillion orgasms, but afterward I didn't like how I felt and I couldn't stop thinking—never mind." She was scowling as she shook her head. "What I'm trying to say is that I'm not here to see him. I wanted to see—"

"Kaia, darling," William said, nearly leaping over a stand of beef jerky in his haste to reach her.

Strider frowned, but he wasn't sure why.

As William pulled her close for a hug, the bastard grinned with utter delight, as if Kaia was just the thing he'd needed to relieve an eternity of boredom. "Are you here to fight the strippers who just enjoyed hours of my company?" He patted her ass in approval.

"Hardly," she said, tossing her glorious mane of hair over her shoulder with a single flip of her wrist. "I'm here to thank them for keeping you occupied. Please tell me they're still with you."

William pretended to wipe away a tear. "Knife through the heart, my sweet. Knife through the heart."

Gods, they were annoying. William had been trying to get into Kaia's pants for months. She, of course, liked to string him along.

Which was another reason Strider would never make a play for her.

Kaia would challenge him more than most, and she wouldn't care if he lost. Hell, she would *want* him to lose, even though the loss would bring him days of physical agony. Her sense of rivalry was just as highly developed as his own.

"We're on vacation, Kaia," Strider grumbled. "You weren't invited."

She waved away his words as if they were unimportant. "Deep down I knew you meant to invite me, so ta-da. Here I am. You're welcome."

"It's scary how well you know us. Here, pay for this," William said, dumping his candy into Strider's arms. "We'll be in the car. Making out."

At first, Kaia remained in place, watching Strider. Whatever she wanted from him, he must not have given to her, because she blew him a kiss and allowed the black-haired warrior to lead her off. Not even trying to hide her actions, she stuffed a Twinkie in the back pocket of her jeans and grabbed a couple magazines before stepping outside.

Strider's jaw ached from the grind of his teeth as he strode to the register. For some reason, people moved out of his way as quickly as possible. Even the ones standing in line, waiting their turn.

"Uh, I wouldn't bring this up, except I kinda have to and everything," the overweight cashier began nervously, "since it's on camera and my boss, like, watches the film sometimes, but, uh, the little lady took a—"

"I know. Just add it all up." After he paid, he stomped outside, the bag filled with candy slapping his thigh with every step. The cool night air failed to dampen his sudden black mood. *At least you're not thinking about Ex now.*

Hardly a silver lining. And one that didn't last. He'd

maybe, *big* maybe, exaggerated his attraction to Ex. If he'd really wanted her, he wouldn't have slept with someone else earlier today. He would have fought for her affections now rather than eventually, no matter how foolish fighting your friends over a woman was.

Look at Paris. Guy needed sex to freaking survive, but he hadn't spent quality sheet time with any of those strippers.

That didn't lessen the sting of being rebuffed, though, and maybe that's why he'd thought he wanted Ex so damn badly. Because she hadn't wanted him. Because she'd been a—what? A challenge. A challenge he claimed he hadn't wanted. And he didn't!

Damn it. No more challenges. He was taking a break if it killed him.

He reached the car, saw that Kaia had stolen his seat in front and practically ripped the back door from its hinges. He climbed inside and settled beside the still sleeping Paris. And what the fuck was that smell? Cinnamon rolls?

He decided to take his irritation out on her. "You wearing perfume?" he growled, kicking her stolen seat so she'd know he was talking to her.

She twisted to peer back at him, a smile clinging to the edges of her I'm-not-wearing-any-panties mouth. He'd known she wasn't wearing any, the little teaser, but he hadn't needed that kind of confirmation.

*Dude. It's a smile, not a glance up a skirt.*

*Oh, shut up.*

He was talking to himself now. Wasn't that just great? "Well?"

"Nope, no perfume, but I did visit a bakery just before I hunted Lucien down. Why? Do I smell as sweet as sugar?"

No, damn it, she smelled like she needed a good licking.

Kaia, in bed. Naked. Splayed. His mind liked the image, and hell, so did his demon. While Strider would rather die than accept another challenge—figuratively speaking, of course—his demon would go insane without them. Beast fed off the high that came with their victories.

But he wasn't going to let himself go there with Kaia. Not today, and not ever. Kaia wouldn't just challenge him more than most; she would challenge him about *every-thing,* and he would never have a moment of peace.

Defeat practically rubbed his hands together in glee.

Strider frowned. *No, no, hell, no. We aren't going there. She's a Harpy. We can't win against her. We'll suffer. Constantly.*

A growl. A whimper. Anger and fear, wrapped tightly together and sprinkled with *Oh, please, gods, no.*

That was more like it. Even if some part of Strider liked the idea of constantly sparring with Kaia, 'cause yeah, matching wits and daggers could be fun and peace was sometimes overrated, he still couldn't allow himself to be with her. Unlike the other warriors, he had never been able to sleep with a woman who had already tasted one of his friends. It was that possessive streak of his. There was simply no way around it.

Although…for Ex, Haidee, he'd been willing to make an exception. Which meant his competitive nature was stronger than his possessiveness. Kaia, though, wouldn't be extended the same willingness.

Defeat gave another growl, this one laced with… disappointment?

No way. *I'm just tired. Imagining things.* His demon only cared about battles, not a specific woman.

Kaia finally gave up on Strider and turned back around. William maneuvered onto the highway, the caddy gobbling up the miles. Of course, he resumed his flirtation with the Harpy.

For a little over an hour, Strider ate his candy and fumed. Yes, vacations sucked. At the next rest stop, he might just ditch his companions and head off on his own. Except, when Kaia giggled at something William said, Strider decided waiting to reach a rest stop was dumb. He'd get out now and hitchhike. That kind of feminine delight was grating to his nerves. Yes, grating. Not enchanting.

He definitely needed distance between him and Kaia. Then he'd stop thinking about her. Stop reacting to her. Stop caring about her past. After all, he'd just gotten out of a bad "relationship" and didn't need to endure another. Plus, that's what had happened the last time he'd left her. He'd left, and all the torment had stopped. Granted, his reactions hadn't been quite as strong back then, but there was no reason to think this time would be any different.

"So where are we going?" Kaia asked no one in particular.

"Nowhere," Strider replied.

"To kill Gilly's family," William answered easily.

Strider needed to have a chat with the man. You didn't undermine your friends. It was worse than cockblocking.

Kaia tossed Strider a shut-your-mouth frown before bouncing in her seat. "Do I get to help? Please! Can I? You may not know this, but I'm very handy with a blade of any kind, a hacksaw, a whip, a—"

"Hey! Someone went through my bag," William said.

"So?" Kaia continued, as if William hadn't spoken. "Whatever the weapon, I'm good with it."

He would not be impressed. "We won't be using weapons. We'll be smashing jugulars."

"Oh, oh! We can play Who Can Smash More!"

"No, we can't because you can't help," Strider said at the same time William blurted out, "I'd be disappointed if you didn't help."

Kaia hmphed at him.

"Just try not to destroy the entire neighborhood," he snapped. Nobody listened to him anymore.

Slitted eyes returned to him. There was no hint of black in the whites, so he knew her Harpy was under control. "Why are you so grouchy?"

"I'm not grouchy. Only women are grouchy."

"You're grouchy," William said.

*"You're* grouchy," Strider said. Realizing he sounded like a child, he leaned forward and propped his elbows on his knees, his face in his upraised hands. What the hell was wrong with him?

William snickered at him. Kaia simply continued to watch him, her expression unreadable.

"Well, grouchy or not, Stridey," she said, "I have news that will cheer you up."

Leaning forward had been a dumb move. The scent of cinnamon and sugar was stronger now, enveloping him, making his mouth water. Would Kaia taste as delicious as she smelled?

Suddenly she stiffened. "You smell like a woman's peach-flavored body oil."

Did he? He thought back to the stripper he'd had on his lap at Paris's ranch, and yep, he remembered smelling peaches. Kaia must have hated peaches, though, because she was obviously planning to murder the maker of that oil.

"I. Will. Destroy. You." And yep, black now bled into the white of her eyes. Her nails had already lengthened and sharpened into claws, and those claws were embedded in the plastic console between the driver and passenger seat. Hello, raging beast.

Mental note: never eat peaches in front of Kaia.

*Win?* Defeat said on a trembling breath, the question

having nothing to do with uncertainty this time, and everything to do with being cowed.

Yeah. *Good luck with that, buddy. She'll eat you for lunch and spit out your scales.* "I'll wash, okay." Strider jerked upright, as far away from *her* heavenly aroma as he could get. "And just so you know, I don't care about your news."

"I cannot kill him," she muttered to herself. "I cannot kill him. I promised Bianka I'd stop at ten bodies a day, and I've already surpassed my quota for the fifth day in a row. I cannot kill him."

As far as pep talks went, that one kind of blew. But it calmed her, the black in her eyes fading and those claws receding.

Strider peered out the window, willing to count the trees that whizzed by rather than peer at that too-pretty face. "Now listen up, buttercup. Stri-Stri is going to take a little nappie-poo. Everyone hush their big, fat mouths." Better to be bored pretending to snooze than accidentally piss Kaia off again.

"Fine. Sleep." All kinds of irritation layered her husky voice. She wasn't squawking, though, which was another excellent sign that the danger had passed. "Just know that while you're catching up on your much needed beauty rest, you'll miss my story about how many Hunters I bagged and tagged this week."

"Good." She'd bagged and tagged a few? He tried not to look intrigued, even as he rethought his strategy. "Go ahead and start your story. I'm sure I'll be so bored I'll nod right off."

"No. You've been a bad boy and don't deserve a reward. Therefore, I won't tell you that there's a certain Hunter on your trail and he's closing in."

"Someone always is."

She blew out a frustrated breath. "I also won't tell you—"

He snored as loud as he could, just to be contrary, and almost laughed when she uttered a quiet shriek. Part of him liked this verbal sparring. Liked annoying her and feeling the sparks that nearly sizzled from that petite body.

"That's it! Do you hear me, Strider? That's it! I challenge you to listen to me. Now."

*That* he didn't like.

As his demon jumped up and down in his head, now desperate to win, Strider glared at Kaia, pretty face be damned. And he didn't give a shit if he pissed her off, either. "I knew you'd do this. I knew you'd challenge me. You're just like every other female I've ever known. No, wait. You're worse. You know what happens to me when I lose, but you challenge me anyway."

Hurt flashed over her features, there one moment, gone the next. Surely he was mistaken. Harpies—especially this infuriating Harpy—didn't do hurt. Ever. "You know you can win this."

"So go on, then," he snapped. "Talk. I'm literally dying to hear what you have to say."

Kaia ran the pink tip of her tongue over her teeth, and his stomach clenched in reaction. She could have refused him and sent him to his knees in gut-wrenching pain. Instead, she finished her little speech. "You captured Haidee. Her boyfriend and his followers have been chasing you. There. Done. You listened and won."

He didn't feel like he'd won. And neither did his demon. There was no rush of pleasure, only a need for a *real* challenge. Something he'd have to work for. *I don't wanna work for anything, remember?* Still. Everything inside him froze. His heartbeat, his lungs. The rush of blood in his veins. "There's more. Tell me the rest."

"Fine. Here it is. While you've been playing around,

*I've* been chasing the boyfriend and those followers of his. There's something odd about each of them, by the way, but the boyfriend most of all. They're…I don't know, darker than other humans I've been around. They made me feel…icky, which is why I made them hurt real bad before I disposed of them. You should have seen them. After I took my blade and—"

"You're digressing, Kaia."

"Am not! Now where was I? Oh, yeah. The boyfriend. I couldn't get close enough to him to figure out what bothered me. He's dark and wily and like I said, he managed to evade me, which means he's good, very, very good at evading because I'm very, very good at tracking. Did I ever tell you about the time I—"

"Kaia!"

"Anyway, *you* haven't been able to evade *him*. He's close, he's filled with piss and vinegar and he wants to make you his bitch."

"How close is he?"

Her chin lifted stubbornly. "Close enough that you're lucky you weren't shot down inside that little gas station."

Yet she hadn't said anything while they were there. Hadn't given him a chance to set a trap. She'd laughed and stolen food and let him take his time. Then she'd carried on a conversation with William, mile after mile, as if there were no pressing issues. To punish him for not welcoming her to their group, he knew. Harpies were as vindictive as they were destructive.

Most. Frustrating. Female. *Ever.*

His fingers dug into his thighs to keep from strangling her, and he knew he'd have long-lasting bruises. "Why were you following him?"

One delicate shoulder, bared because of the lacy pink top she wore, lifted in a shrug. "When everyone left the fortress, going their separate ways to hide artifacts and stash their women safely away blah, blah, blah, I followed *you*. I figured you'd see the most action, and I was right."

Fuck. He must be losing his touch. He'd never even sensed her.

"You're welcome, by the way," she continued. "You grabbed Haidee and carted her off, but you left a blood trail straight to your motel room door. They were set to raid the entire building when I took all but the leader down. That little bastard escaped, and you should have taken him out when you had the chance, because he gathered more men. I've been hot on his heels ever since."

"You're hot, all right. But seriously, how'd you meet up with Lucien?" William asked, inserting himself into the conversation.

"Anya and I keep in touch. I told her I needed to borrow her gentleman friend and she agreed. For a price," Kaia added with a tinge of anger. "And someone in this car is going to reimburse me."

"Gentleman friend. Nice." William opened his mouth to add something else, probably to tell her he would gladly pay.

Strider beat him to it. "Whatever it was, I'll take care of it." He owed her. He guessed. But he didn't like it, and didn't want to be indebted to anyone.

"Good. Then you owe me a ten-minute Frencher."

He blinked, certain he'd misheard. He'd expected Hunter hearts or severed limbs. "Anya made you *kiss* her?"

"Yeah. And at our next stop, I'll expect you to deliver."

"I'll pay," William piped up. "After you describe everything about that kiss you two shared. Did you cop a feel? You did, didn't you, you little hussy. I bet you moaned a lot, too."

"Too late for you to pay," she said in a sing-song voice. "Strider already offered, and I already accepted. And no, I won't do any describing. You can just imagine how sexy it was. Oh, and Willie. Just so you know, your imagination won't do it justice."

She was lying. She had to be lying. But why would she lie about a kiss? What could she possibly hope to gain by forcing him to kiss her? Strider leaned back in his seat and stared up at the roof. No answers were forthcoming, and he doubted they ever would be.

Besides, he had more pressing matters to deal with. Like Haidee's psycho boyfriend. How close was the son of a bitch?

*Win,* Defeat said inside his head. *Win, win.* It wasn't a question this time. On any level.

Great. The boyfriend wasn't even here, but the challenge had been heard, accepted and must now be met.

"Pull over," he told William for the second time that night.

"Why? There's no store."

Kaia flicked Strider another glance and grinned. "Now there's the demon warrior I've come to know and love. He wants to set a trap, Willie, and we're going to help him."

"Nope. I'm getting out and doing this solo," Strider announced. William had people of his own to kill, and Strider didn't want to spend any more time with Kaia than necessary.

Her grin remained in place, though the edges darkened with an emotion he couldn't name. "Oh, really? Well, I seem to recall you telling me I'm worse than a stomach virus, and I think it's time I proved that. I'm challenging you to let me help you, Strider. I'm challenging you to hurt the bastard more than I do, and I'm challenging you to kill more of his men than I do."

*Fuck!* he thought, even as his demon started jumping around again. Nervous, excited. Okay, mostly nervous.

*Win, win, win. Please, win.*

Suddenly hating Kaia with every fiber of his being, Strider gave her a stiff nod. Game on, then. "When this is over," he said softly, "I will make you pay."

"I know," she replied, and her tone was oddly subdued. "Believe me, I know."

# CHAPTER NINETEEN

THOUGH TWO DAYS OF WALKING and monotony had passed since they'd left their cave, and all Amun had been able to do was think and guard Haidee the few times he'd allowed her to stop and rest, he hadn't come to grips with what he'd once done to her. Or what had driven her to hate him and his friends, hate that led her to aid in Baden's destruction. No matter how good Amun's intentions had been, he'd still flung her right into an attacker's blade.

Gods. The blood pouring from her...the agony in her expression...

His friends only remembered bits and pieces of their time in ancient Greece. They knew they'd burned, pillaged and destroyed, but not specifics. Like who and what. Amun, however, recalled every detail. Or rather, Secrets wouldn't allow him to forget. Mysteries of that nature weren't ever allowed to remain unsolved, even within himself.

Very clearly Amun remembered the rage he'd felt as he had followed the Hunters to the nobleman's home. They'd had a particularly violent battle earlier that morning, before the Hunters had cut their losses and retreated. Having none of that, Amun and the others had followed them. The warriors had been sliced, diced and bleeding, and they'd been determined to annihilate those responsible.

What he hadn't pieced together then—the information lost in the tangle of everything else—but what he determined now, was that they'd been herded, purposely led into that house. Not by the Hunters, but by the "he" who pulled their strings. Not the robed being Haidee had seen, but the "he" the Hunters had mentioned when they'd spotted the creature. "He" had known a demon would be there. "He" had wanted everyone inside that room to be slaughtered. Even his own people.

Galen, even then? Or the man who had "rescued" little Haidee and taught her to blame the Lords for her parents' deaths? The Bad Man? Amun might never know, and really, just then, he didn't care. No one's actions had been as despicable as his own.

He didn't deserve the woman behind him, the woman trudging without complaint through cavern after cavern simply to save him. He was responsible for the danger she now found herself in. He might be the cause of her next death.

A death she feared with every ounce of her being. Terror had filled those pearl-gray eyes when she'd spoken of her rebirths. Terror and residual pain, as if even speaking of the events had lanced her with an agony few in the world could even understand. She deserved peace and happiness, a family to cherish her.

Everything she'd ever loved had been taken from her. While his mind had been merged with hers, he'd sensed thousands of hidden memories—the memories she thought had been wiped. They were buried deep, secrets even from herself. His demon had reacted rapturously and now viewed her head as the Holy Grail. Secrets wanted back inside. Amun wanted back on top of her strong little body.

But he wouldn't touch her again, wouldn't deepen the already sizzling awareness between them. Because…damn it! He hated this line of thought, but he didn't allow himself to back away from it. This was part of his penance. He wouldn't touch her again because he was going to give her back to Micah.

Amun's fingers tightened around the blade hilts he held in both hands, and red dots flickered through his vision. Haidee wouldn't come to hate herself for being with Micah, a Hunter. She wouldn't wallow in guilt she shouldn't feel. She wouldn't lose the life she'd managed to build for herself.

With Amun, she *would* come to hate herself. How could she not? Giving herself to a Lord had to top her list of Things Never To Do. She *would* wallow in guilt, berating herself for choosing the very evil she'd fought against for so long. And she *would* lose the life she'd built. No way she could be with him and not cut ties with his enemy.

She must have sensed, or heard, the direction of his thoughts because she sighed, her cool breath wafting down his back. He'd removed his shirt, the heat too much, sweat constantly trickling over his flesh. If Haidee hadn't been with him, that wonderfully cool breeze wafting from her, enveloping him, he might have actually burst into flames.

"Can we talk now?" she said. "About what happened?"

Amun was willing to do anything she wanted. Except that. If he told her of his guilt, his regret, she would do everything in her power to ease him. No matter what she did, she would only increase his guilt, because she would be acting against her nature. The woman could nurse a grudge as stubbornly as his friends. Except with Amun. Him, she wanted to forgive. Him, she wanted to absolve. Him, she wanted to…love. He'd sensed the need inside her.

Because of the blood bond they shared?

"Amun?"

*No.*

"So stubborn," she said, *tsking* under her tongue. "Fine. Let's talk about something else, then."

*No.*

"Please."

As strong as he was, he was helpless against that word. *Very well. What do you wish to discuss?*

"You know some of my secrets, but I don't know any of yours. Will you tell me something that no one else knows about you?"

Had his friends heard that question, they would have rolled their eyes and snorted, certain Haidee was playing Bait, trying to learn everything she could about him to share with the Hunters. And they would have shaken Amun had they realized he planned to answer anyway. That he actually trusted her.

Her, the only person in the world his demon couldn't read automatically. Her, the only person in the world who could read him.

*Point me in the right direction. What type of secret would you like?*

She inhaled sharply, as if she hadn't expected him to respond. Then she expelled the breath with a torturous slowness that caused the sweat on his back to freeze. Rather than numb him, that ice reminded him of her touch, and his shaft twitched in anticipation.

*Perhaps you should increase the distance between us,* he said. He wouldn't turn around, wouldn't look at her to see how she took his request. *Just in case you trip. You don't want to slam into me, do you?*

"If I trip, I need to be *closer* to you. You'd prevent a face-plant."

Logical. Damn it. He increased his pace. So did she. A few minutes ticked by in silence. Sometimes he felt as if he was walking in circles, the cave widening, then narrowing, then widening again, leading up, then down, but never actually taking him anywhere. But there was no other direction to take. This was it.

They snaked a corner, and still Haidee remained silent. Tension bloomed as he considered everything she could ask him. Details about his last lover. His plans for her, the future.

*You have yet to point me in the right direction, Haidee.*

"I'm thinking." Speaking must have distracted her because she tripped, stumbling right into him, her breasts pressing into his back. She huffed. "See? Saved from a face-plant."

The stinging arousal that next consumed him made a mockery of the twitching that had come before. He wanted her to reach around and wrap her fingers around his erection. Stroke him up and down. Perhaps step in front of him, drop to her knees and suck him deep.

Of course, she straightened, ending the contact but not the fantasy.

A moan nearly escaped him. *Don't think like that,* he commanded himself.

"Like what?" she asked, confused.

Gods, he had to be more careful. *Sorry. The command was for myself.*

"Why? What were you thinking about?"

No way he'd tell her. No damn way. *What secret would you like from me?*

A moment passed before she said, "That. I want to know what you were thinking about."

Should have expected that. He could have refused her, but he didn't. She had requested, he had agreed, and he would do as promised. Still. He couldn't speak about what he'd been imagining without begging her to truly do it. *I'll have to show you.* If he could.

"Okay."

When he had lived in the heavens, a minor goddess had performed the act on him, once, only once, and he had loved every moment of it. Sadly, no one had ever done it since. Maybe because he'd never been able to ask for it, and when he'd tried to angle his few lovers into that position, they had resisted. He was big, so he'd understood their reservations and hadn't pressed.

So, before Haidee, the time with the goddess had been the best sexual experience of his life. Just thinking about Haidee sucking his shaft, however, was even better than that.

"I'm waiting," Haidee sang.

And she had called *him* stubborn. *Very well, sweetheart. Just remember, you asked for this.* He pushed the vision out of his mind and into hers, praying it worked.

It worked. She gave another sharp intake of breath, this one shaky around the edges. "Amun," she said on a moan.

A moan of need?

Even as they continued to march forward, her hands slid up his back, then around his sides...playing with his nipples... Her breasts once again smashed into him, but this time her fingers traced a path down...down... *Holy hell.* She would do it, he thought, awed and guilty and so aroused his hunger and need were probably seeping from his skin. She would give him what he wanted, without any hesitation. Right here, right now.

He would have to stop her, couldn't let her—she rubbed his cock through his pants, and his lips parted on a silent groan. He couldn't stop her, would let her—

"I've thought about this, too," she said huskily.

He licked his lips. *You have?*

"Oh, yes. You are a beautiful man, and just looking at you arouses me. You're all I think about anymore. All I crave."

Oh, gods. He was going to spill. She'd done nothing but stroke him, and he was going to spill. *Haidee, I—*

One moment they were surrounded by the rocky walls of the cave, hearing the *drip, drip* of water, the harsh rasp of their breathing, and the next they were encompassed by absolute darkness and utter silence, by sensory deprivation.

"Amun?" Her voice was shaky and soft, but there. Thank the gods, he could still hear her voice. "What just happened?"

They'd entered the Realm of Shadows, he realized, dread joining ranks with his lingering desire. Finally. Progress. Damn the timing, though.

Amun stopped abruptly. Haidee stumbled into him, but his body absorbed the impact. So good, even then. More than hearing her, he could feel her. They weren't so deprived, after all. He reached back to steady her, careful not to let his blade touch her.

"What's going on?" she whispered.

He moved his grip to her wrist and drew her hand to his mouth, pressing a quick kiss into the wild flutter of her pulse. *Do you remember what the scroll said?*

The scroll from the backpack. She'd asked for instructions on how to successfully navigate the next realm, and the backpack had provided them. Only, the instructions had been convoluted and asinine.

*~You must see~*

See through the shadows? Sure. His pleasure. He'd taken the scroll from her as he'd wondered how. A flashlight? Shockingly, the moment the question had formed in his mind, ink had begun dripping over the paper, new words forming.

*~All of you~*

Another convoluted answer. Still. He'd demanded the backpack provide him with a light source that would push through the darkness, but nothing had filled the pack. Which had to mean a flashlight wouldn't work. Which also had to mean the pack could not provide "all of you." And that had to mean he already had "all of you," whatever it was, because the pack was here to help them and wouldn't leave them in the lurch.

He'd then returned his attention to the scroll and demanded to know what awaited them in the shadows if they failed to find the mysterious, *all of you* light. Once again, ink had dripped down the tattered, yellow page.

*~Death~*

Then he'd demanded to know what "all of you" meant.

*~All of you~*

Funny. All of him—his body, perhaps?

"We must see. We must use all of you, or us," Haidee said, words trembling from her and bringing him back to the present. "I still don't know what that means."

Him either, but he didn't tell her that. *Keep your fingers hooked on my belt loop. Whatever happens, we can't be separated.*

"All—all right."

When she complied, removing her free hand from his still burning erection, he released her other one and gingerly started forward. He kept his arms outstretched, hoping to feel his way.

Soon he noticed that as quickly as the darkness had arrived, it was dissipating in spots, leaving little pockets of light. Would have been wonderful, except shadows danced around the light—and those shadows had fangs.

Something sharp sliced into his arm, and he mentally cursed. He shoved Haidee into one of those golden beams, but the beam moved several inches away, returning her to the dark. Something else sliced into his arm. The fangs, he was sure. They must have gotten Haidee, too, because she stiffened, moaned.

Damn this!

*What should I do?* he demanded of his demon, abandoning thoughts about "all of you." They'd gotten him nowhere. As Strider would say, the backpack and scroll could suck it.

At first, Secrets remained silent, still. Sleeping? Now? Or was Amun's other half still beaten to the back of his mind with the others? But the demon must have been searching for answers because suddenly Amun knew to follow the light. The shadows weren't allowed to touch— or bite—anything in the center of those glowing pools.

He watched the macabre dance of light and dark for a moment, enduring several more nibbles, until Secrets locked on a pattern.

*Move with me, Haidee. Now!* Amun leapt forward, straight into the center of one of those beams. Haidee remained directly behind him. One second, two, he waited. *Again!*

They leapt once more, following the light to its next destination. On and on they continued, jumping, pausing, jumping again. For hours. He knew Haidee was tiring, could feel the tremble in her slight form.

*You're doing great, sweetheart,* he praised her.

Before she could reply, a thick, cloying darkness once again enveloped them. No longer were there any pockets of light. No more fangs, either. Thank the gods. He stilled, Haidee pressing into his back. They could rest for a moment, decide what to do.

Secrets prowled through his mind, agitated, and suddenly Amun knew. More shadow-dwellers were coming. Close…closer…

*Be ready,* he told Haidee.

"For?"

*Something worse.* He didn't yet know what a shadow-dweller was, but he knew that much. At least with the total cessation of sight his other senses kicked into hyperdrive.

His ears picked up the whistling sound of wind. Or was he hearing…screams? His nose scented sulfur, and his mouth tasted copper. His palms tingled, sensing a spike of aggression in the air.

*Demons,* he said. Shadow-dwellers were demons. Minions, like the ones he'd absorbed. They approached, and dread detonated inside him. Would he absorb them?

Haidee first, his sanity second, he decided, switching direction. Rather than moving forward, he inched to the side until he encountered the solid length of the wall. He placed himself in front of her, offering what shelter he could.

"What are you doing?"

He wouldn't lie to her. She needed to know the danger they were in. *I told you. Demons approach. I won't let them reach you.*

"I can help you fight," she replied, far from scared.

*I won't risk you.*

A growl of menace sounded beside him, followed by another. And another. Haidee stiffened. So did he. A jumble of thoughts suddenly slammed into his head, each revolving around the taste of his organs. The demons had spotted him, were utterly starved and looked forward to eating every part of him.

And then, suddenly, they were there, attacking from every angle. Amun swiped out with his arms and knew he'd made contact with several of the creatures. Maybe he'd delivered killing blows, maybe not, but it didn't matter how many he felled. There were so many, they converged on him en masse.

He threw off as many as he could, continually slashing, kicking his legs to dislodge those who were chewing through his pants. Like the shadows, they had fangs. Only theirs were a lot sharper. And they had claws, such diamond-hard claws. But at least their evil remained with them, rather than being sucked into him, becoming a part of him.

Despite the rapid movement of his arms, several managed to attach themselves to his biceps. He felt what seemed to be a thousand prickly stings, not just in his biceps, but all over his body.

Warm blood leaked from him, and the scent of it tossed the creatures into a feeding frenzy. They snapped, growled and ripped out hunks of muscle. That quickly, he was losing the battle, weakening, and shit! He didn't know what to do. Didn't know where to find the light, or even how to use all of himself. Unless "all" meant offering his entire body up as a smorgasbord.

When Haidee screamed, the creatures working their way behind him to take little nibbles out of her, he stopped caring about the light and concentrated on killing—however necessary. No one hurt his woman. No one. And those who tried would suffer.

As rage suffused him, totally, completely, Amun bit back, clamping as many of the creatures as possible between his teeth and shaking like a shark that had finally snatched its prey. They were small, he realized, and easily breakable, those he held quickly going limp. He spit them out and snapped for more.

Secrets continued to prowl through his head like a caged lion, wanting to hurt, to destroy, and wipe all conscious thought from the primitive minds around them. Amun held tight to his other half, afraid the beast would hurt Haidee in the process. But when she released another scream, this one slightly weaker than the other, proving she was losing blood and deteriorating, Amun's guard dropped. The agitated demon roared, wrenching control from him and overtaking Amun completely. No longer were they man and beast. They were simply beast.

Some of those minds were indeed wiped, thoughts and

hungers slinking into Amun. Absorbed, as he'd feared. His mouth watered as he imagined tasting blood. Drinking… drowning in the flooding life-force…

The images and urges didn't last long. They quickly joined the muted chorus in the back of his consciousness.

More, he needed more. As his demon's hold on him strengthened, red flicked to life in his eyes, glowing, lighting up the cavern and illuminating hundreds of tiny, piranha-like creatures. They had white, hairless skin and pink-tinted gazes that looked as if they'd never glimpsed a single ray of light.

When they encountered the wash of red, they shrank back with a shriek, trying to escape it. Why would—

All of him, he thought then, understanding. All of himself, and all of his demon. So simple, so easy. He was ashamed he hadn't realized it sooner and saved Haidee from her newest injuries.

Another sin to place at his door.

Secrets continued to roar, out loud this time, frightening the creatures into backing farther away, and with the sound, Amun began to talk, unable to halt the words. Only he didn't reveal devastating truths and vile crimes, the things that had constantly swirled inside his head until Haidee entered his life. He spoke of something sweet and tender.

"I have to tell you something, sweet child." Ancient Greek, a language he'd only recently heard when inside Haidee's mind.

"Mother?" she said now, awed and confused by what she was hearing from him.

Any time the demon spoke through him, revealing something, the voices of those involved were used, rather than his own. So what Haidee heard was indeed her mother.

"Listen well, for we will never speak of this again. You are special, my child. So special."

There was a pause, his voice slipping into a softer, child-like timbre. "I don't understand."

Another pause, the return of the huskier voice. "For years, I could not conceive, and so I prayed and prayed, beseeching the gods to bless my barren body with fruit. And one night, a being appeared to me in my dreams. She told me I had only to promise to relinquish rights to my firstborn, and I would have many children. I agreed. It was the hardest decision I'd ever had to make, but I was so desperate, I agreed, and nine months later you were born."

Another pause, that switch of voices. "Me?"

Yet another pause, yet another switch. "Oh, yes, sweet darling. And soon after, your sister was born. And now, another babe grows in my belly."

Pause. "I shall be a sister again?"

Pause. "Yes. But, darling, listen to Màna. The being has returned. She wants to take you from us."

Pause. "I don't want to leave you."

Pause. "And we don't want you to leave us. Therefore, you will not. We will pack our belongings and flee from this place. I don't tell you this to frighten you, only to warn you. If ever someone approaches you, intending to take you away from us, run, my darling, run. Run and hide, and we will find you."

The voices continued, the mother easing the child with teasing stories and tickles, until both were laughing. The father and sister soon joined them, and their love for each other echoed in every word.

Real-life Haidee wrapped a trembling arm around Amun's waist. Distantly, he thought she might have taken one of his weapons from him, might have been slashing with her free hand to discourage the creatures from approaching his side, where the red light didn't reach, but he wasn't sure.

"Come on, baby," she urged between one of his pauses. "Keep your eyes on those little bastards, and I'll get us out of here, okay?"

He couldn't reply, could only weave the rest of the tale, the family spending what would be their last night together. Haidee never ceased dragging him away from the hungry fiends until finally, the shadows gave way and another cave surrounded them. This one was well-lit.

She eased him to the ground as gently as she could, and he lay there, still talking, unable to do anything else. His mind was consumed by his demon, by the images forming, but soon the memory took a darker turn, the murders clearly imminent.

Amun didn't want to go there, didn't want Haidee to hear their screams, their pleas for mercy. Somehow, someway, he managed to fight his way to the surface and peer up at her. The worst was yet to come, yet she was already staring down at him with horror. Horror she'd never before directed at him.

"Knock…me…out…" he managed between pauses. "Please."

"No."

*"Please."*

She gulped, trembled as she reached down and clasped one of his blades. But when she straightened, she made no move toward him. "I—I can't, Amun. I just can't."

"Please. Must. No other…way." His eyes beseeched her, the memory trying to jerk him back down, escape him. Any second now, and the screams and pleas were going to burst from his mouth. "Please."

"I—I—I'm sorry." Something hard suddenly crashed into his temple.

But he was still awake, still talking. "Again."

Once more, twice more, she hit him with the hilt of the blade. "So sorry." A third time. Harder and harder.

*Good girl.* He smiled as darkness consumed him, at last quieting his demon.

# CHAPTER TWENTY

HAIDEE STOOD OVER AMUN'S unconscious body for a long while, content to watch him, guard him, as he had often done for her. His breathing remained deep and even, and the torment etching his features eventually smoothed out.

He looked like an innocent little boy, she mused, with his dark lashes curling out, his lips soft and parted. Only the dried blood on his temple ruined the illusion. Well, that, and his ginormous warrior frame. Such a beautiful man, and what the hell was dripping on him?

Her gaze narrowed on the red splatter now marring his cheek. Blood. Not his, though. Frowning, she moved her attention to her arm. She still held the blade she'd stuck him with, she realized. She dropped the weapon, heard the clatter of metal against rock, and looked at her hand. There were multiple puncture wounds.

Her frown intensified when she swayed, overcome by dizziness. Wasn't that just typical? She'd felt fine until she actually spotted the wound. But damn, she must have lost quite a bit of blood. Which made sense. Those piranha-like creatures had chomped on each of her limbs. And God, did she remember the pain. Like having acid-tipped pins drilled into her bones.

If she had suffered, shielded by Amun as she'd been, how much had *he* suffered, completely out in the open?

And how had she repaid him? By knocking him into a stupor.

*He wanted you to do it,* she reminded herself, but that didn't ease her guilt. Maybe because, deep down, she had *wanted* to do it. She'd heard her mother's voice, her father's, her sister's, had known their deaths were approaching and had almost collapsed. If she'd had to listen to them die—again—she would have collapsed, no question.

Amun had known that, and had fought to spare her. Always he considered her well-being first, no matter the cost to himself. He'd known what he was saying, what he was about to say, and hadn't wanted her hurt by it.

Until that moment, she hadn't truly realized the constant burden he carried. He ascertained the dark thoughts and vile pasts of those around him and drew them inside himself. Unwittingly, yes, but rather than allow those poisons to spill from him, he held every drop inside himself. That way, no one else had to be tainted.

The strength of will such an act required... Haidee knew she would have crumbled long before now.

"What am I going to do with you, Amun?" she muttered. She hated that he hurt himself that way, that his only means of purging the darkness inside him came at such a high price. For him, for those he loved.

Sighing, she grabbed the backpack and gathered the supplies necessary to clean and bandage him, then herself. Then she ate a turkey sandwich and an apple and drained a bottle of water. Several more hours passed, but Amun didn't awaken.

Had she caused permanent damage?

Concern rocked her, and she paced the spacious cavern. Soon a sense of déjà vu overtook her. The enclosure looked exactly like the one the angel, Zacharel, had brought them to that first night: rocky walls splattered with red, bones in every corner. Had they made no progress?

This was hell. Maybe every cavern looked like this.

As she paced, her heart ached and swelled, any

resistance she still might have harbored toward Amun vanishing. He gave her what no one else had ever been able to give. A past to cherish. A present to enjoy. A future to anticipate.

And he wanted her, too. She knew he did. When he had pushed that image inside her head, the one of her in front of him, on her knees, his pants at his ankles and his hands in her hair, her mouth swallowing every inch of his massive erection, her own hands tugging at his testicles, she had nearly melted. She'd felt the raw need pulsing from him, the consuming hunger...the primal satisfaction.

She'd also felt his reasons for resisting her so steadfastly. Guilt, fear and remorse. Guilt for having inadvertently helped to kill her that first time—she'd known that already. Fear that he would hurt her again—that had been a surprise—and remorse for giving her up, even though it was for her own good. That wasn't going to be tolerated.

He didn't want her to regret what happened between them. Didn't want her to later hate him. He would learn. She wouldn't, couldn't hate him. Not for any reason.

There had to be some way to prove how wrong he was. That the only way he could hurt her was by giving her up. That she would *never* regret being with him.

Amazed, she ground to a halt. It was true, she realized. She would never regret being with him. The Hunters would view her as a traitor, and they would target her as they targeted the Lords, but she didn't care. And Micah, well, he would turn on her, too.

He would feel betrayed, personally and emotionally, but maybe one day, when he finally experienced *the sizzle* for himself, he would realize their split was the best thing that had ever happened to him.

Now that she'd experienced it, she only wanted more. Would do whatever was needed to *have* more. Even seduce Amun within an inch of his life.

No more waiting to move forward until she broke things off with Micah. Yes, she still planned to call him, to tell him they were finished, but their relationship was already over, done. Amun had her loyalty now. Demon, immortal, whatever, he had her loyalty. He deserved her everything.

And really, she was operating under a limited amount of time. If she couldn't reach him before they left these caverns—if they ever left these caverns—he would dump her somewhere and take off. For her own good. That, she knew, as well. Somehow, some way, she had to prove they could make a relationship work before then.

Turning his vision into a reality would be a good start.

She gave herself a once-over. Her clothes were ripped, caked in dirt and dried blood, and she probably smelled like dead piranha. She could clean up with wet wipes from the pack, she supposed, but tiny towelettes could only do so much. And yeah, she could summon another angel robe and that would magically wash away every unwanted speck, but mentally, she would still feel dirty.

"I need a bath," she murmured to the backpack. "A real bath. Can you fit a tub in there? Huh?"

A whoosh at her side had her twisting and reaching for the blade she'd dropped. Though there had been a rocky wall beside her only a few seconds ago, there was now a wide, bubbling spring of water.

Haidee's eyes widened with shock. How had...why... the backpack could manipulate the earth? Seriously? Then she thought, who the hell cared? The urge to soak and scrub overwhelmed her and left her trembling with anticipation.

"Soap, shampoo, conditioner," she said giddily.

The backpack plumped at the sides, signaling it had filled with everything she had requested. After lining the items along the edge of the spring—a real freaking spring!—she stripped herself, stripped Amun, and then shook him until his eyelids cracked open. His spirits needed this. Besides, she was still concerned about him, fearing she had struck him too hard, and if he'd just wake up for a few minutes, she could relax.

He moaned, the sound broken, his throat obviously tender. At least he was rousing.

"Shh," she said, covering his mouth with her hand. "Don't talk out loud, baby. Okay?" Neither one of them was strong enough to deal with the consequences just yet.

His black eyes were glassy as he focused on her. *Something wrong?*

"Something's right. Can you stand? We're going to take a bath."

*A bath?*

"That's what I said," she told him with a grin. And just then she knew; he was going to be all right. "Come on. On your feet, big boy."

He lumbered to a stand and tripped his way to the edge. Then he just sort of fell over the side, splashing headfirst into the water. Haidee jumped in after him and dragged him to the surface before he drowned. His eyes had closed again, his head lolling to the side.

She chuckled as she settled against the rock and anchored him against her, chest to back. "You still awake, baby?"

*Yes.* He uttered a soft sigh. *Just barely.*

"I'm going to scrub us both. Tell me if I hurt you."

*You couldn't hurt me.*

"You're injured and—"

*And I'm in your arms. I'll be fine, I promise.*

Darling man. She tried to be impersonal, she really did. He wasn't ready for the seduction she had planned. Yet.

Still, as her hands lathered the soap and spread the bubbles over his big arms, his corded chest, his strong thighs, her blood heated with desire, a reaction only he could cause.

His silky skin covered a body built for war, and she marveled. He made her desperate, hungry, mindless of anything except pleasure. Maybe because, when she was with him, she didn't belong to herself. She belonged to him. And that probably should have frightened her. Instead, it only made her trust him more. Amun would die before he hurt her—as he'd proven time and time again.

"Amun?"

He gave no response. Poor baby must have fallen asleep again.

"I love your body," she admitted, bold because he couldn't hear her. "Did you know that? Everything about you seems custom-made for me. I mean, it's almost like I ordered you from a catalog. And I wouldn't change anything about you. You'll probably never believe that, but it's the truth."

One day, she hoped he would feel the same about her.

After she shampooed his hair, breathing in the scent of sandalwood, she tilted him backward and rinsed every strand. When she finished with him, she gently shook him awake. Or maybe he'd been awake the entire time. His eyes were no longer glassy; they were blazing.

Her cheeks flushed. "Can you get out on your own?"

*Yes.* He climbed out and settled back on the floor, lying on his side to peer over at her. *Your turn to scrub up.*

The flush spread as she washed herself from top to bottom. Despite her embarrassment, the water soothed the little aches and pains that continuous walking and sporadic fighting—and nearly being eaten alive—had left.

*Haidee?* Amun said after she'd rinsed her hair.

The water splashed as she straightened. She leaned over the edge and stared down at her mighty warrior. His eyes were closed again, lines of tension branching from them. "Yes?"

*Come here and hold me.*

For a heartbeat of time, she could only gape at him. He had just *requested* her touch? No, not requested. Demanded. Such sweet progress already, and his true seduction hadn't even begun.

"Anything you want," she rushed out before he could change his mind. Naked and dripping, she moved out of the water. She didn't bother drying off but curled into his side, spooning him, resting her cheek on his outstretched arm.

He didn't draw her closer.

She didn't let that irk her. Much. She linked their fingers, and though the action wasn't meant to arouse either of them, it did exactly that. His penis grew and hardened against the crease of her bottom, and liquid need pooled between her legs. God, she wanted to arch back, grind into him, beg him to grind into her, but she didn't. Not even when his heat wrapped around her, far headier than it had been in the water, the force of it causing her to tremble.

*Not yet, girl. Not yet.* He wasn't ready for her seduction to begin. That tension… Soon, though. Please, God, soon. "You're not mad at me for bashing your skull in, are you?"

She didn't expect an answer, but a soft chuckle wafted through her mind. *I'm grateful. I'm just too weak to show you how much.*

Show her, he'd said. How? "I'm glad," she said, suddenly breathless. "Now go to sleep and rebuild your strength." *You're going to need it.* She kissed the inside of his wrist. "I'll be here when you wake up." And by that time, she would be doing things to his body that he would never be able to forget—things he wouldn't want her to stop doing.

Unaware of the sensual assault he would soon experience, he obeyed her, his breathing evening out as he drifted back to sleep.

AMUN'S MIND JOLTED into sudden awareness, three things instantly, absolutely certain to him. His body was on fire, his cock was being iced and he was loving the hell out of both. He jerked upright, panting, wondering if he'd had an erotic dream and embarrassed himself.

When he saw a lusciously naked Haidee planted between his legs, licking his hardened shaft from root to tip, then swirling her tongue over the slit, then moaning as if she'd tasted something sweet, he realized he hadn't been dreaming. He hadn't embarrassed himself, either, but was probably going to.

He wanted to come. Desperately.

Secrets was eerily silent, and hiding in the back of his mind. The other demons were silent and hiding, as well. Again. That icy chill of hers must truly scare them. That, or they feared she'd start doing that tugging thing and they were trying not to draw her notice.

*Sweetheart?*

Haidee paused, lifting her head away from him, and every cell he possessed screamed in protest. Cool breath tickled his skin as she offered him a wicked smile, her breasts firm and taunting, her nipples hard and pouting, almost close enough to rub against his thighs.

"Yes, baby?" she asked throatily.

I—I—Shit! He didn't know what to say to her. Except, maybe, *continue*. But he couldn't allow her to do this. She would regret it, and he wouldn't be able to live with himself.

"You're awake, right? You're not in danger of falling back asleep?"

*I'm only in danger of dying.*

"Too weak, then?"

*No.*

The huskiness of her laugh echoed between them. "Do you want me to stop?"

*Yes.*

"Really?"

She gave him another lick and he was rushing out, *No. No, I don't want you to stop.* Oh, gods, he thought. *Yes, you have to stop.*

She blew on the weeping tip of his shaft. "What if I don't *want* to stop?"

Oh, gods, he thought again. The torture…the pleasure… the possible repercussions…he'd never been this torn.

"Amun, darling, say the word and I'll suck you so deep you'll feel my throat closed around you for days." Another chilly breath coasted over his slit. "I've been thinking about this, needing it. Craving it. Let me have it."

His resistance shattered. *Do it. Please, do it. You can blame me later. Hate me later, but please don't stop.* He didn't care about later, didn't care that he was begging. He had to have this, couldn't exist another moment without it.

"I will, I'll do it," she said, fingers tracing up one side of his shaft, then down the other. "And I promise I'll blame you later."

He knew he should be concerned but couldn't manage the emotion. Sweat beaded over him in an effort to purge the intensity of his hunger. She hadn't fit her mouth back over his length, but her breath still stroked him. So good, felt so good. And then that was the only word he could say. *Good.* He was trembling, aching, desperate. *Good, good, good.*

Her voice lowered. "I'll blame you because you're too beautiful to resist. Because you think of my well-being even when you're in danger yourself. Because you're mine. My warrior. My...demon."

The admission affected him as potently as her actions, and he found new words to give her. *You're killing me, sweetheart. You're killing me, yes, yes, yes, please kill me.* Any moment and he would start arching his hips, thrusting up, unable to stop himself.

Her wicked grin returned. "Lie back and conserve your strength, baby. Sweet little Haidee's gonna do all the work."

He didn't lie back. He'd been yearning for this forever. Yearning for *her* forever. He wanted to see every move she made. *Like this. Just like this.*

"Whatever my warrior desires..." Lips of scarlet at last closed over the tip of him. She moaned in delight.

His back bowed. Her cold little tongue flicked the slit it had suckled only moments before, and he had to brace his arms behind him to remain upright. Down, down she sucked him, taking every inch, just as she'd promised, not backing off even when he hit deeper than she'd probably wanted him to go.

No, not true. His little Haidee hummed in satisfaction, in more of that delight, and he felt the vibrations in his bones. He had to grit his teeth to prevent himself from exploding then and there. Then she began to move, up and down, slowly at first, tormenting him, laving him with sensation, sensitizing his skin.

The ice of her touch should have numbed him, but combined with the heat his body exuded, he was kept in a continual state of need, ready to beg for one or the other to finally push him over the edge. And soon he was crying out in his mind, trying not to pump into her mouth.

That blond-and-pink hair bobbed, and with every upward glide, he saw slim, elegant fingers playing at his base. He started thinking about what he wanted to do with his own fingers. Glide them down the bumps of her spine, cup that trim little ass, spread each digit until he hit the warm, wet center of her. Sink deep with one, retreat, go back in with two, retreat, then go back in with three, until he stretched her. Until she squirmed and rode him and gasped and cried.

Haidee groaned, her body trembling, her teeth scraping up his shaft. "Yes," she rasped. "*Yes*. Fingers, deep. So deep."

Amun's heart thundered against his ribs. Was he pushing the images inside her head? He must be, he thought. Was glad. He wanted her to see, to know.

All the while she licked at him, she nibbled, her hips undulating over his legs, searching for something to fill her. He cupped her nape and massaged the muscles knotted underneath. When she began to relax against his hold, he tried to spin her around so that he could please her as she was pleasing him. She resisted.

"No. You first."

*Haidee.*

"No. Just…need a moment…control…slipping…"

He wasn't sure if she meant control of her body or control of the ice, but either way, he didn't care. She wanted him. She needed him. And he wanted to taste her. Needed to taste her, too.

As those tormenting lollipop licks continued, he tossed another image into her mind. One of *his* head buried between *her* thighs, sampling all the sweetness waiting there. Sucking her clitoris, flicking with his eager tongue, his fingers pinching her nipples into hard little pearls.

He'd shove her legs as far apart as they would go, burrow as deep as possible, and make her feel more vulnerable than she'd ever been. She would be helpless, his to control, command…his to own. He would take everything, swallow her up, devour her completely, then rear up and slam home.

He wouldn't be gentle. But then, she wouldn't want gentleness. She would want a hard pounding, a punishing ride onto oblivion. She would scream and she would cry out. She would clutch at him and leave bloody trails on his back, her nails like talons as her legs wrapped around him, ankles locking.

He would make her forget her husband, forget every man she'd ever been with. Only Amun would matter. Only Amun would have rights to her. Anyone who tried to reach her, who wanted to see her like that, taste and touch her like that, would die. He would murder them.

She. Belonged. To. Him. Not even Haidee would be able to doubt that afterward.

"Oh, God," she moaned, then lapped at his pre-come. Her trembling intensified.

*I told myself to stay away from you,* he said into her mind. *I told myself to leave you alone.*

"No," she cried. "Don't."

*But I can't,* he continued. *Let me taste you.*

"No," she repeated. Less savagely, yes, but not completely broken. "Let me finish you. Because I swear to God, baby, you're going to have this memory if it kills me. And it just might. You taste so damn good." With that, her mouth plunged, once again taking his entire length.

Amun finally let go of the gossamer threads of his control. He fell back, hips thrusting up, fingers tangling in her hair. She claimed him wildly, wantonly, as if she couldn't live another moment without his seed; soon he was helpless to do anything but let her have every drop.

Fire rushed through his veins, burning them to ash, allowing the inferno to spread, consume him, burst from him. He bucked up as she slammed down, and that seed rose up his length and exploded from him. Her cheeks hollowed as she swallowed, taking everything he had to give and still demanding more.

She wrung him dry, reduced him to a shell of himself, and he sagged against the ground. She didn't pull from him right away, but licked and purred as if unwilling to give him up even then. His muscles continued to spasm with aftershocks of sensation, pleasure humming through him as potently as she had hummed *on* him.

He would have recovered—eventually—and could have finally possessed her completely. But she wanted to call Micah before they took that step, and Amun wouldn't force that issue now. Not after what she'd just done for him. So he somehow found the strength to sit up, clasp her under the arms and lift her until she straddled his chest.

Her eyes were glazed with passion, her cheeks flushed a deep rose. Those beautiful locks of hair hung in rapturous tangles around her shoulders. Never had a woman looked more mussed, more ready for loving—or better loved.

"What are you—?"

He slid one of his hands between their bodies and thrust a finger deep. Immediately her head fell back and a cry parted her lips.

"Yes! Yes, please, yes."

Just as he'd imagined, he used two fingers on the inward glide. She was so wet she drenched his hand, so needy her inner walls clung to him, trying to hold him captive. This was how a woman should always feel. Ready. On the next inward glide, he used three, just as he'd craved. His thumb rubbed at her clitoris, never ceasing the pressure.

So desperate was her need, she erupted quickly and violently. Her scream echoed from the walls, her knees squeezed his sides so tightly he knew his ribs would crack, and her nails raked his pecs, leaving welts. And when the last tremor left her, she collapsed on top of him, panting, eyes closed, skin sheened by a delicate layer of ice.

Amun was panting just as forcefully. What had just happened...he'd never experienced anything like it. That hadn't been the simple fulfillment of a need. That had been the birthing of an addiction. An obsession. He had to have more. Had to have everything. Now, always.

Haidee's lack of inhibition, her willingness to please him, her absolute claiming of him—for that's what she'd done—had utterly changed him. In an instant, the old Amun had been burned to ash, and a new Amun had risen up.

Haidee's man.

He'd been stupid to try and push her away, he realized now. Stupid to try to ignore the attraction between them. He'd only hurt and frustrated them both. Here, they *could* be together.

No one would ever have to know, which meant she wouldn't be ridiculed, wouldn't be punished or ostracized by her friends. And so they would; they would be together. He simply couldn't be without her. *Wouldn't* be without her.

While they were here, he was forced to remind himself.

When they left hell, they would part. He wouldn't disturb her life any more than he already had.

His hands curled into fists. Gods, even the thought of being without her blackened his mood. He would not be swayed from that course, however. Through his suffering, he would know Haidee lived as she was meant. Happily. Finally.

Secrets gave a little whimper, and Amun frowned. Did the demon not want to lose Haidee, either? *I thought you were scared of her.* He was careful to hold the thought inside his mind.

Another whimper sounded.

Understanding dawned. *You aren't done digging through her mind.*

The demon gave no response, but a response wasn't necessary. He knew.

He and Secrets had never had a true conversation, and he could hardly believe they were (almost) doing so now. *Doesn't matter, though. We can't keep her. For her own good, we can't keep her.*

As if Haidee sensed the direction of his thoughts, she struggled to sit up. Amun held tight, forcing her to remain against him.

*Sleep, sweetheart. We'll talk later.*

"Promise?" she asked, the word slurred with exhaustion.

*Promise.*

"'Kay." She hadn't noticed his failure to specify exactly *what* they'd discuss, and she went limp, slipping into a deep slumber.

## CHAPTER TWENTY-ONE

SOMETHING HARD AND INEXORABLE shook Haidee from the most peaceful sleep of her life. She tried to bat the offender away. The shaking continued. She cursed and blinked open her eyes to see Amun looming above her, his expression tense, his black eyes unreadable.

He pressed a firm finger over her mouth before she could utter a single word. *Something's out there,* his deep voice said into her mind. Urgency radiated from him, as contagious as a virus. *Get dressed.*

Of course someone was out there, she thought dryly. She and Amun were in a division of hell; they weren't allowed a single moment's respite. And now, their long overdue relationship talk would have to wait. Again. Still, this was better than the alternative. Like, say, dying.

As she donned the bra, panties, jeans, T-shirt, boots and countless blade and sheaths he'd laid out for her, she marveled at the change in herself. Only a few days ago, she had jolted to awareness every time she'd awoken, mind already locked on escape. Now, when danger had never been so prevalent, she'd let down her guard. She even had to remind herself not to think about what they'd done last night, how she'd sucked and swallowed him, how she'd ridden his fingers and cried his name.

She shivered as she listened for whatever had disturbed Amun. Nothing, she heard nothing. She wiped the sleep from her eyes and anchored the backpack on her shoulders. When they— Her ear twitched, and she frowned. Was that a...whistle of wind? No, she thought. Laughter. Faint but unmistakable now—and coming from more than one source.

Laughter in hell. Not good. No, not good at all. She glanced at Amun to gauge his reaction.

He looked alert, on edge, as he stood guard at the cave entrance, his back to her. He wore a black shirt and black slacks, and each looked buttery soft and flexible. That way, he wouldn't be restricted during a fight. Silently she moved behind him.

He sensed her approach and started forward. She remained close on his heels as they left her new favorite place in the world. They should have entered another cave, a rocky hallway at the very least. That's what had happened every time before. This time, however, they entered—no, surely not. She shook her head, blinked her eyes. She couldn't be seeing what she thought she was seeing, but the image never varied.

*A...circus?* Amun asked, incredulous.

He saw it, too, then. A freaking circus. Unreal! After the Realm of Shadows, a circus seemed like a spa vacation. Seriously. The restrictive walls of the underground had given way, stretching into what seemed to be a pretty, moonlit night. Stars even twinkled from their perch in the black-velvet sky, a cool breeze dancing past.

A moon...a sky...in a cave. How? She stopped wondering when she saw that several fires crackled nearby, and there were bearded women and jaundiced-eyed men holding their hands *inside* the actual flames, watching her and Amun with palpable menace.

Okay, so "spa vacation" had been the wrong term to use.

"Amun?"

*I don't know,* he said, answering her unasked question. What the hell was going on?

Too-tall men with legs that knifed toward the sky walked by them, thankfully paying them no heed. The animals they led, however…the elephant whined, its trunk lifting, revealing fangs sharper than any demon's. Worse, there were several winged lions, two unicorns that were foaming at the mouth and three crocodiles with blades rather than scales protruding from their backs. Each of the animals was bound to the men by a fraying rope—and each was fighting for freedom, their gazes locked on her, the tasty-looking human.

She gulped, glanced away for fear of egging them on. "I don't like this."

*I won't let anything bad happen to you.*

*Just like I won't let anything bad happen to you,* she thought.

Tent after tent lined either side of her, a graveled pathway between them. At the end of that pathway was a booth, and inside that booth sat an obese man in a sweat-stained wifebeater. A neon sign flashed above him. ADMISSION: ONE HUMAN HEART.

*I understand now,* Amun told her flatly. *We've reached the Realm of Destruction.*

Another realm. She almost groaned. "None of this was here last night," she said. "I would have noticed on our way into the cave."

*Well, it's here now.*

No denying that. But how? Did she and Amun not actually have to hike anywhere to reach a new realm? Could the realms simply come to them? How odd, if so. Was that normal?

Was anything normal in hell? she thought with a humorless laugh.

They stopped at the booth.

"You want tickets or not?" the sweating man demanded

in a voice so low, so deep, there were echoes of darkness bubbling beneath the surface.

Shuddering, Haidee opened her mouth to shout, "Hell, no," but Amun's next words stopped her. *Tell him yes.*

Damn it. Why? Just then, she hated that their mind-connection didn't go both ways. "Yes," she forced herself to say. "We want tickets."

Glittering red eyes swept over them both. He raised his arm, fingers opening to reveal a dull, bloodstained blade in his palm. "First, I'll need your hearts."

"His heart isn't human," Haidee said, jabbing her thumb in Amun's direction.

The big man gave Haidee his full attention and licked his greasy lips. "Yours will do. You can pay for him another way." He stroked himself. "Know what I mean?"

Amun stiffened, and suddenly utter menace poured from him. *Take what we need from the backpack,* he said. His timbre was flat, but all the more fiery for it.

She pulled the backpack forward. *I need two*—she gulped—*human hearts,* she thought and reached inside. What would she do if nothing—

She almost gagged when she encountered two warm, velvet-wrapped…things. "Paying another way won't be necessary." She did gag when she handed both to the man, and he greedily ripped away the material to view the still-thumping organs inside. And when he tore a hunk from both with his teeth, tasting the tissue as he would a fine wine, she had to swallow a surge of bile.

He nodded in satisfaction, all three of his chins bobbing with the movement. "Go ahead and pass." An evil grin split his lips, and she saw the crimson…food stuck between his teeth. "Enjoy yourselves, you hear? I have a real good feeling the performers'll enjoy you."

For a moment, she could only stare at him. He loved to torture females and animals—in that order. How she knew, she couldn't have said. She just knew. And she wanted to kill him. Badly.

Why shouldn't she? she thought next, her skin chilling several degrees. She was loaded down with blades. A simple jab, jab and he would—

*You can't kill him,* Amun told her.

Her eyes widened. How had he known what she was planning? Could he now read her thoughts? Or had his demon—his demon, she thought, nodding. Secrets. There was a warm, dark cloud whisking through her head. The same warm, dark cloud she'd noticed the two times Amun had shown her bits and pieces of her past.

That's how she knew about the man. That's why her temperature had dropped.

When the demon claimed Amun's attention, or sought her own, his skin warmed and hers chilled, the same as when they were making love. Right now, Amun was practically on fire.

"You just gonna stand there?" the beefy man cackled, dragging her from her thoughts.

Shit! She'd allowed herself to be distracted. "Why can't I kill him?"

*Come on.* Amun twined their fingers and started forward, maneuvering around the man—only to twist and strike with his free hand, embedding a blade in the man's spinal cord. *Crack.* There was a gurgle, that beefy body convulsing, slumping, falling over. Skin turned to ash, and bone to liquid, the ash drifting away in the breeze, the liquid forming a black, oozing puddle. *Oh, and to answer your question, you couldn't kill him because the privilege belonged to me.*

When Amun straightened, looking anywhere but at Haidee, he once again started forward. She could only gape up at him, astonished. "Why'd you get the privilege?"

*He planned to find you later and…do things to you.*

"How do you know?" She knew the answer before she finished asking the question. His demon. Again.

*I told you. I read all minds but yours.*

"I remember." She pushed out a breath. "And thank you."

*Thank you? You don't think me malicious? I just killed in cold blood.*

"Malicious? For avenging me? No." Amun must have forgotten that she had wanted to plant a blade in the man, too. "I think you're sweet and maybe even went a little easy on the bastard. I would have forced him to eat his own intestines."

A warm chuckle drifted through her mind as Amun's fingers squeezed hers in thanks of his own. He'd truly expected her to balk, she realized. Later, she would have to tell him about some of the things *she* had done over the years, all in the name of vengeance and, foolishly, world peace.

As if the world would be a better place without Amun.

They remained on the gravel path for several minutes. Over and over Haidee's attention strayed as she searched for the animals she'd seen earlier. She expected them to reappear and launch at her, jaws snapping. Constantly she tripped, but Amun never let her fall. Even better, he never berated her for her lack of concentration as Micah would have done. To him, it was mission first, feelings second.

When you were stalking evil or being stalked by evil yourself, you were to think only of destroying that evil. You weren't to worry about any physical pain you might suffer. You weren't to consider what might happen to the innocents around you. And most assuredly, you weren't to place your fate in anyone else's hands.

"Come," a withered female in front of one of the tents

suddenly called. "I tell you what awaits. You pay me with a scream."

Haidee replied before she could think better of it. "I'm not screaming."

"You will. Oh, you will." A gnarled finger pointed at her, and a cackling laugh sounded. "Best go no farther, hateful girl. Death, death is what awaits you. And pain, so much pain. Soon. Soon you pay me."

The prediction was so close to what Haidee had endured countless times in the past, she couldn't shake a sudden sense of unease. *Soon,* the old crone had said, and the urge to rush over there and shake *the woman,* to demand answers, overwhelmed her. She *would* shake the bitch, she thought, starting forward.

"Oh, I'll pay you all right."

Cackling.

Distantly, she thought she felt something—someone, Amun—tugging at her back. She didn't care. Couldn't care. When she tried to pull from Amun's hold, he tightened his grip.

"I have to go to her. Have to—"

*Don't listen to her. Remember what the angel told us? Trust no one.*

It took a superhuman effort, but Haidee managed to stop and look away from that stooped body. The moment she did, the overwhelming urge left her. "Thank you. Again."

*There's no need to thank me, Haidee.* He stuffed a piece of paper in his pocket. *Come on.*

He ushered her off the pathway. He zigzagged and ducked behind the tents, always maintaining a tight grip on her. She had been chased over the years and had chased others, so she knew what he was doing. Preventing anyone from locking on them, their every move random, unpredictable.

"What's the game plan?" she asked.

*While you chatted with the self-professed seer, I had the pack provide instructions for successfully navigating this place.*

"And?" she asked.

*Another scroll. It said we must find the Horsemen.*

Horsemen? "I don't understand."

*We must find the Horsemen,* he repeated. *Of the Apocalypse.*

Oh, dear God. "You're kidding me." Please let him be kidding.

*I wish I were. Through death or some other means, the scroll said they were our only way out of here.*

She gulped a mouthful of what felt like sand. "And what do you mean by 'some other means'? We're supposed to ride them to safety?"

To her surprise, Amun chuckled softly. *I have no idea. The scroll told me nothing else. But I do know the Horsemen are in some way related to William, and—*

"William?"

*You haven't met him. He's immortal, a god of some sort, I think, and on our side.*

"Our" side. As if they were partners rather than enemies. As if he trusted her completely. As if he no longer saw her as a Hunter responsible for his friend's murder, but as a woman worthy of him. Inside she glowed, tendrils of his warmth traipsing through her.

"So, if the Horsemen are related to this William person, who's on *our* side—" she stressed the word "—the Horsemen should be on our side, as well?"

*We can hope.*

For some reason, that wasn't promising.

A shriek sounded at her left, and she stopped to wheel in that direction.

*Easy,* Amun instructed, stilling beside her. *Someone's playing a game, that's all.*

That was all? The beings here weren't playing with darts, balloons or plastic balls—and the prizes weren't stuffed animals. Severed heads were being tossed at boiling tubs of oil, and though the heads were bodiless, their mouths still managed to scream in pain when splashed with the oil, skin melting away.

The little boy who'd just won jumped up and down, clapping, his hoofed feet clomping hard into the ground and spraying dirt in every direction. The proprietor handed him a beautiful golden bird trying desperately to escape the string around its neck, wings flapping erratically, glitter raining from them like fairy dust.

The loveliness of the bird was surprising, considering the ugliness of everything else down here.

The little boy gently held the bird in both hands, muttering soothing words. Those golden wings gradually stopped flapping. Of course, that's when the boy shoved the tiny creature into his mouth and bit off the head.

Haidee gagged and quickly looked away—right at a group of men who'd locked their sights on her and Amun. Those men were striding toward them, closing the distance. Damn it. She never should have paused to watch the games.

"Amun," she whispered fiercely.

*I see them.* He released her, gearing for a fight they both knew would happen. *If I tell you to run, you run and hide and don't return. Understand?*

As if. But rather than tell him she planned to stay and help, possibly distracting him, she remained silent and palmed two blades in each hand. The men were almost upon them…they were big, bigger than Amun, with paper-thin skin that draped loosely over pitted bone, their eyes merely sunken holes of black…and still they drew ever closer…

Just as he'd done with the ticket handler, Amun stiffened. And not in preparation for battle.

"Can you read their minds?" she asked.

*Yes.*

He said no more, but then, he didn't have to. The men intended to do something vile. To her, she was sure.

"Six against two. Let's see if we can even out those odds." Haidee threw two of her weapons. The first hit the biggest of the men in the jugular, and he instantly toppled. The second hit the man next to him right in the eye socket. He screamed as he fell.

The other four paid their fallen comrades no heed, continuing forward.

*Run,* Amun commanded her.

She didn't.

*Haidee! Now!*

Okay. She had to tell him. "I'm not letting you fly solo on this. I'm here. I'll help."

He growled.

The men reached them and formed a circle around them, effectively surrounding them with a wall of muscle and menace. Wouldn't have been so bad, except the two men she'd felled suddenly rose, jerked the weapons from their bodies and took their places in the circle, far angrier than they'd been before.

Oh…shit. They couldn't be killed. Dread slithered through her, choking her.

"We want the girl," one of them said, and all of them gave her a once-over, lingering on her breasts, between her legs, mentally stripping her and making her shudder in revulsion.

"Well, news flash. You can't have me," she snapped. She would rather die. Again.

"Wasn't talking to you, bitch." The shithead's gaze never left Amun. "Give her to us, and you can go on your way. Alive."

*He'll pay for disrespecting you, I swear it,* Amun told her, and he sounded so calm he could have been discussing his favorite type of doughnut. *But first, since you refused to obey me, and yes, we will be discussing that, ask him if he's seen the Horsemen.*

That, she obeyed. And as her words echoed between them, an almost visible wave of fear swept over the men. They began to tremble, their skin taking on a grayish cast. The Horsemen were so depraved they frightened even psychos, huh? Awesome. Then the fear turned to anger, and the men scowled at Amun with more fury than before, as if they blamed him for what they'd felt.

"Forget those that shall not be named and tell us what you want for her," one of the men said.

Those that shall not be named?

A muscle ticked below Amun's eye as he took each guy's measure.

"Can't you talk, demon?" another growled. "We want the woman. Now."

So they recognized what he was, but they weren't scared of him as they evidently were of the Horsemen. If that was the case, though, why didn't they simply attack him?

"You can have her back when we're done," still another said.

They laughed in eerie unison.

"'Course, she'll be in pieces, and we'll probably keep the good ones, but you can have what's left."

*Run, Haidee,* Amun repeated into her mind. *And this time, do it.* He didn't wait to see if she had—she hadn't—but launched himself at the men. He moved so quickly, she registered only the blur of his slashing hands and glistening blades.

The men converged on him with the same eerie unison in which they'd laughed, kicking at him, swinging their arms like clubs. She couldn't throw herself into the fray because there was no way to tell which body parts belonged to Amun and which to the shitheads. Their positions changed too swiftly.

Blood sprayed, some red, some black. Grunts and groans resounded. Then Amun landed at her feet, wheezing, his face already sliced to ribbons. The men were on him an instant later, their momentum shoving her backward.

She righted herself, that image of Amun filling her with a rage so potent, her blood began to thicken with ice. No one hurt her man. No one. Mist formed a cloud in front of her nose each time she exhaled. She knew anyone who looked at her would see actual crystals glinting in her hair, on her skin. This strong a reaction hadn't happened in so long, she'd almost forgotten she was capable of it.

Hate filled her, joining the ice. So much hate. She hated these men, hated what they'd planned. Hated that they lived.

She couldn't allow them to live.

Amun managed to throw the bundle of bodies off him and jump to his feet. His weapons had been ripped from his grip, so he used his fists now, pummeling with all his might. But every time he cracked one of those fatheads to the side, breaking the spinal cord, the men would shake off the blow and attack with new fervor. Then one of them realized Haidee was alone, seemingly unprotected and disengaged.

His grin was evil.

Hers was worse. "Come here," she said with such calm even she was surprised.

Those black eyes narrowed, a forked tongue swiping over too-thin lips. Though he was obviously suspicious about her sudden eagerness, the man complied, moving closer.

He pushed her down the moment he reached her, throwing himself on top of her, trying to rip off her jeans. Haidee let him, *helped* him, wrapping her arms around him and pressing her lips into his.

His tongue thrust out, hard, attempting to pry her teeth apart. He needn't have bothered. She opened willingly, blowing the ice of her breath, the very hate of her soul, straight into his mouth. He convulsed. In shock, perhaps, or maybe in fear. Or even pain. She wanted him to feel pain. Then he stilled, unable to move, literally frozen, but that wasn't enough. He hadn't suffered enough.

She shoved him off of her and stood, distantly noting the blue pallor of his skin, the unmoving features, the stiffness of his body. More. She needed more. More ice, more hate, more death. These men deserved to die. Her mind locked on that thought—*deserved, deserved, deserved*—and glided to the heap of struggling bodies, brushing her fingers over one, then the other. They, too, froze in place, their skin hardening as the ice flowed over them.

More. Deserved. The remaining three offenders noticed the condition of their friends and leapt away from Amun, watching her through horror-filled eyes.

"What—what'd you do?"

"What *are* you?"

"Don't come any closer!"

Amun pushed to his feet, stepping away from her, as well. His expression was unreadable.

More. Deserved. She walked toward the men, and they scampered backward, tripping over their own feet, falling. More. Deserved.

*Haidee.*

"Come," she said. "Taste me."

*Haidee.*

Amun's voice pushed through some of the ice, but not the hate. She hated these men, knew they had to die by her hand. She reached out. One touch, just a single touch, and she would have what she wanted. Their destruction. Everyone's destruction. Yes, everyone's. She had only to finish with these two, and she could move on, destroy everyone.

They crab-crawled backward, desperate to escape her. One of them wasn't fast enough, and she managed to latch onto his ankle. She grinned. He seemed to turn into stone right before her eyes. More. Deserved.

*Haidee, sweetheart. Look at me.*

Sweetheart. She liked when Amun called her sweetheart. He made her feel special. A little more of the ice inside her melted. Until she realized her final target was only a few steps away. More. Deserved. Destruction within her reach.

*Haidee, sweetheart. Look at me. Please.*

Again the ice melted, and this time Amun's plea reached even her hatred, muting the coldest threads. Slowly she turned to face him. "What do you want?" The frosty rage in her voice stunned her. Upset her. It shouldn't be directed at Amun.

*The last man is gone, sweetheart. You can come back to me now.*

Come back to him? What did he mean by that? She was right here, right in front of him. Frowning, she stepped toward him. She would shake him, make him realize.

Like the enemy had done, he backed away. *Sweetheart. Your eyes are pure white, and even being near you is painful to me. I need you to come back to me.*

Sweetheart again. More of the ice melted, and the hate muted yet another degree, then another, until the emotion was at a low simmer. She hurt him? She didn't want to hurt Amun. Ever. She just wanted to love…him.

Her knees almost gave out. Love? Did she love him?

As the question echoed through her mind, she swayed, a wave of dizziness sweeping her. Just before she hit the ground, strong arms banded around her and kept her upright.

*There you are, sweetheart. I knew you'd come back to me.* Amun held her tightly to his side, and to her relief, he didn't freeze. In fact, his heat wrapped around her, melting the rest of the ice.

"I'm sorry," she said, voice shaking. "I didn't mean to—"

*Don't be sorry. You saved our asses. Now come on. We need to get out of here before reinforcements show up.*

"Ye seek the Horsemen, do ye? Don't deny. I heard," a small voice suddenly said behind them. "Come, come. I show ye."

Amun turned them both, and when she focused she saw a tiny female with the lower half of a bull and the top half of a human. Small hands waved them forward.

"This be fun," the female said with a shady giggle. "Come, come, I show ye." She darted away before they could reply.

*We're going to go with her. We don't have any other choice.*

"Yes, we do. We can choose not to go with her." With Haidee's luck, the creature would lead them into a nest of vipers, piranha and rape-minded giants. Oh, wait. Been there, done that. What came next would probably be worse.

*My demon went silent the moment you—* He stopped himself. The moment she'd…what? Become consumed by the cold? *My demon is still silent, which means I can't figure out where the Horsemen are located. That little female is our only shot. Just don't let anything happen to me, okay?* Amun said with what seemed to be…humor?

No, surely not. She didn't think she'd ever heard him joke with her before. And really, not many men could tease their woman about being stronger than they were. "I, uh, won't."

*Thank you.* The semblance of a smile curled the corners of his lips as he ushered her forward, quickly closing the distance to reach Bull Girl. The almost-grin stunned her more than his teasing. He was just so beautiful, and as amused as he clearly was, he was also distracting.

Love, she thought again.

She couldn't love him. She was careful, always careful, to guard her heart. Yes, she lusted for Amun, cared for him, wanted him safe and happy. That didn't mean she loved him, though. Love weakened, made you vulnerable. Especially love that wasn't returned.

"Here, here," the now-bouncing creature said. She stopped in front of the biggest tent in the area, laughter and smoke drifting from the seams in the front flap. "They be here. This be fun."

Only then did Haidee recall the old woman's earlier warning. Death. Pain. Screaming.

Soon.

# CHAPTER TWENTY-TWO

THEY WERE SMOKING CIGARS and playing poker.

Amun had never seen the four horsemen of the Apocalypse before, but despite the crowd of demons hovering around them, he recognized them instantly. They sat around a table comprised of barbed wire, enveloped in a tobacco-scented haze. Three males, one female, and all four were physically perfect beings. Even more so than Zacharel. Or William.

He studied them. Friend or foe? The female had flaxen hair that waved to her waist, iridescent sparkles woven through the strands, and eyes of the deepest purple. The males were a colorful mix, one raven-haired, one sandy-locked, and one completely bald, his scalp tanned to a golden glow.

They wore clothes very similar to Amun's. Black shirts, black pants. They were relaxed, laughing seductively as they revealed their cards, then ribbing the losers unmercifully. What gave them away was the color of their auras. Amun had never noticed anyone's aura before, but these were undeniable. The shades enveloped them like a second skin, the female's white, one of the males' red, one black and one a pale green.

The Rainbow Brigade, he thought.

Haidee stepped to his side and was given her first full look at them. She gasped.

Amun's jaw clenched—*me, only want me*—but the sound prodded Secrets from his hiding place as effectively as her coldness had driven him there earlier. While Amun had battled the six men who'd wanted to "borrow" her, she'd turned into ice walking. Her hair had morphed into icicles, her skin had looked like crystal and her eyes…her eyes had lost all hint of color.

He'd been riveted by the beauty of her, queen of the winter storm, and awed by the strength of her. His demon had been terrified, retreating as deep into his mind as possible. The others had felt the pull of her again, even though she hadn't touched Amun. They'd fought, screamed. Yeah, they'd done that before, but never that quickly or that determinedly.

He just didn't know what to do about it.

Whatever kept Haidee from dying eternally, whatever brought her back to life again and again, had to be responsible for her change. No mere human could do that. What that made her, what that was, though, he still didn't know, and he wasn't sure Secrets had the balls to try and find out. Still. They were going to have to merge with her mind again.

Amun had to know the truth. And maybe, with the answer, he could find a way to save her from the torture of being reanimated. Of course, that meant she would die permanently one day, and he couldn't even contemplate that without sickening.

She was his.

And he was going to have her. All of her. Yes, the cold he felt while they pleasured each other could hurt him. He realized that now. But he wasn't going to let something as minor as freezing to death stop him from being with her.

He'd already lost the war with his resolve to stay away from her. While they were down here, at least. Up there, they would part, and that knowledge only increased his urgency to have her. Tonight. Tonight, he wiped her former boyfriend from her mind and claimed every inch of her.

At least Secrets wasn't whimpering, or the others screaming, because she stood at his side. That was a start. Secrets was too focused on the Horsemen and their thoughts—or rather, what consisted of their thoughts—enjoying the puzzle of them. There was a strange buzzing noise inside White's head, shrieks inside Red's, moans inside Black's and utter silence inside Green's.

"She the one who iced the congo?" Red asked no one in particular. A cigar hung from the side of his mouth.

The crowd finally noticed Amun and Haidee. Some snarled and flashed their teeth, some licked their lips in glee, but all left the tent as if their feet were on fire. Only the Horsemen remained.

The congo. The men who'd thought to beat him to pulp, allowing them to rape and dismember Haidee without interference? Most likely. Guys had been as big as apes, with a mind-set to match, so the name fit.

"I believe I asked you a question, warrior." Red tossed the cards atop the tabletop and turned, eyes of the cruelest blue leveling on Amun. The shrieks inside the being's head increased in volume. Secrets burrowed through them, still seeking thoughts and intentions. "I'll hear your answer now."

"Yes," Haidee said, answering for him. She sounded confident, unafraid. But for once, Amun could feel the emotions pouring off her. His brave girl was terrified but determined. "I did. I iced them."

If the Horsemen thought to punish her... Amun curled his fingers around a blade the congo hadn't managed to steal from him, ready, almost eager.

"Very cool," Black said, waving them over with a smile that did little to soothe Amun's dark mood. "Sit, sit. We've been expecting you."

They had, had they?

Amun needed a better read on them, and suspected

Secrets would have an easier time sorting through the noise if Haidee wasn't there. Yet he couldn't be without her. Not just to guard her—not that she needed guarding, because damn, he was still in shock over her ability—but because the other demons inside him might use her absence to overtake him. He would lose focus, returning to that mindless state of horror and pain.

*Stand behind me and press your back into the tent flap,* he told her as he moved forward. He gave her a gentle push in that direction. *You've got a weapon?*

"Yes," she whispered.

She didn't question him, but he knew she wanted to. Once again, he wished the connection went both ways, that she could push her voice into his head. Why the hell couldn't she? Just then he wouldn't have minded if she heard every thought he had, knew every urge he experienced. Her safety came before everything else.

He eased into the only empty seat at the table, the horsemen encasing him from every angle. He studied their faces more intently, noting the flawlessness of their skin, the purity of their eyes, the utter amusement in their expressions.

Amusement? Why?

Amun knew the moment Haidee did as he'd ordered and increased the distance between them, because Secrets sighed in relief and homed in on the three males and the female, at last digging past the buzzing, shrieking, moaning and silence.

*—so damn bored…*

*—most fun I've had in a while…*

*—too bad we have to kill him…*

*—girl might be useful, though…*

The other demons cackled, a thousand wind chimes in a storm. They weren't so loud that they overpowered Amun's other thoughts, and they weren't so stalwart they overwhelmed him with dark urges. Oh, he could feel the things they wanted him to do. Taste the Horsemen's blood, cause their screams. They'd been locked away so long, they were desperate. They also sensed Haidee was nearby, the frost of her skin like an invisible tether, and so they behaved. He could deal.

"You want safe passage from this realm," Red said, a statement of fact, not a question.

"As with everything here, you must buy that passage," White added, her voice as lilting and delicate as a snowfall.

Black smiled at him, all teeth and menace. "I hope you're ready for this."

Green, he noticed, never spoke a word. Just watched them all through enigmatic eyes. Amun felt a momentary sense of kinship.

He nodded at each of them.

"We'll play two hands," Red said. "No more, no less. If you lose, you will give me a hand. And I don't mean a round of applause. Feel me?"

Behind him, Haidee choked on a breath.

*I'll be fine, sweetheart,* he told her, even as he arched a brow at his opponents. *Ask them what happens if they lose to me.*

She obeyed, her voice strained. He was proud of her. She was scared but unbending, used to being in control, but allowing him to lead.

Red shrugged one of his massive shoulders, his attention never veering from Amun. "If I lose, I'll escort you out of this realm myself."

Secrets released an uneasy sigh. Over the centuries, Amun had learned the subtle nuances of his demon and knew Secrets sensed something amiss but hadn't yet figured out what.

So now came the real negotiation. *Ask them what*

*happens to you during—and after—all of this,* he told Haidee. *What happens to you if I win, and what happens to you if I lose.*

Once again she obeyed, and all four of the Horsemen grinned.

"Why does the woman speak for you?" White asked in that snowflake voice, ignoring the question. She was frowning, clearly unable to think up a logical reason on her own.

"Tell us what we want to know," Haidee insisted, ignoring the question.

*Good girl.*

Black lost his battle to hide his amusement and gave them another toothy grin. "We keep you no matter the outcome, of course."

Amun leapt to his feet and slammed his dagger into the middle of the deck, causing the table to rattle.

"Do you need me to interpret that?" Haidee asked with false sweetness.

Rather than angering them, Amun's outburst and Haidee's insult increased their enjoyment. Chuckling, Red waved him back in his seat. "Fine, fine. The girl will share your fate. If you lose a hand, she loses a hand. If you win, she wins and leaves with you. Happy now?"

Hardly. *Tell them if I lose the first game, they may take both my hands but neither of yours.*

Of course, Haidee did not obey.

*Mine will grow back, woman.* Eventually. *Tell them.*

Still she remained silent.

He couldn't turn back and glare at her; they would suspect he communicated with her telepathically. Not knowing what else to do, he signed the words, hoping one of the Horsemen knew the language. To his astonishment, all of them did, for they all nodded with satisfaction.

"Very well," Red said, "we will take both of yours and

neither of hers. But then there won't be a reason to play a second game. We'll have what we wanted. Both of your hands."

Why did they want them? *Just pick a different prize for the second. Like...my feet.*

Haidee growled low in her throat, a predator ready to pounce. He knew she could hear his thoughts as he signed, but there was nothing he could do to comfort her. "I don't agree to those terms."

Everyone ignored her.

"Yes." Red nodded. "Your feet will be a nice addition to our collection. We accept. Two rounds will be played, after all."

"Amun—" Haidee began.

Amun held up his hand for silence, and he could feel the malevolence pulsing off her. Later, she would make him pay. But she would have the necessary appendages to do so, so he wasn't too concerned. To the Horsemen, he signed, *What are the rules?*

They looked at each other, genuinely perplexed by his question.

"Rules?" White asked, blinking.

O-kay. Clearly the Rainbow Brigade lived by a code of its own making.

Secrets confirmed the suspicion. Suddenly Amun knew that there was no black and white with them, only shades of gray, and they wouldn't hesitate to lie, cheat or trick to get what they wanted.

Trusting them in any way would guarantee his loss. *Use the backpack to produce a new deck of cards,* he told Haidee.

A few seconds later, she was strolling to his side. Secrets whimpered, the other demons cried out in pain, and then utter silence claimed his head. She angrily slapped the deck into his hand and stomped back to her post without a word. When they were once again distanced from each other, all of the demons peeked from their hiding places.

Secrets was a bit more subdued, afraid she would return at any moment.

The fear would have to be addressed, he realized. Secrets was a part of him. Amun relied on the beast and needed him at his best in dangerous situations. And as each new realm offered more danger than the last, that would have to be addressed *soon*.

Red leaned forward to study the new stack, and their fingers brushed.

In that split second, Secrets soaked up as much information as possible. William had created these creatures. Whether through conventional means or not, the demon couldn't tell. All he knew was that they had purged some of the darkness inside of William and they both hated and adored the man for it, at once wanting to destroy and worship him.

They were too destructive to be loosed on earth, and so they had been bound to this underworld, but those bonds had begun to wither the day William had left them, and were now worn thin. Every kindness they dealt freed them a little more. But kindness was not part of their makeup and they had to actively ponder how to be nice.

One day, they would be free of this place. One day, they would return to their creator. Until then, they waited impatiently, biding their time, amusing themselves as best they could. And they planned to use Amun as fodder for their amusement for a long, long time.

They had no plans to cheat. That was their kindness to Amun—and they'd been considering how to go about this for centuries. Centuries. Here, there was no past or future. Only present, a present that somehow bled into that nonexistent past and future. They had known he would come. Just as they knew he would lose.

"Everything is acceptable, I take it," Red said. "Deal."

He had Secrets; he *could* win. He hoped. He nodded.

Black's lips twitched at the corners, as if he fought another grin. "He wasn't asking if you agreed, demon. He was telling you to deal the cards. You know Texas Hold 'Em, I'm sure."

Amun gave another nod. Tense, he shuffled the deck and tossed the cards. He'd played before. Anyone who was friends with Strider had played. Defeat fed on victories, and between battles with Hunters, he often challenged the men around him.

Amun couldn't afford to lose, and even though his opponents were playing honorably, that didn't mean he had to.

*Secrets. I need you. What do they have?* Even as he asked, he looked at his own hand. All right. Not bad. A pair of eights to kick things off. If there was another eight in the flop, giving him a three of a kind, he just might bring home the first victory.

As usual, Secrets didn't speak to him outright, but suddenly Amun knew that White and Black were his only competition this round. White had an ace and a king, and Black had the potential for a flush.

He knew, too, that the card he wanted for himself waited at the bottom of the deck. So Amun bottom dealt the turn and the river and ended up with three of a kind, just as he'd wanted. His excitement was short-lived, however. Black beat him with the aforementioned flush. That quickly, and that easily.

Damn. His stomach tightened with dread as he leaned back in his chair. If ever a man needed his hands, it was Amun. But he wouldn't fight the Horsemen when they removed his. He had another round to play, after all.

A grinning Black withdrew a serrated blade from his

boot. A blade already coated with blood. "Come on. Let's see the prize."

"How can he play the next round without his hands?" Haidee yelled. "You can't do this. You—"

"I guess you'll have to deal the next round for him," White interjected without a hint of mercy.

*No,* Amun signed. If she remained near him during the next round, his demon wouldn't be able to read the Horsemen and their cards. He would lose his advantage—not that it had helped him so far.

Haidee's clothing rustled, as if she were moving away from her perch. *I agreed to this,* he told her. *It's fine. I'll be fine. I'll find a way to play.* Again, he hoped. *I need you to stay where you are. That's the most important thing right now.*

Thank the gods, the rustling stopped. He placed his arms on the tabletop. Gideon had had his hands chopped off twice in his lifetime. If Gideon could survive, Amun could, too. He only regretted the fact that he wouldn't be able to touch Haidee tonight as he'd dreamed.

Before he had time to move, or protest, or change his mind, Black struck. Boom. Metal sliced through the bone in his left wrist before hitting the barbed table. Blood squirted, and sharp, agonizing pain exploded through Amun's arm, swiftly traveling through the rest of his body. He thought he heard Haidee scream, then soft hands were smoothing over his back, feminine whispers drifting through his ears.

*Worth it,* he thought, panting, sweating. He wouldn't have let them take one of her precious hands for any reason.

"Please, don't hurt him again," she was crying. "Please, take one of mine. Don't do this to—"

Black struck again, taking the other hand.

Haidee released another agonized scream. Dizziness

swam through him, as did more of that pain, but he didn't allow himself to even grunt. He compressed his lips and held everything inside, watching as White lifted the unattached hands and studied them.

"Nice and strong," she said with satisfaction.

"I think I'll like his feet better," Red said. "We can actually walk a mile in his shoes."

Every member of the Rainbow Brigade laughed.

*Tell them...tell them to start...the next round,* he managed to gasp to Haidee. He didn't dare look up at her. She was sobbing, he could feel the icy splash of her tears on his cheeks. Those tears would unman him, enrage him, and now wasn't actually an optimal time to fight the Horsemen.

Silent, ignoring his demand, she placed her own hands over his gushing wrists and an icy sheen spread, stopping the crimson flow and causing Secrets to scramble to the back of Amun's mind...fade. The other demons screamed as Haidee had done, rushing to hide deeper inside him.

"The old cards are covered in blood," she said. "Here's a new set." Then she released him, picked up the new deck and shuffled. She was trembling. Amun couldn't find the strength to send her away, no matter how desperately he needed his demon's aid.

The second game started a moment later, but his brain was foggy, his reactions slow. He wasn't sure how he remained in his chair, but he did. He wasn't sure what cards the Horsemen possessed, or even what kind of cards he possessed. His vision swam, blurring the numbers and pictures.

"What do you want me to do?" Haidee asked him, fear wafting from the words.

"Yes," White said. "Tell us all."

*Do you know how to play?* he asked, ignoring the Horsewoman.

Haidee gave the slightest nod.

He peered at his cards, willing away the haze. His determination paid off, and he finally saw what he had. Better than what he'd expected. He concentrated on the flop, again staring until his eyesight cleared. He needed an ace of hearts and he'd have a royal flush. Anything else, and he'd have nothing.

What did his opponents have?

Nothing with the potential of his hand; he would just have to work that to his advantage.

In the first hand, no one had folded. Because they hadn't been playing for stakes, just the end results. Time to change that. *Tell them we want to up the pot.*

After only a moment's hesitation, she did, and each of the four leaned forward, utterly interested. Amun outlined his demands to Haidee, and she peered down at him for a long while, eyes wide and face pale.

*Do it!* he snapped.

"I have a proposition for you all," she said. "If you lose, each of you will owe my friend here a year of service when you finally leave this place." Something they would find reprehensible, Amun knew. "And if he loses, well, he'll give you more than just his feet. He'll give you me."

*That isn't what I said, damn it!* He'd told her to offer him, all of him. *Tell them what I really said. Now.*

She shook her head, enraging him.

The Horsemen studied the flop, gauging what cards Amun might have. They had to know how close he was to that royal flush—or think he had one already, since he was risking everything.

"If you fold now, however," she went on, "you will be exempt from the new agreement."

*Haidee, damn it. Tell them they can't have you! If you don't, I'll do it. I'll start speaking, and you know what happens then.* He wouldn't risk her, not for any reason.

She didn't.

He opened his mouth.

"The new terms are acceptable," Red said before he could utter a single word.

And just like that, there was no backing down. The stakes had been set. Amun wanted to vomit.

White and Black folded, eliminating fifty percent of the competition and leaving only Red and Green. As he'd hoped. The rest of the flop was dealt, and Red practically hummed with satisfaction.

Green threw his cards onto the floor and spit on them. He hadn't gotten what he'd wanted.

"What do you have?" Haidee demanded of Red.

He flipped one card, then the other. Full house, Amun realized, queen over nines.

Haidee sucked in a breath. "Amun wins." Grinning now, she tossed his cards at Red. "You lose. Both you and your friend owe him a year of service."

Merciful gods. He'd gotten his royal flush.

All four Horsemen pushed to their feet, scowling over at him, their auras pulsing brightly. Red and Green even leapt at him. But everything—the males, the female, the smoke, the tent—disappeared in flash, before a single point of contact could be made.

The cave once again surrounded him and Haidee.

They were alone, he realized just before the haze returned. He was bombarded with relief, and that relief wiped out the adrenaline rush he'd fought so hard to maintain. He collapsed, unable to hold his own weight a second longer. He was panting harder, sweating more profusely, the pain no longer hidden by duty.

*How?* he asked. He was certain he'd won that final round through dishonorable means. Not that he cared. He simply needed to know in case the Horsemen returned and challenged him.

Haidee crouched at his side and placed the backpack on his stomach. "The angel said the pack would give us everything we needed to survive, so I asked for a deck of cards that would stay ordered in a way that would give you an undefeatable hand, even after I shuffled them. And now I'm asking for *literal* hands." As she spoke, she stuffed his arms inside.

The movement blasted the pain to another level, and he passed out before he discovered the results.

# CHAPTER TWENTY-THREE

STRIDER POSITIONED HIMSELF on the thick branch of an oak tree, surrounded by lush foliage and darkness. The clouds were thick and gray tonight, shielding the moon and stars and scenting the air with promised rain. The perfect atmosphere for fighting. Of course, he would have said the same thing if the sun had been shining brightly.

Planning an ambush was a lot more fun than vacationing with a horny immortal of questionable morals, a depressed, drugged-out warrior looking for his lost love and a forked-tongued little Harpy who rubbed his nerves raw.

William had decided he wanted no part in the coming battle. Said he couldn't risk injury when he had more important things to do, or some shit like that. So he'd taken off for Gilly's family home. Paris had just screwed a random stranger, his strength returned, his body healed, and was in the process of gathering weapons for The Stupid-Ass Chase, as Strider was now calling it. But Kaia, well, she was perched in the tree across from Strider's, waiting for the Hunters to find them.

They'd left a subtle but clear trail, acting as if they only wanted to camp and screw.

Below them was a tent, a crackling fire that cast only the barest hint of gold, hot dog weenies roasting on a portable grill—turned to its lowest setting, of course—and a lawn chair with a CPR dummy lounging on the plastic. How Kaia had produced the thing, he didn't know and wasn't going to ask. The stupid thing looked like him and had clearly been stabbed. Repeatedly. In the groin.

He thought she might have used the dummy for target practice, and tried not to be offended. Key word: tried. What had he ever done to piss her off? Well, besides annoy the hell out of her. But that had only happened recently, and she must have had that dummy for weeks. There were just so many slashes.

Suddenly his branch bounced, the leaves rattling together. He bit the inside of his cheek. He didn't have to look to know what had just happened. Kaia had decided to join him. She still smelled like cinnamon rolls, and his mouth still watered every time she neared him.

"You have your own tree, woman," he pointed out. "You said you'd stay on yours, and I'd stay on mine."

"Yeah, well, I lied." Kaia settled next to him, completely at ease. "That happens. Get used to it. Besides, yours is prettier."

He didn't allow himself the luxury of looking at her. One, he'd already memorized her features. In his mind, he saw the glossy red of her hair, so much like flames. Saw those gray-gold hawk eyes framed by lashes the same shade of red as her hair. Saw that pixie nose, those siren lips. Two, she would distract him—more than she already was. And with her litany of challenges still ringing in his head, she'd made certain he couldn't afford a distraction.

He wished his demon would get the message.

Ever since she'd opened that fire-and-brimstone mouth of hers in the car, Defeat had been supercharged. Eager, humming with nervousness, but also with great waves of anticipation. She was a worthy opponent, strong, brave and fearless. Besting her would be a thrill unlike any other, and a sexual high the likes of which he'd never experienced. As many battles as he'd fought over the centuries, he knew it, felt it. Wanted it.

And yeah, some of Strider's anger with Kaia had drained as they'd staged the campsite. She was just so unabashedly female, so unrepentantly aggressive, and he admired those qualities. But that didn't mean he *liked her* liked her.

The burn of her gaze brought him back to the present. She was studying him, taking his measure.

"Why are you here?" he asked, checking the site on the rifle mounted beside him. "Why did you ask Lucien to find me? The truth this time."

She sighed, her breath warm as it drifted over his shoulder. "Maybe I wanted to be with Paris."

"Nope. Try again. You've slept with Paris, and you know he can't have you again." Irritation had crept into his voice, and he didn't know why. What did he care if this gorgeous Harpy had welcomed his friend into her bed? She wasn't his, and he felt no sense of possession toward her.

"Maybe I wanted to make William jealous."

"Please," Strider said, his irritation rising for whatever reason. "Lucien said you'd specifically asked for me, and you don't need me to make William jealous. He'd offer himself up for your pleasure, even if you just wanted to carve the Chinese symbol for dumbass in his chest."

She paused, tensed. Then she grumbled, "Fine. I admit it. I wanted to be with you."

Harpies were notorious liars, as she'd admitted, but in this instance, he suspected she was finally telling the truth. Not because he was hot and most females wanted him. Well, yeah, he was hot and most females wanted him. But there had to be another reason.

"Why?" he insisted. "And don't give me that shit about being bored, because I also want to know why you tracked *my* Hunters."

"*Your* Hunters?" She snorted, every inch the warrior. "When you weren't tracking them yourself?"

"Kaia. Please."

She sighed again, the second caress of her breath making his muscles go rigid. "Lookit. You don't know this, but I was in the clouds with Bianka when you brought that female Hunter to the fortress. You...desired her and hated yourself for it."

He stiffened. If there was one topic guaranteed to blacken his mood, it was Haidee. "How do you know that?"

"Duh. While I'm in the clouds, I can watch anyone I want."

And she'd wanted to watch him? "Why me?" he demanded again.

Another pause, this one brittle with increased tension. "I...like you," she eventually admitted.

The words had him stiffening all over again. There was so much longing in her tone, he wanted to cover his ears. "As a friend, right?" He did *not* need a Harpy crushing on him. Especially now. Harpies were more determined, more stubborn than a pack of rabid pit bulls.

"No," she said, tracing something on the space between them. "Not as a friend."

Defeat's attention switched from the coming battle to the Harpy. Winning her heart would be—

No. His hands curled into fists. No. He didn't want to win her heart. Her body, yes. His cock was filling, hardening, suddenly desperate to feel the slick glide of her inner walls. He shook his head when he realized the direction of his thoughts. He didn't want to win her body, either.

Gentle, he had to be gentle with her. If he hurt her feelings with a rejection, she would hurt his face with her claws. The situation was as simple as that. "Kaia. You slept with Paris. One of my best friends."

"I made a mistake," she said hoarsely. "Haven't you ever made a mistake? I mean, you still smell like the stripper you banged. The one wearing the peach-scented body oil."

He understood her hatred for peaches now. She'd been— was—jealous. That did not please him. "Okay, so, yeah. I've clearly made mistakes, and I don't blame you for yours. But I'm not going to sleep with you." Defeat might have whimpered. *You're afraid of her, remember?* "Some of the guys can share. I can't."

"I—I wouldn't be with anyone else while we were together," she whispered, and his chest ached.

If he didn't know better, he would think she was...vulnerable right now. But he did know better. Harpies were as hard as steel. Nothing intimidated them, nothing softened them. They wanted something badly enough, they took it, and that was that. She probably just saw him as a challenge, something to tame. Gods knew enough women had tried and failed over the centuries. Gods also knew he understood the allure of a challenge.

"That doesn't matter," he said, still using that gentle tone. "It doesn't change the past."

"You wanted to share with Amun," she replied, trembling now. "You wanted his woman. Would have taken her if she'd wanted you in return."

"But I didn't, and I won't. Why do you think I left the fortress?"

"Well," she huffed, "just so you know, I didn't ask you to nail me. I just wanted to go on a date with you, maybe get to know you better."

So she could hop into bed with Paris, no preliminaries, but Strider needed to wine and dine her first?

*And don't you dare take this as a challenge,* he snapped at his demon. The beast had gone quiet, ceasing that annoying humming, waiting for Strider to reply to her, waiting for Kaia's next response.

"Let's backtrack a little," he said. Maybe, if he prodded

her enough, her desire for him would fade. "You saw that I wanted the Hunter."

"Yes."

"And?"

"And I realized I didn't like it."

Again, he doubted she lied. "So you tracked the other Hunters because…"

"I didn't want you distracted by them."

"Because…"

"I wanted you focused on me."

He was not pleased by that, either. *When are you going to stop lying to yourself?* "On dating you, not sleeping with you."

"Yes."

"Even though I wanted someone else?"

"Yes," she snarled.

Time to go in for the kill. "I'll be honest with you, Kaia. Ultimately, I need a woman who won't challenge me." *Which will bore the hell out of you,* common sense piped up. Strider ignored his stupid common sense. "I hate what happens when I lose, and with you, everything would be a challenge." *And exciting. And nerve-racking.*

"No, I wouldn't—"

He held up his hand for silence. "You wouldn't be able to help yourself. Look where we are, think about what we're doing. You challenged me to kill more Hunters than you do, for gods' sake."

"That was for your own good," she protested. "You were depressed or something and not taking care of business, which placed you in all kinds of danger. I was *helping* you, damn it!"

Maybe. Maybe not. "Well, your help has ensured that I slaughter anyone who's foolish enough to track me. Your help ruined my much-needed vacation."

Silence.

Finally he allowed himself to look at her. She was still watching him, those beautiful gray-gold eyes wide and glassy, as if she was fighting tears. A Harpy, cry? Not bloody likely. She was just disappointed that she wasn't getting her way, he rationalized, but that didn't stop the ache from blooming in his chest again. Didn't stop a wave of guilt and remorse from winding through him. He had hurt her.

"Kaia," he began, then paused. He didn't know what else to say.

In the distance, a twig had snapped.

Both he and Kaia stilled, not even daring to breathe. They waited...waited...but no other sounds were forthcoming. Neither relaxed their guard, however. They knew.

The Hunters had finally arrived.

How many men had Haidee's man brought with him?

Defeat started humming again, prowling through Strider's head as he focused on the battle. *Win. Win, win, win.*

Strider leaned into the rifle he'd propped at his side, studying his surroundings through the night-vision scope. Night-vision was both a blessing and a curse. Using the scope cut through the darkness, sure, but afterward, he wouldn't be able to see shit without it, even in the light.

There. He spotted...six men inching toward the camp. A slight adjustment of his alignment, and he saw...six more men doing the same on the other side. Twelve soldiers, then. Unless there were more behind him, of course, and he would bet his ass there were.

His heartbeat quickened with a hot surge of excitement. Much as he'd chastised Kaia, he really did love to fight. He loved the adrenaline rush, the knowledge that he was one step closer to finally winning the war with the Hunters.

The branch he perched upon suddenly shuddered the slightest bit. His jaw clenched as the leaves rattled together, announcing his location. Kaia had just jumped down. No one seemed to notice her, or him, however.

*Win,* Defeat said. *Win!*

*I know. I will.*

A shriek rent the air. A Harpy's high-pitched shriek.

A second later, he heard a *pop* and a *whiz*. The sounds of silencers, bullets. Next he heard a *crack*. The sound of a target being hit. The lawn chair shook, the dummy's body jolting.

Strider lined a target of his own in his sights—chest, dead center—and softly squeezed the rifle's trigger. There was a scream, then a grunt, and his victim tumbled down, face-first in the dirt.

The rest of the Hunters rushed into the camp, a few attacking the dummy.

"It's a fake," someone snapped.

"Ambush?" someone else said.

"Maybe."

"Stay on alert."

"Always."

"Spread out. Anything moves, anything at all, shoot to kill. I don't give a flying fuck about setting some crazed demon free. I want the host dead. The keeper of Defeat deserves to die."

"Hate that bastard," another murmured.

There was another scream, this one shrill and desperate. Kaia must have struck—with her claws. Damn it. He couldn't allow her to best him.

Strider angled his gun. Fired. Hit someone else in the chest. Angled. Fired. Hit again. Over and over he repeated the process, quick, so quick, before anyone realized what he was doing or where he hid. Bodies piled around his tree.

Finally the Hunters gained their bearings and spotted him. They peppered his branch with round after round.

Strider jumped, only one bullet grazing him as he fell. Fire lanced through his arm, but it wasn't enough to slow him.

*Win!*

As anticipated, he only had one good eye, the other shrouded with black. He could see there were quite a few Hunters left standing, and they'd already ferreted out his new locale. They converged, firing as they approached; he fired back. Before meeting them in the middle, he was struck twice, once in the shoulder and once in the stomach. He mentally blocked the pain.

*WIN!*

Guns were dropped and knives grabbed. This close together, bullets were simply too risky. Strider slashed. Someone screamed. He slashed again. Someone else screamed. A blade slicked through his wrist, but he maintained his grip and ducked, punching, tip extended. *Contact.* He hit all the way to the spine.

On and on the lethal dance continued. He was bleeding profusely but still energized. He was winning. He even managed to toss someone into the fire. Screams, grunts, groans and whimpering abounded. But by the time the last Hunter fell, Strider was losing strength fast.

He was also grinning.

He had done it. He had won.

"Who's your daddy, bitches?"

Defeat chortled inside his head, jumping up and down, glorying in the victory. Heat filled his veins, pumped him up. In a little bit, he would feel the sting of every slice, the rest of his energy gone, but for now, he felt invincible.

"Strider?" Kaia stepped into his line of sight. Firelight licked at her, illuminating her beautiful skin. The makeup she always wore must have sweated off, because she glimmered with every color of the rainbow.

In seconds, his cock was painfully hard. *It's just the*

*sexual high,* he told himself. *You don't want her. Not really.* Gods, her skin…his mouth watered for a taste.

Concentrate, he had to concentrate. He hadn't seen her fight, but he had heard the results. Now her hair was in tangles, and blood was splattered over her cheeks and arms. "Well?" he demanded. "How'd you do?"

Frowning at his waspish tone, she gestured behind her. He wanted to curse when he spied the pile of men she'd defeated. He didn't have to count to know she'd won their challenge. His stomach tightened with dread as he waited for his knees to buckle and acid to fill his veins, destroying the pleasure.

One minute passed, then another. Nothing happened.

"I didn't kill any of mine," she said, buffing her claws. "I just knocked them out. So feel free to do the honors yourself."

Wait. What? She'd *let* him win? Surely not. That was as un-Harpylike as, shit, baking an apple pie with ingredients she'd purchased—with money she'd actually earned. "Kaia—"

"No, don't say anything. The main guy, the one who wants you a lot more dead than even these guys did, isn't here. I checked. I told you he was wily, so there's no telling where he is or what he's doing."

"Kaia," he repeated, trying again. What he would say, though, he didn't know.

She spun away from him, as if she couldn't bear to look at him a second more. "I'll leave you to it, then. Goodbye, Strider."

Before he could say another word, she was gone, the tiny wings on her back giving her a speed he could never hope to match.

He stood there for the longest while, peering down at

the mound of unconscious men she'd left for him. He'd won, she had made sure of that, yet in that moment, he'd never felt more like a loser, and he didn't know why.

# CHAPTER TWENTY-FOUR

HAIDEE KNEW SHE WAS DREAMING. How else would she be seeing flashes of Amun's life? How else would she hear what he was thinking? Currently, she saw him pacing through a sunlit bedroom she didn't recognize, his hands alternating between scrubbing over his eyes and pressing into his ears as he fought to subdue the many voices chattering inside his head. Voices that whispered one human memory after another.

He could deal with them, he knew, but his friends could not. They had enough to agonize over and didn't need to know the vile things people thought about them, the atrocities committed every day in the homes around them.

He shouldn't have patrolled the city for Hunters tonight. Strider and Gideon could have handled the duty, no problem, despite their recent injuries. They'd offered; he'd turned them down, already sensing trouble on the outside and wanting to keep them safe.

Thankfully, he'd only found three enemy soldiers, and killing them hadn't been a hardship.

The Hunters hadn't planned to engage. Amun's demon had sensed that right away. The men had wanted their female, their Bait, on the inside first. They thought she had succeeded, but they were waiting for confirmation. The moment he'd realized that, Amun knew he'd have to wipe one of the Hunter's minds to find out who "she" was and when and where she would contact them. He'd have to absorb memories, perhaps even memories of mutilating his own friends. 'Cause yeah, he'd see through Hunter eyes, as if *he* was a Hunter.

"Amun, man," someone called from outside his room. It was Sabin. "Chow time."

He walked to the door and knocked, signaling he'd heard. Just as soon as he cleared his head, he'd join them. The memories were still unfolding, even though he'd already uncovered the information he'd wanted. The "she" belonged to Kane, keeper of Disaster.

The warrior rarely dated, too afraid of hurting those around him, but the human female had captured his interest. He'd have to be told. Amun would have to be the one to tell him.

Amun was always the one to break the bad news.

First, there would be denials. Then rage. Then sorrowful acceptance. But damn it, they shouldn't have to live like this! They shouldn't have to suspect everyone they encountered of using them.

For a moment, Amun's image faded from Haidee's mind and his thoughts quieted. She was shrouded in darkness and thought she might be lying down. What was that tickling her belly? she wondered.

Before she could discover the answer, those images of Amun returned, shifted. Now he was whaling on a human male, knuckles drilling into bone. The human was average height, on the thin side, and begging for mercy Amun refused to show.

Haidee didn't have to wonder why. Like Amun, she somehow knew what this man had been doing to his little girl. And when Amun was done, when the man was dead, he used his demon to find the little girl a safe, loving home.

Images, fading again. Voices, quieting again. Seriously. What was tickling her belly? Whatever it was brushed whisper-soft heat over her sensitized skin. But again, before she could reason out what was happening to her, the images in her head returned, shifted and claimed her full attention.

This time she saw a shirtless, cut-up and bleeding Amun playing basketball with his friends. He was grinning, laughing silently and slapping each of his buddies on their backs between cheap shots.

The boys shouted good-natured insults at him. Insults he could only return with the lifting of a single finger. No one stuck to any rules, so there was lots of tripping, elbowing and even punching, and Amun loved it. No one could beat him because he knew every move everyone planned to make before they actually made it. Only, any time Strider went for the ball, Amun let him have it, even slowing his steps and pretending to stumble.

His past was as varied as hers, Haidee mused. But while she had always been a Hunter, driven by hate, he was so much more than a Lord of the Underworld. Which should not have been possible. A demon should be a demon. Evil, ruined. Amun cared, though. He uplifted.

He shouldered such a heavy burden. A burden he shared with no one because he would rather suffer forever than cause one of his friends to suffer a single moment more. That was love, not evil.

Love.

The word echoed through her mind. Maybe because she felt utterly connected to Amun just then, she couldn't keep secrets, even from herself. She loved him, she realized. There was no denying it now, no questioning it. For all that he was, all that he'd been and all that he would be, she loved him. He was a warrior to his very soul, would always fight for what he believed in, would never buckle under pressure. When he cared, he cared deeply, intensely, and nothing and no one could shake that affection from him. Oh, yes. She loved him.

How did he feel about her?

She wanted him to care for her. Desperately. Because if they were going to be together, and she prayed that they were, his friends would be angry. Actually, "angry" was too mild a word. She doubted there was a word to accurately express the rage they would unleash upon him. But if he loved her in return, he could bear it.

How could she ask him to bear it? Even if he did, in fact, love her?

How could she ask him to carry yet another burden?

God, what a mess. If they were together, her friends—no, that wasn't the right word. They'd never truly been her friends. Her *coworkers* would fume at her, too. They wouldn't understand how she could adore a demon. They would attack Amun; they would punish her. And she knew that was exactly why Amun had pushed her away. He didn't want her to suffer. Didn't want her to have to "bear it," either.

That bespoke caring, right?

What he didn't know, however, and what she had to somehow show him, was that nothing would cause her more suffering than trying to live without him. For him, she could bear anything.

Perhaps he would one day feel the same for her. If he did, losing their friends wouldn't be something to bear because they would have each other, could rely on each other, comfort each other...cling to each other.

They had shared each other's blood all those centuries ago, creating a bond far more powerful than the hatred always simmering inside her. They belonged together; she knew it. She'd have to show him that, too.

Yes, she had loathed his kind for centuries. Yes, she had hurt him, and yes, he had hurt her. But that was in the past. Now, she only wanted to look ahead.

Look ahead. Again, the words echoed through her mind,

and she was forced to face a hard truth. She couldn't ask Amun to give up his friends. She couldn't allow him to cut those friends from his life, whether he could bear the loss of them or not, whether he would cling to her or not. How could she expect such a thing? Those warriors had helped shape Amun into the wonderful man he was. He needed them, and they needed him.

If Amun would just give her a chance, she would do everything in her power to smooth things over. After a time, if his friends still couldn't accept her, no matter what she did, she would leave.

So many ifs…so many possibilities.

Leaving would kill her, but for Amun, for his happiness, she would do it. All she needed was that chance.

*Haidee. Wake up for me, sweetheart.*

Amun's deep voice reverberated inside her head, much louder than in her dreams, jolting her into awareness. She blinked open her eyes. Several seconds passed before she was able to orient herself, and when she did, she took stock. Muted light filled the cave. In the distance, she heard the *drip, drip* of water. She was sprawled flat on her back, practically…sweating?

*Haidee, sweetheart. Can you hear me?*

Amun again. "Yes," she drawled. She stretched her arms over her head, back arching. The ground beneath her was soft, as if she rested on pillows.

*Finally. Now look at me.*

"Where are you?" Something tickled her belly again, causing goose bumps to sprout in every direction. Her gaze descended, and what she found left her gaping. A shirtless Amun was on his knees in front of her, her spread legs braced on his thighs. He wore pants. She wore panties. Only panties.

Both of his hands rested on her stomach, his fingers tracing designs around her navel, on her hips, just above the tiny patch of curls guarding her where she already ached.

"You have hands," was the first thing she thought to say. She'd been so afraid, so uncertain.

His lips quirked at the corners, revealing an amusement he rarely displayed. *Yes. I have my hands. I'm glad you noticed.*

She'd stuffed his injured arms into the backpack, eased him to his back when he had passed out, and then she'd paced, checked on him, prayed, bathed, checked on him, prayed some more, cursed, checked on him and finally fallen asleep beside him. At last check, he had still been handless.

"How?"

*The backpack, as you thought. Just took a while for everything to regrow. Now, enough about that. Do you remember when you woke me up with your mouth on my cock?*

She gulped, licked her lips. "Yes."

His eyes darkened and he flattened his palms on his thighs, as if he didn't trust himself to keep them on her. His gaze drifted to her core, and a ragged breath left him. *Good. You can't dispute that it's my turn to wake you up properly.*

Meaning it was his turn to taste her…oh, yes, please, yes. Yet he didn't lower his head. Didn't make any other moves toward her, and every nerve ending she possessed went on alert, readying for his touch. *Craving* his touch.

"Amun," she pleaded.

A muscle ticked in his jaw. *First,* he said, reaching back, *you're going to call Micah.*

Wait. What?

He lifted a small black cell phone. *I asked the pack for a phone that would reach the outside world.*

"But—it's okay." She shook her head. "I don't have to… not anymore, because I—"

*You wanted to call him, and so you will.* He held out the phone, forcing her to accept it.

She stared at the device for a long while, unsure whether Amun was trusting her or testing her. If she made the call, would she hurt him? Make him think she wouldn't take him anytime, anywhere, without his meeting certain conditions?

*As soon as you're done, I'll start.* The sensuality in his tone left no doubt as to what he meant. *Just know that by doing this, you're giving up your friends. You'll never be able to return to them. They'll despise you.*

Was he…giving her a chance? The very chance she'd wanted? "I know," she replied softly.

*They might even hunt you.*

"I know that, too."

*And you don't mind?*

"No. I'll have you."

*Oh, yes, you'll have me.* His expression became fierce. *I thought I could let myself have you for a little while, but I know now that a little while isn't going to be enough. I'm going to find a way back, and I'm going to keep you. Now, always.*

He wanted her now…always; she almost couldn't process the news. Amun, with her, forever. He hadn't offered any words of love, and she wasn't going to ask for them. That could come later. For now, this was enough.

*So what are you waiting for? Make the call.*

Maybe he was trusting her as she hoped, maybe he was testing her as part of her feared, but in the end, anticipation decided her. She dialed, shocked when the sound of ringing filled her ear. She wanted this over and done with, Micah out of the picture completely.

Her former boyfriend answered on the second ring, a snarled, "What?"

"Micah?" she asked hesitantly. Her gaze locked on Amun, gauging his every reaction. He wasn't looking at her, was looking just beyond her, his expression now a blank mask.

"Haidee?" Micah sounded baffled, relieved and over-joyed—and still angry—all at once. "Where are you? Tell me. Now." With every word, his emotions were overtaken by determination.

She experienced a pang of guilt. "Yes. I'm alive. But no, I won't tell you where I am. I—"

"Are the bastards monitoring this call?"

"No." Not really. "Listen, I—"

"Tell me where you are, then, and I'll come and get you."

"No. That's not why I'm calling. I just wanted you to know—"

"I thought you were dead," he interjected, once more cutting her off. Now he sounded accusing. "I mourned you. I tried to track you, tried to save you. Tell me, damn it. Tell me where you are."

"No. I'm alive, and that's all you need to know." Except… "I really need you to listen to me. I—"

"Who's that?" a female voice murmured sleepily from Micah's end of the line.

There was a beat of static, then a shuffle of footsteps as if he was pounding away from the intruder. In that moment, Haidee knew that he was sleeping with someone. Might have been sleeping with someone else even while they were dating. She couldn't bring herself to care.

Had he ever wanted her, though? With her, he'd been content to keep things mostly hands-off. She hadn't won-dered why because she'd been happy with the status quo. But if he hadn't wanted her, why had he stayed with her?

"If you're alive, that means you're helping them." She didn't have to ask who "them" was. And he didn't even address the fact that a woman had spoken. "Otherwise, they would have killed you by now."

"Yes," was all she said on the subject. Let him take that answer however he chose. "I just wanted to call and tell you that we're over. I don't want to date you anymore."

Amun, she noticed, had tensed, his fingers digging into his thighs and probably leaving bruises. He had no idea what Micah was saying, no idea why she'd said yes to the man. Yet he wasn't interfering.

He *was* trusting her, she realized.

"Now you listen to me, you fucking bitch," Micah suddenly growled, and there was so much hatred in his tone she was momentarily speechless. "You tell me where the hell you are, who you're with and what you're doing. I'm going to find you and take back what's mine. Then I'm going to cut your fucking throat and dance in the blood. You don't deserve—"

*Click.* Haidee severed the connection before he could finish berating her, shocked, at last upset, and unsure what had just happened.

Amun's gaze finally met hers. He didn't ask questions, just took the phone and tossed it over his shoulder. Then, without another word, he lifted her hips and stripped the panties from her, pulling her legs in front of him, one at a time. Mouth set in a grim line, he tossed the panties beside the phone. He repositioned their bodies the way they'd been.

Tears suddenly burned her eyes. How could Micah have said those things to her? *Fucking bitch. Cut your fucking throat. Bitch, bitch, bitch.* He'd been her friend. Hadn't he? And yes, she had expected the Hunters to turn on her, but not that quickly. Not that violently.

*You're that distressed to lose him?* Amun asked, and

though the words were soft, she heard the fury—and even the insecurity—behind them.

"No." She was the one who couldn't meet his eyes this time. "He—he called me a terrible name, said terrible things." And she didn't want Amun to ever think of her that way. Even though he, more than anyone, had the right.

*Like what? What name?*

Amun hadn't been furious before, she realized then. *Now* he was furious. If Micah had walked into the cavern, Amun would have killed him without hesitation. "Do you think I'm a…a bitch?"

*No,* he answered without any hesitation. His expression softened, gentled. *I think you're perfect, sweet…mine. And now I also think he can't be related to me. He's an idiot.*

"Really?" She swiped her watery eyes with the backs of her wrists. "You don't think badly of me, I mean."

*Really. We're together, now and always, remember?*

"I remember." The hurt inside her eased. She was with the man she loved. *That* was all that mattered. "Amun?"

*Yes.*

As she finally met his gaze, her heart skipped a beat. His expression was heated, his gaze heavy-lidded, his brows a determined slash. His lips were red, as if flushed. Did his blood race as swiftly as hers?

Wonderfully dark skin pulled taut over the muscles of a warrior. She couldn't see his butterfly tattoo, but she vowed to trace every inch with her tongue one day soon. Between his legs, his cock stretched past the waist of his pants, the head already beaded with moisture. Her mouth watered. She knew his taste, would forever be addicted to it.

"I want you," she whispered.

*Then by gods, you'll have me.*

Yes. Finally, they were going to make love. The restriction she'd so foolishly placed on their physical relationship had been vanquished. But even if she hadn't spoken to Micah, she still would have given herself to Amun this night.

*Such a pretty pink,* he said, gaze moving to her sex. *So wet for me already.*

Even his words were a turn-on. "I ache for you. There, everywhere."

His hands slid to her inner thighs, and he spread his fingers, almost, but not quite, brushing her where she most needed. Soft. One finger, two, glided up her slit, and she quivered, whimpered.

*Like silk.*

She wanted those fingers on her again, gliding yes, but lingering, too. Pressing. She lifted her hips, silently beseeching. He gave her what she wanted—sort of. He traced between those pouty lips, and he did linger, but not where she so desperately needed. He allowed one fingertip to push past her opening, but not deeply. He pushed just enough to swirl and stoke her need higher.

*Play with your breasts. Let me see how you like them touched.*

Not for a single moment did she consider objecting. She plumped them, kneaded them, pinched her nipples while he watched. The heat inside her grew…grew… "I want you to take me the rest of the way now," she gasped out. She wasn't sure how much more she could take. "Please."

A long moment passed in silence before he nodded. He didn't fall on her, licking and sucking and tonguing between her legs as she expected, thought she wanted, but leaned forward, pressing them together. Since her thighs were draped over his own, the action spread her wider, brought her core into contact with his pant-clad erection, rubbing, creating the most delicious sense of friction between her legs and on her breasts. Her nipples rasped his chest.

"I thought you were going to…"

*I am. First, though, I'm going to prepare you.*

She gasped, hands sliding around his neck, nails sinking into his back. His head lowered, and his mouth opened up on one of her nipples. The heat was nearly unbearable, so much greater than what swirled inside her, but so necessary she didn't even think about trying to shove him away. Then he was at last licking and sucking and tonguing her there, shooting startling sensation after startling sensation through her entire body.

She knew he was a big man. How could she not? He probably outweighed her by more than a hundred pounds and was nearly a foot taller than she was. But just then, the width of his shoulders practically engulfing her, she felt almost…dainty.

"Take off your pants," she managed to gasp out as she arched against him. Sweet heaven, that felt good. "Let me feel all of you."

*No. Moment I do, I'll be inside you.*

"That's the point. I'm prepared, I swear."

*We're taking our time, woman. Get used to the idea.*

She loved that he could talk to her and continue tormenting her nipple at the same time. And he did. Torment her. His teeth scraped the sensitive bud, but then he would quickly kiss away the sting.

When she was writhing against him, begging him for more, he gave her other nipple the same treatment. Hours seemed to pass as he contented himself with her breasts, plumping them, kneading them as she had done, never ceasing to bathe her nipples in the wet heat of his mouth.

*You're so beautiful,* he said.

"Amun, please. More."

*You're so strong and brave. And mine. Did I tell you that already? Mine.*

"Yours," she croaked. She tugged at his hair, forcing him to raise his head or lose a handful of strands. Onyx eyes shimmered, lines of tension branching from them. He wasn't as relaxed as he would have her believe. "Kiss me. I need your taste in my mouth."

With a moan, he surged up, curling her body higher, tighter, and crushed their lips together. His tongue immediately pushed inside to roll and mate with hers. He tasted of mint and something sweet. Something uniquely his own.

He released her legs to cup her face, and she locked her ankles around his back. She slid herself against the thickness of his erection, probably wetting his clothes, but she didn't care. Her need was too strong, and just as she'd kissed him the other times, her mind became focused only on climax.

Soon he lost his pretend nonchalance, his movements becoming jerky, his arousal slamming against her, grinding into her, ringing gasp after gasp out of her mouth. He swallowed every one of those gasps before angling her head, allowing his tongue to thrust as hard and deep as she wanted his cock to thrust.

Only with him had she ever felt feverish, burning, the heat of him continuing to pulse inside her, spreading, consuming. Somehow, that freed the chill she'd managed to hide. In seconds, she was a writhing cauldron of both fire and ice, thoughts fragmenting, muttering incoherently.

"Please," she might have said. She needed to be filled, needed some kind of release. This was too much, not enough, and her heart couldn't take much more. "Please, baby." She rubbed her legs up his sides, squeezing him, encouraging him. She tangled her hands in his hair, she scratched at his back, probably drawing blood. "Please. Give me more."

He pulled away from her, and she groaned. He didn't

disappoint her, though. He finally, blessedly, oh, so sweetly, licked between her thighs. Her cry of delight pierced the passion-scented air, and her hips shot up, drawing him closer. Over and over he licked, nibbled, sucked.

*I could do this forever, sweetheart.*

"Forever."

*I'll never get enough.*

"Never." She knew she was only repeating part of what he said, but she couldn't help herself. Couldn't concentrate on anything but the pleasure. But always, she maintained a sharp hold on her inner chill, never allowing the ice to seep to the outside, to Amun.

He pushed her to the brink, and then, with one swirl of his tongue, he pushed her over. She screamed her release, bucking against him, unable to still for a long while. When her tremors eased, she sagged against the ground, panting. She realized then that her body had gotten what it needed—for now—but her mind had not. The ice, still churning inside her... Her mind wouldn't be completely satisfied until she gave Amun everything.

He flipped her over, and the swift action startled her. Before she could gasp, he was kissing her back. Her tattoos. Laving them with his tongue as she'd wanted to do to his. He was offering absolution, apologizing for what she'd lost in the most basic way. And oh, God, tears filled her eyes.

*I've imagined taking you in every position, but this first time, I want you facing me. Looking at me. Seeing me.* He turned her back over. *So open your eyes, sweetheart, and I'll give you all that I am.*

She hadn't realized she had squeezed her eyelids closed. She pried them apart and peered up at the man who had won her heart. He had straightened, was now merely staring down at her. Sweat dripped from his forehead. The moment their gazes met, he reached between their bodies. His knuckles brushed her sensitized clitoris as he unfastened his pants, and she again bucked wildly, already needing more, already verging on desperate.

She wanted total satisfaction this time.

He didn't waste a single second shoving his pants off. They were open, and as he'd promised, he lost track of everything else. The thick head of his cock probed her entrance, seeking full penetration. Except, still he held back.

His white teeth were chewing on his bottom lip. His sweat began dripping off him and onto her. *You're mine, Haidee, all mine. I'll take care of you...always...won't risk you...don't think you can get...pregnant...no worries... Just let me...*

He was trying to reassure her, she knew, but she was past the point of caring. "Do it. Please, do it. I need you. Have to have you. All of you. Dying without you. Please, Amun, please. Let me give all of me, too." He could take it. Please, God, let him be able to take it.

Before she could finish her prayer, Amun slammed all the way home, and she arched up to meet him, to drive him so deep they might never be able to part. Haidee released another scream, her relief so potent she couldn't keep it contained. She'd waited for this moment forever, it seemed.

She hadn't been with a man in a long, long time, and she had never been this aroused, this willing to break apart and reform into someone new. To experience every sensation, nothing held back.

"Everything," she said, a promise.

*Everything,* he agreed, a vow.

Then he was kissing her, and he was in her mouth, her blood, her bones, her soul. And yet that still wasn't enough. She wanted to be inside him, too, a part of him always.

*Mine, you're mine.*

"Always."

He began to move, pounding forward, withdrawing, pounding forward again. Stretching her, burning her up, catching her on fire. Driving her higher and higher, toward that edge of insanity. She thrashed and she clung to him, almost afraid to fall this time.

*Let go, sweetheart.*

"The cold…" It was there, waiting.

*Let go. I don't care what happens. I need you. All of you, just as you vowed.*

She heard the strain in his voice, knew he was near the edge, as well. And so she did it. She finally let go. She trusted him completely, opened herself up totally and let down her guard inexorably.

Instantly satisfaction slammed into her with the same ferocity that Amun did. Her body splintered, flew to the heavens, stars winking behind her eyes as she lost sight of his beautiful face. All the while, the fire spread…hotter and hotter… All the while, the ice stormed…colder and colder…

Amun trembled and bucked against her as wildly as she bucked against him, and then he was roaring, loud and long, coming, coming, coming so hard. She thought distantly that her body had been starved for him, was now drinking from him, and she might never be thirsty again. Would probably be sated forever. But still the fire spread, hotter and hotter. The ice, though, was fading, no longer storming inside her—because it was seeping into Amun.

At first, she loved the heat. Welcomed it, wanted more and tried to get it, pulling every bit she could from Amun's body while giving him the ice, unable to stop herself. Soon, though, he was gasping, groaning, shoving away from her and severing contact.

Even without his touch, however, it was too late for her. She felt bathed in flames, no hint of ice left.

She screamed in pain, in agony, not knowing what to do. The flames should have lit her up, blazed bright, but they somehow surrounded her in darkness, darkness she couldn't find her way out of.

She was dying. She had to be dying. That was the only time she'd ever battled such darkness and pain.

*Sweetheart, oh, gods, sweetheart. What's wrong? Tell me what's wrong.* His hands smoothed over her face, and for once, it was not heat she felt from him. He was as cold as a meat locker, and she was envious.

*I don't know what's wrong,* she wanted to shout, but her jaw was locked together, the pain knotting her muscles and preventing her from moving, even in the slightest way.

Somehow, Amun heard her and replied. *I don't know, either, sweetheart.*

*Help me. Please.* Any more and she really would die. Just then, she *wanted* to die.

*I'll find a way. I swear to the gods I'll find a way.*

The vow was the last thing she heard from him. The darkness thickened until she could see the slick texture of it, the evil that oozed from it. Like black oil, coating her… destroying her.

Demons, she realized with a moan. The demons—*his* demons—were now a part of *her.*

# CHAPTER TWENTY-FIVE

WHAT THE HELL HAD HE done to her?

Amun was in a panic. Physically, he had never felt better; he was clearheaded, sated, both energized and relaxed. Cold, yes. He was far colder than he'd ever been. Rather than destroy him, as the cold had done to the congo, he was strengthened. And yet, his woman now suffered unbearably. Her beautiful skin was flushed a bright red, but not from pleasure. She was racked with pain, her body curled into itself, her fingers actually gnarling as she screamed, over and over again.

He'd promised to help her, but he didn't know how, had no medicine, could only ask for—the backpack, he thought suddenly. Some of his panic eased as his gaze landed on the angel's gift. Of course. So simple. *Please be simple.* The backpack had given him back his hands. Now it would give Haidee back her life.

Amun grabbed the pack, his grip so tight he feared he would rip the material. *Give me something to help her, something to save her.* Though urgency bombarded him, he waited one second, two.

Trembling now, he reached inside and found—nothing. *Help me help her,* he demanded. Again, nothing appeared inside. Cursing, Amun upended and shook the material, but still he found nothing. The bag remained empty.

That didn't mean…couldn't mean… No. *No!* He refused to believe Haidee was beyond saving. She would survive this, whatever "this" was. She had to; he needed her. Had never needed a person more.

He didn't care that she would be reanimated if she…if she…he couldn't even think the word. She hated when that happened, hated the pain that followed. Hated her loss of memories.

She *would* survive, he thought again. She was the missing piece of his soul, a necessary part of his soul. How he'd ever lived without her, he didn't know. But he did know that he loved her. Loved her strength, her courage, her wit and the tender way she cared for him, so at odds with the sexy, tough-girl look of her. He loved the way she gave herself to him, her body his to do with as he pleased, inhibitions vanquished.

He had only to kiss her, and she became a live wire in his arms. No other woman had ever responded to him like that. She truly reveled in his touch and wasn't ashamed to beg for more. She made him forget they were on a mission, made him forget that anyone or thing existed beyond the two of them.

And she had chosen him. She'd known the consequences of cutting ties with the Hunters, of becoming Amun's woman—he'd made sure of it—but she had chosen to be with him anyway.

He wasn't giving her up. Once, he'd thought he could. Once, he'd thought their time together would end the moment they left this realm. Wrong. He was keeping her. Now, always. Just as he'd told her.

*Hot*, she whimpered. *Hot.* Tears trickled from her closed eyelids, catching in her lashes before running down her cheeks.

She was talking inside his mind. He'd thought he'd heard her earlier, had convinced himself he was mistaken, but now there was no denying the truth. The connection was complete. The barrier that had kept her out of his head, whatever it was, had clearly been shattered. Probably because he had utterly lowered his guard the moment he'd penetrated her.

He had been defenseless against her, vulnerable, and hadn't cared. He had welcomed her, every part of her, inside and out. He had craved an unbreakable connection, no matter the consequences, wanting no secrets between them. The good, the bad, he'd wanted to share all of it. With her and no other. Just as she had said. All, everything.

He had to save her.

Amun eased beside her and gently, so gently, lifted her in his arms. He sat with his back propped against a rocky wall and settled her on his lap. At first, she struggled against his hold, every motion probably torturing her. Then the new coolness of his skin seeped past the new burn of hers. She rubbed her cheek against his chest, moaned and cuddled against him.

*So evil,* she whimpered.

He traced his fingertips over her brow, trying to ease the fever there. *What's evil, sweetheart?*

*The demons.*

Demons? Amun stilled, not even daring to breathe. He'd felt her tugging on them, felt them resisting her, but his pleasure, the cold, he'd lost track of everything else. *They're...inside you?*

*Yes.* Another whimper.

*Mine?*

*I think so.*

How could that be? He closed his eyes, searched his mind—and found no evidence of the vile essence that had nearly destroyed him before Haidee had entered his life. There were no disgusting urges waiting to pounce, no creatures writhing deep in his cognizance, no painful memories desperate to spring to the surface.

He should have been happy, but he was infuriated. With himself. He would rather deal with the evil himself than subject Haidee to a single moment of *this*. Damn it. He had to help her. Another thought struck him, and he flinched.

If Secrets had left him, too, Amun would die. For the moment Secrets had possessed him, they'd become two halves of a whole. One could not survive without the other. Not really.

*Secrets,* he found himself rushing out.

His voice must have nudged the creature. Secrets sighed with relief. Relief and joy. Once again, it was just the two of them. And though Haidee's chill—Amun's chill now—cloaked them, there was no more fear. They'd faced the storm and survived. Hell, they'd thrived.

How had Haidee taken the other demons but not Secrets?

He didn't know, but he could find out. And perhaps, in doing so, he could save her. Determination replaced every other emotion inside him. *You're going to find the answer, all the answers, and you're going to help her.*

Information was the demon's crack. Eagerly Secrets forced his way into Haidee's mind. Actually, "forced" was too strong a word. The demon glided on in, as if the welcome mat had been placed at the front door, the windows left open. Even more astonishing, there were no barriers. The floodgate had opened. Whatever the demon wanted to glean, he gleaned.

Amun swam through the churning, never-ending sea of memories, searching for what he needed and discarding what he didn't. He discarded most, in fact, but at long last, his efforts were rewarded. The story of Haidee's life unfolded as if he were turning pages in a book.

After the Lords of the Underworld were kicked out of the heavens and tossed to earth, Themis, the Greek goddess of Justice, decided to balance the scales. The world had been given demons, and so, to her, the world required demon executioners. Executioners *she* could control, as the angels—demon-slayers in their own right—refused to do her bidding. Unable to simply create beings from air as Zeus, the god king, Themis was forced to find another way.

When she heard the prayers of Haidee's parents, the answer came to her. The couple was childless, barren and desperate, and in their desperation, they agreed to the bargain Themis proposed. The goddess would bless the mother's womb, and that womb would bear fruit. The couple would raise that child for ten years, and at the end of that tenth year, they would give her to the person of Themis's choosing, so that she might be trained. They weren't to worry, though, for the goddess would bless them with other children. Children they would be allowed to keep.

All was set.

The parents tried to distance themselves from their little girl and save their love for their other children. But one smile from the sweet little angel, and they fell. Unlike other babies, she was not fussy or contrary or even temperamental. She watched the world around her, thoughtful, always thoughtful.

As her tenth birthday approached, they realized they would rather die than lose her.

Themis, being Themis, granted their request. The couple had prevented a demon executioner from learning how to fulfill her purpose, and so they would die at the hand of a demon. Justice would once again be served.

And so the goddess commanded the keeper of Hate to slaughter the entire family, Haidee included, for she would start again, find someone new, someone she would raise from birth herself.

Hate was more than happy to comply.

After murdering Haidee's parents and little sister, the demon-possessed immortal turned his sights on the god-touched child. But as he peered into her eyes, he remembered how Themis had once planned to use her and realized she might be able to save him. For if she could destroy the demon inside him, he would finally be free.

So Hate grabbed Haidee, intending to hide her until he figured out how exactly her ability worked. Only the moment he touched her, a strange cold infused him, tearing at his insides. He reacted instinctively, stabbing and releasing her, then running from her, the pain too much to bear.

As the days passed, he realized she had ripped a small piece of his demon from him—like a human losing a limb. And as time passed and he came to discover what happened to keepers who were severed from their demons... Well, instead of yearning to break ties with the creature, he wanted to reclaim that missing part of it. But each time he found Haidee, she died before he could touch her, as if Themis had forever cursed him to fail in his quest because he had failed to destroy the girl as promised.

Secrets marveled at the deluge of information, a child at Christmas.

And still so many questions remained... How had Haidee taken a piece of the demon High Lord? How had Hate's host not died? How had Haidee never known Hate was inside her? How had she not known what the demon was thinking, feeling or wanting? Amun always knew. So did his friends. How had she not known Hate was the cause of her reanimation and memory loss? Or was Themis the one responsible?

How had the demon stayed with her even after she died, when Baden's demon had been freed after his death? When Aeron's had been freed after *his* death?

More answers flowed... That small piece of Hate had hidden inside her, strong enough to influence but too weak to do anything more. That's why she hadn't known the being was there or what he felt. His wants and needs had simply seemed like her own.

And Hate had not brought her back to life all those times; Themis had. Inadvertently. Since Haidee had sprung from a womb blessed by the goddess, she'd never been fully human. So, like the souls who reanimated in hell, she never really died. Only difference was, her corporal form could walk the earth, as well as hell.

So much information...too much...not enough.

As she'd done for Hate, Haidee had taken the demon minions from Amun. Not just pieces, though, but every part of them. Secrets, a High Lord, was stronger, however, tethered to Amun by godly bonds, while the others hadn't been.

Still, she could have taken Secrets, but she hadn't. She'd been careful, even though she hadn't realized what was happening to her or to Amun.

Were the new demons forever a part of her now?

No. *No!* He couldn't allow that. He knew how evil those beings were, how disgusting their thoughts, and he would not leave Haidee to suffer like that. But what could he do? He waited for Secrets to tell him, but this time, no response was forthcoming. The demon was still lost inside those memories.

Haidee was curled in the fetal position, whimpering, her tears burning his chest as they streaked down his skin. He reasoned out the rest on his own. She'd been a little girl when Hate first attacked her, and she'd probably clung to the dark piece of the demon she'd drawn inside her, needing the emotion to survive the terrible deaths she'd witnessed her parents and sister suffering.

Hate was as much a part of her as Secrets was to him,

but these other demons were new and hadn't had time to bond with her yet. He hoped. They wouldn't want to bond with her, either, and would fight the connection. After all, Themis had ensured Haidee was a demon executioner. That meant Haidee had the power to defeat the darkness inside her, even if she didn't realize it, and the bastards had to sense that.

No wonder they'd been so afraid of her, of her pull and her cold.

Guilt filled Amun, surpassing every other emotion because, with this new knowledge, he realized he alone was responsible for her current torment. She had saved him, and he had harmed her.

*Haidee, sweetheart,* he said, squeezing her tight. *I need you to listen to me.*

*Hurt,* she moaned. *I hurt so bad.*

*I know, darling, but fight past the pain and listen to me. Can you do that?*

A pause, another whimper. Then a hesitant, *yes. Yes. Amun, you're reading my mind. How are you reading my mind?*

*I think I instinctively built a mental wall to block you out when those demons were inside me. The moment you took them, that wall fell. Now I need you to fight the demons, sweetheart. Push them out of your body. Out of your skin.*

*How? Every time I mentally approach them, they dart away.*

*Corner them.*

*I can't!*

*You can. And you will. Do it. Now.* He put enough steel in his voice to anger her. *Do it, or I'll hand you over to Strider. You think you're suffering now, well, wait until he gets you. He will torture the living hell out of you, and*

*I'll cheer him on. Then I'll make love to another woman in front of you.*

Every muscle in her slight, trembling body stiffened. *B-bastard.*

*I know. Get well, and you can punish me.*

*T-trying.* Her body uncurled, stretching taut as a bow. *They're still darting...like little flies...no, close, I'm close... they can't go anywhere else...there they are...*

Her back arched as an agonized groan ripped past her lips.

*Haidee? Talk to me. Tell me what's going on.*

*Pushing, I'm pushing them. They're screaming, want out. Out, out, out.*

*That's the way, sweetheart. You're doing so good. I'm so proud of you. Keep pushing them.* He flattened his palms, his cold, cold palms, on her and stroked. He stroked her everywhere, every inch of her body, willing the cold out of him and back into her. *Push them out, and then cut any tether that binds them to you. Understand?*

Slowly her skin began to darken. Not tanning, not becoming a lovely gold, but becoming a dark, sickly gray. She was doing it. She was expunging them. He could feel the malevolence pulsing off her.

Relief only increased his urgency. His hands moved faster, trying to touch every inch of her at once. *That's the way.*

*The ice. Yes, the ice. Need it. Need it. Need—* She screamed. Screamed until her voice broke, until his eardrums nearly burst just to escape the noise. Darkness was now pouring off her, drifting into the air like dust motes before darting out of the cave entirely.

Her nails raked at him, drawing blood. She thrashed, she fought, but he never released her from his hold. Finally, thank the gods, *finally*, she sagged against him, silent, not even trembling, as if every bit of strength had been sapped from her and she could barely even manage to breathe.

Amun never stopped cooing at her. He whispered everything he'd learned about her past, knowing she would want every detail. He promised he would never allow anyone—not gods, demons or humans—to hurt her. Finally, she rallied.

*I suspected you were part goddess, you know,* he said.

A small, sad smile. *I almost can't take this in. Chosen and betrayed by Justice. Targeted by Hate. Part Hate myself. I mean, I'm a demon and I've fought demons all my life. Lives. It's ironic and weird and…and…I hate it. Hate.* A bitter laugh. *Makes sense now.*

*No one can blame you for what happened.*

*I can. I do.*

*You shouldn't.*

*I want to deny it all, so damn badly, but I can't.*

*You are a wonderful person, and what we've learned today doesn't change that.*

*I—* Whatever argument she meant to give, she changed her mind. *Thank you, Amun. For everything you did, everything you said. For liking me despite this.*

Liking? He more than liked her, but she'd endured enough revelations for the moment. *Sleep now, sweetheart.*

*Yes.*

The gray cast eventually faded from her flesh, returning her skin to that lovely golden shimmer. The fever even cooled. He, too, sagged, his relief so great he practically choked on it.

Hours passed while she dozed, her body trying to fortify itself. Though he was exhausted, he never allowed himself to drift. He remained awake, alert, keeping guard. And as always, just being near Haidee aroused him. More so now, considering how close he'd come to losing her.

She was naked, he was naked, and her soft scent was imprinted in his sinuses. Her breasts were pressed into his chest. Breasts he'd held, suckled. Her legs were twined with his. Legs he'd spread, caressed. Soon he was sweating, the chill inside him gone as if it had never been. He needed to reaffirm that his woman lived, that their bond hadn't been shattered.

*She's too weak. She needs a little recovery time.* More than that, making love had almost killed her. He would not risk her again. Ever. He would be with her, safeguard her, pamper her, but never again would they be together in a sexual way.

"I'm not too weak," she murmured sleepily, the coolness of her breath tickling his chest. "I'll never be too weak for that."

He inhaled sharply. In that moment, he knew. He knew she was going to be all right. His arms tightened around her, squeezing so tightly he feared he would crack one of her ribs. But he couldn't temper his reaction, couldn't dilute his need to hold her and never let go.

"Make love to me," she said. She raised her chin and looked up at him, though she never lifted her cheek from his chest. "Remind me that I'm alive."

*No, sweetheart. No. We're just going to hold each other.*

"But why?" Was she…pouting?

His cock twitched in response. *What if there are other demons hiding inside me? Or what if you draw Secrets out this time? Secrets is a High Lord, and the demons you took from me were merely minions. High Lords make minions look like infant children in need of a bottle.*

"But there were hundreds of those minions."

*Thousands of minions could not compare with one High Lord.*

She sighed. "That's probably true."

*Is that piece of Hate still inside you?* he asked. *Or did you expunge it, too?*

"It's still with me. I can feel the emotion, weaker than before, but there."

*Good.*

"Good?"

*I don't want to risk losing you. I'll die if I'm separated from Secrets, and I fear the same will happen to you if you're separated from Hate. Even so small a piece.*

"Oh...yeah," she said, disappointed. "I forgot about that."

His heart stuttered to a stop. *Does it bother you that I will always be a demon?*

"Not at all." She slid one of her hands to his neck and pressed a fingertip against his pulse, jump-starting his heart into action again. "I accept you for who and what you are."

He hadn't realized how badly he'd needed to hear those words until she'd said them. *As I accept you.*

She placed a soft kiss on his sternum. "I'm still in shock. But God, this explains so much, you know? Why I have so much trouble loving, why people tend to dislike me when they first meet me. Why moods are sometimes blackened in my presence."

*I'm sorry. Sorry that happened to you.*

"I should be sorry, too. I want to be—well, more than I am—but it brought me to you, so..."

He kissed her temple in thanks. *I wonder how you drew that piece of Hate inside you without killing the host. I wonder how you took Hate, but not Secrets.*

"From what you told me, the host of Hate *wanted* me to free him. Until the pain started. Then he changed his mind. You didn't want me to take Secrets. Maybe that has something to do with it."

*Maybe.*

"Or maybe I wanted to hurt him, but didn't want to hurt you."

*That makes more sense. But either way, I never want you to go through a purging again.*

Frowning, she sat up, turned, and straddled his waist. "So you plan to deny us both for the rest of our lives?"

*Yes.* Even though the word passed from his mind to hers, his tone still managed to drip with all kinds of irritation. He wanted her, damn it, and resisting her was nearly impossible. Practically riding him as she was, her breasts uptilted, her nipples hard, she wasn't making it easy on him. She was making it hard. Very, very hard.

One of her brows arched, and a calculating gleam entered her eyes. She flattened her palms on his pectorals and leaned forward, as if she meant to push off him and stand. "I can't believe you're making me resort to rape, Amun."

*Haidee—*

In the next instant, she raised her hips and impaled herself on his erection. She was already wet, and took him easily. His lips parted on a silent moan of bliss.

Her head fell back, and her nails dug deep. "A girl will do what a girl has to do to prove to her man that the only way to hurt her is to deny her. But then, I guess I'm not a girl. I'm borderline demon, so you should have expected this kind of behavior."

*You shouldn't have—you need to—oh, gods...* Unable to stop himself, Amun arched his back and surged the rest of the way inside her, hitting her deep, so deep. A hoarse cry left him this time, echoing around him, and in the back of his mind he expected words to start falling from his lips. They didn't. So he forced himself to return to that motionless state, panting, afraid and hopeful.

As her knees squeezed his sides, her stomach quivered from the pleasure of having him inside her. She'd never looked lovelier, he thought. Never looked more pagan, more...his.

*Haidee,* he gasped into her mind. *I shouldn't have thrust the rest of the way. You have to...move...off me...on me... you just have to move, damn it.*

She didn't. She remained still, watching him.

His fingers banded around her waist, holding tight. She was so wet, so wonderfully cool inside, and she was killing him with every second that passed, refusing to move off him—or on him.

Finally he sagged against the ground. He didn't have the strength to push her away. And he damn sure didn't have the courage to urge her on. He wouldn't hurt her. He wouldn't risk her.

*Haidee,* he said, trying again.

"Just hold on, baby," she whispered huskily. "This little lady is gonna do all the work."

# CHAPTER TWENTY-SIX

*ALL THE WORK...*

Holy hell, she really would kill him.

Especially since there were no more secrets between them. Not anymore. Amun knew she could now read him as easily as he could read her, and knew why she was doing this. She had felt his fear, his determination never to touch her like this again, and even though *he* had felt *her* fear, she was willing to risk herself. To try this again.

But more than he wanted the exquisite pleasure he could find in her body, the utter bliss of feeling her inner walls clamp around him, holding him close, the thrill of sliding inside of her, retreating, then sliding back in, he wanted her safe.

*Secrets,* he gritted out. *Do you know what will happen to her if we...if I...take her again?*

His demon was still lost in her mind, soaking everything in.

Damn this! Haidee hadn't moved since her announcement. She merely sat there, his shaft buried deep inside her, giving him time to adjust to her plans. If he'd been a stronger man, he would have shoved her off. But he wasn't. He was a warrior who had finally found his woman. A warrior who wanted to possess her, body and soul. A warrior who needed to stake his claim, to warn every other man away.

"I'll go slow, all right? Just release my hips and I'll rock us both to paradise."

*No,* he managed to growl into her mind. He'd grabbed her again? Yep. He had. *I will protect you. Even from myself.*

"You want me to go fast, then?" she asked, ignoring the other things he'd said.

*No!* Gods, yes.

"Well, what do I have to say to change your mind? I need your fire, Amun. Your heat." As she spoke, she leaned down, shifting the slant of his erection inside her and making him groan. She braced her hands beside his head, her breasts meshing into his chest, her nipples stabbing at him, her wanton mouth poised about his. "And I think, maybe, you need my chill?"

That slight hesitation revealed something her thoughts and tone hadn't. Uncertainty. She was afraid she couldn't please him sexually. That she was too cold for him, that *she* would hurt *him.*

He couldn't allow her to find fault with herself. To question her power over him. Some men might not like their women knowing just how badly they were whipped, but Amun wasn't one of them. The better she understood the depths of his feelings, the more confident she would be. He wanted her confident.

As she nipped at his lower lip, he released her hips, slid his hands under hers, beside his temples, and twined their fingers. She peered down at him, those pearl-gray eyes luminous—and confused, as if she didn't understand what he was offering.

*I'm not wearing a condom this time, either,* he said.

Her pupils expanded as she realized what his comment meant. Surrender. He was giving in, giving her what she wanted. Risking her, the most important part of his life, to share this moment with her.

"Do you mind?" she asked, her radiant expression lighting her up from the inside out.

*No.* He imagined her pregnant with his child, as radiant as Ashlyn was with Maddox's twins, and almost came inside her without a single thrust. *Do you?* His voice was choked now.

"No," she whispered.

*Then move on me, sweetheart. Let me give you fire, while I luxuriate in that ice.* When she tried to rise, to ride him, he squeezed her hands, holding her in place. *Just like this.*

"Yes." She used her knees as leverage and glided up his length, making both of them gasp.

*Now kiss me.*

On the downward slide, she pressed her mouth into his. Immediately he opened, welcoming her tongue. Cool, wet, just the way he liked her. She tasted of his wildest fantasies and unending passion, both of which wiped his thoughts, his concerns, and left only need. He fought the urge to hammer at her, hard and fast, driving them both to the sweetest insanity.

They would go slowly this time. If, at any point, she seemed to be in pain, he *would* find the strength to pull from her.

Up and down she moved on him, savoring. Savoring until they were panting in each other's mouth, silently gasping each other's names, her nipples rasping against his chest, creating a decadent friction. His blood was heating, and that heat was seeping into her. Her blood must have been cooling because that chill seeped into him, wrapping them both in fire and ice, one sensation feeding off the other.

*Too fast,* he said, even though they were moving at such a leisurely, languid pace, hips rolling together, her clitoris grinding against him, her desire providing such a tight, perfect glide. *Hurting?*

"So...good..."

He licked his way to her jaw. Her ear. He nibbled on the outer shell, then dove inside. A shiver raked her spine and her lower body jerked against his. Another nibble and then he was licking down her neck. He stopped at the wild thump of her pulse and sucked, drawing the blood higher, just under his tongue. That earned another shiver from her.

"Amun?"

*Yes, sweetheart.* Gods, he would never tire of hearing his name on her lips. *Tilt your head farther to the right.*

She obeyed, and he sucked at the tendon between nape and shoulder. Her movements quickened, but the thrusts became shallow, her body riding him only part of the way. Sweetest. Torture. Ever. She kept him in a state of unwavering desire, his skin so sensitized even the caress of air stoked him higher.

"I—I love you," she said.

*W-what?* Dare he hope she'd said—

"I love you."

*Oh, sweetheart.* She was everything to him. Simply everything. After her declaration, there was no holding back. No going slowly, no taking their time, playing it safe, easing their way to climax. Amun rolled her over, releasing her hands to grip her knees and shove them as far apart as they would go. *Tell me again.*

"I love you."

He pulled nearly all the way out before slamming home. *Again.*

A cry spilled from her lips. "I love you."

*Again.* In, out. In, out. Hard, fast. The heat spreading, the ice consuming. He stared into her eyes, so deep, losing himself, glad.

"I love you." Her nails dug into his back, drawing blood. Her head thrashed from side to side.

In, out. In, out. He released one of her legs and placed

it between his own, his testicles suddenly rubbing against her thigh. The new position diminished the space between her core and his hammering erection, the rounded, weeping head scraping against her clitoris with every insistent inward pounding.

Soon she was gasping, incoherent. So was he. From pleasure, no hint of pain. And if he'd thought their first time intense, he learned the error of such a mind-set. She loved him. He owned her heart, just as she owned his. They were melded by more than their bodies. They were melded in spirit, part of each other forevermore.

Relief and ecstasy poured off him, enveloped them both, and without thought he closed his teeth over that well-sucked tendon. Immediately she gasped, went rigid. Her back bowed, her hips lifted, forcing him as deep as he could go, her inner walls clenching on him, milking him.

Amun erupted. He gave her every drop, filling her up, branding her, staking that claim.

*Mine, mine, mine.* No secret. Not to him, and not to his demon, and not to Haidee.

Finally, when he had nothing left, he collapsed atop her. She didn't complain. She sagged to the ground, as depleted as he was. He barely managed to angle his body so that he wouldn't crush her, but he didn't move off her all the way, didn't pull out of her. He was where he belonged, and he was loath to lose the connection.

*Hurting?*

Her eyes were closed, the long length of her lashes creating a fan of shadows over her cheeks. "No. Dead."

He chuckled. *Then my woman is pleased? Even though she had to do most of the work herself?*

She blinked open those pearl-grays. "So I *am* your woman?"

His humor drained in the face of her doubt. *Now. Always.*

"Will you—?" She licked her swollen, well-kissed lips. "Will you say the words, then?"

He smoothed his hands over her brow, not surprised to note that he was shaking. He had needed the words, so it stood to reason that she did, as well. He was ashamed he hadn't said them before now. Had been so selfish, enjoying her declaration but not offering his own. *I love you, Haidee. I love you so much I ache.*

Tension seemed to drain from her, though he'd never felt her stiffen. "Do you forgive me for what I did? All those centuries ago?"

*Sweetheart. What is there to forgive? You were as consumed by your demon as I was by mine.*

Tears sprinkled from the corners of her eyes, then rained down her cheeks, streaking down her lovely skin. "My demon. I don't think I'll ever get used to hearing those words in conjunction with myself."

*But it's true. You took a piece of Hate, but didn't know to purge it. That piece bonded with you, became a part of you. That piece drove you.*

She placed her palm over his heart. "Your friends will never understand that. They'll never accept me."

He cupped her jaw and angled her head, forcing her to peer up at him. *You're first with me. They'll accept that or they'll lose me.*

"But I don't want *you* to lose *them*. You need them."

*I need* you.

"What if I accidently take their demons?"

*You won't.*

"How can you be sure?"

*Just like with me, you won't want to. Therefore you won't.*

"You trust me that much?"

*Yes.*

Her arms banded around his neck and drew him down, allowing her to bury her face in the hollow of his neck. The tears continued to flow, icy crystals that broke his heart. Her lithe body rocked against him as she sobbed.

*What's wrong, sweetheart? I wanted to make you happy, not sad.*

"I am happy. I've never been first before. I mean, for a while, with my parents, I was. After they'd decided to keep me, I guess, and before my sister was born. But then, when Hate tortured them, they begged him to take me, and that hurt me. Here, now, I know you'll always put me first and I shouldn't let you do that. Not for me. Not for anyone, and I'm babbling, I know, but if I let you do this, you'll just be unhappy later on."

He rolled to his back, fitting her atop him like a well-placed puzzle piece. *Unhappy? Why, are you planning to leave me?*

"No, you deliberately obtuse man. I'm too greedy."

He found himself chuckling again. *As long as I've got you, I can never be unhappy.*

"Your friends—"

*Will accept you.* Or else, he thought.

Secrets remained quiet. Perhaps the demon knew the truth of their reactions, perhaps not. Either way, Amun planned to do everything in his power to ensure his friends did, in fact, accept his woman.

If they couldn't, fine. He'd go. He'd miss them, always love them, but he'd go. If they threatened her, he'd go—but he'd hurt them before he did. If they tried to make him choose between them and Haidee, they'd lose. No question.

His heart beat for this woman. He lived for this woman. She'd endured travesty after travesty when she only deserved pleasure. He would now provide that pleasure. Nothing would stand in his way.

She was amazing. She had survived the only way she'd known how, with grit, courage and determination, never realizing she was battling herself as well as the forces poised against her. With Hate a part of her, she probably shouldn't have been able to love—by her own admission, loving wasn't easy for her—but again she had proven just how amazing she was. Her love was stronger than the darkness inside her.

He held her until she settled, caressing her and whispering to her, then kissed her temple. *I want you to know that I'm not going away, sweetheart, and I'm not going to regret choosing you. I'm with you, now and always, just like I said.*

"How can you love me?" she asked between hiccups. *How can you love me?*

"I just do. You're a part of me." *Exactly.*

Her arms squeezed at him again, and he felt her chilly sigh. "The demons have been purged from you," she said sleepily. "We don't have to stay down here anymore."

She was right. He should have realized. He'd already planned to leave, but now their mission was actually completed. Funny, but he found he wasn't quite ready to abandon their cave. He wanted his woman all to himself for just a little longer. *Let's get some rest, and when we wake up, we'll find a way to summon Zacharel. He brought us here, so he can return us to the fortress.* If he didn't, well, they would simply find another way.

Nothing was impossible. He knew that now.

"All right," she said.

*Before we go, though, we're going to use the pack to summon the proper tools to tattoo you.* He wanted Micah's name erased and his own added. All over. On every limb, finger and toe, so that she would always know the name of the man she belonged with.

"Good idea. Yours can be the first name on my un-inked arm."

*More than my name. There's going to be an entire paragraph dedicated to how much you love me.*

She chuckled, and the husky sound delighted him. Turned him on. Hell, everything about her turned him on.

*Who are the others tattooed on your arm? Skye? Viola?*

"Skye saved my life once. We were prisoners, and I was too injured to escape on my own. And Viola is possessed by the demon of Narcissism. See how the *i* is dotted with an *x?* We fought. I don't remember the outcome."

Secrets could help her with that.

*We'll need to send you notes about me, then. Pictures, too.* If he could find a camera that could capture his face, that is. Somehow his demon managed to distort even drawings of him. Still. He wasn't taking any chances. Yes, he was going to do everything in his power to defend her, would even die for her, shield her with his own body, but damn it, all their bases were going to be covered. Just in case.

"Another good idea," she said after a big yawn.

*Sleep now, sweetheart.*

"Yes." She drifted into sleep almost immediately, her body relaxing against his.

He wanted every night to end exactly this way. With Haidee on top of him, sated and trusting him to keep her safe. And he wanted to awaken each morning with her still in his arms. They'd make love, talk and share, drown in each other.

He was smiling as he, too, drifted off to sleep.

# CHAPTER TWENTY-SEVEN

CLAWS SCRAPED AGAINST A nearby wall. "Haidee." The eerie howl of her name echoed, blending with the swish of a robe.

*Blood, a river between her mother and her father. Both helpless...dead.*

Haidee's eyelids popped open, dread already curling in her stomach. She knew those sounds, knew that voice. Only a nightmare, she told herself, or another realm of hell. Trust no one and nothing. Except Amun. A lesson she'd learned well.

"Little Haidee," the voice sang, a whisper. "I know you're close by. I can smell you."

Please be a nightmare or another realm of hell, she thought desperately.

"You cannot hide from me, little Haidee. You have what's mine. Mine, mine, mine." *Scraaape.* "Hay...dee... finally, you're going to give it back."

*Blood, a river between her mother and her father. Both helpless...dead.*

"Hay...dee... You hid when you were a little girl, too. Do you remember? I do. The screams, the splatter. The pleas. Your sister squealed like a pig when the blade sank into her belly. Your mother begged me to stop, to take you away. Your father, well, he was the first to die, wasn't he?"

She cringed, fought a wave of sickness. No, not a nightmare, not another realm. There was too much glee in that tone. Too much truth to the memory.

Hate was here.

Somehow, the demon had found her. Had come for her. Again.

Denial roaring through her head—*not now, please not now*—she jackknifed to her feet, wild gaze already searching. She didn't see him, but that didn't lessen her dread. She was still in the cave, Amun lying on the pallet he'd made for them.

He must have awoken at her movement, or maybe he'd heard the bastard's taunts. His eyes were already open. He sat up stiffly, pulled on a pair of pants and grabbed two blades without pausing to clear his head.

He asked no questions. Maybe he didn't have to. Since making love that second time, they'd been utterly attuned to each other, and she'd actually felt his emotions for her, the sweet depths of his love.

"Haidee." Hate was closer now. "Come out, come out wherever you are."

*Blood, a river between her mother and her father. Both helpless…dead.*

No. No, no, no. The memory would not consume her. Since meeting Amun, she'd barely thought of that night and thought perhaps she was finally healing. She would *not* be distracted. Not this time.

She dressed as swiftly as Amun had, then weaponed up. She'd known this day would come. She just hadn't expected it to come *now*. No warnings, no sensing Hate's approach. Just hello, terror.

Actually, no. The old crone at the circus had tried to warn her, hadn't she? "Soon" had finally arrived.

Amun tugged her toward the only entrance to the cave, pressed her to the side, out of striking distance, then turned and waited, ready to attack. His shoulder pressed into the center of her chest, holding her in place.

"Haidee girl. Dead girl. You have what's mine. You're not going to die before I can take it. Not this time. That will come after."

*Blood, a river between her mother and her father. Both helpless…dead.*

Her molars ground together. "What are you planning? He's not like your friends," she whispered. "Not human in any way."

*I know,* Amun finally said, dark and menacing as their thoughts merged. *Secrets knows. He is more than immortal. He is a child of a goddess. Of Themis. Her son. Always he enjoyed killing, suffering. That's why he was sent to Tartarus.*

She couldn't hide her sudden spike of terror. Not from Amun. Her breathing grew shallow. Hate was the child of a goddess. A god himself. How would they defeat a god?

Secrets flashed images of Hate through Amun's head, which in turn caused them to flash in hers. He was fast, too fast, his strength unparalleled. Haidee was the only person who'd ever walked away from him, and she'd done so only because the cold had surprised him. He wouldn't be surprised this time.

"We can't fight him. We'll lose."

*I fought gods all the time when I lived in the heavens.*

"Yes, and that was thousands of years ago, and you had an immortal army as backup. Right now it's just me and you. He'll slaughter us."

*We'll think of something.*

Secrets disagreed, and his certainty swam through her.

"No matter what we do, I'm going to die today," she said flatly. The demon wasn't even trying to hide the realization, the knowledge now as much a part of her as Hate. She wasn't ready, though. Needed more time.

*No. No, you're not. I won't let you.*

Just as surely as she could discern Secrets's knowledge, she could feel Amun's rising panic. She had to fight her own panic all the more stringently or they would feed off each other, make each other worse. Someone had to stay calm. Someone had to get Amun out of this alive.

It was already too late for her.

"Listen to me." As she spoke, she forced herself to accept her fate. She would die—in her way—and she would hurt. So what. She'd done it before. And this time, she'd do it for Amun. There was no greater reason. "In a few days, I'll be in my cave. No," she rushed out when his gaze swung to her. "Don't say anything. And don't… don't come for me. I won't remember you, and I'll attack you. But I think—" hoped "—I'll dream of you again and when the hate settles, I'll come for *you*. We'll be together again."

*You're not dying. Not this time.* I'll *die first.*

That's what she feared most. "Just…let him have a go at me," she pleaded. "You heard him. He wants his demon back, and he's not leaving without it."

*He won't be leaving, anyway.*

Oh, Amun. Stubborn to his core. "Something's changed. Always before, he kept his distance when he found me, afraid to touch me. This time, I don't think he's afraid."

*He is. A little.*

But not enough. "Good," she forced herself to say. "I can work with that. You'll stay here, and I can—"

*No!*

She knew she'd just insulted Amun's warrior core, but she didn't want to risk his life. She would come back. He would not. "Amun, just listen to me. I don't want you to fight him, either. He's a freaking god."

*Demigod. And you can't stop me.*

"Whatever. You know the outcome. We both know the outcome. Your demon is not—"

"Haidee…mine…mine, you have what's mine," that despised voice from her past said. Hate didn't sweep through the cave's only opening. He simply walked through the wall to stand in front of her and Amun. "Together again, at long last. The thief will finally have her due. You took what's mine. I want it back."

"Repeat ourselves much?" As the past collided with present, she wanted to vomit. As always, he wore a hooded black robe, his face cast in thick, impenetrable shadows. His feet floated just above the ground, a wind she couldn't feel ghosting around him.

*Don't approach him,* Amun growled, inching away from her, severing contact. *And don't touch me. Okay? We need to engage him verbally if we're to learn how to best him without engaging him physically.*

*Okay,* she said. Lied. Maybe. She wasn't sure. And why couldn't she touch Amun? When his shoulder had pressed into her, she'd read his mind, his demon. Now, there was… nothing.

Amun gave a jerky nod to let her know he'd heard her reply before their connection had been severed.

Hate hadn't spoken during the byplay, had merely watched them. Now a low growl erupted from his throat. "You've been together. Demon and Hunter." The words carried a hint of fire. "You do not deserve pleasure, Haidee my girl. Mine. After what you did to me, you deserve only pain."

"What happened here is none of your business," she said, raising her chin.

*Haidee, watch your words. I said engage him, not infuriate him.*

Good, they could still talk to each other. *And just what*

*can I say to make him want to stick around and chat,
rather than do what he came to do?*

*I don't know.*

Before she could respond, Hate's growl sharpened like
the deadliest of blades. "I want what's mine, and you will
give it to me."

Amun's arm stretched out, a hard block that prevented
her from moving forward—or Hate from launching at her
directly. She almost pushed that arm aside, but remembered his command not to touch him. Damn it. She wanted
to save him, not offer him up as a replacement dinner.

"Do you have no response, little Haidee? Dead
Haidee?"

Even as Amun warned her to keep quiet, she said,
"What if I decide to keep it?" She didn't want the bastard's
attention riveted on her man. Hate could move too quickly,
kill before his victim could even blink. Hell, Hate could
walk through walls, as he'd already proven, and simply
attack Amun from behind. "Forever."

*Damn it,* Amun cursed. *Are you trying to ring the starting bell? I just need a little more time. I'm having trouble
reading him.*

Clawed hands curled into fists, peeking out of the long
sleeves of that dark robe. "You will give me what's mine.
Give it now."

"No," she said with false calm, "I don't think I will."

The wind whipped up, agitating the hem of his robe.
"I'll make you."

"Will you really? Then why haven't you already?"

Wind, wind, so much wind.

If she wasn't careful, the bastard would attack no matter
what she did or said. "Will I die if I do give you what you
want?" she asked, pretending she was thinking it over.

*Good. That's good.*

"Give. Me."

He hadn't answered her question, she noticed. "You know what? If you want that piece of the demon back so badly, you come over here and take it."

*What?* Amun shouted, the wind rocking through the entire cavern.

*Like I said, he can't do it on his own or he would have already. He has to have my cooperation. I'm just reminding him of that.*

Dark tension pulsed from that floating body. "Now, Haidee. Is that any way to speak to your lover?" For the first time in their sporadic, centuries-long acquaintance, Hate flipped back the hood of his robe, freeing his features from those too-thick shadows.

She gaped, horrified. He was grotesque. His skin was rotted, pitted, and most of his hair was missing. The few patches there were were thin and coarse, frizzed. Rather than eyes, he watched her through two black holes of despair.

"You have never been my lover," she spat.

"Are you sure?" Before her eyes, his skin smoothed out, darkened. His hair grew, thick and black, glossy like silk. Beautiful brown eyes appeared in those fathomless holes.

Soon, beautiful Micah stood before her. Nearly identical to Amun, but without the sizzle of awareness.

"No," she said, shaking her head violently. "No!" She would have known. Would have sensed. There would have been a clue. Something, anything. Right? Like the fact that he'd gotten it wrong. She and Micah had never been lovers. Not really.

*He wasn't the Micah you were with, sweetheart.* Amun's voice soothed her rising disgust.

"Yes," Hate said. "I know you better than you know yourself, and knew you wanted this face. Therefore I gave you this face."

*He's lying, I swear to you. But keep him talking. My demon is still rooting through his head and we're close, so close to discovering how to defeat him.*

"How did you find me?" she growled.

Hate glared at her, but he said, "The phone call, how else? Once I locked onto your voice, it was only a matter of hours before I found you, wherever you happened to be. I admit, I didn't expect to find you here, reeking of another demon."

"So how do you have Micah's face? How long have you been Micah? Where is the real Micah?"

Familiar lips curled into a smile. "Perhaps I was your Micah all along."

*No,* Amun said. *He became Micah a few days after Strider grabbed you.*

Was Secrets revealing the truth to him? Because she believed Amun. Always. Which meant she *hadn't* kissed this creature, hadn't completed missions with this creature. Only Micah. Her relief was palpable. "And now the human is…?"

"Dead? Yes. I killed him. And do you know what? While he lay dying, I showed him your face." For a split second, she saw her own face staring over at her. Then he returned to Micah's image. "I told him how much you despised him."

*That is the truth. I'm sorry.*

Dead. Micah was dead. And he'd been killed so cruelly, thinking she loathed him. Even though she had never truly loved Micah, she found that she mourned his loss. He'd had many flaws, but he had fought for what he'd believed in.

"Have you nothing more to say, dead Haidee, before I kill this warrior, too? And I will, you know. I will force you to watch—unless you give me what I seek. Now, now, *now.*"

He would, too, which meant they'd run out of time. Her gaze shot to Amun. *Have you learned the way to kill him without fighting him yet?* Please, please, please.

A muscle jumped in Amun's jaw, and several seconds ticked away. *No.*

That hesitation... He was lying. And suddenly, even without touching him, she knew what he was keeping from her, what he'd tried so hard to prevent, so desperate to find another way. And she couldn't believe she hadn't thought of it before. *Removing his demon completely will kill him the same way it would kill you. Won't it?*

His head whipped in her direction, his eyes giving the briefest flare before he refocused on Hate. *Haidee. You cannot do that. Because there are only two possible outcomes. You'll be stuck with all of Hate, perhaps losing yourself to him, or, when Hate is finally put back together, you'll expunge him and die.*

*I don't care. If I die, I'll come back.*

*And I don't want your hands on him.*

She didn't want her hands on him, either. Didn't want to touch the being that had slaughtered her family. For Amun, though...anything.

"All right. I'm willing to give you what you want," she said to Hate.

*Haidee,* Amun warned.

She continued anyway. "For me to return your demon to you, you'll have to let me touch you. And as you know, I can't touch you without hurting you. That tiny piece of the demon hurt you coming out, right, so it stands to reason it'll hurt going back into you. So don't fight me, okay?" Because she wasn't going to give him the demon. She was going to take it. All of it.

No matter the consequences to herself.

A long while passed in silence, Hate rigid as he pondered whether or not to trust her. Finally, perhaps realizing he could not have what he wanted any other way, he nodded. "I will let you touch me."

She experienced another beat of hope. Until—

"*After* I ensure your cooperation," he finished. "Betray me, and your warrior dies. See?"

Hope, completely dashed. And there was no more time to think, to prepare. One second Hate was in front of them, the next he was behind them, just as she'd feared. He shoved her out of the way, careful not to connect with her skin, and slammed a mighty fist into Amun's head. Her warrior stumbled to the side but was quick to right himself—and just as quick to spin, blade slashing out.

Hate anticipated the move and dematerialized, reappearing behind Amun. Again. The creature had no weapons, but then, he'd never needed them before, so why would he now? He always used his claws. He slashed those claws at Amun, scraping the back of the warrior's neck.

Amun howled inside his head, no sound escaping his lips. He spun, launched himself at Hate a second time. That black robe swished as the creature danced out of the way, and an eerie laugh filled the cave.

"You are stronger than the others I killed on Haidee's behalf, but like them, you will fall. I won't slay you, though. No, I'll just keep you close to the brink. And afterward, when I have all of my demon, I'll let you go."

A lie. She knew that soul-deep. He had no plans to let either of them go.

Haidee narrowed her eyes on the creature responsible for so much of her pain. He was Hate in its purest form. And she had a piece of him inside her. She had Hate. She drew on the emotion now, letting it fill her, consume her. The ice always churning inside her blossomed in her veins, turning her blood to sludge. Good. Yes. This was her purpose, after all. This was what the goddess had wanted her to do.

Destroy.

The warriors continued to fight, lashing out, connecting, blood spraying. Amun was faster than she'd realized and managed to land several blows. In fact, the more he fought, the faster he became, until he seemed to anticipate exactly where Hate would reappear. Soon Amun was landing more punches and slices than his enemy.

Still. That wouldn't stop her from doing what needed to be done. Finally, she would end this.

The two slammed into the rocky walls of the cave, dust pluming around them. One would throw the other, and they would spring apart, only to fly at each other again. Snarls and growls reverberated, followed by the crack of broken bones, the sick whisper of flesh splitting apart.

She would have to jump into their midst.

A strange turn of events, one she'd never seen coming. She'd fought all her life to stay alive, to avoid the sting of death and rebirth. Not this time, though. Better to die herself than to allow Hate to live. Better to die herself than to allow Amun to be hurt. She'd hurt him enough. She loved him more than her own life. More than that, she owed him. Hell, she owed his friends. They'd lost one brother because of her. She wouldn't be the cause of Amun's loss.

Though she trembled, knowing deep down that this was going to hurt her more than it would hurt Hate, Haidee focused on Amun. On his thoughts. They weren't touching, but he was too busy to block her and soon she heard a whirl of commands, absorbed his knowledge and his fury, all the while sifting though the massive influx to find what she needed—the urgings of his demon.

There! Suddenly she knew what Hate planned, three moves in advance. She watched. Waited. Amun was so focused on his opponent, he paid her invasion—and her intentions—no heed. She counted down…still watching… still waiting…finally launching herself into the fray. She plowed into Hate just as he reappeared, her head connecting with his middle and her hands wrapping around his neck. They were skin to skin as they plummeted to the ground. Better yet, they were out of Amun's range.

The moment they hit, she unleashed the cold. Hate screamed as ice formed on his heated body, connecting them, and he was unable to jerk away.

*Haidee,* she heard Amun scream inside her head.

She tuned him out, concentrating fully on her task. When she'd taken those demons from Amun, she'd had to lower her guard. She'd had to stop fighting him and let him in. Welcome him. She did that now, with Hate. Lowered her guard. Fighting him no longer.

She wanted his demon, and she would have it.

At first, the demon—that hot, hot darkness inside him, scaled, with glowing red eyes—ran from her as the demons she'd absorbed had done. She was having none of that, however, and gave chase, the ice spreading. Soon there was nowhere else for the terrified demon to run. She had consumed Hate's entire body.

She latched on to a sharpened claw. At the first moment of contact, pain exploded through her. She wanted to balk, to jump as far away as she could, but she merely held on tighter, heaving the being from Hate's body into hers. Tug-of-war, and she would win.

Despite the ice, Hate thrashed against her, pushed against her. Still she held on, still she tugged. Then that ice began to melt, leaving her. Just as before, fire bloomed in its place, spreading, and acid started flowing through her veins. Spiderwebs winked through her vision, and dizziness bombarded her.

The darkness that had been a part of her for centuries cried out in welcome as the demon High Lord slipped into her little by little. No longer did she have to tug. The demon wanted inside her now, was even aiding her, desperate to crawl in, to be whole again.

Almost over, she thought, hurting so badly tears were streaking down her cheeks.

Suddenly there was a pain of another kind tearing through her neck, her back—Amun started shouting again, perhaps crying, but she hardly noticed. Her insides were too busy burning to ash.

And then she was being pulled away from the former keeper of Hate. She didn't protest; she had the demon now. All of the demon, and it was zipping through her mind, banging into her skull, filling her up, consuming her.

*Haidee, sweetheart. Please. Let me see those beautiful eyes.*

Her eyelids fluttered open, and she saw that Amun was looming over her, bathed in red. Blood? But blood had never glowed like that before.

*Sweetheart, oh, gods, sweetheart.* He'd never looked so tormented.

She opened her mouth to reply, but something warm flowed from her mouth rather than words. *Is he dead?* She didn't have the strength to push the words into his mind, but somehow he heard her anyway.

*Yes, sweetheart, he's dead.* Tears glistened in his black gaze.

*You're sad? Don't be sad, baby. We won.* She tried to reach up, to brush those tears away, but again, she didn't have the strength.

*Oh, sweetheart.* Soft fingers smoothed her brow.

Her heartbeat was slowing, then fluttering, almost nonexistent. Thankfully, though, the cold was returning to her limbs, dousing the fire. Once the ice returned, she thought, she could expel the demon, right? And she and Amun could be together.

Amun had feared she wouldn't be able to expel the

demon, that he would forever be a part of her. If that were the case, she would deal.

*He...fought you. He ravaged your throat.*

She blinked, not understanding.

*Sweetheart, you're...fading.*

Fading? The red glow bathing his face was dimming. Did that mean... *I'm...dying?*

*No! I'll do something. There has to be something.* Amun leapt into motion, dragging the backpack next to her. With shaky hands, he reached inside and withdrew bandages and other materials to try and save her. *Stay with me, sweetheart. Okay?*

She was. She was dying.

She tried to obey him, she really did. Not because she feared the pain that awaited her, but because she wanted to be with this man always. She didn't want him hurt by images of her death the way she'd been hurt by images of her family. So she fought the cold, the weakness. And while she fought, she realized she *could* expunge the demon, because a scaled, fanged and clawed creature rose from her skin, its eyes bright red.

Amun watched, horrified. She watched, too, amazed that she hadn't had to corner him and force him out. Amazed that she didn't hurt anymore. But when the beast darted out of the cave, roaring hysterically, she found there was nothing left to tether *her* to her body. Darkness was pulling at her.

Her organs were shutting down, the ice that had saved her now killing her. She knew the feeling well. Had experienced it hundreds of times before. This was the end of her.

*I love you,* she told Amun.

He never stopped bandaging her wounds. *Then stay, damn it. Fight this. Haidee! Do you hear me? Don't you dare leave me!*

*I love you,* she repeated, and then, because she couldn't fight any longer, she allowed herself to be pulled the rest of the way into the darkness.

# CHAPTER TWENTY-EIGHT

AMUN WAS GOING CRAZY. Haidee had died. Died. Her heart had stopped, her ruined body had gone still and her eyes had glazed. She'd had no breath left inside her lungs, even when he'd pumped at her chest for hours, her blood all over his hands. And then she'd disappeared. Simply vanished, as if she'd never existed.

He screamed for hours more—and Secrets screamed along with him.

While Amun had been making love with Haidee that second time, the demon had realized that she would never hurt them, no matter how powerful she was. That she would always strive to make life better for them.

With the realization, affection for her had grown. Not just because she possessed so many secrets, but because of *her*. Even though she was a demon-slayer, a justice-dealer, she was the demon's favorite playground.

How could Themis have sentenced such a precious female to die? Where was the justice in such a vile action?

Amun was suddenly happy the goddess was currently rotting in Tartarus with the rest of the Greeks. After everything she'd done, she deserved that and more.

Only, if she hadn't acted, Amun never would have had this second chance with Haidee. Or even met her at all. She was a gift. His gift. And he'd failed her. In every way that mattered, he'd failed her. Twice she'd died because of him. And she hated to die, feared the pain, the loss of her memories.

*My fault,* he thought.

The first time had been an accident on his part. This second time, she had rushed headlong into danger to save him. He'd been too focused on slaying their enemy to take note of her plan. Foolish of him. He was the keeper of Secrets, damn it! He should have guessed her intentions, and he should have stopped her.

When she had locked on Hate, Amun hadn't known what to do or how to separate them. All Secrets had known was that breaking the link between the pair would hurt Haidee far more than letting her finish drawing the demon into herself. But then Hate had begun fighting her, chomping at her, clawing at her, and Amun hadn't cared about her pain—he'd cared only about saving her life. He'd ripped them apart.

But he was too late.

The wound in Haidee's neck had been fatal.

Amun paced. If he summoned the angel, Zacharel, he would be escorted home. His demon knew this, sensed it now as if the knowledge had always been there, yet Amun could not force himself to do so. This was the last place he'd seen Haidee, the last place he'd held her, tasted her, and he didn't want to leave just yet, didn't want to give up the sweet scent of her that lingered in the air or the chill of her that was wrapped around him like a cloak.

He needed to formulate a plan. *Without* interference from his friends.

Haidee had told him not to try to find her cave. That, he would ignore. He would find that cave. He would help her through those waves of hate. *If* she still possessed any hint of the demon inside her, that is. The creature had risen from her, and had seemed intact. Nothing missing.

But even without the demon, she wouldn't stay dead. She'd said so herself. She would come back to him.

And if she *was* without even that small piece, she could very well remember him.

Suddenly hope welled within him. First, he had to find her. And he would. She was out there. She had to be out there. If she *didn't* remember him and fought him, he would let her go, wouldn't hurt her, even to save himself. But then what? What if she returned to the Hunters?

He would just have to follow her, guard her from a distance. He'd slipped past her defenses once. He could do so again.

All he had to do was reach her.

Decided on his course of action, he grabbed the backpack and at last shouted for Zacharel in his mind. A few seconds later, as expected, the angel appeared. No bright light, just blink, and the winged warrior was there. Those wings arched over the wide expanse of his shoulders, white threaded with gold. He still wore a colorless robe, his dark hair slicked back from his face.

Those brilliant green eyes regarded Amun with satisfaction. "And so you are saved."

*Yes,* he signed. *Now take me to my woman.*

His demand elicited a single shake of that dark head. There was no sorrow in the angel's expression. No emotion whatsoever. "I cannot do so. She is dead."

So simply stated. Amun almost pounded over and stabbed the bastard in the heart. *She will be reanimated in Greece. You will take me to her. Now.*

"No. She is not in Greece."

*Yes. She is.*

Still emotionless, the angel said, "When she drew the rest of Hate inside her, the demon reformed in its entirety. When she released it, she released every bit of it, even the part that had bonded to her. A bond that was never supposed to happen. She was supposed to draw and release. But because she did bond, she could no longer live without Hate. Just as you cannot live without your demon." The layer of truth in his voice was devastating. "This, you already know."

Still he fought the very idea of it. *She's alive, I tell you. Aeron died, but then he lived.*

"Amun, Haidee had already died. She was already a soul, like those in the heavens and hell. A soul that has now withered once and for all, its source of life gone."

*No! She's out there. She's alive.* She had to be. *Souls reanimate in hell. I've seen them. You said so yourself.*

"Those souls never bonded to a demon. Never then lost that demon."

*No!* he repeated. *She was blessed by a goddess.*

"A goddess who later turned her back."

*Haidee is alive, damn you. A blessing is a blessing, and cannot be taken back.*

"Just as the favored cannot fall into disfavor and be kicked from the heavens?"

*That is not the same, and you know it. Why did she keep coming back to life after the goddess turned her back, then?*

"Because she was still intact. This time, she was not. I can take you to her cave, if you'd like. Though I warn you now, it is empty. I checked, just to be sure."

He didn't panic. Yet. He concentrated on his breathing, on drawing the still-chilled air through his nose, letting it fill his lungs, clear his mind. But with the breath, his demon—who didn't like the angel, but couldn't stay out of his head, searching for answers—at last discerned what was the fantasy Amun desired and what was the reality he feared.

Haidee had not returned to Greece.

There was no way to save her.

She. Was. Dead.

Forever.

Zacharel had spoken the truth. As always.

A roar nearly split Amun's head in two. He gripped his ears, trying to block the noise. That didn't help. On and on the roar tormented him. His eardrums shattered. Blood leaked onto his shoulders. Eventually, his knees gave out. He fell to the ground, hot tears springing into his eyes. No. No, no, no. She couldn't be dead.

She was dead.

*She* is *waiting for me in her cave.*

She wasn't waiting for him in her cave.

*She* will *remember* me.

She would remember nothing. She was dead. Now, always.

Any illusion he tried to create, his demon instantly destroyed. In that moment, he hated his demon. Hated so much he could have been possessed by the essence of the demon Haidee had harbored inside her. The truth…oh, gods, the truth. Nothing had ever hurt him so intensely. She was dead, she was dead, she was dead, and there was nothing he could do to bring her back.

She shouldn't have died. *He* should have died.

Why hadn't he died?

Other questions swirled through the crushing grief, and he found himself glaring up at the angel. *Did you know she would…that she would end up that way when you brought us here?*

"Of course," Zacharel offered without any hesitation. "Her death was the only way to save you."

No reaction. Not yet. *What do you mean?* She had pulled the demons from Amun and successfully released them, all without messing with Secrets. Afterward, she had been healthy, whole. Until Hate. But Hate had not been a part of Amun. So, after healing him, she could have walked away.

Oh, gods. She could have walked away.

If he had called for Zacharel then…

"Have you not realized yet? You never needed to visit hell to release those demons. You had only to learn to trust each other. That was the only way Haidee could discover the truth about her abilities. That was the only way you would let her close enough to use those abilities on you."

*Then why did you send us here? Why? I would rather have died myself. Me!*

"You were sent here because nothing draws people together faster than perilous situations. More than that, I was not told to save Haidee. Only you."

*But she didn't have to die.* His motions were jerky now. *We could have left before Hate found her. You could have swooped in.*

"She was going to die whether Hate found her or not. She loved you. Eventually, that love would have weakened her demon. Just as your demon feeds on secrets, hers fed on hate. Ultimately, that love would have killed her."

*No. She loved before. Others loved her.*

"Did she? Did they? No, she did not. No, they did not. Many overcame their dislike for her, some even came to care for her, but no one loved her with their whole heart. Until you."

Secrets found no deception in the confession.

So Amun *had* killed her. Again. His love for her had doomed her for eternity. She would have lived if he'd left her alone, if he had refused to bring her down here. If he hadn't given in to his craving for her.

He hated himself.

He hated Zacharel now, too.

They had moved her around like a chess piece. They had set her up for failure. And why? To save him.

If Haidee had survived this, Amun could have continued on with his life. Even if she'd hated him, he could have continued on, happy in the knowledge that she was out there somewhere. But this...this shattered him. She was gone forevermore, and he was responsible. The knowledge ruined him. He was raw, eternally wounded, unable to heal. And he didn't need Secrets to confirm that.

There was only one thing left to do.

*Take me home,* he signed, as determined as he was defeated.

"I find I am oddly...troubled by your reaction. I did not expect this, nor do I understand what I am feeling. What I know is that I do not like it and something must be done."

In less than a heartbeat of time, Amun's surroundings changed. Gone were the bleak rocks he'd shared with Haidee, and in their place were the smooth white walls of his bedroom. He took no comfort from the familiar setting.

He moved to his bed and sat down on the edge. The angel never reappeared, and that was probably for the best. Amun wanted to kill him for hiding the truth—however he'd done so—and for allowing Amun to save himself and condemn his woman. And he *would* kill the angel. Soon, but not yet, for the action would earn him a death sentence of his own. A sentence he would welcome just as soon as he said goodbye to his friends.

That was all he had left to do.

He wasn't going to live without Haidee; it was as simple as that.

AFTER ZACHAREL BRIEFED TORIN on everything that had happened to Amun and Haidee, gathered the rest of his angels and finally left the fortress for good, their job now done, the keeper of Disease studied his friend on several of his computer monitors. The cameras Strider had placed in Secrets's bedroom hadn't yet been disabled, so Torin had a clear view of his friend from multiple angles.

The warrior might be back to normal, but he wasn't even close to being happy. Desolation seemed to cling to him. His dark skin was dulled, and his eyes were bleaker than Torin had ever seen them.

Torin ached for him. Even though he didn't understand how Amun had fallen for such a woman, he still ached for the man. And he wouldn't judge. Amun would get enough of that from the others. What he needed right now was compassion and unconditional support. Support Torin would give him.

Once upon a time, Torin had killed a woman he lusted after. He'd worshipped her from afar and had finally given in and touched her. Just a simple brush of his knuckles on her soft cheek, but soon afterward, he'd been forced to watch her sicken and die. He'd been helpless to save her.

Knowing he was responsible had torn him up inside. And if Zacharel was right, Amun blamed himself for Haidee's loss. And the fact that Torin had merely lusted but Amun had loved…well, he doubted his pain could compare.

Torin tugged at an earlobe. Things were still calm here. Hunters were still missing, still disappearing for seemingly no reason, but now Rhea had disappeared, as well. As Cronus had done with Strider, he'd just popped in and informed him. So…

Whether the warriors here would judge Amun or not, Amun needed them. Needed a distraction from his guilt. That wouldn't be the same as compassion and support, but those things would follow. Hopefully.

So Torin lifted his cell phone and sent everyone the same message. Amun's here & sane. Angels gone. Return ASAP. He needs help.

Replies began arriving seconds after he pressed send, and soon every single one of the warriors (besides William) had agreed to come home.

On way. He OK? Aeron.

Coming. Something wrong? Lucien.

Take me out of your address book. William.

Will make it. Gideon.

Cameo & me just hit town. We'll be there in 10. Kane.

Let me get Ash situated 1st. Maddox.

Done & done. Sabin.

Me & Paris R in the States. Might take a bit, but we'll B there. Strider.

Had a tail 4 few days. Will show as soon as I lose it. Reyes.

Pleased at their show of loyalty amid this crisis, Torin settled back in his chair and waited.

# CHAPTER TWENTY-NINE

AMUN'S FRIENDS TRIED TO CHEER him up, they really did. They hugged him, slapped him on the back and told him what they'd been up to. Strider, fighting Hunters. Aeron, playing with his Olivia in the clouds. Lucien, guarding the Cage of Compulsion with his Anya. Gideon, honeymooning with his Scarlet. Kane and Cameo, scouring the city for any sign of the enemy. Maddox, playing nursemaid to his Ashlyn, who was "big as a house." Her words, not Amun's. Sabin, begging the Unspoken Ones to give back the artifact Strider had parted with. Reyes, guarding his Danika while she painted glimpses into the future. Paris, getting high on ambrosia and preparing to go to war in the heavens.

Amun spent two days with them. No one mentioned Haidee. They all avoided talk of her. But as he seated himself at the dinner table, he decided to change that. They didn't know it, but this was to be his last dinner with them. Tomorrow he would leave the fortress. Tomorrow he would challenge Zacharel.

Tomorrow he would lose his head.

He knew what Aeron had experienced after his death. Knew the warrior's soul had gone to another realm, a place where formerly demon-possessed immortals were supposedly to be trapped, unable to taint any other souls with their darkness. Baden was there. Pandora, too.

But Aeron, Baden and Pandora had merely died as

mortals did. Their souls hadn't been burned to ash, as an angel's sword of fire could make happen.

That's the death Amun wanted for himself. An end. Totally, completely.

First, though, he wanted these men to know the kind of woman Haidee had been. To know her as he had, as sweetness and light. As worthy. As the best among them. He wanted them to know what she had given up. And so, while they piled their plates high with food, he started talking.

"Haidee was not the monster we painted her. She was strong and courageous."

Conversations tapered to quiet as everyone stared at him in shock. He'd never begun a conversation before. Had rarely spoken anything but other people's memories since his possession.

He continued before his demon decided to take over and spill the secrets hiding inside everyone around him. "She had every reason to despise us. A demon killed her mother, her father, her sister and her husband. A demon, just like us. Hell, maybe one of us killed her husband. We were there when it happened. And then I helped kill her. Me. I threw her in front of my enemy's sword. Little wonder she came back for us. For vengeance. We would have done the same. We *did* the same."

Thankfully, no one tried to stop him. Not even his demon.

"The same demon who killed her family managed to infect her, give her a piece of himself. Of Hate. Yet somehow, though she was little more than a human, she managed to defeat that demon's darkest urges. Then she was killed again and again and again, and even though every good and decent memory she had was always wiped from her, even though she knew only sadness and pain, she found a way to love me, to save me…to die for me. That is the woman we have hated all this time. Someone we hurt first. Someone with the power to kill the rest of us, someone who could have been used against us, yet chose to save us instead. Through her own death."

A thick, heavy silence enveloped the entire room.

Still Secrets made no attempt to speak through him. Perhaps because the taint of memories had been purged inside that cave. Perhaps because the demon mourned Haidee's passing as he did.

His friends continued to stare at him, not moving, not even daring to breathe. Their thoughts and emotions grew in intensity, finally piercing the quiet. Some felt sorry for him. Some felt guilty for having condemned Haidee. Only Sabin refused to back away from his own hate.

Strider, though... Strider was the worst. *Her death is for the best,* the warrior thought. *Ultimately, she would have turned on him. She wouldn't have been able to help herself. And when she hurt him, or us, he would have blamed himself. He wouldn't have been able to forgive himself, either.*

The statement pushed Amun over the edge. Hell. No.

Amun didn't realize he'd launched out of his seat until he had his hands around Strider's neck. Until he was tossing the warrior into the wall, plaster dusting around him.

"What the *fuck,* man?" a scowling Strider demanded as he stood.

"Her death wasn't for the best! She was lovely, damn you. She deserved to live. *I'm* the one who should have died. And you can wrap up your excuses as prettily as you want, but that doesn't change the fact that you just don't care that she's dead."

"Okay. Okay. Whatever. Just relax. You're entitled to your opinion, and I'm entitled to mine."

"Mine is the only one that matters!" With a roar, Amun

launched at Strider again. They fell to the floor in a tangle of violence.

"Stop," Lucien commanded. "Now."

"Let them finish," Sabin said.

Amun tuned them out. His fists pounded at Strider, his legs kicked. Strider, of course, began fighting back. They rolled together and slammed into the table. Plates shattered, food splattered. Both of them knew how to fight, and fight dirty. Knew how to stop a heart from beating, how to break a femur with a well-placed kick, how to smash a trachea and prevent oxygen from making it into greedy lungs. They did all of that and more.

And still they kept fighting, no one trying to separate them. Amun's hands soon swelled from continuous impact with bone, his fingers refusing to bend. Dizziness washed through him, black winking over his vision, but even that didn't slow him. When this was over, Strider was going to regret his thoughts and words. Strider was going to admit how special Haidee had been.

Defeat's nose broke under the next strike of Amun's palm. Blood poured. That crimson flow reminded him of what Hate had done to Haidee—fangs digging into her beautiful neck—and that only increased the depths of his rage.

"Tell me you appreciate what she did for us. Tell me!"

"You want me to lie? She was a Hunter," Strider shouted, a few of his teeth missing. "A killer."

"*We're* killers!" Another strike. Another direct hit. Two pearly whites sailed through the air.

"Damn it!" Defeat's rage increased as well, and he kneed Amun in the groin. "She couldn't be trusted. I realized that. Why can't you?" The words were slurred as they pushed through the empty spaces where his teeth had been.

Amun shook off the pain. What was physical pain after the emotional agony of losing his woman, anyway? He dove into Strider's middle, sending the warrior flailing to the ground. On impact, Strider lost his breath. The warrior was quick to recover, and they rolled, still pounding on each other—until they slammed into one of the table legs and cracked the wood.

Amun stilled, glaring down at the man he'd once called brother. "I trusted her more than I trusted anyone else. Even you."

Strider pushed, sending Amun stumbling to the other side of the room. "How can you say—"

"No, you don't get to speak." Once again, he closed the distance between them. No mercy. Secrets knew Strider planned to kick, and so Amun jumped out of the way, spun, punched and ducked, punched and ducked. "You wanted her, but you would have tortured her. You would have ruined her."

"No." Somehow, Strider dodged every blow.

"You might, *might,* have been able to love her, but only after you'd broken her." Finally, contact.

Strider hunched over, trying to catch the breath he'd only just found. "Don't you see what's happening? She's dead, but still she's pulling us apart. I love you. I left this fortress for you. So you could have her."

"You left this fortress for *you.*" No mercy, he thought again. "You couldn't win her, and you knew it." Amun kneed him in the chin, sending Strider tumbling back into another wall. "I would have married her, pampered her, and I would have expected every single one of you to accept her. But you wouldn't have, would you? She was just another challenge to you. But you know what? She rejected you, and you walked away from her without a flicker of pain. That changes *now.* You will feel pain. You know why? Because I challenged you, and you just lost."

With that, Amun punched him. Punched him so hard his jawbone dislocated completely.

Strider was knocked unconscious. Even then, he was in physical pain, moaning from the mental anguish of his defeat.

Amun kicked him while he was down. Again and again.

Someone grabbed him from behind and jerked him away, holding him so tightly he couldn't quite draw in a breath. Yet still he fought. His woman had been slighted. He wouldn't stop until he was appeased. And he would never be appeased.

"I'm going with her," he shouted. "Do you hear me? I'm going to die with her! And if you don't watch your stupid mouth, I'll take you along, too!"

Strider released another moan, this one far more pained.

The warriors holding Amun must have sensed his determination because they ceased trying to hold him and started trying to subdue him.

"We need you," he heard.

"Don't talk like that, all right."

"You'll get through this."

"No. No!" His body was already badly beaten, weakened, but still he fought, his rage like a living entity.

"It's gonna be okay, buddy."

"No!"

They squeezed tighter.

"Let us help you."

"What if we spoke to the angel? What if something could be done?"

"Something *can* be done," he snarled.

Tighter still.

*Haidee,* he screamed inside his head then. *Soon, I'll be*

*with you soon. We'll be…* His thoughts fragmented. His motions were slowing. *We'll be together again.*

Darkness rained down like poisoned arrows. He welcomed the storm with open arms.

# CHAPTER THIRTY

"Amun," a gentle voice called.

Amun fought his way through the darkness, slashing at it as determinedly as he remembered slashing at Strider. That voice, so familiar, so necessary. Forever lost.

"Amun, baby. Wake up."

His struggles increased until finally, amazingly, he was able to blink open his eyes—and what he saw took his breath away. Haidee. His beautiful Haidee. She loomed above him, peering down at him with those pearl-gray eyes.

Had the warriors killed him as he'd wanted? he wondered. No, they couldn't have. Inside his head, Secrets was sighing with relief, picking up on something, a mystery, a truth, but was unable to sort through the details.

How was Haidee here?

*Am I dreaming?* He didn't dare speak again. Just in case. He would not spoil this moment with a spew of secrets. Besides, if this moment was steeped in falsehood, he didn't want to know. *Wait. Don't tell me. Just stay right where you are.*

"No, baby. I'm here." She smoothed the hair plastered to his brow, and he felt the coolness of her touch. "We're in your bedroom, the place we first met."

He studied her, certain this had to be a trick. Her pink and blond locks were in tangles around her shoulders, and her lips were swollen from where she'd chewed them. Her eyes were aglow with love and warmth.

"This isn't a trick," she said. "I'm real."

*But you died. I watched you die. Was told you couldn't be reanimated by Hate any longer.*

"And that's the truth. I was reanimated by something else this time."

*I don't understand.*

"That's okay—I barely understand it myself. What happened to me was kind of like what happened to Aeron—and yeah, I got to hear all about that—only I didn't need a new body because I was already in soul form. Anyway, this is how it was explained to me. The demons are the negative, and the angels are the positive. Happiness, Joy, Strength, and so on. So, just like I had taken a piece of Hate, I could take a piece of one of those without killing the giver. And I did. First from you, then from someone else."

*From me?*

"Oh, yes. I took your love. Just a little, and I expunged most of it when I expunged Hate. But the little bit I kept was enough to bring me back. I was fading, though, and fading fast."

*What else did you take? And from whom?*

"Well." She massaged those swollen lips together. "Zacharel kind of…gave me another piece of Love."

*Zacharel? The angel?* Jealousy sparked, but vanished just as quickly. Haidee was here. Haidee was alive and with him. Zacharel could share whatever he wanted with her.

"Yes. The angel."

*Why? Why would he give you something of his? And how was he the keeper of Love?*

She stopped massaging, and her lips twitched at the

corners. "Funny story. Apparently there are several keepers of the more overwhelming emotions, and he was keeping his portion of Love in a jar on his nightstand. Weirdest thing I'd ever seen. It was kind of like his personal Pandora's box, but a treasure chest rather than a prison. He said he wasn't using it, and that I was welcome to a little pinch of it. A few of his angel friends were upset about it, and I heard them say it would cause some problems for him, but now I'm—I'm babbling, aren't I? Say something!"

*First, I owe that angel an apology. And a thank-you. Second, I can't believe this is happening.* He reached up with a shaky hand and caressed her cheek. Her skin was as cool as before. As solid. For a moment, he was too numbed with shock, hope and joy to move again.

She was here, he thought again. She really was here. Here, with him. Alive.

And there was the truth Secrets had been trying to reach, to understand. She had defied death, defied what should have been truth, what *was* truth, and come back for them. She was no longer Hate; she was Love. Just as she'd said.

Joy quickly overshadowed the other emotions. Amun jerked her on top of him, his arms squeezing her as tight as possible without crushing her ribs. *I thought I'd lost you, and it was more than I could bear. Tell me you remember me.* He knew she did, but he had to hear the words. *Please, tell me. I know you do, you're here, but like you, I need the words.*

"Oh, yes." She squeezed him just as tightly before lifting her face and grinning. "I remember everything about you."

*Gods, Haidee.* He pulled her back down. Every part of him needed to touch every part of her. *Tell me the rest. What happened to you...after? I have to know.*

Secrets was even then unraveling the rest of the details, but Amun wanted to hear them from his woman.

She burrowed her head in the hollow of his neck and flattened her palm over his heartbeat. "After I died, I opened my eyes and found myself—my soul, I guess—in my cave. With Zacharel, as I said."

*Wait. Maybe I won't apologize to that bastard, after all. He let me think you were dead, and that there was no way to reach you. Because of him, I've done nothing but mourn you. In fact, I was going to challenge him in the morning and allow him to kill me. I can't live without you, Haidee.* When he'd told her "now and always," he'd meant it.

"He didn't lie, Amun. I did die. For a little while. Believe me, he was as shocked as you when I was reanimated. He was visiting my cave, you see, because something you said really got to him. At least, I think that's why. He wasn't big on explanations. And just so you know, I can't live without you. So don't you ever, *ever* think of dying for me again. I'll always find a way to get back to you."

He rolled her to her back, covering her with his body. *I won't die for you if you won't die for me,* he said, happier in that moment than he'd ever been. His woman was in his arms, underneath him. His. *Are you still somewhat immortal, able to come back again and again?*

"Definitely. You're stuck with me for eternity." She wrapped her arms around his neck and kissed his chin. "Now, no more talk of dying."

The kiss wasn't enough, not nearly enough, but he didn't press for more. Yet. *How did you get here?*

"As soon as Zacharel realized I was going to survive everything," she said, tangling her fingers in his hair, "he flew me here."

*How do we thank an angel? Somehow I don't think a fruit basket will do the trick.*

Her lips twitched with amusement. "I don't think so, either."

He couldn't help himself. He licked his way into her mouth, enjoying her sweetness, her taste. Her legs spread in welcome, and he fell deeper into her, his shaft lengthening, hardening. Groaning, she arched her hips to press more fully against him.

Any moment now, and they would both lose control.

With a groan of his own, Amun lifted his head. Haidee's cheeks were flushed, her lips even more swollen. She'd never looked lovelier. *The rest. Tell me the rest. How did my friends react to you? If they offended you, we'll leave. I told you, I can't live without you. I* won't *live without you.*

Haidee's amusement returned. "Oh, they've accepted me already."

*So you* have *spoken to them?*

She nodded. "I didn't expect to be welcomed with open arms when Zacharel dropped me off at the front door. He rang the doorbell and disappeared like a coward." She shouted those last three words, as if she'd been angry at the time and still harbored a bit of the emotion. "But a few minutes after that, the one named Torin let me inside. I thought I'd be taken straight to the dungeon, but no. I was asked a few questions, and then brought here to you. I think they realized they would rather put up with me than see you hurting."

*Back up. What questions?*

"Everything you asked me and more."

His attention snagged on the word "more." *Such as?*

A blush stained her cheeks. "Like was I going to have telepathic sex with you at the dinner table. Did I know how to cook something other than a PB and J. Was I okay with naked Thursdays. *Anyway.* After I saw that you were okay and sleeping, I asked some questions of my own."

*What questions?* he repeated.

She shrugged, trying for an innocence he didn't buy. "Who you had fought. Where Strider was."

Amun arched a brow and tried not to laugh. *And?*

"And Torin told me. I marched to Strider's room, prepared to...well, please don't be mad," she said, stiffening, "but I was going to stab him. That piece of Love wanted me to forgive him, but I was still going to do it."

*I like where this story is headed. Continue.*

A sigh left her, seeming to drain the tension right out of her. "I didn't. Stab him, I mean. He was in pain. Awake, but in pain, and I guess Love got to me more than I'd realized. He and I had a little chat."

Amun was the one to stiffen now. *Did he insult you?* If he had...

"No. Nothing like that, I promise." She traced her fingertips along his jaw. "He said that he never wants to fight you again, even at Xbox. He said a determination like yours is a rare and precious thing, and something he respects. He said he loves you and one day, he'll love me, too. Like a sister. But not to expect *one day* anytime soon."

*Truly?*

"Yes. Truly."

That was completely unexpected. *I will forgive him, then. Maybe. One day,* he added.

"You will." Her expression became fierce, that intense determination returning. "I won't be responsible for any more hate. And why should I? I'm Love!" She laughed. "I don't think I'll ever get tired of saying that."

Amun was willing to give her anything she desired, even that. *You're right. I will forgive him.*

"Thank you."

*I'm sorry for the pain you've experienced, sweetheart.*

"I know, baby." She stopped caressing, settling her hands against his cheeks. "I know. Just like I'm sorry for the pain you've experienced. But we're going to look ahead now. Together."

*I'm going to do everything in my power to make you happy, I swear it.*

"You must have been reading my mind."

Finally, he kissed her the way he'd needed to kiss her from the first, a kiss that was more than a kiss. A kiss that was a promise. A kiss that was forever.

Until, of course, forever was interrupted by the sudden unhinging of his bedroom door. A loud boom echoed, and wood chips rained. He and Haidee sprang apart. Amun grabbed the knife on his nightstand before moving back over his woman to shield her. He calmed when he saw tiny, redheaded Kaia looming in his doorway.

Perhaps he should have panicked.

"Don't hurt him again, Secrets," she growled. Her eyes were completely black, her Harpy having taken over her mind. "He deserved what you did this time, so I won't punish you. Do it again, though, no matter the provocation, and I'll have to hurt you. Bad."

He didn't have to ask who "him" was. He balanced his weight and signed, *Strider is my friend and brother, and despite everything, I love him. As...you do?*

Kaia offered no reply. She simply stalked away.

"Who was *that?*" Haidee demanded from beneath him.

He focused on her and grinned. *I think that was Strider's downfall. Now, where were we...*

"You were in the middle of adoring me."

*A middle suggests there is an end. What I feel for you is forever.*

"Prove it," she said with a grin of her own.

He kissed her. *I will, at least five times a day, and probably more on Thursdays, considering we'll be naked.*

She laughed. "I have a feeling Thursday will be my favorite day of the week."

*Mine, too, sweetheart. Mine, too.* That said, he got busy proving each one of his claims.

\* \* \* \* \*

*Look for more Lords of Underworld
in THE DARKEST SURRENDER,
coming soon from Gena Showalter
and HQN Books!*

# Lords of the Underworld
## Glossary of Characters and Terms

Aeron—Former keeper of Wrath

All-Seeing Eye—Godly artifact with the power to see into heaven and hell

Amun—Keeper of Secrets

Anya—(Minor) Goddess of Anarchy

Ashlyn Darrow—Human female with supernatural ability

Baden—Keeper of Distrust (deceased)

Bait—Human females, Hunters' accomplices

Bianka Skyhawk—Harpy; sister of Gwen and consort of Lysander

Cage of Compulsion—Godly artifact with the power to enslave anyone trapped inside

Cameo—Keeper of Misery

Cloak of Invisibility—Godly artifact with the power to shield its wearer from prying eyes

Cronus—King of the Titans, keeper of Greed

Danika Ford—Human female, target of the Titans

Dean Stefano—Hunter; right-hand man of Galen

*dimOuniak*—Pandora's box

Galen—Keeper of Hope

Gideon—Keeper of Lies

Gilly—Human female

Greeks—Former rulers of Olympus, now imprisoned in Tartarus

Gwen Skyhawk—Half-Harpy, half-angel

Haidee, aka "Ex"—Immortal Hunter

Hate—A demigod and keeper of the demon of Hate

Hera—Queen of the Greeks

Hunters—Mortal enemies of the Lords of the Underworld

Kaia Skyhawk—Harpy; sister of Gwen

Kane—Keeper of Disaster

Legion—Demon minion, friend of Aeron

Leora—Human friend of Haidee (deceased)

Lords of the Underworld—Exiled warriors to the Greek gods who now house demons inside them

Lucien—Keeper of Death; leader of the Budapest warriors

Lucifer—Prince of darkness; ruler of hell

Lysander—Elite warrior angel and consort of Bianka Skyhawk

Maddox—Keeper of Violence

Marcus, aka. "The Bad Man"—an ancient Hunter

Micah—A Hunter

Olivia—An angel

One True Deity—Ruler of the angels

Pandora—Immortal warrior, once guardian of *dimOuniak* (deceased)

Paring Rod—Godly artifact, power unknown

Paris—Keeper of Promiscuity

Reyes—Keeper of Pain

Rhea—Queen of the Titans; estranged wife of Cronus; keeper of Strife

Sabin— Keeper of Doubt; leader of the Greek warriors

Scarlet—Keeper of Nightmares

Sienna Blackstone—Deceased female Hunter; new keeper of Wrath

Solon—Husband of Haidee (deceased)

Strider—Keeper of Defeat

Taliyah Skyhawk—Harpy; sister of Gwen

Tartarus—Greek god of Confinement; also the immortal prison on Mount Olympus

Themis—Greek goddess of Justice

Titans—Current rulers of Olympus

Torin—Keeper of Disease

Unspoken Ones—Reviled gods; prisoners of Cronus

Warrior Angels—Heavenly demon assassins

William—Immortal warrior, friend of Anya

Zacharel—A warrior angel

Zeus—King of the Greeks

# GENA SHOWALTER

| | | | |
|---|---|---|---|
| 77535 | THE NYMPH KING | ___ $7.99 U.S. | ___ $9.99 CAN. |
| 77530 | JEWEL OF ATLANTIS | ___ $7.99 U.S. | ___ $9.99 CAN. |
| 77525 | HEART OF THE DRAGON | ___ $7.99 U.S. | ___ $9.99 CAN. |
| 77524 | THE DARKEST PLEASURE | ___ $7.99 U.S. | ___ $9.99 CAN. |
| 77523 | THE DARKEST KISS | ___ $7.99 U.S. | ___ $9.99 CAN. |
| 77522 | THE DARKEST NIGHT | ___ $7.99 U.S. | ___ $9.99 CAN. |
| 77461 | THE DARKEST LIE | ___ $7.99 U.S. | ___ $9.99 CAN. |
| 77455 | THE DARKEST PASSION | ___ $7.99 U.S. | ___ $9.99 CAN. |
| 77451 | INTO THE DARK | ___ $7.99 U.S. | ___ $9.99 CAN. |
| 77392 | THE DARKEST WHISPER | ___ $7.99 U.S. | ___ $8.99 CAN. |
| 77391 | PLAYING WITH FIRE | ___ $7.99 U.S. | ___ $9.99 CAN. |
| 77359 | THE VAMPIRE'S BRIDE | ___ $6.99 U.S. | ___ $6.99 CAN. |

*(limited quantities available)*

| | |
|---|---|
| TOTAL AMOUNT | $ _____ |
| POSTAGE & HANDLING | $ _____ |
| ($1.00 FOR 1 BOOK, 50¢ for each additional) | |
| APPLICABLE TAXES* | $ _____ |
| TOTAL PAYABLE | $ _____ |

*(check or money order—please do not send cash)*

To order, complete this form and send it, along with a check or money order for the total above, payable to HQN Books, to: **In the U.S.:** 3010 Walden Avenue, P.O. Box 9077, Buffalo, NY 14269-9077; **In Canada:** P.O. Box 636, Fort Erie, Ontario, L2A 5X3.

Name: _____

Address: _____ City: _____

State/Prov.: _____ Zip/Postal Code: _____

Account Number (if applicable): _____

075 CSAS

*New York residents remit applicable sales taxes.
*Canadian residents remit applicable GST and provincial taxes.

# HQN™

## We *are* romance™

www.HQNBooks.com

PHGS0411BL